Enoch M. Marvin

The Life of Rev. William Goff Caples

of the Missouri Conference of the Methodist Episcopal Church, South

Enoch M. Marvin

The Life of Rev. William Goff Caples
of the Missouri Conference of the Methodist Episcopal Church, South

ISBN/EAN: 9783337850159

Printed in Europe, USA, Canada, Australia, Japan

Cover: Foto ©Lupo / pixelio.de

More available books at **www.hansebooks.com**

THE LIFE

OF

Rev. William Goff Caples,

OF THE

MISSOURI CONFERENCE

OF THE

Methodist Episcopal Church, South.

BY

E M MARVIN.

SAINT LOUIS:

SOUTHWESTERN BOOK AND PUBLISHING COMPANY,
510 AND 512 WASHINGTON AVENUE.

1871.

PREFACE.

I must have my little prefatory chat with the reader.

The writing of the Life of Caples was not undertaken upon my own suggestion, but in compliance with the request of the Missouri Conference, made by formal resolution at the session of 1867, at Macon City.

I had no time to devote to it until after my return from the Pacific coast last fall. As I felt unable for hard service in the pulpit at the time, I proposed to devote the winter to the preparation of this Biography, preaching only on Sundays near home. But before the work was more than fairly begun I was drawn into a series of revival meetings that kept me from home nearly all the while. Away from home inevitable engrossments of time prevented all writing, and at home a heavy correspondence, with other claims upon me, demanded attention. The greater part of this book has, therefore, been written by snatches, as a few hours could be commanded now and then. I feel persuaded that, as a literary production, I could improve it greatly, if I had leisure.

Perhaps the friends of Brother Caples will be disappointed to find so little of *narrative* in the book. But I had not the facts, nor could I procure them, unless I had taken time to go and see hundreds of people, and interest them in conversation about him until their memories might have yielded me their store of hid treasures. In response to letters, with but two or three exceptions, I got only *generalities*. It seemed impossible to get incidents, to any great extent, by correspondence, and I gave it up at last in despair. I had to depend largely on my own memory, which, when I put it to the test, served me better than I expected. I found that I could recall the substance of many conversations I had had with him much more fully than I supposed.

That there may be inaccuracies in the book, I can not doubt, but I have taken every pains to get the exact truth, and trust that I have generally succeeded. Of the general accuracy of it I feel fully assured.

The plan of the work is somewhat peculiar. I had not the material to make a book of much size as a mere biography, and so determined to make the narrative the vehicle of other matter, which seemed to me of great importance. This matter is pertinent, and always suggested by the facts.

My object has been to make this biography a means of doing good, and not simply a memorial of one so highly honored amongst us.

If, in some parts of the book, the style should appear too familiar or offensively egotistical, I have but one apology to make: It was written with the consciousness of a Missourian talking to Missourians about Caples. Was it possible that, with this feeling, the author should avoid the free use of the personal pronoun? I am sure the immediate friends of my honored brother will accept this feature of the work with generous allowance, at least.

It has been written with prayer and an earnest desire to glorify God. If it shall lead any soul to Christ, encourage any young minister or console any of the older ones; if it shall contribute to more wholesome views of truth and obligation in the Church, or bring any to a more perfect consecration, the labor of preparing it, which has been considerable, will find ample reward.

E. M. MARVIN.

St. Louis, April 28, 1870

CONTENTS

LIFE OF CAPLES.

CHAPTER I.

BIRTH, AND THE NEW BIRTH.

WILLIAM GOFF CAPLES, son of R. F and Charlotte Caples, was born April 23, 1819, in Jeromeville, Wayne county, Ohio.

Of his parents and his early life I know nothing beyond the fact that his educational advantages were limited, and that he was converted and joined the Methodist Episcopal Church in his seventeenth year. It is, therefore, to be inferred that he had enjoyed Christian training, and I should judge that his parents were of the better class of that adventurous multitude that have been ever pushing into the West. But whether his father was farmer, merchant, mechanic or professional man I know not. Nor do I care to know. I feel quite certain that good ancestral influences were upon

the man.   He was possessed of that sort of deep,
unassailable principle that is apt to be hereditary.
Whether it be in the blood or in a species of tra-
ditional family honor, I shall not undertake to
say, but my observation is that where there is
very high moral tone it may be traced to an
honorable line of ancestry.   There are exceptions,
no doubt, but this is the rule.

There are two vital facts in human life, and
individual character is the result of their combined action.   The first is *personal liberty*, and
the second *reciprocal influence*.   Character comes
of the action and reaction of the individual will
upon all the multiform moral influences that come
upon the man.

All observation compels us to admit that much
depends on early influences.   It is a rare thing
that the character of a man is the reverse of the
character of the external agencies brought to bear
upon him in the formative period.   So fully is
this true that the declaration comes with divine
authority, "Train up a child in the way he should
go and when he is old he will not depart from it."
This is literally true.   It is the declaration of God.
Yet many who accept the Bible as the book of
God either disbelieve the affirmation or *explain*
it until the meaning is all gone.

True, many children of Christian parents turn

out wicked. But who can affirm that they were trained up in the way they should go?

Training means much more than mere instruction. Even this part of it is sadly neglected by many parents who are in the Church. But even where there is thorough instruction in the things of God, still the training may be very imperfect, or positively bad. Let it be remembered that training goes on as actively (often more so) in the street as by the fireside. It is imperative on parents to secure their children, as far as possible, against such *associations* as will lead to an evil life. Let their surroundings, as far as may be, tend to salvation. After the utmost care and vigilance the precious soul of the child will be sufficiently exposed. The carelessness that lets them run at large, the parent knows not where, and the weakness or pride that sends them to the mouth of the pit that they may enjoy themselves, or that they may establish a footing in "fashionable society," betrays either a thoughtlessness or a degree of carnality on the part of the parent that quite unfits him for his great responsibilities. It is safe to affirm that where the children of religious parents turn out irreligious—permanently so—they have not been *trained* "in the nurture and admonition of the Lord."

A child baptized in infancy and properly trained is almost sure to desire a place among the people

of God when it is from eight to twelve years old.
After that there will be many temptations, much
backsliding of heart, in many cases, and much
mere formality; but with the due exercise of
parental influence and authority mingled, aided
by proper pastoral fidelity, in a living Church,
with the stated means of grace regularly enjoyed,
and the revival seasons—those "seasons of refreshing from the presence of the Lord" that are
sure to come in every vital Church—the child is
certain to come, sooner or later, to a sound experience of grace, and a stable, consistent, Christian
character.

Even as it is, with the very imperfect training
realized amongst us, it is the children of religious
people that constitute the staple of the Church.
Christian families are the salt of the earth.

An important factor in the problem of character as it results from training, is the actual character of the parent. A man's influence proceeds
out of himself, and is, in the long run, just the
out-going of his inner life. He may greatly
desire to exert on his children an influence above
his own standard. He gives the best possible
advice, and now and then goads himself up to a
measure of piety on their account that is not
habitual with him. The motive is a good one;
the only trouble is that he falls back again to the
old level of nominal religion, and the force of his

influence comes from his whole life, and not from the better and exceptional part of it. I have no doubt that there is a great deal of true piety in the Church, and in proportion to this our religion will reproduce itself in our children.

The great work of Mr. Wesley was to bring personal religion in experience and practice up to the scriptural standard. The experience of the love of God, felt and known, the new birth taught so distinctly and with such emphasis by our Lord and by all the apostles, was the key note of the Methodist movement. No less vital was the averment, that where this is found in truth it will be seen in the fruit of it—that is, in holy living. This heavenly birth realized in the soul and bodied forth in a life of habitual devotion to God, with proper instruction and training of children, and the prayer of faith earnestly, constantly offered to God in their behalf, will reappear from generation to generation, and in this manner, chiefly, will heaven become populous with redeemed spirits from the earth.

From what I know of the *man*, Caples, I doubt not that the *boy* was very wide awake and full of fun. If I might venture to make a little history, after the manner of the rationalists, I should say that this boy was a recognized chief among the youth of his neighborhood. Both from intellectual superiority and force of will he was a leader, even amongst boys older than himself. Then there was such boldness and activity, so much dash and enterprise, and withal such an unceasing flow of wit, combined with the most genial humor, that he would inevitably attract every thing to himself.

An inborn hatred of everything little and mean, and a sense of justice that was little less than a passion, often no doubt called him to a noble championship in instances of insolent tyranny such as are constantly recurring amongst boys, while at the same time the impulses of a master spirit probably made him overbearing himself, at times. But the genuine nobility of his spirit would always appear in the end.

The casual observer would see in him only a very bright and a very irrepressible boy, running over with vitality and fun. But his *mother* would discover something much deeper. *She* would see the young spirit opening itself to everything divine in nature and in the Bible. I can not doubt that the awe of God was often upon the child, that the voice of a conscience wonderfully authoritative made itself articulate in his soul, and that the check of these often brought him to pause in the midst of wayward adventures, when none but himself was aware of it. As he grew into youth there was an ever-deepening sense of God.

I know not what the fact was, but can scarcely

doubt that it was in a *revival* that he was con
verted and joined the Church. He lived in a comparatively new country It was not at a camp-
meeting that he was brought into the fold, for it
was in the winter. Perhaps it was in a rude
schoolhouse. Many of the princes of Israel in
the West have been born into the Kingdom where
all was in a very crude state. But it matters not
whether amid the grandeurs of some costly Gothic
structure, or the still more imposing grandeurs of
" God's first temples," a soul first comes to the
knowledge of its Creator. The supreme fact of
our life is independent of all that is accidental.
He that is once an actual partaker of the divine
nature will feel it to be a matter of no consequence whether the consummation was reached at
a camp-meeting or in a cathedral. Every thing
else becomes insignificant in the presence of the
love of God. All other beauty is lost in the
beauty of Him who is "chiefest among ten thousand and altogether lovely." *All else is nothing*
compared with " Christ crucified." Worldly ad-
juncts are forgotten in the " knowledge of sins
forgiven."

The experience of our departed brother was
clear and positive. I think he never doubted his
conversion. Always after I knew him he was at
rest on that point. There was nothing equivocal
either in his views of the doctrine of the new birth

or in his experience of the fact. It was a great reality to him.

> "What we have *felt and seen*
> With *confidence* we tell."

He was never concerned to bring within the terms of a vain philosophy this chief of all the affirmations of revelation and of the experience of the people of God. With him it stood on its own everlasting foundations—the testimony of God and the responsive testimony of the saints of all ages. His own experience was a divine preparation for the work God had for him to do in the world. It was so full, so distinctly and deeply a *fact of consciousness* with him that "the trumpet never gave an uncertain sound." He delivered the fact of the spiritual birth not only out of the Holy Scriptures, "opening and alleging" that it is so, but also out of the depths of his own soul.

This great epoch in his life dates from December, 1835. Thenceforward he was a "new creature in Christ Jesus." "Old things passed away, all things became new." Not that the essential personal traits that constituted his identity and differenced him from other men were destroyed; but the spiritual nature was raised to a new life, which was thenceforth to give complexion to the whole man. The views and hopes of his life now sprang from this new fountain. The unconquerable energies of his soul came under control of motives thence arising. His whole being adjusted itself to God, to his law, to Christ and eternity That wonderful emotional nature of his, which was, for volume, like the tides of the ocean, swelled and subsided under the attraction of the Son of God.

"The Spirit itself bore witness with his spirit that he was a child of God." I have heard him dilate upon that passage in private conversation until I would

> "Taste unutterable bliss
> And everlasting rest."

None but a man who had *felt* its truth could talk about it as he did. Once when we were alone together he dwelt upon it until, when he passed to the latter clause of the text, "if children then heirs — heirs OF GOD and JOINT HEIRS WITH CHRIST," his very recitation of the language opened its unfathomable depths to me. His own experience taught him the import of all the richest passages of the Word of God.

His conversion determined the course of his after life. He had other views, indeed, ambitious views, which sprang out of conscious intellectual power, and prompted him strongly to a career in which he might win fame and gold. He studied law, and had an intuitive foresight of the illustrious career that his peculiar mental endowments would have secured him in that profession. He had none of that contemptible sort of vanity which makes small men ridiculous, but he did have that quiet consciousness of power which is the prophesy of success in minds of the highest order. But "the law of the spirit of life" was in him, and an awakened and dominant conscience curbed what would otherwise have been an indomitable ambition. It opened his ear to another voice—a voice felt to be from God—a voice articulate within, summoning him to the ministry of the word. It offered no emoluments and no gold. He knew that it involved much toil and poverty. There was no charm in it then for a carnal heart, for Methodist preachers in those days saw no well furnished parsonages nor "fat salaries" in the perspective of the future. For such a man as Caples it was a sacrifice, and a great one; such a sacrifice as a man may bear for himself very well, but to involve his wife and children in it touches to the quick.

I get hints of a period of conflict. There was a time when temptation was strong, and when the flesh warred against the spirit with such force that the issue was doubtful. He was in poise between contending motives. There was agony in the struggle. But, as we shall see, in the end the spirit triumphed. He "was not disobedient to the heavenly vision." The spiritual momentum already received became the determining force of his life.

A man is not, therefore, yet perfect when he is born of God. He will soon find himself in the midst of a great warfare, the flesh lusting against the spirit. Like his Lord, he will find that, in his measure, he must be made perfect through suffering. The cross is to be borne. The flesh is to be mortified. Doubtless, some attain to a full consecration much sooner and with less pain than others, for "faith the conquest more than gains." And those of us who linger in a protracted struggle triumph at last only through Christ—only by *faith*. And how self-abased we must be that, with the victory always in our grasp, through Christ, we have maintained an impotent warfare in our own strength so long.

I have not the data from which to give an account in detail of the agonism through which Brother Caples passed. I only know that he struggled and that he triumphed.

Since this chapter was written I have received the following in a letter from John F. Caples, Esq., a lawyer of high standing at Portland, Oregon, and a brother of Rev. W G. Caples. It contains some information I did not before possess, and confirms other facts already given. I feel quite sure, however, that Brother Caples came to Missouri an exhorter only, and received

2

license to preach soon after he arrived. The
letter of Rev B. R. Baxter, in another chapter,
confirms the information I had before, and which
I had always understood to be the fact. This is
not a material point, however, and the letter from
Portland will be read with interest. To me it was
of great interest in giving an insight into the
home influences under which the character of
Mr. Caples was formed. The father and mother
were the manner of people I had supposed them
to be :

"PORTLAND, OREGON, *December 10, 1869.*

"Brother William was born at Jeromeville,
Wayne county, Ohio, April 23, 1819; was the son
of Robert F and Charlotte Caples; emigrated,
with his parents, to Seneca county, Ohio, in 1831;
experienced religion and joined the Church in
1835. I presume you do not wish to go back
very far as to parentage. His father, in his early
life, had studied and been admitted to practice
law; served as judge of the Common Pleas Court
in Wayne county, Ohio, for four years, but devoted the balance of his life to farming.

"William, as a boy, was of studious habits,
but his literary opportunities (outside of his
father's early instruction) were only those of a
common school in a new country He was accustomed to labor upon a farm until about eighteen
years of age, when he engaged as a clerk in a

store at Findlay, Ohio, and was most of the time thereafter engaged in mercantile pursuits, until he left Ohio for Missouri, which, we believe, was in the spring of 1839. He studied law at Findlay during the years 1836 and 1837, but never practiced the profession that we know of.

"His parents were religious from early youth, members of the M. E. Church, and their house in Seneca county was for many years a home for Methodist preachers, and served as a preaching place, class rooms, and other religious services of the Church.

"For some years before leaving Ohio William served the Church as an exhorter and local preacher. In his younger days he was distinguished for his energy, cheerful and hopeful disposition, and extreme kindness of heart."

CHAPTER II.

APPRENTICE WORK IN THE GOSPEL.

Young Caples was appointed Class Leader within a year after his conversion. My data simply says this appointment was made in 1836. At what time in the year this occurred I have no means of knowing; but as his conversion took place at the very close of the preceding year it is likely that very soon after the close of his probationary term, possibly even before the close of it (for such a thing would not be without precedent), he became the Leader of a class. He was not only young in religion, but also young in years, for in April of this year he attained his seventeenth year.

Not only must his religious life have been very decided, but, for one so young, his personal character for intelligence and stability of purpose must have commanded great respect, or he would not have been placed in so responsible a relation to the Church. One can imagine how warmly the sympathies of the Church clustered about the young disciple, so sprightly was he, so intelligent, and so fully trusted. No doubt the simple-hearted members already predicted that he would be a *preacher*, and felt all that generous interest in him so near akin to family pride, which constituted one of the most beautiful traits of the old-time Methodist piety And I am thankful to believe that this trait is not obsolete now. Every truly pious heart must feel a devout interest in a young man who is "called of God to preach the gospel." In the eye of faith there is in him somewhat that is not in other young men of the Church. He seems nearer to Christ, and in one sense actually is so. He is a chosen vessel, to whom God has committed a dispensation of the gospel. The freshness and ardor of his young manhood have the air of consecration upon them. If he be more deeply pious than is common with those of his age, there is a recognized spirituality and self-abnegation in him the odor of which is a "sweet smelling sacrifice." No genuine Christian can fail to be touched by all this. Accordingly, there has ever been in the Church a rich sentiment of prayerful regard toward the youth who are looked upon as being destined, by the call of God, to the ministry. In the local Church where he resides, and where he was converted—the Church that was in travail when he was born—the Church that was

in sympathy with his penitential anguish, and
heard his first shout of praise, and thrilled under
the sunburst of immortal joy when it blazed out
of the thick darkness, changing, it may be, in one
moment, his midnight into day—there is a sort
of proprietary interest in him. Much note is taken
of every hopeful fact, and many a sage prediction
of the coming greatness of the young worker for
God is delivered.

But while this is always so, it was eminently
the case among the Methodists of forty years
ago and less. At that period, when there was so
much energy in the administration of the itinerant plan, a heroic character invested the preachers, in addition to the sacred interest always felt
in their office. A young man caught up by this
whirlwind might be let down almost anywhere.
Wherever he might be he would have a circuit
large enough for a principality, with all the incidents of bridgeless streams and pathless forests
and consuming labors. There was a sort of rail-
road activity in the itinerancy, while all else was
in the heavy jog of the sober old time. Friends
and neighbors, therefore, followed the young
Evangelist with a romantic interest as he disappeared in impossible distances, with no railroad,
nor telegraph wire, nor scarcely an old-fashioned
stage line to disenchant the scene. He was out
swimming rivers on horseback, wandering of tem-

pestuous nights in morasses, with the howl of the
wolf and the scream of the panther making
chorus in the song of the wind and thunder,
attacked by robbers or, "mayhap" (as Hugh
Miller would say), by savage Indians. All this
on an errand of love, with nothing that could
be called pay as the world goes, moved by the
self same motive that brought the Master down
from heaven to suffer and to die. He was out on
the Master's business—to seek and to save the
lost. This gave the early preachers a commanding place in the affections of the Church.

The tie was strengthened by the fact that the
preachers lived among the people of the Church.
No preacher on a circuit thought of *boarding*
anywhere. He had no time to board. He was
never in the same neighborhood more than a day
or two in three or four, or maybe six, weeks. He
lived with his people. Many of the preachers
were unmarried, and if one had a family he was
at home but little. They were almost always on
the hospitality of the brethren, and the brethren
loved to have it so. It was a bright day when the
preacher came, especially if he came to stay all
night. The children looked on him almost as an
angel of God. The faces of the servants (where
there were any) glowed, and the preacher and the
preacher's *horse* (always a notable animal) were
at *home*.

These old Methodist people were *not* miserly, as they have been slanderously reported. True, they had no idea of paying the preacher much money They had not been so taught by the fathers. The preachers did not want much money, did not need much, ought not to have much. They were not hirelings. Their reward was on high. And this was all very well while the preachers followed Asbury and the fathers, and remained unmarried. But when they began to have many mouths to fill with bread—mouths that relished butter, too, if they could only get it—wives and children to buy calico and shoe leather for—poor fellows, it operated hard on them. No wonder if, in the bitterness of their souls, they said the Methodist people were stingy But they were *not* stingy They had only been trained not to give much money to the preachers. Yet, when was it ever known that a dozen of these same preachers came up at nightfall, on their way to Conference, before the cottage gate of a Methodist brother of the old time—a poor, hard-working man, with a large family to support, it may be—that they were not cheerfully hailed as the servants of the Lord, and man and beast welcomed to the very best the place afforded, in the most cordial manner? Many a brother who felt it a hardship to pay twenty-five cents a quarter would cheerfully open his house for preaching every two weeks, and feed every one who would stay for dinner. And how many would he *not* feed at the camp-meeting?

The fact is he did not *get* much money, but of that which he had in abundance, the product of his labor, he gave freely.

Such was the relation between preacher and people when Caples, in the flush of youth, became a class leader and began to be looked upon as one devoted to the work of the Lord. There must have been an exalted sympathy between the young leader and his class very much after the model of apostolic times. His own nature was generous and responsive in the highest degree, and it could not have been otherwise than that their social meetings were seasons of the richest spiritual communion—occasions that must ever more glow in the firmament of memory with a lustre all the brighter as it recedes.

The simplicity of early Methodism appears in the appointment of such a mere youth as class leader. The case was not so very uncommon then Gifted young men—especially if they were thought of for the ministry—were often put in charge of classes—young men who would scarcely be tolerated in such a relation anywhere now. They had not much knowledge, nor any maturity of experience. Many members of their classes would be in advance of them in both of these respects. But if the young brother was truly pious, "fervent in spirit serving the Lord," and had the "gift of utterance," he was welcomed joyfully as the leader of their meetings. True, he could not instruct them much, but there was that glow of spiritual sympathy which furnishes a species of nutrition for the soul scarcely less important than instruction itself. The worshipers were very devout and child-like in their religious life, and went to the meeting to enjoy communion with God and with His people, and were not disposed to criticise each other's performances. It was not felt to be a *performance*—in fact, it was a meeting of the children of God to build each other up on their most holy faith. The rhetoric might be very poor, and, for the matter of that, the grammar barbarous and the matter crude, but they did indeed grow in grace and in the knowledge of our Lord Jesus Christ, and the earnest, gifted, unconscious young leader, though a very inexperienced and incompetent instructor in the things of God, was greatly loved, and was sure to find many an Aquila and Priscilla to teach him the way of God more perfectly Meantime this spiritual athlete was being trained for a wider field, where his prowess would be called into play in a more important contest. In the course of a few years, with hardened and practiced muscle, he would wield the sword of the Spirit in the very midst of the combat, and be ready to speak with the enemy in the gate.

Without doubt " William," or, as he was, per-haps, affectionately named among them, " Billy Caples," was the object of much godly interest in his class. The heart of many a Christian matron told her that there was the making of a master in him. Many an aged saint rejoiced that God was still raising up young men to bear the banner of the truth aloft when the veterans then in the field should be no more.

The fervor of his own spirit, and the pathos of his wonderful voice, among Methodists of that day, could not fail to secure lively class-meetings. Newly born of God as he was, the overflowing of his soul would be sure of a full and deep response from the members. The singing led by him would be loud and full of the soul. There would be many tears, the most hearty amens, and I should say much shouting of praise to God, the Giver of Salvation; and the little company of believers would go away as giants refreshed with new wine.

The next year, 1837, introduced our brother into another office in the Church—one which, in the custom of those days, looked more decidedly to-ward the ministry. He was licensed to exhort. It did not follow, as a matter of course, that he would become a preacher, for many were officially recognized as exhorters who never went beyond that point. There were many men gifted in exhortation who could never be useful in the regular ministry. As leaders of prayer-meetings their services were invaluable. I have known some in this office to be instrumental in the conversion of many sinners to God. They used sometimes to carry on protracted meetings in which there would be no formal preaching, but in which many souls were converted. Would to God there were more of such labor in the Church in our day.

But while it was true that not every exhorter became a preacher, yet, in that day, almost every young man looking to the ministry first received license to exhort. While it opened to him at once a door of usefulness, it served also to afford the Church an opportunity to judge of his gifts. If it became apparent that he had the capacity for a higher work, and he felt himself to be called of God to preach the Gospel, the requisite authority would be conferred upon him.

I presume that in the case of Brother Caples the Church understood that they were advancing him toward the regular ministry. This advancement is in proof that he had acquitted himself to the satisfaction of the brethren as a class leader, though so young, not only so far as gifts were concerned, but also in maintaining a consistent Christian character. This is the more noteworthy

In his case for the reason that his nature was of that buoyant sort that involves young men in great temptation. He was the *heartiest* companion I ever knew; but he had also a strong will, and having set himself to be a Christian he no doubt resisted in the most decisive manner every solicitation of the world that might have compromised him as a Christian. The hilarious nature that was so strong in him—that was born in him—must have been under decided control at this period. Not that I imagine he wore a long face at this time; I can not suppose that he was otherwise than genial and joyful, often jocular, in social life; but that he kept himself within the limit of associations allowed by the Church must have been due, through the abounding grace of God, to that decision of character which he possessed in a remarkable degree.

The office of exhorter he held for two years. It was very common in those days that young men of decided gifts should pass from the office of exhorter to that of preacher in a few months. Many became preachers and entered the traveling connection no older than he was when he was licensed to exhort. Ardent and eager as he was in everything that he undertook, it is a noteworthy fact that he lingered so long at the threshold of the ministry. It is not in keeping with his general character. It could not have been that the Church was doubtful of his capacity; I suppose that was never doubted. There must be some explanation of this hesitancy.

If my information is correct there are two facts that furnish the clue to this mystery One is, that at this time he studied law; the other is, that within this period he was married. This was a momentous era in his life. His temptations were fearful. Every great soul has great struggles. Men of Caples' class must, through much tribulation, enter into the Kingdom, if they ever do enter.

Naturally he was as ambitious as Julius Cæsar. The kingdoms of the world and the glory of them were in his eye. They dazzled him. For a time he allowed the gorgeous vision to master him Its force was greatly augmented, just at this critical juncture, by his marriage. Miss Charlotte Gist, the daughter of Gen. George W Gist, formerly of Maryland, was young, beautiful, intellectual, witty Her father was of an old, wealthy Maryland family, but had been reduced to poverty by being "surety for his friend" The exquisite personal beauty and vivacious intellect of Miss Gist were an irresistible attraction to young Caples, and the brilliant, ambitious student of law was accepted by her with all the noble trust of young womanhood. They were married, and none were ever joined with a deeper love. Mrs.

Caples' views and hopes of life were all colored by the chosen profession of her husband, while his love for and pride in her would intensify his own ambitious impulses.

The wonder is that he did enter the ministry at all. His wife felt it to be a cruel involvement of her in the poverty and humiliations of a calling with which she was not in sympathy—a blight of all her hopes. *He* felt the same, for he was always most tenderly regardful of her. Besides that, in devoting himself to the itinerant ministry, he crucified *self* in its most sensitive consciousness—his ambition.

CHAPTER III.

CALLED OF GOD TO PREACH THE GOSPEL.

In 1839, General Gist, with his family, accompanied by his son-in-law, Mr. Caples, and his wife, emigrated to the State of Missouri, and settled at or near Westport—I think in the town.

Whether Mr. Caples engaged in any business here, or if any, what it was, I know not.

He came to Missouri, with his certificate of membership in the Church and his license as an exhorter. Promptly uniting with the Church in his new home, and becoming active in the public meetings, his remarkable talents were at once recognized. He was put forward on all occasions, and always listened to with great interest. In a very short time he was induced to take license to preach, and in the fall of the same year was received on trial into the Missouri Conference.

From himself I learned that from the moment of conversion he had a conviction that it was his duty to preach, that he was strongly tempted to another vocation, as I have already stated, and that conscience, after considerable delay, was master. But, minutely, what were the incidents connected with the final decision I do not know. Whether the long continued struggle was terminated by some special, marked interference of Providence, some immediate quickening of the spiritual life, or was an act done in homage to the will of God without any unusual excitement, I know not. I do know, however, in a general way, that it resultèd from a profound conviction, long felt, that God had laid on him the burden of the ministry. As his consciousness of the new birth was clear, so the sense of his vocation was profound.

Young men, feeling impelled to preach the Gospel, are not unfrequently uncertain as to the nature and source of the impulse. They know not how to decide as to what may safely be regarded the call of God. There is, also, very often, great reluctance to enter upon the life of a preacher. Nor does this reluctance always arise out of worldly motives. Sometimes there is a solemn fear of assuming these sacred and awful obligations uncalled. A tender conscience dreads to assume them presumptuously. To speak in God's name, unauthorized, is no light matter, and the force of this is felt in proportion as the conscience is enlightened and sensitive. Nor is it

3

easy—perhaps it is not possible—to define the call of God as it is realized in the soul. The experience of it, I suppose, is not identical in every individual, but varies according to character and circumstances. With some it is an overwhelming conviction from the first. In other instances it may be less distinct and impressive; but in all cases where God has chosen a man for this work He will, in one way or another, bring the duty home to his conscience.

No doubt some run who have never been sent on this errand. It is not every impulse toward a good work that comes from God. I think it very likely that some good men suppose themselves to be called when in fact they are not. Brother William Shields, of Columbia, once told me that he never heard a talented man preach that he did not feel a strong impulse to be a preacher himself. This he discriminated from a call to preach, no doubt very justly But others, not accustomed to an intelligent analysis of their own mental state, fail to make this discrimination, and infer that every impulse toward the pulpit is the call of God. The disposition to be a public speaker is not uncommon, and that, in a religious man, it should associate itself with the pulpit is not surprising. The fact of such a desire is not proof of its divine origin.

Others who are called, resist. So it falls out

that some are in the sacred office uncalled, and others in secular life who have been designated by the Holy Spirit to this work. The ideal Church is perfect, but the actual Church is not. The basis of the Church is divine. Its doctrine is of God, and is perfect. Its essential constitution is of God, and is perfect. But the human material in which it takes its organization is very stubborn and impracticable—often cranky. No wonder things get out of joint at times, and that there is more or less of friction in the working of the Church. That it does not go to pieces is due to the power of the indwelling Spirit "We are builded together for the habitation of God by the Spirit." The Holy Presence, counter-working the depravity of man, sanctifying believers and helping their infirmities, preserves the Church as God's great agent in saving men.

How, then, is a young man, under an impression that he is designated to the work of the ministry, to judge of the character of his impression? How is he to know that it is from God?

1. Let him live near to God. Let him, by prayer —earnest, constant prayer—put himself in God's hand to be guided whithersoever He will. Let pride and self-will be thus cast out. When he is, in fact, ready for God's will to be done he will be led by a way he knows not. If he is really a chosen vessel, and gives himself up to be any-

thing or nothing, as it may please Him that called him, God will "set his feet in the way of his steps."

2. Where there is a call to the work of the ministry there will be a corresponding Providence opening the way. The good man's steps are ordered of God. The inward spiritual prompting will find corresponding opportunity and encouragement in outward conditions. There will be an open door.

3. The Church will find out her messengers. There is a wonderful intuition among the people of God in such matters. I have never known it to fail. Often the young man designed by the Head of the Church for the ministry of the Word is pointed out by the Church before he has any definite conviction in himself. Where there is a truly spiritual Church, and the members concur in a spontaneous selection of a young man, it is very strong proof of his vocation.

4. The discipline contemplates a period of apprenticeship. There can be nothing more repugnant to modesty and good sense, not to say Christian feeling, than the custom of making young men preach *trial sermons*. The effect must be bad—bad on the candidate and on the Church. Rather let him hold prayer-meetings and exhort, as occasion may serve—not under circumstances where he will expect criticism, but with a view of

doing go d. In this apprentice work, often awkward and embarrassed enough, the heart of the Church will respond to the voice of the true worker. The questions of the discipline can then be answered—"Has he gifts? Has he grace? Has he fruit?" The fruit may not have ripened into great results. It may appear more in serious congregations and in the comforting of the Church.

Where there is any sense of duty, an open door and a concurrent selection by the Church, it may be safely understood that the man is indeed chosen of the Lord to bear the message of salvation to the lost.

At the same time, when the harvest is white and the laborers few, as now, it becomes the Church to be on her knees. We must pray the Lord of the harvest to send forth laborers.

Many, resisting a conviction of duty, fall into great temptation and distress, and many backslide. The biographies of old time Methodist preachers abound with details of dreadful anguish suffered and fearful struggles of soul, with the words resounding continually within, "Wo is me if I preach not the gospel." To be a Methodist preacher then was extremely repugnant to flesh and blood. The call in those days required to be uttered in a most authoritative tone. No slight impulse would move a man to the great undertaking. To be a laughing-stock for many, to forego domestic pleasures, to be a wayfarer all his days, to suffer great exposures and perform herculean labors—this was what was in the perspective on the worldly side of the picture. When they sang,

"No foot of land do I possess,"

they used no metaphor, but sang just the plain truth.

At the threshold of such a ministry the struggle was sharp, and many a refractory spirit was lashed forward with a whip of scorpions. Days of bitterness and nights of groaning preceded the final decision.

But when a man is not contumacious he usually escapes the horrors of such a struggle. Every man, however, must realize the solemnity of the work. I can not conceive of a man being set between the living and the dead and made responsible for souls for whom Christ died without feeling himself oppressed. What an awe of God must be upon him! A man so flippant as not to tremble at the thought of occupying such a place is not fit to represent the Son of God in the world.

Such a man as Caples, we may be sure, realized his position fully The consecration of himself to this work, in the midst of the temptations mentioned in the last chapter, with his sensibilities, at once quick and profound as they were, is sufficient evidence of the power of God felt to be upon him.

Nothing short of an adequate sense of the majesty of a righteous God—an overwhelming view of the Infinite Authority—could have caused him, tenderly and considerately as he loved his wife, to involve her in the fortunes of a life to which she felt a repugnance almost amounting to horror.

He did not often speak of his deepest experiences. Now and then, with a trusted friend, he would. When he did, it was with deep feeling and solemnity. Not that sort of feeling which expresses itself with tears, but that profounder sensibility which appears in the countenance and in the whole aspect. His voice—who that ever heard that voice when fully laden has lost the echo of it?—was the most adequate vehicle of such emotion that I ever heard. Once in public and once or twice in private I have heard him refer to the offering of himself on the altar of God, and well do I remember the impression it made on me. I never after doubted that he had talked with God (so to speak) in the secret place of thunder.

The momentum of Godhead, delivered upon his soul, set him forward upon the course of his ministry Nothing less than this could have changed the direction of his life from its ambitious course. This divine momentum came upon a most forceful soul. It contended even with the Omnipotent for awhile; but it was at a greater disadvantage in such a contest than a feebler spirit would have

een.   A soul *feels God* in the measure of its own
capacities, and agonizes under the weight of Him
in the measure of the power it puts forth in the
struggle.   In his case the contest was an agony
insupportable, and the victory was God's.   It is
due to a will, stubborn almost to desperation, that
the agony was protracted at all.

When he did capitulate he did not attempt the
folly of making terms with God.   He gave himself up to the Infinite Conqueror.   Soul, body, wife,
children, all were lawful spoils, and, with a single
exception, to be mentioned hereafter, were thenceforth surrendered to the Lord.

God's best steel is always tempered in a hot
furnace.   Moses, David, Isaiah, Paul, Wyckliffe,
Luther, Wesley, all passed through the fire.   Every
keen blade has been in the fire and on the anvil.
Caples was, and took a temper and edge that held
to the very last.

Sometimes the fiery trial is entirely within,
sometimes largely without.   With Caples it was
chiefly the former, though not exclusively.

The secret of the agonism is with him and God.
Only sufficient sign of it to intimate its intensity
was seen by any mortal eye.

CHAPTER IV.

HOW HE WAS EDUCATED FOR THE MINISTRY.

I have made two statements in reference to Mr. Caples that, to some, will seem to contradict each other. One is, that his educational advantages in early life were very limited—that he had not a liberal education. The other is, that he had prepared himself for the profession of the law. Both these statements, however, are true.

It was no uncommon thing in the West, at an early day, for ambitious young men, not even well grounded in a common English education, to study law and gain admission to the bar. Many of them became respectable; some of them attained great eminence. Hon. James S. Green, who at one time was the recognized peer of the most distinguished men of the United States Senate, had no collegiate education. Henry Clay, peerless in the Senate, when it *was* a Senate, was in this category. Caples would have been another if he had not turned to a higher calling.

Our Church at present is all agog on the subject of " an educated ministry." The changes are rung on this phrase until one is almost confused by the din.

I suppose no man of good sense doubts that a liberal education is of great value to a preacher of the Gospel. The knowledge acquired is itself an important advantage. It gives a man confidence to be able to make his exegesis of a passage of Scripture from the original text. But the chief value of literary advantages, I take it, is in that training which gives facility both in acquiring and using knowledge.

Caples had a definite theory on this subject of ministerial education, as indeed he had on all subjects, for he was a man of positive ideas. There was nothing negative in him. His views on this subject are well known in the Missouri Conference. He did not undervalue education. He saw as clearly as any man the importance of it. He felt more deeply than most men on the subject. His connection with the educational history of the Church in Missouri, which will be given in its proper place, will show this.

His conviction was that if the Church would do its full duty in sustaining colleges and high schools, under positive Christian influence, there would be an ample supply of educated young men raised up in the ministry. This he regarded as all-sufficient. Consequently, he laid himself out to establish a grand system of schools in his Conference—a system to be noticed hereafter.

Theological Seminaries were an abomination to him. He had come in contact with many poor specimens of their work. The conclusion reached by him was that they made sermon-readers and not preachers, copyists and not thinkers, pretenders rather than men. To learn theology and put it to use, acquiring the facility of using it as you acquire the knowledge of it—and at the same time to be learning men in the actual circuit work—he regarded as the method that had turned out the best specimens. The young man formed thus will never have a sophomoric manner. He will be free and original — and an original he thought better than a mere copy, even if it did lack somewhat in polish. The polish is very well, provided a man does not become prim and angular in taking it on, and the young preacher on a circuit, if he is anybody or can be made anything of, will take on refinement in an easy way, escaping the conventionalities and imitations that will come into vogue in a theological school, where the students take their cue from one set of men for a quarter of a century. Intercourse with society will refine him if he was not refined at home, and hearing a great many good preachers will break up any tendency to ape one. He will take his manner, as the Irishman did the small-pox, in the natural way. An easy, self-possessed bearing in the pulpit and in society will be the result. That is, if he be of good material. If he be too knotty or stolid to come to anything with this training, he will turn the edge of all the tools in the preacher factory. The most skillful work-man can never whittle him into shape.

Such were his views, though I have given a poor idea of the vivacity with which they were often expressed.

As to the value of theological schools, the la-mented Col. Thos. C. Johnson, late President of Randolph Macon College, held much the same opinions. Give your young preachers, he said, a thorough literary and scientific training, and with the mental power thus acquired, the habit of systematic thinking, let them enter the ministry and take the regular course of study prescribed by the Church. The fact is, if the young man has been trained in a Christian family, or in the Sun-day School, or has even been a regular attendant of church, he will know a good deal of theology to begin with, and that the most vital part of it. And, after all, it is not theology that requires to be preached so much as *religion*.

But Caples, while he was anxious to have young men well educated, would never consent to making a liberal education a condition of reception into the Conference. A young man of good capacity, if he could do no more than read tolerably well, and was studious, he held, would make a man of himself, and that in a short time. In fact, he declared that if the Methodist itinerancy did not make a man of one, nothing would. All the colleges in the world would leave him where they found him—a two-legged *thing*—a mere "biped without feathers."

The members of the Missouri Conference will never forget his College on Horseback. The students were the young traveling preachers. The college edifice was "all out of doors." The library was not on so magnificent a scale, though very convenient, it being in one end of his saddlebags. Watson's Institutes he held to be equal to a course of mathematics for mental discipline. Wesley's Sermons could not be read with care without inducing a habit of exact thinking. Then the Bible, God's own text book in the science of salvation, studied with reference to excellent commentaries, and in communion with nature, was the best educator in the world. At the same time, the literary course prescribed was sufficient to give the young student a taste for general studies to be prosecuted in after years. While these studies are going on he is on horseback every day—in the open air—in vital sympathy with nature, and with God through nature. He is also preaching every day or two, reducing what he learns, in the crucible of his own thought, to a new coinage out of his proper mint. The analytical powers of a man would thus be cultivated, he maintained, much more fully than would be possible in school. The student would at the same time be gaining confidence in his own thought. Best of all, he would be in condition to "grow in grace and in the knowledge of our Lord and Savior Jesus Christ."

In point of fact, he maintained that the Horseback College had turned out the best preachers in the world. The *average* Methodist preacher was above the average in Churches that required a classical education of every preacher. The class of men distinguished in the pulpit, he affirmed, from this College, was largely in excess of those from the Theological schools. As for the great names that tower above all the rest, the master spirits that stir a continent, he claimed the same distinction in favor of this Methodist College. Nor was he at a loss for instances. Joshua Soule, Lovick Pierce, H. B. Bascom, H. H. Kavanaugh, and I know not how many he gave in illustration and proof of his assertion. His auditors would be sure to think of *him* as another.

He would sometimes add, with great gusto, that what was the matter with us was not the want of education among the preachers, but that we had given the people so much first-rate preaching that they were spoiled. They had been fed too high. Anything second-rate was insipid to them. A preacher that any other Church would be proud of, Methodists would turn up their noses at. (He did not, on occasion, hesitate to use a very expressive phrase, though it might be wanting in elegance. His style in the pulpit, however, was uniformly elevated.) The alternations of the Itinerancy, the quarterly visits of the Presiding Elder, and the free interchange of ministerial services on revival occasions, had familiarized all the people with the best preaching, and every circuit had begun to feel itself entitled to preaching of a high order. If a man of good, plain common sense was sent, such as a congregation of another church would honor, they felt themselves aggrieved, wronged. Their claims had been overlooked.

He had a good humored way of saying very plain things in a very cutting manner. Half the severity sometimes used by him would turn a congregation into a swarm of wasps coming from almost any one else He had Dr. J B. McFerrin's faculty of delivering the most unpalatable truths in a way to be felt without exciting anger. I have heard him say from the pulpit that in one respect the Methodists were the *meanest* people in the world—that was in criticising their preacher. When the new preacher arrived the church con-

stituted itself into a committee on his case, and if
any flaw might be discovered it was sure to be
the topic in all circles. "The Conference has
treated us badly," they exclaim, and so prejudice
the public against their pastor. If he had preached
the very same sermon, or one not half so good, as
the pastor of a congregation in connection with
the Presbyterian or Baptist Church, his people,
overlooking what might have been open to criticism in it, and fastening upon the real gospel
teaching it contained, would have said, "What a
good sermon we did have to-day! It brought
home the truth with such force. Such preaching
must do good." And this, said honestly and with
real feeling, would go far to propitiate the public,
and secure such influence for the preacher as
would greatly aid him in his high calling.

I have more than once heard Mr. Caples indulge in this vein of remark. I think his view of
this evil was somewhat exaggerated, yet there is
cause of self-examination among us on this very
point. I believe, verily, that no other people go
to church for the *pleasure* of hearing fine preaching so much as the Methodists. It may be gravely
questioned if this be not an unwholesome condition. If our motive were rather to be reminded of
duty, if we were occupied more with the weighty
matter that is in every—even the poorest—sermon, we could never fail to be fed, and grow

thereby. Far better would it be if we were more occupied with the truth of a sermon, and less with the rhetoric. If we did but look on the minister as being (what he is in truth) God's messenger, bearing to us God's message touching our sin and our Savior, we should never go away from the house of God unprofited. A church rallying to a preacher earnestly will communicate a measure of its enthusiasm to the community at large; and if this enthusiasm arise out of interest in him *as the servant of the Lord*, and not *as a fine preacher*, the effect in the end will be the deeper and better. Mr. Wesley said he would no more dare to preach a fine sermon than to wear a fine coat. His followers, I fear, too many of them, consider both a desideratum.

Mr. Caples, so far, however, from being opposed to the education of preachers, held every man in the sacred office deeply culpable if he failed to use every opportunity to study. There was during his lifetime a popular belief that he himself did not *study*. This belief arose out of the fact that his acquaintances could never imagine what time he had for study amid all the official and social demands to which he responded without stint. "I never saw him with a book in his hand" was on the lips of many Yet he *did* read, and to much better purpose than most of us. As a student he was, as in most other respects, *sui generis*.

4

No young man could, with safety, make him his model.

No other man that I ever knew read so much in so little time. Not that he was a fast reader— the reverse was true. He read with deliberation, and took time for thought. He masticated his mental food. He did not bolt it. Yet there were very few books that he had read through straight. Prefaces and introductions might as well never have been written, so far as he was concerned. Much of the body of a book would go unread and yet the book itself be mastered. Getting the analysis of it, and reading carefully the parts that gave the hinge, the rest would be so open to him as to require only to be glanced over. He had a wonderful faculty of absorption.

I doubt if any preacher in Missouri had so good a library, or knew so much that was in it. He was a great devourer of the best old English authors. South's sermons—how he luxuriated in them! Some books of this class he read *through*. With pabulum like this he could feel himself fatten. His style in the pulpit betrayed the company he kept. It was *his own*, but you could see the stuff out of which he had made it. I speak not only of language, but also of the style of thought. Watson's Institutes had actually been soaked into him. Only the Bible, with him, had precedence of that book.

He had eminent facility in learning from original sources — communion with himself, with men, with nature, and with God. His powers of observation were very remarkable. His mind would fasten upon a fact and use it up directly. He consumed a world of raw food as he found it—stuff that the rest of us never thought of eating until it came to us from some accredited caterer, all duly prepared and spiced, and served in respectable platters, with appetizing condiments. Much that "books are made of" was appropriated and in use by him before he ever saw it in books.

From what has been said it will be seen that Mr. Caples had no specific education for the pulpit. Some important training he had, as a class leader and as an exhorter. His law studies, also, were of great service, no doubt. The Bible had been read with care. This was his equipment for the great work, so far as mental culture was concerned.

His *spiritual preparation* was much more ample. It consisted of a sound experience of converting grace and a solemn conviction of duty.

From this point of departure he went forward, and became—I say it without qualification—the greatest preacher in Missouri. His rank would have been with the first class anywhere on the continent.

I take this opportunity to say what is in my heart on the subject so much agitated in the Church now—the education of young men for the ministry. Above I have given Mr. Caples' views; I propose now to give my own.

The great body of Methodist preachers in America have been what is popularly phrased "uneducated men;" that is, they entered the ministry with nothing more than a common school education—many of them with much less than that. Many of them have become, in the course of a few years, men of large information and ripe scholars in Biblical learning, so far as this is attainable in "their own language wherein they were born."

In point of fact, they have influenced American society, in religious matters, more effectually than any other class of preachers. The census of Methodism is the astonishment of the world. But the literal census gives only a very partial statement of the result of these men's work. The fruits of Methodist revivals abound in other churches. I have known flourishing churches of other denominations which were replenished from scarcely any other source. It is proverbial what numbers go from the "mourner's bench" (this is purely Methodist termonology) into other communions. Other churches have fallen largely into the methods of labor and the character of preaching which have been so potential amongst us. Beside all this, these "uneducated" men have revolutionized the popular theology of this continent.

On the human side the causes of this astonishing success are apparent. These preachers were men of the people. They were fresh from the various callings of life, and were in the fullest sympathy with the masses. Their doctrine, in some aspects, was new and striking, and on the mere statement of it commended itself to the common sense of men. Their sermons were not burdened with unintelligible theological terms. Every word was in the mother tongue, every sentence was fully comprehended, even by the less intelligent classes. They were very ardent—their words took fire in their own hearts and went out blazing among the people. They were bold men, never hesitating to denounce the most popular vices. They rebuked sin with no feeble generalization, but a pointed and barbed shaft was driven into the profane swearer, the Sabbath-breaker, the drunkard, the man who did not pay his debts, the gambler. Theaters, balls, circuses, grogshops, were pointed out as so many gates of hell. Sinai was altogether on flame before their congregations. Ah! these men knew where the conscience lay, and with what probe to touch the quick of it.

Then when a man fell, thunder-smitten, among the crags of Sinai, with what skill they lifted him

and laid him at the foot of the cross, under the
stream that dropped warm and healing from the
very heart of the Victim who "tasted death for
every man."   Themselves knew his *power to save.*
"*A* FREE *salvation—a* FULL *salvation—a* PRESENT
salvation—conditioned upon faith—this was their
theme.   *Sin* they pictured "in all its blackest
hue," and salvation in all its richest fullness, its
present plenitude and power.

"Gaining knowledge is a good thing, but saving
souls is better."   This came from Mr. Wesley,
and who can tell the power his words had over the
early Methodist preachers?   Their prime business
was to save souls, and they were all their time
engaged in it, redeeming at the same time every
possible moment for study.   At the cabin fireside
in the winter evenings, under the shade of a tree
in the spare hours of a summer day, in the saddle,
they would be reading some important book.
Preaching almost every day, what they had
learned they put to service at once.   Thus, not
unfrequently, they became men of extensive
knowledge — real Doctors of Theology   This
knowledge came from them to the people in popular language, in the form of impassioned extemporaneous sermons.

Then on the spiritual side they were men of
deep experience in the things of God, men of
much prayer and great faith.   Their word was in

power. They ever heard the sound of their Master's footsteps behind them, and His voice saying to them, "Lo, I am with you always, even unto the end of the world." And He *was* with them. They *felt* it, they knew it. They had wrestled with the Angel, and had power with God and with men. Each one was an Israel — a Prince of God. They were much with God in secret, and He rewarded and honored them openly

But I shall be told that things are changed now—that there is extemporaneous preaching all over the land with much of the Methodist fervor and power, by educated men of other denominations, and that the people at large are themselves more intelligent, so that our preachers must be up to the level of their hearers or lose credit. I doubt not there is much truth in all this, and on this point I have these remarks to make:

1. No one desires that preachers should be educated more than I do. Let it be done as far as possible. Let the Church tax her resources to the uttermost. Let us have a theological school. Let us have a chair of divinity in our colleges, where it can be done.

2. But when the utmost has deen done we will not turn out educated men as fast as the demands of the work will require.

3. Large classes of men will always be found to whom men of good sense, though not highly

, ducated, will be acceptable; more acceptable than the learned man, if he have the air of a pedant

4. Many men in the Church now who are in demand in the very best and most cultivated communities are such as have had no early advantages beyond the common school.

5. The college will not make a brilliant, attractive man of a naturally dull one. Many educated men never become acceptable preachers. If a man has no "gift," no training can *give* it to him. My conviction is, that if a man does not become a respectable public speaker on the basis of a fair English education, he would never do so with all the help in the world. You must have the "timber" to begin with.

6. I apprehend that exaggerated hopes are entertained of the results of a college course. Yet I do not deprecate the present agitation of the subject. Good will come of it—has already come of it. But brethren will be disappointed in many of the young men that will come to their pulpits out of the colleges.

7. I should deplore most deeply any legislation that would make a liberal education a *condition* of membership in the Annual Conferences. The hand of God will be on many a man who can never take a classical course. I am not sure but some men — very useful men, too — whom I have

known, would have been spoiled by any attempt of the sort. I am almost tempted to give names. H. S. Watts will pardon me for writing his.

8. If in any measure Methodist preachers lose their simplicity through affectation of learning, it will be a black day for us. If ever geometry and Greek, "the objective and the subjective," come to reduce our estimate of personal holiness as the prime condition of a truly useful ministry, we may write "Ichabod" upon our altars—for Methodism will be dead.

There is in some places an actual vice, which may properly be denominated a lust for fine preaching. Men go to church from very much the same motive that takes them to the theatre — not to be edified, but to enjoy fine declamation.

For these reasons it behooves our colleges to maintain a high order of Christian life. Let the young men being formed for the ministry be made constantly to feel that our great qualification is a holy life — a faith that gives men power with God, and a depth of spiritual experience that gives power with men, and that all their knowledge is mere chaff if the kernel of holiness be not in it.

There is danger that preaching may become too scholastic, that the pulpit in the pride of learning may displace the Cross by other themes; or if the Cross be not displaced, the egotism of knowledge and of display may hide it by a heavy drapery of alien matter.   The profoundest philosophy, the most consummate knowledge, is an impertinence, a shame, a crime, in the pulpit, if it shade Christ.   Only when it pronounces that Name, adoring, trembling — only when it gives a deeper, fuller utterance of that Name is it of the slightest value.

Preaching is nothing — worse than nothing — it is a mockery — if it does not bring men to the cross.   All we know must be felt to be of use only as it helps us to get God's truth before the eyes and into the ears and hearts of men.

CHAPTER V.

CAST DOWN BUT NOT DESTROYED.

In the fall of 1839 Mr. Caples was received on trial into the Missouri Conference. In a brief diary which he kept the last year of his life I find the following outline of the work he did:

"November 2, 1863.—I this day enter upon the duties of Glasgow station. Eighteen years ago I was appointed to this station by Bishop Soule. Prior to this I had traveled, first Plattsburg circuit in 1839–40, then Weston circuit in 1840–41. At the close of this year I was in debt, having received the first year $47, and the second $105. I cut cord wood during two or three months, paid off my debts, and in April was appointed by Wm. W Redman, Presiding Elder, to the Keytesville circuit, which I traveled until Conference, last of August, at Jefferson City. Bishop Roberts appointed me to Keytesville again. The two following years I traveled the Huntsville circuit. Then two in this station. Then two in Brunswick station. Then two in Hannibal station. Then four on the Weston district Then one in Weston station and High School. Then two as agent of Central College. Then one on Fayette district. Then one in Brunswick station. Then three on Brunswick district, and am now again appointed to this station."

When he entered the Conference he had a small family, for the support of which he received, as stated above, forty-seven dollars the first year, and one hundred and five the second. Without private resources, he found himself at the close of the second year *in debt*. Of course, a family could not subsist, by any miracle of economy, on this amount. Debt, or actual starvation, was the inevitable alternative A man can not see his family perish. The consequence was *debt*, and to him this was intolerable.

There is abundant evidence that from the very first he was more than acceptable as a preacher. Indeed, as Judge James H. Birch, of Plattsburg, informs me, there are still traditions of his wonderful power as a preacher there in the first year of his ministry. Even then he was an able minister of the New Testament, capable of defending the doctrines of his Church so as to put opposition and controversy to silence. An attack made upon him by a party given to controversy provoked a reply which was so triumphant as to end the matter at once. From the time he first made his appearance in the Platte country he was the object of admiration above any other man. The meagreness of his support is not to be accounted for on the ground of any opposition to him, nor any want of zeal or industry on his part. The people gave him more, I imagine, than they would have given most men. But the country was new, money was scarce, and the people had not been trained to just views of duty in this matter. Want of ability goes far to explain the fact. The first settlers of a country, for some years, are straitened in their means. All they can command must go to the most necessary improvements. The fruits of industry are swallowed up in subduing the wilderness, building houses and getting ready to live. Both in the Plattsburg and Weston circuits this was the condition of things when Caples traveled them. No man had a dollar for which there was not immediate and pressing use in his own affairs.

Yet an enlightened conscience in the Church would have turned an amount to Christian uses sufficient, at least, to keep the preacher's family above want. Intelligent faith would have seen in Christian agencies a prime necessity But this high ground had not been reached by the Church. So this preacher, popular as he was, was starved out.

Nor was there any prospect of a better state of things the next year. If he should get a circuit for the next year on which he would obtain sufficient support, there would be nothing over to pay debts. To him debt, where there was no prospect of paying, was intolerable. His sense of honor was acute. His character before the world was at stake. What was more sacred still, his integrity, was at stake. He might afford to sacrifice the respect of others, but there was *self-respect*. Without that he could not be a preacher of the Gospel. Without that, to a man like him, existence itself would have been insupportable.

He never hesitated long about anything. On the contrary, he was a most decided sort of man. He always took his measures promptly So now he resolved to ask to be discontinued. This was accordingly done. Just when his probationary term expired, and his connection with the Conference ought to have been consummated, his name disappeared from the list of appointments. It was his purpose at the time never again to take work as a traveling preacher. So he himself afterward declared.

Here, then, he stood face to face with the world and with—poverty Without any property, without a dollar, he was in debt. Now, what was he to do? He had studied law, but had never been in the practice. It would require time to get into professional business. His case was exigent and required instant relief. Bread, daily bread, it must be had, and that without delay. Hunger never waits on a perplexed man long. It never defers to embarrassing situations. It has not the delicacy to wait awhile and see if "something will turn up."

Well, there was *one* opening. Cord wood was in demand, and at a good price. As has been already said, he was not a man to hesitate. He never belonged to the class of animals that will starve to death between two piles of hay Here was money to be had for work, and here was muscle. He cut cord wood.

I give no incident of his life with greater satisfaction than this. It does honor to his head and heart alike. He was too great a man to be whining around in a helpless way, with the tone of an injured man, waiting for some gentlemanly employment. He would invoke no sympathy. He would not parade his wants. With God to help him he would help himself.

Which is the more honorable, to cut cord wood or leave debts unpaid—to defraud creditors of their due? Which is the more honorable, to cut cord wood or to whimper around, make new debts, and wait for something to turn up? Caples cut cord wood. I thank him for it. I can see him now in the heavy timber of the Missouri river.

bottom, above Weston, with his coat off, spurning the snow with heavy boots, and swinging the ax from dawn to dusk, in the short days of that memorable winter of '41–'42. I can see his open, honest face as he carries one instalment after another to his creditors. He lived close, labor was remunerative, his debts were small, and by midwinter he was free. By the first of February no man in Weston would have hesitated to loan him money, for he had proved himself *an honest man.* His was not that sort of honesty that is glad enough to pay if it may be convenient, but that other sort that *will* pay, whether it be convenient or not.

My recollection is that, before the winter was over, Wentworth employed him as a clerk in his store in Weston. But he did not remain there long. One thing had become evident on all sides, that he could not only make a living, but make money. With no untoward providence he would have been as likely to make a fortune as any man in Platte county. This he felt. The force was in him, and so was the mother wit.

In the face of all this, in the face of his own deliberate purpose only six months gone, and with a wife to whom poverty was most grinding and unwelcome—a wife, too, whom he cherished with uncommon tenderness—whose feelings and views he treated with the utmost delicacy and deference in every other matter, in April he takes an appointment to the Keytesville circuit from the Presiding Elder. Why this change of purpose?

There can be but one single reply to this question. The exigency that compelled him to locate was out of the way. Keytesville circuit lost its preacher in the middle of the year. It was in an older portion of the country. The Church was better organized and better able to support a preacher. His expenses would be met, at least. He was in demand as a preacher. Even while he was local the people would give him no rest. He was compelled to go here and there to meet incessant demands. He felt that the hand of God was on him. His life must be devoted to this work or the wrath of God would overtake him. The wrath of God would smite his family. Conscience uttered its imperious mandate. Its voice was obeyed. Wife and children were committed to God again with a faith purified and strengthened by trial. He had been in the crucible and came out with a deeper, richer experience.

The circumstances under which he was called to the Keytesville circuit were embarrassing and painful. The preacher who had been appointed to that circuit from the preceding session of the Conference was an Abolitionist. To that the people did not object. He was received to their altars and firesides with all that affection habitually

5

given to their pastors. He greeted his dear brethren, slaveholders as they were, with a cordial manner, encouraged their faith in the class-meeting and made long prayers for their prosperity in the family circle. He came and went about their houses as an honored guest, a pastor and a friend. After a time the negroes began to report to their masters that the preacher was persuading them to run away, and offering to assist them in doing so. Thus had he, in the guise of a Christian pastor, and accepting their hospitalities, betrayed them. More than this, he was guilty of a crime, infamous in the eyes of the law, and exposing him to the degradation of a term in the penitentiary His crime having become public he fled. But the odium remained. Methodist preachers were suspected men. It had been demonstrated that one of them could smile at your table and talk piety as a friend, and at the same time, taking advantage of your confidence, tamper with your servants.

The Presiding Elder at once selected Caples as the man to meet the emergency. His popular address, his pulpit power and the high tone of his character would restore confidence. The selection was a most happy one. Before the year closed the fair name of the Church had been redeemed. Those old Missourians were a most generous and confiding class. Honorable themselves, it was unnatural to them to be suspicious of others. Especially would such a candid, open nature as Caples' win them at once. After his first round the recent troubles began to be forgotten, and he was at once enthroned over the affections of the Church and the confidence of the public. It was felt that the perfidy of one man could not be justly charged upon a whole class. After Caples, Methodist preachers were at par, or above, in Chariton county.

At the next session he was admitted into the Conference on trial a second time and returned to the Keytesville circuit. At the close of this year he had been traveling actually three years and a half, but the irregularity involved in his discontinuance had caused the delay of his election to Deacon's orders, so that he was not yet ordained. Even now he was, technically, only in the class of the first year, and therefore ineligible as a traveling preacher. But he had been preaching four years, and the President of the Conference allowed him to be presented for orders under the law governing the ordination of local preachers.

At this point occurred an incident which he felt most keenly. Indeed, I think nothing ever mortified him so much. His election was opposed and defeated. Rev. N. M. Talbot, as true a man as the Church has ever had, objected to his ordination, on the ground of extreme levity. He spoke at some length and urged the objection strongly. There was not that gravity, he said, which became a Deacon in the Church of God. He did not himself mind a joke now and then; in fact he rather enjoyed it, and thought a hearty laugh once in a while innocent enough. But this young man was at it all the time. It was incessant. His jests were often irreverent, if not actually profane. The Most Holy Name would be used to give pith and poignancy to his wit. In the pulpit he was great. He had few equals there. But out of the pulpit he ruined all. The brother, he continued, was like the cow that gave the bucket *full* of the richest milk and then kicked it over.

Whether the application was withdrawn or voted on and defeated, I do not now remember. At any rate he was not ordained at that time, and always blamed Uncle Nat for the failure. Dating, however, from his last admission on trial he graduated in due course to deacon's and elder's orders.

I plead guilty to the enthusiasm of a friend in writing of my brother Caples. But I can not consent to play the part of an indiscriminate eulogist. There was ground for brother Talbot's censure of him. He was a man of most exuberant spirits. His vivacity was astonishing. He saw a ludicrous side to everything. Wit and humor gushed up from a perennial fountain, down deep in his very being. Without intention he would say the most laugh-provoking things. He often went too far. The brakes ought to have been down, hard, many a time when they were not down at all. Sometimes there was a species of recklessness in his jesting that made me shudder. It seemed that he would sacrifice anything to the triumph of a first-rate joke. I always felt that he could and ought to have been more temperate in this respect.

Yet there never was a man with whom I could more readily fall into the most edifying conversation on the subject of religion. At the same time I feel it to be due to the truth, in writing an account of his life, that I should record my unqualified disapproval of such excessive levity. But in *him* it was less objectionable than in any other man I ever saw, because it was so evidently of his very nature to be so.

He used to say, facetiously, that he did try once for three weeks to be sober, like a preacher. He wore his face of an edifying length. At last he began to feel "the solemn" striking in, and felt that it would kill him. After that he never made the experiment again. It was too dangerous. Thus jocularly would he put aside expostulation. Reproof did no good. He would turn it aside so adroitly that the reprover himself would end in uproarious laughter in spite of the most serious purpose.

In making missionary speeches, and preaching what he called "money sermons," he gave full play to his wit. But the most laughable things were often such a natural outgrowth of the deepest pathos that the effect was rather hightened than otherwise. At any rate it loosened the money in a man's pocket most effectually. But in his ordinary sermons there was not the slightest trace of it.

He had another fault — the use of extravagant epithets in denunciation. It was an incident of the decisiveness of his character. He saw everything in a strong light. He could excuse the foibles of a brother, but all meanness he hated with a perfect hatred. He loathed it. His soul poured itself out in red hot invective. His vehemence was like Luther's and required strong adjectives. Often the man would not be distinguished from his meanness. It was part of the man. The odious thing was not an abstraction, but was actually here in town, standing on two legs, and showing its face in the sun. It was embodied, and had a name. He would exhaust a whole arsenal of blasting epithets upon it.

Not that it was wrong to condemn decisively, sharply, or point out the infamy of an infamous transaction, and of the author of it. But there were occasions when he put too much brimstone in. Where saltpetre would have been strong enough, he used fulminate of mercury. His adjectives were terrific.

He saw more in an incident than any common observer would, and hence his anecdotes seemed to most of us like exaggerations. Many of his statements had an extravagant air. Yet I am sure that he told the story as he saw it. He had insight that others lacked. He saw below the surface. Sometimes, I doubt not, his imagination supplied features that were not present. But *to him* they were present.

And, now, I do verily believe I have told the whole story of this man's faults. I am confident that no just censorship will add to the catalogue. If there were others, they were virtues in excess.

These that I have mentioned were on the surface. They pained his friends, and at times did harm. They did in some cases, as I have reason to believe, interfere with the effect of his ministry. They were the first things you would see. They invited attention and criticism. But those who were closest to him, and had the deepest insight into his character, saw that these things were incidents of natural temperament rather than elements of moral character. There were no covert wickednesses in the man. He had no politic concealments of traits consciously evil. What was to him came out freely He was without guile. After a long acquaintance, in the intimacies of a close relation, you would feel that all the settled purposes of his life were pure, all his habitual aspirations holy To the voice of the Spirit of God his innermost soul gave a solemn response and a free allegiance. The will of God was his supreme law.

Perhaps it ought to be said, in addition, that these faults had their ground in that geniality and heartiness of nature which gave him so great an influence amongst men. Who was there that did not love Caples? Even when he provoked you, you still loved him. The very quality that you were tried with was the outgrowth of an attractive trait.

Baffled as he was, first by want of support, and secondly, by the delay of his ordination, he was all the while gathering force for the great part he had to perform in the history of Missouri Methodism. If he was cast down he was not destroyed. From the very fall he secured a firmer footing, and stood the more safely afterward. The momentum that bore him forward was too great to be overcome by this resistance. The current of his spiritual life gathered head upon the obstructions until every thing was swept before it. It was no feeble stream that might be arrested until it would evaporate or be lost in the sands, but a iver, which, though checked for a moment, would soon force its way Its volume was swelled by the resistance, and went forward to a larger destiny.

I have not a doubt that his life was better and more fruitful from these early embarrassments. They deepened his sympathies. They enlarged his soul. They made him a better preacher, a better pastor, a better presiding elder. He could enter into all the perplexities of the preachers. He could reassure them in the hour of trial with a more inspiring word.

But the period of temptation did not end here— I mean special temptation to abandon the work of the ministry He has been heard to say that as late as the time of his first term at Glasgow he had a fearful conflict with himself on this point. He knew that in the profession of the Law he could both rise to distinction and amass wealth. Year after year the devil followed him with this temptation. In Glasgow, at that time, one of the principal centers of business and wealth in the interior of the State, it came upon him with new force. In this elegant society he might establish himself permanently, and soon become rich and great. Here were personal admirers who would throw a lucrative practice in his way He saw himself standing at the threshold of the temple of fortune. As he stood in his poverty outside, the light and glory within shone with exaggerated splendor. A growing family demanded his care. Ought he not to give up this work of the Gospel, in which there would never be more than bare subsistence, and amass something for his children? Thus was a bribe offered even to his conscience. That stronghold won, the enemy would have easier work at every other point. The defenses were not very formidable on any other part of the line. For a time he was in suspense—a state of mind he could not bear. He resolved to end the strife.

For this purpose he went alone into a forest adjacent to the town. There the matter was to be settled and then. He would get an answer from God that should keep his soul in rest, or failing in that, from that day the star of fortune would become his cynosure.

The secret of that day is with him and God. Only the result is known. From that time he never vascillated, even in thought. He conquered in being conquered. God mastered him, but he gave him His name, and with that he triumphed over all else.

What passed between him and the Creator in the solitude of the forest, what felt shadows of the world to come were on his soul, how he bowed himself and opened himself to the Holy Ghost, what visions were given him, we can only imagine. One thing we know: he rarely spoke of that day, and never but in the tone of deepest reverence.

I have often thought it remarkable that any such thing should occur after all that had gone before in his life. There had been a first and second offering of himself to the work, with the utmost deliberation, for he had twice come into the Conference. There was a third when he was admitted into full connection and received deacon's orders. There had been a fourth, the most solemn of all, when he took the vows of an Elder in the Church of God. Yet there remained this final consecration to be made in the depths of consciousnsss that had not yet been reached. Or, if they had, his polarity had been disturbed by alien influences afterward. There was required this awful interview, face to face with God, to restore fully the divine magnetism. Thenceforward there was no perceptible disturbance. It cost him no effort at any moment to say, " Get thee behind me, Satan." He gravitated toward God and duty with sustained, undeviating purpose, until he went up.

> " Henceforth let no profane delight
> Divide this consecrated soul ;
> Possess it Thou, who hast the right,
> As Lord and Master of the whole."

Reference having been made to Mrs. Caples' repugnance to the life of a preacher, it is proper to say that about a year before her death, at a session of the Conference in Glasgow, in 1847, she became deeply concerned on the subject of religion and presented herself for prayers. From that time she seemed reconciled to the calling of her husband. The following year they were in Brunswick. Near the close of it she died, having been happily converted some short time before she passed away. She was a woman of most decided character, and without any experience of the love of God, it was inevitable that her position as a preacher's wife would involve many things distasteful to her. But she was a true wife and mother, a woman of fine intellect and many noble traits of character. If she could have lived after her conversion to God, no doubt her husband's calling and character would have been the joy of her life.

Nor can I doubt that it was his steadfast devotion to his work that led her at last to the foot of the Cross. If he had vascillated both would, perhaps, have become worldly, and been at last involved in sin and destruction. As it was, she saw that religion was with him the one great concern of life, and though she held out against the strivings of the Spirit for years, he had the satisfaction of seeing her at last yield to the supreme attractions of the Cross; and when called to mourn her departure to the world of spirits he "sorrowed not as others who have no hope."

When she died, the light of his life, so far as this world's pleasures were concerned, went out. It was a sad hour when, returning from the burial scene, he looked upon his motherless children. But she was with God. Already the angels had welcomed the new-comer to the joys of heaven, and she was at home in the midst of the innumerable company and Church of the First-born. He was again "cast down but not destroyed."

His second marriage, with Mrs. Bailey, of Brunswick, was in every respect happy She was a true mother to his children. She had been converted under his ministry, and married him in view of his high calling. All its privations she accepted with cheerfulness, and even joy. Without grudging she saw the insufficient support of the Church supplemented out of her own resources. Ever a cheerful presence in the midst of his household, she made his home at all times a happy retreat.

She lived to share with him the calamities of the war and to see him die. After that dreadful hour, nerving herself to the task of a widowed mother without resources, she was faithful to the last. But the time was short. Her Father in heaven soon called her away from over-taxing labors and anxieties and "received her into rest."

CHAPTER VI.

THE PREACHER.

There are many thousands of people in Missouri who remember Mr. Caples in the pulpit. There are thousands whose character took more or less complexion from his sermons, thousands whose Christian life commenced, other thousands whose Christian life started into new power, and became more elevated and intelligent under his preaching. A chapter may well be devoted to this one part of his life. In truth, *preaching* constituted a large part of his life — the largest part, perhaps, I might say The man culminated in the pulpit. He was great everywhere — greatest of all here. Let us pause and contemplate him as he stood at the head of the Missouri pulpit.

He bestowed no great amount of labor in the immediate preparation of sermons. Some few of his sermons may be exceptions to this rule. Of some sermons he made brief notes, indicating the analysis of the matter; of others he made no notes at all. I think he rarely, if ever, took notes into the pulpit. I do not mean to say he made *no preparation* for the pulpit. He devoted much time in this way, with travail of soul. No mind ever brought forth like his without the pains of parturition. He was all his life engaged in this work. Laying up and digesting matter for the pulpit was a constant habit. He read and often conversed with reference to this. There is no man living with whom I have had so many and such earnest conversations on the great themes of religion. Invariably, when we were alone together, we would drift into this channel. He told me once that in talking with an intelligent friend he often got the deepest insight into spiritual truth. From other men's sermons he would get here and there a thought in a new attitude. At once a whole theory would be evolved from it. At times he would get a clew, and for weeks, at every unoccupied interval, he would be threading the labyrinth of unexplored thought into and through which it led, and at last come out with matter for from one to a dozen sermons.

To reduce the ·mass — to bring the chaos into shape — never cost him the labor it does most of us. The crude matter once in hand, the greater and lesser lights, standing in their appointed places in the heavens, would soon blaze forth on sea and dry land, each crowded with its own ap-

propriate population. The real labor was in the
creation; all that came after was little more than
re-creation, and, as I have good reason to believe,
was often — not always — left to be done in the
pulpit. He would at any moment block off a
section of the mass, knead it and shape it into a
world, and populate it with the living forms of
truth, coming and going upon their errands and
sweeping forward to their destinies. What worlds
they were sometimes! They were never just mere
mechanical structures. Living things innumerable were in them. They were all aglow with the
divine splendor of truth.

He never announced the "heads" of his sermon. Such an announcement, proper as it often
is, would have been out of place in his preaching.
Generally his sermons were evolved, each one out
of a single thought. Everything had direct relation to a common point. But it was not a mechanical relation, it was vital. His sermons were not
built, they grew. He could not announce, therefore, beforehand so much stone for the foundation, so much lumber for frame and flooring, so
much glass and so many pounds of nails — the
painting and finish to come last. The whole tree
is in the acorn, but you can't well bring it under
the square and compass while it remains there.
Such were Caples' sermons while yet they were
in his own mind. Each one was all there before

it was delivered, but in a germinal form. It was impossible to tell beforehand the exact shape this intellectual oak would develop into; how high the shaft might rise before the first great branches would start out, or how heavy the top might be; how rich the foliage or how abundant the acorns. You might predict, safely, a big tree, of fine symmetry, perfect of its kind; but it would be the symmetry of a tree, not of a statue. His mind was a forest, not a gallery of art. It was large, free, vital. Order there was, but of the sort that allows striking, surprising varia-tion; so large in conception that many a grand, but not unmeaning divergence might find scope within its lines.

I remember he told me once that he had two reasons for not announcing his analysis before-hand. One was, that such announcement would put the sermon into a straight-jacket. He wanted liberty. His mind did not work well under the constraint of inflexible lines. The other was, that he thought the effect better if every new point reached in the progress of thought should take the hearer by surprise. The sudden discovery of an old thought in new relations, giving it a new significance, would at once delight and edify.

Often a sermon was just a mere elaboration of his text, taking up, point by point, the matter of the text, in the order in which he found it. Still

6

what has been said was, in the main, true even
of that class of his sermons.   One of these he
preached in the Centenary Church, St. Louis, two
or three years before the war, from Phil. ii. 15,
16: "That ye may be blameless and harmless,
the sons of God, without rebuke, in the midst of
a crooked and perverse nation, among whom ye
shine as lights in the world, holding forth the
word of life."   I remember that the sermon produced a deep impression on the minds of the
young men of the Church, with whom I was at
that time in very intimate relations.   He gathered
up all the points in the text, somewhat leisurely,
and no one saw the underlying thought which
was the basis of unity in the discourse, until at
last, in a few striking statements, everything that
had gone before was made to re-appear in the last
clause of the text, "holding forth the word of
life."   The import of the whole passage was
brought into this clause, until every syllable
seemed bursting with the truth that was in it,
and you could almost see flames and tongues of
fire breaking out through every crack.

He never followed beaten ways in his preaching.
When you went to hear him you knew you were
not just going to hear the same old thing that you
had been hearing all your life, in the same old
way.   The same old thing it would be, indeed—
just the gospel; nothing else—but with what new

life and power! His mind was too big to get into a rut—too broad. Nothing is capable of greater variety of statement and illustration than the simple doctrines of the Cross. Nothing else that can be stated in so small a compass contains so much matter. Why, if a man had the insight he could talk about Christ and His Salvation forever, without repetition. There is no excuse for want of variety in preaching, unless it may come of mere irremediable dullness. If it does not come of that it comes of what is infinitely worse—laziness. Caples would have preached in the same house all his life and kept his congregation alive with expectation of something fresh to the last.

His style was elevated, but not without faults. It was not what it would have been if it had been formed under good tuition in boyhood. His chief defect was an occasional want of precision in the use of words. This was not so glaring as to attract notice of any but men of literary tastes. The common run of hearers would never think of it. Sometimes his sentences would be quite clumsy. Yet, I must add, it was not an offensive sort of clumsiness. They had a look as if they had a right to be awkward.

These defects, however, disappeared when he became fairly enlisted. When his mind was a little heavy at the outset, or when he "made a failure," as he did sometimes—not often—they were very noticeable. But when he was well sprung, everything was transformed. There was no want of precision then, nothing was clumsy. The word suited the thought, and the thought seemed as if it might have been fresh-born out of a celestial brain. Yet it was not beauty that you would predicate of his style, even in its best estate. It was grandeur. It was not the flash and polish of the diamond, but the play of chain-lightning in black tempests.

His sermons were not ornate, nor yet were they destitute of ornament. It was not, however, the adornment of gorgeous drapery, hung loosely about them; it was carved into their substance—or rather, it was of the very essence of them. He never went about hunting up fine things, but a gorgeous efflorescence would often appear on the high branches of the goodly tree.

I have witnessed greater effects under his preaching than under that of any other man. In 1851 there was a camp meeting at Thrasher's Chapel, in Marion county. The Hannibal and Palmyra stations and Hydesburg circuit united in it. It was commenced on Friday, and we intended to close it on the next Wednesday. But a revival of such extent sprang up that it was protracted over the second Sunday. Next to the conversion of souls, Caples' preaching was the great feature of the meeting. He preached in the morning on both Sundays. The crowds were immense. But when Caples rose every straggler came in, and a hush settled upon the whole scene that was almost oppressive. I *felt* the silence. On the second Sunday his text was the CX. Psalm. The theme was the inauguration and triumphs of the Son of God. It was no mere declamation. It was all thought. The speculative and the practical were combined. Christ wielding the resources of the universe in the interest of his kingdom, man redeemed, cleansed, exalted, glorified; and the issue of the sublime movement when the kingdom shall be delivered up to God, even the Father—this is the outline. I will attempt no description; but three thousand immortal spirits will carry the memory of it into the eternal world. Toward the close, every sentence was a shell, which, on reaching its objective point, exploded. The "slain of the Lord" were many There could not have been one who escaped unwounded. Many who resisted the Spirit that day have gone into eternity, and others still carry their scars.

In the pulpit his manner and speech were uniformly grave—often solemn—as became the great matter of which he treated. That wit, which was of his very nature, and which was so freely indulged in social life and in public speeches on ordinary occasions, even in Missionary meetings, was never suffered to appear there.　He felt that it was incongruous with that sacred place.

Many extensive revivals attended his labors.　I was with him in several.　In 1849–'50, while I was on the Monticello circuit, I had an appointment in Quincy, Ill.　I went there under the direction of my Presiding Elder, Rev Jacob Lanius.　He held that the Church North having violated the covenant of separation, we were not bound by it.　A society of twenty-five members having been organized there, I was directed to take it into my circuit.　My congregations were large and serious from the first.　After some months I invited Mr. Caples up from Hannibal.　In a meeting of less than two weeks there were over one hundred accessions to the Church, and a greater number of persons were converted.　A good many joined other churches, though their pastors kept aloof from us.　I found there that in the altar he was scarcely less effective than in the pulpit.　His instruction of penitents was wonderfully apt and helpful.　One case of a young lady I still remember.　She was in great distress, weeping as if her heart would break.　Brother C., approaching her, heard her exclaim repeatedly, "O! my Savior!" "Did you say *my* Savior?" he asked.　"Yes, sir." "*Is* He *your* Savior?"　To this point he held her mind until she found peace in believing.

As a preacher he was sound, "in doctrine showing uncorruptness." He would hear to no improvement of Watson. Evangelical Arminianism was with him the very truth of God. Calvinism on one hand and Pelagianism on the other he held to be equally false. By one man sin came into the world, and all have sinned. But Christ died *for all*, and all *who will* may be saved through Him. "That we are justified by faith only" was to him a most wholesome doctrine and full of comfort. The new birth of the human soul through the immediate agency of the Holy Spirit, and the direct witness of the Spirit of God with our spirit that we are accepted in the Beloved, were facts most precious to our ascended brother.

He was given to speculation, and was an adventurous thinker. But his judgment was sound, his discrimination too clear to allow any involvement in heretical opinions. He surveyed the field of Christian theology too comprehensively to construct a little, perverse theory in conflict with the scope of doctrine given in Holy Scripture. Many a man who has a crotchet and thinks himself wiser than the fathers, if he only had half of Caples' breadth, would find that his knowing so little is the secret of his thinking that he knows so much. Men sometimes construct theories from a small portion of the entire data, and are over-bold because they do not see the other side of the case. They have this, plus that, which gives a grand

·esult. They are so full of this, so proud of having discovered it, that off they go, shouting Eureka, like one possessed, never suspecting that they have stopped in the midst of the process, and are in fact far from the solution. A great, well-poised mind like Caples' has almost intuitive perception of the missing factors, and sees that all truth is *not* reached in this summary way—just by putting two and two together. There is a world of multiplying and dividing and subtracting, with taking of angles and dimensions, to be done before the goal of investigation is reached. At last, having gone down to the foundation, he finds that there was wisdom in the world before he was born, and that Watson and Wesley held their beliefs, not because they had not seen these wonderful depths which some of us are so proud of having fathomed, but because they knew how very shallow these depths are.

The purity of Christian doctrine was held by Mr. Caples as of vital consequence. His vow as an Elder in the Church of God bound him by solemnities equal to an oath to banish and drive out erroneous and strange doctrines. Toward error his attitude could not be that of neutrality Nor could he stand merely on the defensive. Error in vital doctrines was fatal. He must *attack it*. The great danger of our day he considered to be, *Sacramentarianism and Ritualism.* They are acceptable to the carnal mind. If a man may attain salvation through the rites of religion, it is, indeed, an easy process The sinner may be expected to receive with facility a system which might properly be entitled, " Salvation made easy " The dreadful fruit of all this is the carnal security of countless millions who live unregenerate, die in a false hope, and drop out of the Church into an unexpected hell.

His preaching was largely doctrinal. He not only maintained the true doctrine, but pointed out the antagonistic error. This involved him sometimes in controversy, which he did not court—nor yet shun. He had two public debates: one at Hannibal, with Dr. Hopson, of the Campbellite Church; and one at Brunswick, with Elder Moses E. Lard, of the same sect. At the former of these I was present. It afforded a fine opportunity of studying the man in several particulars. The contrast of him with his antagonist was striking. It was the difference between heavy ordnance and small arms. The big gun does more execution at one shot, the other is quicker loaded.

Dr. Hobson was *au fait* in minute verbal criticisms He knew well how to wield them for popular effect. He showered small propositions upon the audience, numerically distinguished, so as to make a formidable array. From what I knew of Mr. Caples' ready wit, his electrical quickness

in repartee, the flash and spring of his mind in
emergencies, I had expected him to show great
dexterity in this by-play of sophistries. On the
contrary, he seemed to have no taste for small
verbal criticisms, and really no skill in them. Of
the dexterously paraded sophisms he took little
or no notice, except now and then to ridicule—
not to answer them. One instance of this I
remember. The Doctor announced, with great
solemnity and formality, a grand rule—his auditors were at liberty to call it a rule of grammar,
of logic or of rhetoric—he was not particular
about that—but it was a rule decisive of the controversy. After due flourish of bugles, the rule—
the grand discovery of Dr. Hopson—this miracle
of learned criticism that was to be the last word
of all dispute, and send the whole world straight
off to the Jordan, was announced, in the terms
following: "An active transitive verb must terminate on an object that is capable of receiving
its action." "For instance," he proceeded, "I
may say, I eat bread, because bread is capable
of receiving the action of eating. But I can not
say I eat a stone, because a stone is not capable
of receiving this action. I may say with propriety,
I immerse a man, for a man is capable of receiving
this action, but I can not say that I *sprinkle* a
man, because a man is not capable of receiving
this action. I sprinkle water, for water is capable

of receiving this action." This was accompanied by significant gesticulation with the fingers.

I called Caples' attention to the language of the Apostle: Moses " sprinkled the book, and all the people," and other like passages. But he disdained to answer in any sober way a sophism so shallow. He only alluded to it jocularly, saying he would like to see the Doctor try the action of eating on a stone. He would find the stone very capable of receiving the action; the only question was, whether the Doctor was capable of performing it.

In the same debate his opponent stated sixteen propositions, consecutively, all duly numbered. I wrote them all down and offered the note to him. He paid no attention to it. In his next address he stated *one proposition*, in few words, that swept away fifteen of them, leaving one forlorn little fellow standing by himself. There he stood, and was never noticed.

At the close of the debate Mr. Caples, who had the closing argument, made one of the most remarkable addresses, on the work of the Spirit, that it was ever my fortune to hear. No heart was untouched. Argument was blended with appeal in a torrent of eloquence that swept the whole congregation before it. The old Methodists said, Amen. Emotion was irrepressible. Campbellites wept, the wicked were melted, and I felt that the word of God had been fully vindicated. How long he would have gone on I know not, but the gavel announced the half hour out, and he sat down.   Silence did homage for some moments to this sublime utterance of "the truth as it is in Jesus," after which Dr. Hopson made a few very graceful remarks, acknowledging the Christian courtesy of his antagonist throughout the debate. This was heartily reciprocated by Mr. C.   The whole congregation then sang the Long Metre Doxology to Old Hundred, the benediction was pronounced, and the congregation dispersed as if from a solemn Sabbath service.

I am indebted to Rev. W M. Rush for the following facts connected with his debate with Elder Lard, at Brunswick:

Mr. Lard's friends employed a stenographer and had the debate taken down, intending to have it published.   Neither Mr. Caples nor his friends took any part in this.   But after the reporter had prepared the manuscript, it was courteously submitted to him that he might revise his part of it. He did so, and gave his consent to the publication.

For some cause, I know not what, the book never appeared.   Whether those who had been at the pains and expense of having it prepared for the press concluded that it would not advance their cause, or feared that the sale of it would not cover the cost of publication, I do not know.

One thing often struck me: the contrast of his treatment of other subjects with his treatment of that of religion. In contests on other matters he did not himself disdain sophistry if he might gain his end by it. At the Educational Convention in St. Louis, when the question of the location of Central College was up, there were but two places in nomination—Fayette and St. Charles. I advocated the claims of St. Charles. The friends of Fayette did not desire discussion. Without it they were sure of their point. By discussion they would gain nothing, but might lose votes. I made an elaborate speech, expected a formal answer, and was prepared for it. The other party looked to Mr. Caples. He met the emergency, not by a reply to the facts and arguments, but by ridicule. Dr. Brown Maughs helped him. They raised a laugh at my expense. I had nothing to reply to—was confused and mortified. The vote was taken, and I was floored. After adjournment he saw that I was annoyed, and coming to me with his invincible good nature, "Ah! old fellow," said he, "did you think I was going to work on your timbers? I had too much sense for that. My only show was to nibble your ropes," and he finished with that laugh of his, half exultant and half humorous. I said something about nonsense being at a premium in this grave body, charged with vital interests of the Church. He replied that I must console myself as John Randolph did, referring to an anecdote he had seen to this effect: Randolph being defeated in a Congressional struggle, after one of his greatest speeches, met his servant, and relieved himself by saying to that friendly auditor, " We carried the day in the argument, but they got the advantage in the voting." It was impossible not to love him.

I have said that he never indulged his wit in the pulpit. I never heard of but one exception to this. It occurred at Savannah. Elder Hudgins, of the Campbellite Church, had been carrying on a meeting for some time, and had immersed great numbers of people. The preaching had been largely, of course, on the mode of baptism. A popular *furore* was raised on the subject of immersion. Methodists and others insisted that Caples should preach a sermon to meet the current. He was reluctant, but at last yielded For once he determined to preach *ad captandum*. The result was a sermon altogether unique, and such as he alone could make. No one else need ever attempt one on the same plan, unless he wishes to make himself ridiculous. But he could do it to perfection. The sermon was allegorical, the basis of the allegory being a military campaign. My account of it was from his own lips.

First came the preliminaries—efforts on both sides to secure the alliance of the *Greeks* At this point he reviewed the controversy on the meaning of such Greek words as are involved in the baptismal contest. The result was a firm alliance with the Greeks. No trouble about soldiers now. The Greeks love to fight. They will enlist to a man, if need be, and take the front in every battle. The army now organized, every phalanx takes the field. Active operations begin.

He is at no loss where to find the enemy, who is in force *at the ford of the Jordan.* The argument on John's baptism was here gone over, and the Greeks all in phalanx, with spear and buckler, fresh, confident, invincible, make the charge. There is desperate courage in the immersionist ranks. This ford is the key of their position. They are conscious of it. This lost, disorganization and overthrow are imminent. They fight like heroes. But one phalanx after another, imperturbable as truth itself, bears down upon them, until they waver, their columns break, and they fly The retreat is rapid, made in some disorder, and in the direction of *Enon.*

He predicts that they will rally at Enon. There is water there, much water; and the line of the Jordan lost, this point is vital. Taking no time to breathe, he marches his Greeks, flushed with vic tory, upon Enon. As he expected, the immersionist forces are massed here. No time is lost. The attack is brought on at once and furiously Here he gave the argument on this passage. The enemy makes a better stand than he expected. He had calculated upon their being disheartened from defeat, and the loss of their most important line of defense. But they fight with absolute desperation now. They "fight for their firesides and their altars." They seem eager to die. But on come the Greeks; they never falter. Truth knows no pity. Whoever stands in its way must be run over. The phalanx of Truth receives no check in the desperate bloodshed that stains all the springs of Enon. At last the shattered columns of the enemy break. They fought till hope was gone—long after it was gone they still fought—fought from sheer desperation, and from the instinct of fighting. Immersionists are all born fighters. But it avails nothing. What the maddest bravery could do has been done. All goes for nothing. Enon is lost. Nothing remains now but to surrender at discretion or maintain a hopeless, desultory warfare for awhile. The last line of defense is lost. A sound discretion would dictate peace on any terms in such a situation. But who ever knew an immersionist to surrender? Like the Mamelukes, they keep slashing with their swords while they are dying.

At last they fly. The Greeks hold Enon. The retreat is precipitate. With as little delay as possible he brings on his forces in pursuit. The enemy has fled to the desert toward Gaza. There is, however, no difficulty in following. The desert is strewn with abandoned *impedimenta*, and with the exhausted, the wounded and dying. He hastened forward and soon came upon them. They had found water in the desert; probably not much—possibly enough to cover a man. At any rate it was *water* The Jordan lost, and Enon lost, every little puddle in this scarce country was worth a fight. Here, accordingly, was another battle, and another defeat of the enemy. In this case it was an utter rout. It would seem that this must end the unequal conflict. Yet he would make thorough work of it, so he led his Greeks forward. Not an enemy was to be found. They had certainly disbanded and given up in despair. He goes into camp, however, prudently resolving not to disorganize his forces, for he dreads guerrilla operations. Beating around the country in search of any trace of the fugitives, he hears a melancholy voice—a sort of wail. "It is a voice from the tombs," said he;" "they have taken to the tombs! Hark! Do you hear that? '*Buried with him in baptism.*' I knew it. They have intrenched themselves in the tombs."

Deprecating the violation of the tombs by the din of war, but determined at all costs to secure the fruits of so many victories, he made the last attack and took the tombs.

7

It is not to be understood that this allegory constituted the staple of the sermon. Argument, illustration, exposition of Scripture, formed the substance of the discourse. The allegory, managed as he alone could do it, secured a popular effect, kept attention on tiptoe, and well disposed his audience to receive the more important and substantial matter which he gave them.

I feel in this, as in every instance, that I have given no just idea of the vivacity, vigor and taking character of his public efforts. It is not in me to do it. Indeed, if they had been taken down, word for word from his lips, the printed speech would give no idea of the spoken speech. Voice, face, that peerless eye, the very attitude of the man, gave more meaning than the words did.

The first time I ever saw him was in the summer of 1842, at a camp meeting in the Peery settlement. Constantine F Dryden was on the Trenton circuit, in the bounds of which this meeting was held. I was on the Grundy Mission, which lay higher up on the branches of Grand river. It was my first year in the ministry I had not seen much of Methodist preachers beyond the neighborhood where I was born, had not attended a session of Conference, nor met with any preachers during the course of this year, except my Presiding Elder, William W Redman, and brother Dryden. Every new preacher I met, if he was a man of mark, impressed me deeply. I am conscious to this day of a sort of romantic interest in all the preachers whom I met this year. At this meeting I saw, also, for the first time, Daniel A. Leeper. He was about my own age, and was just beginning to preach. One afternoon he preached at the camp-meeting. His text was: "Behold I stand at the door and knock," &c. It was properly an exhortation. He wept and all the people wept. My soul clave to him from that hour.

There I became acquainted with those princes of Grand river Methodism, the Peerys, Wynns, and others. There was among them a sort of elegant plainness that realized all that is best in refined manners under Christian conditions. I began to get a better insight into life and society My horizon widened, perceptibly. No one fact contributed more to this than my contact with Mr. Caples. He had been sent up (being on the Keytesville circuit) by the Presiding Elder to supply his lack of service, he being unable to attend.

Something may be inferred of his standing at the time from the fact that Brother Dryden, an older man and preacher, cordially yielded him precedence in everything. He took the management of the meeting and preached at 11 o'clock on Sunday. Of the sermon I only remember these facts—that I did not see the connection of the thought, did not perceive the *unity* of it—that it was very long, and that it magnetized the congregation. The feeling among the people became more and more intense to the very last. All seemed instinctively to recognize in him a leader of God's Host.

A few weeks later I heard him at Old Franklin, at a meeting attended by several preachers on their way to Conference. He preached on Sunday morning. I remember, more distinctly than I do the sermon, a conversation I heard between two elderly laymen, expressing devout gratitude to the great Head of the Church for raising up such a young man for his service in Missouri. It was to them a mark of the favor of God.

Some years elapsed before I heard him again. It was when he was stationed at Glasgow and I was on the Weston circuit, in 1846. He visited the family of Gen. Gist, his wife's father, then living in my circuit. I had appointed a meeting in anticipation of his visit. It was then, for the first time, I saw the grandeur of his mind. His word was in power. The only time I ever knew him to be at a loss for a word was at this meeting. In that instance he was so completely at fault that after a pause of some moments he used a word that, in the connection, was really ludicrous. He intended to say the wounded deer forsakes the herd, but the word *forsakes* forsook him, and he said slopes— and there the sentence ended. The strangest thing was that the congregation, all in tears, did not seem to observe the blunder. He recovered immediately. I question if there was ever another instance of his hesitating for a word.

He never healed the hurt of humanity slightly. He probed to the bottom of the sore. The guilt, the hell-deserving character of sin, the absolute helplessness of the sinner, he portrayed in their deepest colors. The danger of souls he felt, and made his congregations feel it. Nor would he tolerate any empirical treatment. The all-healing blood of Christ alone could save. That blood could be reached only by faith, and faith could not exist without a deep repentance. The test of all true repentance was the *forsaking of sin. Thorough work must be made* when the soul was at stake.

He dealt faithfully by the Church. Outward sin in the Church he rebuked with authority. He had great skill in setting it in every odious light. Sins against light, against knowledge, against covenant engagements—were these sins in the Church? The guilt of them was heavy. Especially would he lay the soul bare for its own inspection, and detect and bring to shame the lurking secret corruptions that were there, corroding it, defiling it. Lust, pride, mercenariness, anger, malice, often ruling the heart when the outward life is without reproach, he would charge upon his hearers with such convincing speech that every one would go home convicted of sin. The foundation of revivals under his preaching was thus deeply laid. The motives he appealed to were of the highest order. He did not at all depend on touching anecdotes — rarely related incidents. The tears that fell in his congregations were not started by graphic descriptions of death-bed scenes; or, if ever, very rarely. The Word of God was his weapon — the very sword of the Spirit. "The Word of God is quick and powerful, sharper than any two-edged sword, dividing asunder the soul and spirit, and the joints and marrow, and is a discerner of the thoughts and intents of the heart."

I have witnessed revivals that were marked by a species of flippancy, from the low class of motives appealed to. Not much lasting fruit is gathered from such.

All the duties of a holy life were urged home by him in times of revival with most solemn enforcement. The doctrines, the great fundamental doctrines, he would set forth largely at such times. But didactic sermons from him were not *dry*. There was not much mere exhortation, but almost all he said had the force of exhortation. It at once enlightened the understanding and appealed to the conscience.

Oh! what a comforter of the Lord's people he

was when they were in distress. He had himself been in the depths. Every consolatory form of truth had at one time or another met some great need of his own soul. Out of the Word of God and his own experience he administered abundant consolation to those who were cast down. His *voice* at such times made the words richer and more healing.

His preaching was never empty declamation. He did not understand himself to be a declaimer. The arts of oratory he had not studied with much care. He was a *teacher of Christian truth.* To accomplish this mission most effectually was his study. Whatever was impressive and effective in manner and voice was a natural gift, perfected by the aim and effort I have mentioned. There was no merit aside from the matter — no merit of *mere manner* — though, as a vehicle of the matter, his manner was most effective.

His sermons were eminently *suggestive.* I scarcely ever heard him preach that he did not give me some germinal thought which started into immediate growth in my own mind, so overflowing with vital thought was all he said. Some sermons, full of important matter, have an architectural character. Everything is finished. They have high value and great beauty But every part is finished. You see nothing beyond just what is contained in the structure. Mr. Caples' were not f that class. I have already, in another trait of them, compared them to a tree. The same illustration is in point here. A thousand germ points, in each one, were ready to start into fresh and indefinite development.

I have said that he **rarely** " made failures " in preaching. A few times in his life he did, but very few. The most notable instance of the kind in the memory of his friends occurred at Nashville, at the General Conference of 1858. To those who knew him it seemed almost a miracle that a mind so vital could so completely break down. There was neither thought nor spirit in it. I knew what few did, that for two days he had been sick, and that, as the result of it, he was suffering from great physical debility Almost any other man would have excused himself from the task. To do so, however, seemed to him a sort of affectation.

To the debilitating effect of sickness must be added the fact that he had been spoken of for the Episcopal office, and he suspected that many of the members of the Conference were there to decide upon the question of his capacity for that position. He became self-conscious. There was no help for him. In pain and weakness, aggravated by this consciousness, he dragged through a most miserable *effort* of near an hour. I had heard him, at St. Charles, only a few months before, from the same text. The sun unobscured and the sun in total eclipse have not an aspect more in contrast than these two sermons.

His preaching was original, often unique—but not eccentric. He used, however, to relate an anecdote of his early ministry to this effect: Expecting to attend a camp-meeting (I think it was in Jackson county—of this, however, I am not sure), he memorized one of Wesley's sermons, intending to deliver it in case of being called upon to preach. Not yet confident of his ability to preach extempore on such an occasion, he thought this the better policy. He had fully mastered the sermon, and entered the pulpit with confidence. Singing and prayer ended, he arose and announced his text. On the instant his mind became completely inactive. Memory would render up none of her store. That precious sermon was under lock and key, and the key was lost. Such was the effect of it on his nervous system that he lost consciousness and fell. On coming to himself he discovered that he was lying on a bed in the preacher's tent, and that there was no one present. Upon an impulse of shame he crept under the bed. After some minutes of mortifying reflection he seized his saddlebags, hoping to elude observation, and fly from the place. Fortunately, the Presiding Elder met him at the tent door, and, with brotherly force, detained and soothed him—perhaps saved him.

He was thus effectually cured of plagiarism. He set up a thinking shop of his own, and carried on business on a grand scale. To be sure he did not disdain to get lumber at other men's mills. He laid in material from every source of supply—from books, from observation upon men and society, and from the primeval warehouses of earth and heaven. But all that he put on the market was *made in the shop*. He kept no second-hand furniture for sale. When you once knew him there was no mistaking his work. I should have known one of his sermons if I had met it on the Isthmus of Panama. They were of a type as peculiar as that of his own physique. Indeed, between the mental and physical conformation there was a striking resemblance.

I had not heard him for several years before his death, but from all I gather he grew to the last. His preaching at the Mexico Conference will never be forgotten. The sad events of the war, probably, deepened his character.

But I must stop. I shall weary the reader. I am in a garrulous mood. I can not tire of talking about this preacher. I see him now in the rude camp-meeting pulpit, a little stooped as he announces his text. With what deliberation he unfolds his theme for the first twenty minutes.

His voice now deepens. Electric streams begin to pour out of his eyes. Soul and body dilate. The current of ideas widens. The volume and momentum of thought is augmented. The congregation is hushed. There is much weeping. There is deep sobbing. Will he not forbear? Justice appears with the hot thunderbolt in his lifted hand. Mercy pleads. Guilt darkens eternity, pardon lifts the pall. The Judgment Throne and Heaven and Hell sweep into the field of vision. The sentence of the Judge sets the seal on destiny!

"Come! sinners, come! It is *not* too late. You are not dead yet, thank God! thank God. Come! God calls you! Fly! Death is on your track. Your steps take hold on hell. The pointed lightning-shaft quivers at your breast. COME TO CHRIST! COME NOW!"

The altar is crowded with the slain. There are shouts, and groans, and sobs, and cries, and songs, all mingled, and above all the voice of the preacher: "HE IS ABLE TO SAVE TO THE UTTERMOST ALL THAT COME TO GOD BY HIM."

In confirmation and illustration of what has been said in this chapter, Rev. W M. Wood sends me the following account of his preaching at a camp meeting near Shelbyville in the summer of 1850. "The meeting had continued," brother Wood writes, "some days with great success.

Monday came, and with it a continuous rain. The preacher had no thought of service. The tent-holders had a consultation; the result was a proposition to Caples that if he would preach he should have a congregation. He consented, and appeared on the platform, partially protected by a temporary cover. The people gathered around, some with umbrellas, others without, standing in the falling rain, like statues, listening to the word of life as it fell from his lips—one of the most impressive illustrations of the power of true eloquence I ever have known. S——, a bright candle in the ministerial ranks in the East, who having come West intending to invest a little surplus money in lands and continue his ministerial labors, was induced to engage in speculation, and, Lucifer-like, had fallen, heard the sermon. He came to Caples at the close, with tears, and asked if there was any hope for him, and if so, what he must do. C. told him to go and sell all and give to the poor, and with sincere repentance engage in the work of the ministry. He promised he would, but when Caples was gone it was all forgotten, and, poor man, the night of his death he said he was wrecked, soul and body "

This incident not only illustrates his wonderful power as a preacher, but his clear sense of the *exclusive* character of this calling Preaching once on the spread of the Gospel, he was dilating on the passage of the Apocalypse in which the angel appears, flying through the midst of heaven, having the everlasting Gospel to preach. Seeing in the congregation some preachers who had once been devoted exclusively to the work of God in the itinerant ranks, and had, as he believed, great power for usefulness, but who were now local, and immersed in business, having large farms and mills, he suddenly pictured the angel weighted down with a mill on one wing and a farm on the other, laboring in painful and embarrassed flight. The brethren felt the force and acknowledged the justice of the rebuke, but held on to their mills and farms.

Amos Rees, Esq., gives the following account of an exhortation he once heard from him at Parkville: "After a long, tedious sermon by another man, Caples arose and seemed to be at a loss for something to say. At last he announced one of those passages of Scripture where Christ is spoken of as a rock, which was suggested by something said by the preceding preacher. From that he branched out into one of the most powerful exhortations I ever heard in my life, either before or since, and for thirty or forty minutes the whole congregation was spell-bound and in tears; no doubt much more so from the contrast between this exhortation and the sermon preceding. He went on to say that Christ was that rock. To be saved we must get on that rock. How shall we get on it? There is an immense chasm between us and the rock, all deep, dark and fearful. We must get on it *by faith.* He would bring the poor, halting sinner up to the verge of that chasm, and require him to take a step forward. Trembling and alarmed, he could not do it. But ruin was behind him and destruction before. Then he interposed the *promise of God* that he should be saved if he went on, and assured him that ruin would follow his halting. At last he pressed him to take a step *by faith. His foot was on a rock.* And so, hesitating, doubting, fearing, he made him take step after step until he was safely landed on the rock.

"Now, as you received Christ, so must you walk. You received him by faith—you must go out and walk by faith. He pressed him out in the same way he had got him on to the rock. He got him to take a step by faith, and his foot was *on a rock,* although he could not see it. And so he got him out, step by step, until, at last, *in his* peculiar style, he exclaimed, in all the fervor of his soul, 'Bless God, the way to heaven is a macadamized road!' The effect was overwhelming. The house was in tears."

A statement from Rev. W M. Rush will close this chapter:

"I first met Mr. Caples at a session of the

Missouri Conference, held in Jefferson City, commencing on the 31st day of August, 1842. He was there for admission, on trial, into the traveling connection. I remember him at the altar upon his knees, engaged in most earnest, pleading prayer for penitent sinners. His prayer impressed me greatly, and I remember it with a distinctness with which I remember no other prayer that I heard during that Conference session. Mr. Caples' prayers were always edifying, but there were times, as in the above instance, when he would seem, in an extraordinary manner, to come into the immediate presence of God, and there talk and plead with his Maker as I have rarely ever heard any one. I remember him as the faithful pastor, the efficient and ever popular Presiding Elder, the advocate, friend and agent of our literary institutions, and I can never forget him as I have seen him upon the platform at our Missionary Anniversaries, pleading the cause of the poor in the sparsely settled sections of our own country and the cause of the perishing heathen. But above all do I remember him in the pulpit, the messenger of God to the people, and I think I never saw a man in the pulpit whose whole spirit and bearing were in better keeping with the character of his message than were his. Here, indeed, he was a master—a workman that needed not to be ashamed. Who that heard his sermon on the

Judgment, preached at the Conference at Richmond, in 1855, can ever forget it? His text was Rev. xx. 11–15: "And I saw a great white throne, and Him that sat on it," &c. He argued the necessity of a judgment. He described the solemn and awful grandeur of the attendant circumstances—the great white throne and Him that sat on it—the dissolving universe—the opening graves and the dead, small and great, standing before God, were all dwelt upon in his own peculiarly graphic and lucid style. But the interest of his discourse culminated in the opening of the *books*. Prominent among the books was the book of memory. Memory, faithful to her trust, had borne an impartial testimony. Every thought and feeling and desire of the heart was legible as if written with an iron pen and graven in the rock forever. Every word echoed afresh through all the chambers of the soul, and every transaction of life, whether good or bad, was a living consciousness. Next was opened the book of life; and this was not a *mere* record of names—names, indeed, were there—but it was also a record of the way of life. Each redeemed one could plainly read the record of his own recovery Drifting down to the abyss of woe, guilty, polluted, ready to perish, he came, penitently, trustingly, to the Father, through the Son, and obtained mercy; was lifted up, washed, purified, refined, clothed in righteousness; his name written in heaven, he now stands approved in the presence of his Judge. I can give no adequate description of this sermon or of its effect upon the vast congregation that heard it. Some one said he preached an hour and a half, but I made no note of time. The preacher was himself moved and inspired by his theme as I rarely ever saw him, and he carried his audience with him at will as he ranged amid the grand topics of his subject; and in the close of his discourse we saw the righteous saved, the wicked damned and God's eternal justice approved.

The sermon was the subject of remark for days. A visiting brother, who is himself a man of distinction in the Church, and who had heard most of the leading pulpit men of the country, not only of the Methodist Church, but of other Churches, remarked to me the next day, that he had heard some of the most distinguished men of the country preach upon the judgment, but that Caples' sermon was the grandest thing he ever heard on that subject. Such are some of my recollections of our mutual friend and brother."

CHAPTER VII.

THE PASTOR.

Mr. Caples was in the active work of the ministry more than twenty-four years. Eight years of this time he was a Presiding Elder and two years agent of Central College. He spent over fourteen years as a Pastor, on stations and circuits. He never imagined that he had filled up the measure of duty when he had met his regular appointments.

There are, on one principle of classification, just two sorts of men in the pastoral office. The two classes are not in fact separated by a sharply defined boundary, but shade into each other by imperceptible degrees of approach. One class is composed of men who seem to have no idea of anything beyond the routine of stated and well-defined duties. They go to the regular appointments; if they find prayer and class-meetings already established, they attend them (provided it may be convenient); and if any one happens to volunteer a subscription for the *Advocate*, why they will forward the name. I once inquired of an excellent and very sensible layman, living in a circuit, how his preacher was doing. " Well," said he, " he's goin' around." This told the whole story. The routine was steadily gone through with. Every four weeks, about eleven o'clock or a *little* later, you might look down the road, assured that your eye would be rewarded by the vision of the preacher advancing at a leisurely pace, his whole aspect and bearing seeming to give assurance that nothing could move him any faster, and nothing stop him, unless it might be " bad weather."

Everything is perfunctory, both in the doing and in the spirit of it. You begin to feel sleepy the moment you see him. He evidently has a serious, complacent sense of the fact that he is " doin' the duties." No sooner is he fairly established on a circuit than the Church subsides. It will hibernate so long as he remains.

Take an example of the other sort. He comes to his circuit to do whatever he may for the Master. He is full of his mission. The affairs of the Church must be attended to. He never whimpers about this or that being the duty of some one else. If no one else will, he does it, or sees that it is done. If Church property is not regularly deeded or cared for, he sees that it is no longer neglected.

He stirs around among the people and wakes them up to organize Sunday-schools. When there are no prayer meetings or class meetings, he appoints them, and if he can induce no laymen to lead, he will lead himself. He talks about the *Advocate* with hearty interest, and asks for subscriptions with the manner of a man who means it, until there is a *subscribing mania* on his circuit. He has the broken lights in the Church windows replaced. His eye is on everything; his hand touches everything. Think of *his* circuit hibernating!

In the pulpit there is the same vitality. This man never drones. He may not be boisterous; he may be very quiet. But he is *in earnest.* You feel it. He is not going *through a discourse*—he is *preaching the gospel*

How soon such a man is *felt* in every part of his work. The man is vital. Everything around him wakes into life and energy. All the agencies of the Church become active. He sets the whole machinery in motion.

"Like priest, like people." With rare exceptions, the private members of the Church will not be active under an inactive preacher. By the ordination of God the pastor is chiefly responsible, as he, mainly, is charged with the welfare of the flock committed to him—over which the Holy Ghost hath made him overseer. *It is his business* to work for the Church. He has nothing else to do. If other men, private or official members, neglect some duty, they may plead the engrossment or fatigue of secular affairs with some show of plausible pretense. But *this is his business*, and negligence can offer no excuse. The more so as his negligence is certain to be a precedent. Not only his own idleness, but the idleness of the whole Church, which it is his business to lead into active labors, he must be held to account for. Some men in the sacred office will have a heavy account to meet at the last day

The true pastor will interest himself in the welfare of every member of his charge. So far as possible he will become acquainted with every one. In the largest churches this may be difficult. In such cases the pastor must make the wisest and most industrious use of his time. He can ascertain if any are negligent of the means of grace; and if their circumstances make it impossible for him to see them in a private way, as is often the case with young men in a city, he can write them an affectionate letter. I have known such a manifestation of affectionate interest on the part of a pastor to produce the happiest effect. The man who realizes in any adequate degree the worth of souls, will make it his study to keep all those committed to him, that he may present them at the last day without grief or shame. That none may have hurt or hindrance through his fault or negligence, will be the object of chief solicitude with him. To this end he will make himself accessible to all, and invite approach. He will interest himself in their troubles and perplexities, even if it should seem to him absurd to be troubled and perplexed about such things. It will be enough for him to know that they are in difficulty. The wicked one is taking advantage of some mere trifle, it may be, to tempt them. An endangered soul will arouse his interest. With patient care he will lay himself out to defeat the adversary.

The pastoral relation is realized when there is active intercourse between the minister and his people; when there is capacity of intelligent instruction on his part, and respectful confidence on theirs; when he is ready to enter into all their dangers and perplexities, and when all are edified and established through his influence and instruction.

It is not merely the instruction given in particular cases, the special attention given here and there, that builds up the members of the Church. There are subtle, spiritual influences going out from a true man of God which accomplish more, for aught I know, than any special effort he may put forth. While he is intent upon this duty and that, going about on the Lord's errands, results follow that he never dreams of. I once knew a very faithful man in charge of a circuit, always doing something for God, who was on the road early one morning going to meet a Bible class. A wicked man, seeing him in the saddle at that early hour, and knowing his character, and that he was spending his life in doing good to the souls of men, fell under conviction and was soon converted. It was but a short time until the whole country was in a flame of revival.

To be effective this work must proceed out of a sanctified heart. There must be the tone of a true and deep spirituality in it. If it is forced work it will fall into mere cant, which is the farthest imaginable from genuine religious sentiment. Out of a deep experience of the things of God a man will speak freely, fearlessly, naturally. *Cant* is constrained, forced, affected. The words which come out of a heart overcharged with the love of God have body and weight. They sink into the minds of others, and command a serious, thoughtful hearing. *Cant* is chaffy. It has no specific gravity, and men put its exhortations aside lightly, often with a feeling of petulance, as if the effort were felt to be intrusive. All genuine work in the vineyard of the Lord must proceed out of a substantial Christian character. A man must himself be in the Spirit in order to make the voice of the Spirit articulate to others.

The minister must be often in the "mountain," or his coming into the multitude will amount to but little. Jacob comes to be *Israel*, "a prince of God," who PREVAILS WITH GOD AND MEN only after he wrestles with the angel to the last extremity—till his thigh is out of joint. Thus disabled he wrestles still, even when ready to die under the weight of his Omnipotent Antagonist—never faltering in the importunate purpose of the struggle: "I will not let thee go except thou bless me." Thus prevalent with God he goes forth to conquer men.

Mr. Caples understood this. In his diary I find this entry: "Spent the evening in reading, meditation and prayer." The prayer seems to have been prompted by a sense of his own need. But beyond what he knew, he was getting strength for his great work. With a sick wife and a Church distracted by the war upon his heart, he went into the secret place of the Most High. He prayed in secret, and He that heareth in secret rewarded him openly.

An important incident of the pastoral office is visiting the sick and comforting those that mourn. In times of sorrow men turn, if ever, to the contemplation of divine things. In bereavement, in sickness and in the presence of death the heart, with unerring instinct, recognizes in religion the only source of consolation. Many who, in the midst of health and good fortune, slight the word and ministers of God, will call for help from on high in the last extremity And to the faithful people of God how comforting is the presence of the trusted pastor in the dark hour!

Dr. Richard Bond, when he was agent of the American Bible Society, spent some days with brother Caples in Glasgow. At the next session of the Conference, during the examination of character, when the name of brother C. was called, Dr. Bond stated as a matter to be especially noted, the considerate and tender attention he gave the sick of his charge. In his diary I find abundant evidence of the same fact. It not only appears that he was attentive to those who were in distress, but that there was also a deep, abundant fountain of sympathy in him. His visits were not merely official; they were the attentions of a friend. He entered into their trials. He went to the house of mourning not because he must, as a part of his calling, but from a real interest in his people. His relation to them was not a formal, ecclesiastical one, so much, in his own consciousness, as it was real and spiritual.

One thing in his diary is especially suggestive. Wherever a funeral is mentioned, it is certain to be noted in the entry of the following day that the bereaved family was visited. The day after the funeral is a sad day in the household. A solemn hush is upon the whole scene. The shadow of death lingers. The presence of a gossip, to chatter about the trifles of the neighborhood, would be an impertinence. Not so the coming of the pastor. His face, full of sympathy, serious but not gloomy, brings a ray of light. His voice, reading the twelfth chapter of the Epistle to the Hebrews and raised to God in prayer, brings a sense of the divine love, and the graciousness of the divine severity, though not yet seen, begins to be felt. There is no better day for a pastoral visit than the next day after the lost one has been laid to rest.

In other instances the diary shows that his visits were not made at random. There was much going from house to house. There was also much attention to circumstances—much thoughtful adjustment of labor to the actual condition of individuals in his charge. From his knowledge of human nature he chose the best time to approach men. There are times when almost every man is accessible and impressible. He excelled in that sort of insight which enabled him to take advantage of such times.

He makes mention of an aged sinner, very sick, whom he visited. On the occasion of the first visit he was inaccessible, evincing no interest in religious concerns. The claims of Christ were not pressed upon an unwilling mind. The sufferings of the helpless man were mitigated by a little thoughtful attention. When the man of God came again he found a willing ear and a heart open to his message. Another unconverted man he visited constantly through a period of many weeks, witnessed a happy result of his care, received the prodigal into the Church, and parted with him at the gate of death, in joyful hope of the resurrection.

As an example of the heart of this man in his pastoral work I make the following extract from his diary:

"Nov. 4, 1863.—Returned to town. Called at brother Henry Lewis'. Stayed at brother J. O. Swinney's. Little Billy very ill of scarlet fever. The Lord spare him to his fond parents.

"5, noon.—Billy is no better. Dined and prayed with father Lewis, John and wife.

"6.—Dined at Dr. Walker's. Visited brother Swackers, brother Dunnica's (Thomas suffering very much with his arm); Mr. Hutcheson (found Rebecca sick with fever); visited mother Watts, brother Pitts, etc. Little Willie Swinney died this afternoon at 3 1-2 o'clock—a lovely child. He was five years old the 20th of April last. I hasten to offer such consolation to my afflicted brother and sister as I may be able. An interesting conversation with brother Swinney, sister Thompson and others, on the providence of God and the state of the pious dead. Brother S. tempted to doubt the goodness of God in permitting such suffering in the case of innocent childhood. Billy had learned to love God, yet suffered so much. Is satisfied as he remembers the necessity for the violence of the storm to drive one into port so soon, and the eternity in which God rewards for these short sufferings.

"7.—Billy's funeral at 2 1-2 o'clock. The day interspersed with pleasant conversations about him. Brother and sister S. resigned and tenderly submissive. God's grace, so far, has given victory.

"After religious services, with a short address, we buried little Billy. Peace to his ashes!"

This extract is literal, except that in two or three places I have supplied connectives and omitted one sentence foreign to the matter.

Several other passages might be culled from his diary to illustrate the deep interest he felt in all the sorrows of the people of his charge. He rejoiced with those that did rejoice, and wept with those who wept. Though of a very joyous nature himself, he never shunned the house of mourning. It was better to be found there than at the house of mirth. Yet, while he always had sympathy to give, he did not seem to demand it for himself. He was a very self-contained man. He had a helping hand for all without seeming to expect much help from others. He was an example of those two striking passages in Gal. vi. 2–7: "Bear ye one another's burdens, and so fulfill the law of Christ:" "for every man shall bear his own burden." Resting on God he bore his own burdens, not weakly demanding help from every one in hearing. Yet was his hand ever stretched out to aid an overburdened brother.

The poor were never overlooked by him. At one time he was himself, to use his own language, in "poverty, bordering on want." The houses of such he never shunned. Perhaps his own poverty was part of the training by which God prepared his heart for the pastoral office. Possibly it was a better training than a full course of Divinity would have been. At any rate his education was not deficient in this particular branch of it. He knew the wants of the destitute, and the sensitiveness and solicitude of modest and meritorious poverty. He knew how to deport himself amongst them. They never felt that Caples *patronized* them. He never came with the air of condescension, but with the easy, natural manner of a friend. He came with the spirit of one who came of his own choice, and not because it was one of "the duties." Nor was his kindness in word only, but also in deed. Even when pressed in his own circumstances he would help the poor of his Church liberally out of his own short supply. And there was a homely sort of matter-of-courseness and genuine heart in the giving that forestalled all embarrassment and awkward, mortified self-consciousness on the part of the recipient of his alms. Indeed, it did not seem to them that they were receiving alms, but rather a compliment, an expression of friendly regard. Of course this refers to the worthy poor of his flock, and not to professional beggars and trifling vagabonds, whose highest ambition it is to prey upon the charities of the preacher. It was a real luxury to him to divide the last dollar with one who was truly unfortunate. That his charities were in deed and not in word only I happen to know from personal observation in two or three cases; and in further illustration I cite the private diary which has been placed in my hands.

"Dec. 16, 1863. Visited sister C.; found her in trying circumstances (in want); prayed for her and gave her $5 in the Lord's name. Oh! the suffering poor! The Lord pity them this cold and stormy day. The storm has continued now forty-eight hours."

What a heart he had! No man destitute of true sympathy would have made such a note in his private diary. Beside this, these two days of winter were spent visiting the sick and poor. He was out a good portion of both days. He was no hireling, doing routine duty for a piece of bread; but a faithful under-shepherd, caring for the souls and bodies of those whom the Lord had bought with his own blood. His chief ambition was to share the labors, and he was ready even to enter into the sufferings of Christ, in his measure, ever looking forward to a final participation of the joy of his Lord.

An important function of the pastoral office is the maintaining of godly discipline. On this as on all subjects his views were broad and comprehensive. He did not understand, as some seem to do, that the administration of discipline consisted only in expelling members to keep the Church pure. He considered this only as the last resort. Sensitive he was, indeed, to any dishonor the Church might suffer from sin amongst the members. He was alive to the purity of the Church. But he did not conceive that expulsion of the offender was the only method of maintaining purity If, on the contrary, the offender might be reclaimed, two objects would be secured — the Church would be purified and a soul saved. It is as important a work of the Church to recover a member from his first backslidings as it is to bring sinners to Christ. The grand object of the Church is to save men, whether by getting sinners converted at first or saving them from apostasy afterward. This last is not to be accomplished by a hasty, harsh expulsion on the one hand, nor by a loose, careless administration on the other. It must be well understood that incorrigible offenders are to be expelled in due time—that the Church is not to be trifled with; yet every effort must be made in each case to bring the delinquent to repentance and confession In cases of infamous crime, no doubt, the extreme penalty ought to be promptly inflicted. But in most cases the most prayerful and earnest effort ought first to be made. Very often, probably in a great majority of cases, the labor will be crowned with success. The Church is more honored in recovering her members from their backslidings than just in expelling the backslider.

The best thing of all is, to keep the Church in a spiritual state so positive and high that there will be little or no backsliding. This preventive discipline is the best of all — infinitely. The preacher that does nothing to keep up the spiritual activity and warmth of his Church, to maintain a center of spiritual attraction, or to keep the members alive to their duty and danger, but suffers it to sink into inanition, so that when temptation comes there is nothing to counteract it, and then with great satisfaction resorts to the ax the first thing when one of his young people steps the least aside, may have a very comfortable pride in maintaining the purity of the Church. I can not doubt, nevertheless, that the Good Shepherd would have been much better pleased with him if he had kept the lambs in good pasture, so that they might not have been tempted to stray.

All this Mr. Caples felt. I remember he said to me on one occasion that we must keep something going on in the Church. We must have some point for the young people to rally to. A mere negative condition will not do; there must be something positive. Keep up a *positive* religious interest in the Church. If we do not, the wicked one will create a positive interest somewhere else, and no mere negative condition in the Church will keep our young people in safety. If they are suffered to fall into a negative state in the Church the world will offer a positive pole, and they will gravitate to it in spite of all threatening and scolding. In fact, scolding will highten the negative condition, and the attraction will thus be made all the more irresistible. But keep them well enlisted in the prayer-meeting, the class-meeting, the Bible-class; get them to strive with intelligent perseverance for the conversion of every scholar in their Sunday-school class, and you will find little or no trouble to keep them from the theater or ball-room.

Well he knew how destructive of all true piety these places are. They are of the world—corrupt and corrupting. No sophistry could blind him to the fatal character of all such godless diversions.

9

Young preachers are often perplexed by the shallow but specious sophistries of those carnal professors who defend dancing as an innocent recreation. Good people in the Bible times danced, say they No one ever approached Mr. Caples with that pretext without being made to feel his own wicked silliness. To parade those sacred dances, keeping time to the solemn pulses of religious music, with constant praise of God, the men and women always apart, in justification of the modern dance, betrayed either an ignorance or a want of candor that offered as fine an object for his good humored but most cutting sarcasm as he could ask. He was the most skillful sharp-shooter I ever saw, and such a target always called out his most pungent wit. He certainly did have the most consummate knack of shaming one without offending, and these bare-faced sophistries he considered just occasion of such rebuke. He thought it was the best way they could be treated.

A young lady once asked him if he really thought dancing—just mere dancing—dancing in the abstract, was wrong. Poor child! I felt sorry for her. And yet there was an undertone of tenderness in all he said that had a most happy effect. The question, he said, was not pertinent. What she was seeking to justify was not just *mere dancing*, it was dancing for pleasure; men **and** women dancing together to the strains of voluptuous, not to say lascivious, music, with suggestive touch and movement, the whole scene so sensuous that it is actually sensual. Even Gibbon says that the midnight dance, with its accompanying incidents, offers both the temptation and the opportunity to female frailty. Many a young member of the Church was saved by the plain and faithful warnings of this servant of God from the fatal fascination of this most insidious snare of the devil.

He had no patience with circuses and circus goers. The grossness and vulgarity of them he considered as most hurtful to piety and damaging to delicacy. It pained him for any lady friend to go. He felt that she must come away with some loss of womanly sensibility

I remember that, in Dr. M'Anally's office, when he was in St. Louis on his agency of Central College, he condemned, in most unmeasured terms, our agricultural fairs. He maintained that while they might in some slight measure promote the improvement of valuable farm products and stock, they would a thousand times more stimulate horse-racing and gambling. He would no more encourage them than he would the race course. When occasion offered he did not hesitate to denounce them from the pulpit. In doing so he encountered a clamorous public opinion, both in and out of the Church. But he never quailed before public opinion. He was true to his own convictions. When they were clear and well settled he would announce them in the face of any sort of derision, and stand by them against any weight of social pressure.

At the time I differed from him as to the character and tendency of the agricultural fairs. But I have lived to see that he was right and I was wrong. And here, while I commemorate the wisdom of my departed brother, I renew his warnings. I do most solemnly and earnestly advise Christian men to keep clear of these places, and above all to keep their sons away from such schools of vice.

In Caples' hand the trumpet gave no uncertain note. He never destroyed the force of his own warnings by lowering his voice before imposing contradiction. No prestige of personal opposition could cause him to lower his front or bate the utterance. The truth was of God; with God he could stand against the whole world.

It will appear from what has been written that he had strict views of the Chistian life. This is true. It is not to be inferred that he was an ascetic. Very far from it. He concurred most heartily in Mr. Wesley's condemnation of "such diversions as can not be used in the Name of the Lord Jesus." Especially did he condemn all that class of amusements which tend to immorality Amongst them he placed the dance, the theater, the circus and card playing. He was also opposed to the habit of playing chess, back-gammon and the like, as a useless frittering away of time. Such recreation as involved healthy exercise and did not lead to gambling he did not condemn, unless it was carried to an extent that involved too much time and was an actual dissipation.

He saw the necessity of keeping the Christian life free from worldly tendencies. Whatever subordinated the spirit to the flesh and made carnal things a capital object of pursuit was to be condemned. He knew that if young people began to run eagerly after mere pleasure the spiritual life would wane. The heart filled up with such vain desires has little room for Christ. Sobriety is a prime element of the Christian character.

Sobriety, not gloominess. There is a distinct boundary, not easily described in generalities, but easily discerned in actual life, beyond which cheerfulness degenerates into levity—into chaffiness, Solidity of character is lost. This is incompatible with true religion.

Our brother was a most joyous man. Perhaps we must admit that he had this trait in excess. Naturally there was in him the most exuberant mirthfulness. Perhaps he had not sufficiently restrained this disposition. I believe, in fact, he had not. But yet he saw most clearly that the Christian character must be preserved from such associations as lead to excessive gaiety. Life with him could be very bright on the social side and yet not given up to pleasures of this world. Cheerful, witty conversation he could sometimes indulge and yet not become a "lover of pleasure more than a lover of God."

His views of Church discipline, therefore, contemplated the most positive restraint upon the natural tendency of the human heart to forget God in worldly follies. He well knew that a Church of dancing people and theater goers would have no spiritual life. All sober, earnest consecration of soul and body to God would be out of the question. Religious joy would die out and earthly follies take its place. Heaven, in any true spiritual view of it, would cease to be the great object of hope. He felt that the Church must curb with a steady hand the strong tendencies evermore present in this evil direction.

It will never be laid to his charge in the last day that he was too cowardly to take a bold, firm stand on this subject. We must follow his example in this matter. As wealth increases in the Church the pressure upon discipline in these respects will become greater. Great firmness will be required in the young people of the Church to resist social beguilement. The pastor must be a man of no little courage to avow himself unequivocally in every presence.

But if he shall falter the world will come in like

a flood. All deep spiritual consciousness will be lost. We will no longer be a "peculiar people, zealous of good works." We will come to be ashamed of being peculiar. We will then no longer be Methodists. We will no longer be Christians. We will just be of the world—proud, vain, carnal. Scripture holiness will be at an end with us. May every preacher be as firm and full of courage in this matter as Caples was.

If ever we are shorn of our strength by conformity to the world, the apostasy will lie at the door of the preachers. It will be when they become pusillanimous and shrink before the sneers of the ungodly in and out of the Church that the evil time will be upon us. When we cease to be willing to be the filth and offscouring of the world we will begin to make terms with the world, and Methodist discipline, experience and purity will all go together. Then the Wesleyan work will be at an end, and God will have to raise up some other people to do the work that we will be no longer able to do.

I dwell on this subject because it is vital. We are in greater danger here, as I have no doubt, than at any other point. The problem of personal salvation lies in great part in the fact of *self-denial.* It will do us no good to be worldly people in the Church. If we are determined to be wordly people at all hazards, it is far better to sail under the world's colors at once. If we are of the world in heart and practice, to belong to the Church is only an affectation — a hypocrisy. If the devil is our master, let us openly confess him. "If the Lord be God, serve Him, but if Baal, serve him." Let us not mingle the stench of the world with the incense that goes up from the altars of God. If we offer a vain oblation, the stench of a carnal devotion, let us lay it boldly on the altars of Baal.

One capital qualification of a good pastor Mr. Caples had in the fact of his *industry*. He was no idler. There was but one way in which he was tempted to spend time unprofitably That wonderfully susceptible social nature of his never tired of conversation with congenial spirits. I am sure he wasted time in this way But he was no mere lounger. He was essentially active. In the midst of his charge he would be employed either in his studies or in domestic duties, or in visiting. The diary, so often referred to already, shows great activity.

It shows also the liveliest interest in the prayer and class meetings, and in the Sunday-school. He often refers to the social meetings as precious seasons, mentions whether they were well attended or not, and makes remarks which show his high estimate of them. He organized a Bible class of the Sunday-school teachers, to aid them in preparing the lessons, so that they might more adequately instruct their classes. Not only was he habitually in attendance at the Sunday-school, but often, also, at their special meetings for singing. The freshness of his spirit, the tenderness of his heart, caused an unflagging interest in children. He was idolized by the young people of his congregations. They were always glad when he noticed them, and his word had great weight with them.

I mention all these matters under the head of " discipline." This, as I understand it, is where they belong. That Church is under good discipline where every method is resorted to and every agency brought into play to elevate the tone and augment the activity and spirituality of the Church. By whatever means the pastor gains a legitimate influence with the young, so that he may restrain them from evil, so that his voice may be potential with them in shaping their character, he may turn it to high account in maintaining godly discipline. And how much better is this, on every account, than to make all discipline to consist only in Church censures, trials and expulsions. He is the best disciplinarian who avoids this as far as possible by leading his Church into such a state as shall bring about few or no occasions for extreme remedies.

Many hundreds who read this book will do so with devout gratitude, thanking God that in His merciful Providence they ever had this man for their pastor.

CHAPTER VIII.

——

THE PRESIDING ELDER

At the Conference of 1851 Mr. Caples received his first appointment as Presiding Elder. His field was the Weston District, which he had in charge for four successive years. Then, after an interval of three years, he was appointed on the Fayette District, where he remained but one year. After another interval, of one year, he was placed on the Brunswick District, which he served three years. This last term was, however, greatly interrupted by the war. He held this office eight years in all. The history of his administration in this office well deserves a separate chapter. My data is not so full as I wish it was, otherwise this chapter might be invested with greater interest. Still I shall give the material I have, and feel well assured that it has sufficient value to justify the prominence I give it.

From the first there have not been wanting men who have doubted the utility of this part of our

Church economy. It has been characterized as a fifth wheel. Especially is this feeling found to exist in the cities. It has been often affirmed that the Presiding Elder does no good. His quota must be paid, adding to the burdens of the Church, while he accomplishes nothing to compensate the outlay. Often the stationed preacher fills the pulpit better and more acceptably than he, and the quarterly meeting is an occasion not felt in the Church. Therefore, why take a man out of the regular pastorate where he might do much good, and give him this office in which he does none?

This argument takes for granted as a fact what can by no means be admitted. That many Presiding Elders do, apparently, little or no good may be granted. The same is unfortunately true of many pastors. Too many men on Districts render only a perfunctory service. They do not take hold of things with the spirit that insures results. They attend the quarterly meetings, preach Saturday morning (may be) and Sunday morning, go through the business of the quarterly Conference in a languid way, hold the love feast, receive their "quota," and take their departure, not greatly regretted. This is the history of too much District work. Yet it may be maintained that even this species of service has considerable value. It holds the administration of the pastoral charges to a responsibility that has a wholesome effect. It brings the affairs of the Church under official review, and in that way secures an attention to many important interests that would be otherwise left at loose ends. A good many things are done because the quarterly meeting is coming on. But for this spur they would not be done at all. The condition of the Church, of the Sunday-schools, of the finances, is brought under review. There is something in human nature that recognizes the prestige of office, and respects it. "Governments" are of divine ordination, and one of the chief securities of government is found in that sentiment which is ineradicable, and which is an essential constituent of our very being—the sentiment of reverence for dignities. The official character of the Presiding Elder, though as a man he may have no great weight, has a good effect in causing the business of the Church to be attended to and keeping some vitality in the organization.

But, as a general rule, the Presiding Elder is a man whose intelligence, industry and personal character enable him to exert an influence beyond that which attaches to his office. His intelligent eye discovers much that is loose and damaging in the management of Church interests as the business passes under his review in the quarterly meetings and conferences, and he interposes

in authority that is corrective. The very fact
that affairs will be brought under his eye prevents
much loose administration in the circuit or station. I am sure that this office promotes thor-
oughness of organization. The *value* of this, perhaps, few comprehend. It has been observed
with perfect truth that Mr. Whitfield's work soon
came to nothing, while Mr. Wesley's continues
and extends itself even to this present. Yet the
immediate effect of Whitfield's preaching was
greater than that of Wesley's. One word explains
the whole matter—*organization*. Whitfield did
not organize in any efficient way, while the world
has rarely had such an organizer as Wesley was.
The organization that he effected *conserved* the
fruits of his ministry, and put them in condition
to be *reproductive. Organization conserves vitality and renders it reproductive.* This law is
fundamental in human society *It is fundamental
in nature.* Nothing preserves itself amongst the
active forces of this world that is not organized.
Nothing developes otherwise. No life accomplishes anything that is not posited in organic
forms.

The Methodist itinerancy is a singularly compact, well contrived, vigorous, reproductive organization. Its utmost vitality has been realized in
America, where the Presiding Eldership is incorporated into it. Those Methodist bodies that

have discarded it in this country have never done well. The fault is, the itinerant organization is not complete without it. The *fifth wheel* is indispensable. Its regulating and balancing function is vital. It prevents friction and derangement, and keeps things in good tone.

If the incumbent be a man of good administrative ability he will start new enterprises every here and there and impart new vitality to old ones, and the Church will go forward with more and more vigor, and a better growth, through the agency of every new activity set on foot. It is a thing greatly to be desired that this officer should be a man who can comprehend the possibilities of the situation in each charge of his District. There are agencies at hand every where which escape the notice of most men, and which, if brought into requisition, would insure prosperity We have all known Presiding Elders, a few of them, who excelled in this. Sometimes the men most successful in this office are no great preachers; but they have an instinct of organization and administration that makes them a power. They seem to have been made to *have work done.* They work with a will themselves, and put springs into everything they touch. This class of men, men of fine administrative faculty, realize fully the value of this office.

If, in addition to this, again, they have unusual

power in the pulpit, there is an effectual door open for them. In this case the quarterly meetings are fruitful occasions, especially in smaller towns and country places. Who is there in the West that has not many recollections of such occasions? The Church is edified. Religion takes deeper root. The way is prepared for revivals. Very often the work begins under the labors of the "Elder." The doctrines of the Church are vindicated and established by his preaching. Every thing is toned up, and the operations of the Church acquire new force.

Many a preacher, perplexed and discouraged in his work, particularly of the younger class of preachers, has been enheartened and set forward with a new hope and a fresh zeal by the quarterly visits of his superior officer. Many a steward and class leader has been made to realize the obligations of his office under the admonitions given in quarterly Conference.

Movements may often be set on foot having a wider scope than the limits of a single charge. Large results may often be secured by concentrating the agencies to be found scattered over a considerable area. The connectional character of the Methodist organization, especially as it appears in the form of a District, may often be made available for most important ends. It often embraces a scope of country just large enough to be kept well in hand and concentrated on one object. Let it be, for instance, the building up of a school of high grade.

Much that has been accomplished in the last few years in the St. Louis District has been done by this sort of concentration. The Missionary work was for some time done with a good degree of efficiency. The sagacious administration of Rev. T. M. Finney, making available this connectional feature of our polity, secured the erection of St. John's Church, and so added another prosperous congregation to our existence in St. Louis. Thus, much of the growth and power of Methodism has resulted, unquestionably, from this office.

As a Presiding Elder Mr. Caples magnified his office. He was always thinking or working for the Church. Full of plans, he was also fruitful of resources in executing them. The whole Church in the District lay upon his heart night and day He could never rest unless the ark of the Lord was moving forward. The troubles of the Church were his troubles, her successes were his triumphs.

He seemed to charge himself with every interest of the Church in his District. Any want of prosperity in the most obscure places would trouble him. Nothing short of activity and progress at every point satisfied him. He animated the preachers by word and example. He exhorted the official members to zeal and diligence.

The finances of the several charges were never overlooked. He had had bitter experience in the beginning of his ministry—had been literally starved out. It was the duty of the preachers, no doubt, to economize closely, to live on the least possible amount; but then there was a minimum below which no pressure could reduce expenses. To go in debt was ruinous. A preacher in debt, with no resources but what the Church is likely to give him, has little prospect of paying; and to go in "debt without a probability of paying" is not strictly honest. The preacher must be *strictly* honest. Otherwise he is himself wanting in a fundamental virtue while he is a teacher of Christian purity. In view of all this he brought the full weight of his great personal influence to bear to raise for each preacher in his District so much as would subsist his family. He did great good in this way. The views of the Church were elevated, and the effect of his labor at this point is still apparent. To secure this result he labored both with the official members in the quarterly conferences and with the Church generally in the public congregations. As Presiding Elder he could talk freely on this subject in the pulpit. This the pastor could not do without giving offense, on account of his direct inter-

10

est in the result. In this office, however, he could appear as the advocate of the pastor with the utmost propriety. For the following instance of labor in this department I am indebted to Rev. S. W Cope:

At a camp-meeting in Howard county, in 1859, " he made a most singular and effective appeal to the stewards in this wise: They stand in the future general Judgment. The Judge asks, 'Where were you living in the year 1859?' 'In Howard county, Missouri.' 'Did you have any preaching that year?' 'Yes, Lord.' 'Who were your preachers?' 'Brothers Cope and McMurry' 'How much did you allow them as a necessary support?' 'We fixed the claim of the two at one thousand dollars.' 'Did you pay them that amount?' 'No, Lord, we lacked a hundred dollars or more.' 'Did your preachers do you a good year's work?' 'Yes, Lord, we believe they did the best they could.' 'Was there not means enough in the Church to pay them their entire claim?' 'Yes, Lord.' 'Why, then, did you allow them to go away unpaid?' They were speechless. This appeal was most singular and wonderful in its *manner* and *effect*. The amount was nearly or quite all made up in a few minutes, one man not a member of the Church giving twenty dollars."

It must ever be borne in mind in reading incidents of this class that not even *what* he said can be accurately given from memory, much less *how* he said it, and with what vivacity and pathos.

Brother John Stone, of Plattsburg, referring to his having to cut cord wood at one time to pay his debts, says: "This incident in his life served him a great purpose in after years, when Presiding Elder of our district, in raising *Conference claims.* He always presented ministers of the Conference as a living, active body, who, rather than starve out, would chop out; but the poor, worn out preachers, widows and orphans must starve without assistance, for they had no bonus to depend on, as the life of the itinerant minister was all worldly sacrifice without gain."

From this it will be seen that it was not only the support of the preachers in the active work that he looked after, but that he took in the whole department of Church finances. He was especially alive to the Missionary work. In the same letter brother Stone writes: "I well remember, at a district camp-meeting at Mt. Moriah, a Missionary sermon which he preached on Sabbath had such a powerful effect on the congregation that they were imperceptibly drawn around the stand, and the whole congregation, consisting of about four thousand persons, were all standing on their feet. He made a call for Missionary money and raised two hundred dollars." Be it remembered this was in a country comparatively new, and where money did not abound as it does now. Two hundred dollars at once, then and there, was the next thing to a miracle.

So, as will elsewhere appear, he neglected no interest of the Church, but delivered the full force of his being upon every object of importance to the cause of his Master.

Brother Stone adds: "It is my opinion that the Church has furnished to the world but few of his equals." I agree with him.

He took a lively interest in every preacher in his district. They were all *his boys*—at least the younger ones. If there was a sort of patronizing of them, it was accompanied with a spirit so genial and a friendship so whole-souled that they never regarded it. While ever they did about right they were sure of a champion in him. He would correct their faults, rally them upon their weaknesses, ridicule their foibles, and strive to bring them up to a high standard of intelligence, purity and usefulness; and then before the public, in their work, at Conference, he was their friend and advocate.

The sufferings and self-denials of the preachers touched him. If one of his preachers, especially one having a family, endured unusual privations, and bore it all cheerfully for the work's sake, the man was thenceforth enthroned in Caples' affections. More than once he related an incident of

Rev. M. R. Jones, now of the Illinois Conference. He went to brother Jones' circuit to hold a quarterly meeting, taking his wife along with him. They found the preacher in a poor hovel. The weather was severe. The circuit had made no provision for any comfortable house for the preacher. But Jones had what Caples, in his good humored way, called *grit*. He did not understand that he was called to preach on condition of the Church doing its duty by him. God had laid on him the responsibility of the sacred office. He must meet it. If he could put his family in a comfortable house he would be thankful. If not, still he must *preach*, for his vocation was from God. Better that he and his family should live poor than that he should betray the trust committed to him. That is a sublime faith in which a faithful husband and tender father commits his family to the care of the Great Head of the Church in the face of suffering. How it contrasts with the course of those who refuse to suffer for Christ's sake and turn to some secular calling unless a fat salary is guaranteed.

Brother and sister Jones, with their little ones, were crowded around the fire in their poor cabin, all cheerful, taking joyfully the incidents of their high calling, however trying to flesh and blood. The Presiding Elder and his wife were welcomed to such hospitalities as the place afforded, and shared the self-denials of the preacher's family with a sense of the preciousness of the fellowship of saints which might have been wanting in a better house. How these common trials endear men to each other! Ever after that these men were as David and Jonathan to each other.

Rest assured the finances had an overhauling at that quarterly meeting. I can imagine how he talked and with what hearty interest he set himself to get the preacher comfortably provided— not withholding personal aid.

He took a fatherly interest in young men who were looking to the ministry. I believe I never knew a man who showed so much gratification in bringing men of more than ordinary promise into the Conference. His face beamed all over when he introduced the names of such. No father could be more gratified in a son than he was in the lamented H. H. Hedgepeth. He thought he had unearthed a gem. Nor was he mistaken. The boy proved to be all that his great friend predicted.

A pleasant incident occurred in connection with the introduction of Hedgepeth into the Conference, which many of the preachers still remember. When his case was up for admission on trial, Caples, among other commendatory traits of the young brother, announced that he was not going to get married for four years at least. He had, without hesitation, given a distinct pledge to that effect. In the course of the year the *Advocate* contained a notice of the marriage of Rev H. H. Hedgepeth. At the following session of the Conference his Presiding Elder, Caples, gave a most flattering account of him as a man and preacher, and sat down. Some one rose and asked how about the pledge to remain unmarried for four years. Either there was a mistake abroad or the young brother had violated his pledge, which was an offense against good morals. Caples laughed after a manner peculiar to himself. " Mr. President," said he, " I hoped no one would remember that." He then proceeded to inform the Conference that he had taken the young brother to task on the subject, and that he had denied having made any such promise. " Why you certainly *did*." "Indeed, I did *not*. You never asked me to make such a promise. You asked me if I could let the girls alone for four years, and I told you that I *could*, but never said I *would*." Caples was outwitted, and enjoyed it prodigiously. Nevertheless he most earnestly and wisely dissuaded the young preachers from marriage until they had attained to such a character in the Conference as would command work that might afford subsistence for a family Many a poor fellow has been in great straits in his early ministry—many a one driven to location—from pursuing the opposite course. Alas! that men should learn only from experience.

His quarterly meetings, especially in the country, were great gatherings of the people. His fame as a preacher was such that the whole country would assemble. The official and other members came from the remotest portions of circuits, and for miles around the place of preaching the roads were alive with people on Sunday morning, the moving multitudes converging to a common centre.

His energy and punctuality in meeting his appointments are well illustrated by the following amusing anecdote, for which I am indebted to Rev. W G. Miller:

"While he was Presiding Elder of the Weston District he had to pass from Gentry to Nodaway county, along the Iowa line. It was in midwinter. He had a ride of near forty miles to meet his next quarterly meeting. So, sunshine or storm, he must go. The route was entirely new to him. There was no leading road. Indeed, it was unbroken prairie.

"So he must take the chances of keeping his course without a single way mark to guide him, or missing his way and spending the night on the naked prairie, with a fair prospect of freezing. But nothing daunted, he started off, holding his general course as best he could, facing a driving northwest snow storm, over 'boundless prairies, unbroken by a single pathway But the snow was drifting into heaps in all the low places, so that he often found it difficult making headway Thus obstructed, long before his journey was ended he found night coming on. But fortunately he was now occasionally crossing a narrow neck of timber running up some little prairie ravine. But no sign of human habitation was to be seen. His situation was rendered still more desolate by his frequently hearing the howling of wolves, and there is nothing more desolate in this world than the lonely howling of a wolf on one of our wide prairies as night begins to darken upon you. A single wolf will so change his tone that you will think there are a whole half-score of them in a pack.

" But, fortunately, as the twilight was deepening into the gloom of night, he came upon the lonely habitation of a backwoodsman in one of these skirts of timber. It stood all alone, with no out-house or stable or barn—a single round-pole cabin He rode up and halloed. The man opened the door. He asked if he could stay all night with him. Without the least hesitation he was answered in the affirmative. By this time half a dozen little heads were peeping out around the legs of the sturdy sire. They ranged from a girl about fourteen down to the toddling little youngster of two years. Our hero alighted, fastened his horse to a sapling near by and entered the cabin, nearly stiffened by the cold. His supper, which consisted of corn bread and wild meat, was treated with due respect, even cordiality, as he had had no dinner. But pretty soon the question of sleeping became an all-absorbing one. There were only two beds in the cabin, and it was entirely innocent of any pretension to up stairs, as they were in full sight of the board roof. He cast a calculating glance around to see what his prospect was for a bed, and with dismay he saw that they would be as thick as four in a bed, without including himself. While many of us have crept into bed with a dirty, greasy urchin on each side of us, still beds, like everything else, have their capacity and will hold no more. These certainly were pre-empted. It, therefore, became the all-absorbing problem, 'shall I have where to lay my head?'

"Finally his host arose and said, ' Wall, stranger, as we gits up in the morning here, I reckon it's time we were abed.' So saying he took a light and said, ' Come with me.' They went out of the door, and round in the rear of the house, where he found a shed by the side of the cabin. As they entered it a little less than a dozen hounds came sneaking out. He was here shown a bed made after the following fashion: A pole, with one end stuck into a crack of the cabin, extended to the centre of the room, where it rested on a fork driven into the ground. Another pole rested by one end on the cross-piece of the shed, the other end also in the fork in the centre of the shed. On this frame boards were laid, and the bed made on them—a little shaky, but pretty comfortable. The man remarked as he went out that he must put up the door well or the dogs would get in. But Caples had scarcely begun to get warm in bed when, sure enough, the dogs began to demand entrance, and with very little effort the rickety door was down and they inside. He drove them out, and as well as he could reconstructed the door, but was only snugly tucked in again when the dogs assailed the door, and down it went, and in they came. Finding it impossible to barricade them out he concluded to take the next best chance, which was to let them stay in. They, of course, all piled up under the bed. But just as he was getting into a sweet dream of home and its comforts, a lot of wolves set up a howl near the cabin, and all the hounds rushing out at once, came in collision with the dreamer's centre of support, that is, the fork supporting the poles in the centre, when down came poles, boards, bed, preacher and all.

"He stretched his legs out to see if any bones had been broken, and finding them all sound, he quietly adjusted himself to his situation, and was soon sound asleep, from which he did not awake till the full dawn of the following morning. But on awaking he attempted to move his legs, when they utterly refused to obey his will. 'What,' thought he, 'am I frozen as stiff as a poker? No, that can't be, for I am in a general perspiration. It can't be that I am paralyzed?' But drawing the cover a little off his face, what should meet his astonished eyes but the nose of the biggest, ugliest hound in the pack, within three inches of his own nose.

"This old fellow had seemingly claimed the distinction of sleeping at the head. On looking down he saw the set had just arranged themselves, *ad libitum*, literally covering him from head to foot, until he was scarcely able to move a single limb. With a few vehement begones, and sundry, uneasy, spasmodic movements of his lower extremities, however, he soon dislodged his impertinent bed-fellows, and rose, congratulating himself that, after all, many a man had slept with meaner dogs than these hounds of the backwoodsman."

This anecdote brother Miller received from Caples himself. No doubt he could have given many like it from his frontier travels. The hospitality of the pioneer settlers is unbounded. They never turn the stranger from their doors.

However inadequate their means of entertainment they always receive the traveler with the utmost cordiality, and this amply compensates the lack of much else that might be desirable.

The District meeting was anticipated by him. I am not sure whether he embraced any other than the traveling and local preachers in his plan or not But he conceived the idea of infusing new vigor into the work by an annual convocation of the preachers—all the preachers—those who were local as well as those in the regular work. It was in the scope of his plan to enjoin upon the local preachers a course of study and to habituate them to intellectual labor by requiring of them an essay at the District meeting. Various matters, doctrinal and practical, were to be discussed and opportunities of Church extension to be canvassed. One object, especially, he hoped to accomplish—that is, to get all the local preachers into a way of regular work in appropriate fields. That there should be so many men in the Church declaring that they were called to preach, and bearing the name of preachers, doing so little, was intolerable to him. He believed that an open door might be found for them, and great good accomplished in that way. Thus he sought to bring an agency comparatively dormant into activity.

Besides that, he held that just to get all the

preachers of the District into consultation with each other on the interests of religion would do good. An intensified interest would be felt by these men of God—an interest which would diffuse itself and reappear at many points in actual prosperity

The success of the effort did not answer to his hopes. It was new to the Church, and the preachers did not enter into it with the spirit that would have secured success: It was not a part of the regular machinery of the Church, and men felt no obligation to attend. Yet much was accomplished. His personal influence gave the movement character. Many attended, and under his management much interest was infused into the business sessions.

At any rate we see the *man* in the undertaking. His busy brain was ever at work devising plans to increase the efficiency of the Church. The horse going his ceaseless and unvarying round in the mill is not the type of this man. It shows, also, the breadth and scope of his views. His methods were co-extensive with his opportunities. His plans were bounded only by the limit of his field. If he had been at the head of affairs in an entire Church his comprehensive organizations would have swept the continent. When he was in charge of a single congregation he concentrated on that. The affairs of a whole District he comprehended as readily and handled with as much facility. With equal perspicacity and power he grasped the interests of Central College, as will appear elsewhere. In fact, the compass of his mind and the force of his will were sufficient for any work the Church might call him to perform.

This largeness of ideas came out in another form while he was on his first District. He projected a general system of education for the entire Conference, and, as a grand initiation of it, he established two High Schools, one at Weston and one at Plattsburg. By a grand outlay of personal effort he secured the erection of adequate buildings at each of these places. All this, however, belongs to another chapter. I mention it here because it was an incident of his Presiding Eldership, and shows his breadth and power. His conceptions, I have no doubt, will modify the development of Missouri Methodism for ages to come. Even when his name shall be no longer a household word with the people, and only an occasional copy of this memorial of him that I am now writing shall exist in old, forgotten libraries, the activities of the Church will still be, in some measure, adjusted to methods that originated with him. There are only a few men who deliver themselves upon society with sufficient momentum to give shape and color to the work of successive ages. One of this few was Caples.

He had no opportunity of showing his power in District administration after he left the Weston District. He was on the Fayette District but one year; not long enough to evolve the latent agencies of the Church by a wise and potential method. Beside which the interest and energy of that part of the work was concentrated, even to agony, at the time upon Central College. Soon after his appointment to the Brunswick District the war came on, and that great upheaval was an effectual estoppel of ordinary Christian enterprise. But on the Weston District his opportunity was ample, and he appears to better advantage there, perhaps, than any where else in the course of his life. The country suited him to an iota. It was filled up with first-class men, the soil was as productive as the valley of the Nile, and wealth was multiplying rapidly Cities were growing, commercial activities and resources were working such miracles as he had never witnessed, and amazed at the new empire of wealth and intellect that was organizing itself around him, he entered into the spirit of the country and the period with the utmost enthusiasm. Over all this population, this commerce, this wealth, this irrepressible, ambitious life, religion must assert its dominion, otherwise these wondrous activities would precipitate themselves upon ruin. Alas for the country where so much human force was expending itself if the purifying power of religion were wanting. It was his mission to put the Church on a footing that might command this tumult, to evoke out of these industries and this commerce some homage of God, to evoke churches and Christian schools, and put Christian shape upon affairs. He fulfilled his mission. He stood for God in an attitude that commanded every eye; he spoke for God with a tone that commanded every ear. He seemed made for that time and that country And he loved his work. If the worldly activities, the ambition, the lust of money, rendered the task of Christian organization a herculean one, it was a challenge of the power of the Gospel and of the courage of the minister, that roused a sanctified ambition in the man which made him actually sublime. These very forces, depraved as they were, and tending as fearfully to a deeper depravity, contained in themselves the grandest possibilities for religion, if only they might be redeemed and elevated to Christian conditions. There he stood in God's name, extorting from Mammon himself the agencies that were to undermine his throne. He was conquering this magnificent region for Christ, and establishing a powerful ecclesiastical garrison under most efficient drill and thorough Gospel discipline at every point. With sleepless vigilance and Napoleonic

11

energy he was reducing these elements to Christian forms.

In the midst of this push and hurry he could not bear an easy going, insipid preacher. Such might do in places where everything was stagnant. But *here* the servant of the Lord must be a live man. He once asked a preacher visiting him at Weston to preach on Sunday morning. After moving rather sluggishly through the preliminary services he announced his text. Then followed a considerable pause. At this juncture several persons left the house. Caples was on thorns. Still the preacher stood silent. Others left. Caples could bear it no longer. " Fire, brother, fire quick! Don't wait to take a rest. Fire off-hand. The people here are all in a hurry. They won't stand for you. *Fire quick*, or the last one of them will be gone."

CHAPTER IX.

IN CONFERENCE.

Mr. Caples never appeared in a better light than at the annual sessions of the Conference. There he was in his element. Among the preachers he was fully himself. Socially, in the business sessions, in the Missionary meetings, in the pulpit, he was, unless some distinguished visitor may be excepted, the center of interest.

His active and influential participation in the business of the Conference came about by degrees. When young in the body he was not obtrusive. For several years he never spoke on the floor except some occasion made it imperative. In that early time he never initiated measures. He was never obtrusive. Gradually his good sense commanded recognition, and he fell naturally into a leading position. Once he had grown into full sympathy with the affairs of the Conference he became the leading spirit in almost all important affairs and debates. For some years before his

death he almost always carried any measure that
he advocated. This was the result of various
facts. Being a man of great good sense, his
measures were generally just. They were such
as commanded the approval of his brethren.
Then he was a fine debater. He got at the heart
of the matter in few words. He never bored the
Conference with long, unwelcome speeches. Beside the clear statement of his case there was
always a dash of humor to spice it. The brethren
were always glad when he began, and ready to
hear more when he quit.

If the opposition was formidable, he drew upon
his knowledge of human nature. If he could not
carry the Conference by argument, he did not
hesitate to resort to his unfailing fund of wit. He
would raise a laugh, confuse his opponent and
end in triumph. In fact he had the advantage
from the outset, in every case, in virtue of his
great personal influence. If the younger preachers
did not quite understand the case, they were sure
to think that *Caples* must be right. He always
had their hearts, and once you command a man's
heart you may be sure of his ear, and generally
of his judgment. For all those reasons there was
nothing that could stand before him in the Conference.

In fact there was rarely any collision of parties
in the Missouri Conference. The conflicting claims

of St. Charles and Fayette in educational enterprises form the principal exception to the pre-
vailing harmony of the body If there were ever
any little personal jealousies or rivalries they
were so slight as to be mere ripples upon the
great stream of love and confidence, which continued to flow on with unbroken current. Brother
Monroe was the father of us all, full of parental
care and ripe and sanctified views, and Caples,
the great, gifted young man, the leader of the
host. Then there was Smith, who preached Methodist doctrine like Watson's Institutes, but never
said much in Conference; and Brown, whose sermons on any topic were conclusive and exhaust-
ive—a little disposed to criticise, but always heard
with great respect on the floor; and Jordan, who
might have been a leader but for one fact—that
was, that he always carried an overload of modesty,
which broke him down; and Ashby, whose face
was a sermon—all old men in the body, all
revered, and all proud of Caples. We had, also,
our dead prophets, Greene, and Bewley, and Redman, and Lanius, and Patton, and many others,
whose names we often repeated and whose unseen
presence seemed like a luminous cloud hovering
over our assemblies. As for the rest of us, we
were all boys together, in the rank and file, gratified with the character of our old men, having
confidence in each other, deeply loving each

other, and all proud of Caples, awarding him heartily the first place.

I do not believe that there has ever been a body of men associated the same length of time with less friction than the Missouri Conference. I doubt if the primitive Church offers anything that excels it. May this harmony ever continue. May there arise no vain men, with little personal ambitions to gratify, to be firebrands here.

LET BROTHERLY LOVE CONTINUE.

What occasions our Conferences were. I have them in my mind's eye now. Late in the afternoon of Tuesday there is the bustle of much coming and going about the Methodist Church. Men come in buggies, on horseback, from the depot on foot, all making their way to the church. One squad is no sooner disposed of than another comes. Each one is assigned to a "home" for the session. After a little the first comers, having been duly installed in their homes, return to greet the fresh arrivals. Caples comes leisurely along from his boarding-house in company with two or three others. I can see the sunshine in his face now. They are in earnest conversation. Caples stops and halts the others. I know from his very attitude that he is telling an anecdote — an uncommonly rich one. Presently he bends forward and laughs one of *his* laughs. They all join, not boisterously, but convulsively — laugh until the tears run down their faces. They move on and meet others. Caples quickens his pace. "Why," says he, "there's Billy — *God bless you, old fellow!* Why, they have fed you high up there on Grand river." "Why, Ben., bless your soul, is this you?" Then the shaking of hands! Commend me to a Methodist preacher when I am to shake hands. It is not an art with them, but a natural gift.

As these men come and go every here and there you will hear a voice, quivering with pleasure, say, "Yonder's Caples," "Caples is here," "How are you, Caples?"

Then there is the hum of voices in friendly inquiry — inquiring after wives and children; for news from old fields of labor and old friends; messages from one and another; information of one married, another dead, a young friend coming up to join Conference, another backslid from God, and a thousand other things. Ah! the heart that is in these reunions. Every preacher meets others fresh from fields where he had labored a year or two or ten gone by. Every one meets preachers with whom he has been in common labors, perils, privations and triumphs. What a bond of hearts the itinerancy is.

I will not describe the preaching, the coming of the Bishop (usually a portly, imposing personage—

not always), the opening of the Conference and the business. But there is one part of it that I must note — the opening hymn, sung by the preachers:

And are we yet alive,
    And see each other's face;
Glory and praise to Jesus give,
    For His abounding grace!

When I was a boy in Conference Rev John F Young used to lead the singing. In 1842, at Jefferson City, I heard it for the first time! Was there ever such singing? It was religion set to music! There was no swallowing of the voice there, no letting of it out thin through closed teeth, none listening while others sang. There was a contagion of singing all through the house. If a brother had no control of his voice, still he was not afraid to make a noise, for his discord would be drowned! It was no mere medley of voices neither. It was *music*. The time was perfect, the melody good, the harmony above criticism, and the tone and emphasis superb. I would have gone a hundred miles to Conference if for nothing else but to hear the preachers sing. From 1842 to 1867, the time of my last visit to the Missouri Conference, the *personnel* of the body had changed almost entirely. Not more than four or five of the same men were present. But the old *animus* was there and—the old singing. The individual voices were different, but the complement of sound was exactly the same, and the spirit unchanged. I said to myself, surely there is no better music this side of the River.

After Caples came to be a little flush of money he was the first in every generous suggestion. If a brother had lost his horse or met with any special misfortune, a purse must be made up for him. There was in those days a Conference Missionary Society. Each member was expected to pay a dollar a year. For this purpose the roll was called and every one responded with his dollar. He often responded for absentees and superannuates. A brother once having given away his last dollar, at one session, borrowed five dollars of him to pay his expenses home. At the next session he refused the amount. He had intended it from the first as a gift. He abounded in such acts of generosity at every session. He knew what it was to be embarrassed for want of money, and if it had been in his power he would have saved every one of his brethren from the bitterness of his own experiences.

He has often made what is technically called the begging speech at the Missionary anniversaries. In this he was at home. He put no restraint upon his propensity for humor. But the humor was near akin to pathos, and often hightened it. It was, in a very high sense, a "feast of reason and a flow of soul." He would ridicule and shame the miser with the most unheard-of invective. Every man in the audience would be ashamed not to contribute.

On these occasions the preachers always gave the greater part of the whole sum contributed. He never hesitated to urge them. God would reward their uncalculating liberality. Let to-morrow take care of itself. " May God bless the Methodist preachers," he would say, " there never has been such a set of men on earth since the times of the Apostles. They get less money and give more than any class on earth. What do they care for money ! They labor for souls, and their reward is on high. Never mind, brother, God will take care of your wife and children. You are not squandering money to pamper pride or gratify lust. You are using it for your Master !" Having drained these willing givers, he would shame others by their example.

His own contribution, if he had the money, was never a whit behind the chiefest.

I never heard of his seeking to influence his own appointment. My conviction is that he never did. He was a Methodist preacher, ready for any work the Bishop might give him. He was as far above all intrigue as it is possible to conceive. It is true that he was above the temptation to be an intriguer. He was in demand everywhere But I feel quite certain that he would have taken any work without a murmur, so long as he could get anything to eat and a roof to shelter his family.

After he had been a Presiding Elder for some time he came to have a sort of patronizing manner among the younger preachers. He was, or had been, the official superior of many of them, and had introduced several of them into the Conference. His personal superiority they all felt. He was very much deferred to by them. They looked to him for counsel and sympathy. His greatness was not of the oppressive sort that causes a young man to tremble and hesitate in its presence. The genial spirit that was apparent in everything he did, in his entire demeanor and intercourse, invited confidential approach. No young man, after the slightest acquaintance, felt any embarrassment in his presence. There was the most perfect mingling of respect and freedom in their feelings and manner toward him. It was the most natural thing in the world that he should take a sort of paternal relation toward them in his own consciousness. There was nothing officious or offensive in it. His age, his prestige, the genuine goodness of his heart, brought it about in an inevitable way.

Many of the young men had received some substantial kindness at his hands, such as a father might be expected to extend. He had some amusing anecdote to tell on each one. Some of them had personal habits that he ridiculed. But no matter whether he had helped them to a new coat, or told an amusing story on them, or turned the laugh upon some personal trait, they had an intuitive perception of the loving spirit out of which it all came. It was Caples, and he might say what he pleased; nothing could disguise the genial heart which overflowed upon a man even when he was making fun of him.

His patronizing was not an affectation of superiority It was the interest of an elder brother, and was called into this species of expression by the confidence and deference manifested toward him. If to a stranger it seemed a little demonstrative, in the family it was all natural and pleasant.

His representations of the young men of his District, when he was a Presiding Elder, always showed the most hearty appreciation. Indeed, a partial, paternal spirit often colored what he had to say of them. Most of them were first-rate preachers, "for yearlings," or "two year olds." Regular-bred theological graduates were not to be compared to them! If there was a dash of extravagance in all this it came out of the heart.

No man ever more fully realized the *esprit du corps* of the Methodist preacher than he. He had acquired it through the double baptism of suffering and of triumph. More than any other man

he was the *heart* of his Conference. He took an
honest pride in the work and in the workmen.
As he saw the country growing into opulence and
power, and the plans and operations of the Church
taking on a type and assuming a magnitude somewhat in keeping with surrounding conditions, this
pride swelled into a generous enthusiasm, which
the annual convocations brought into full play.
It brought him into communication with the whole
field, and with all the good and great things that
Missouri Methodism represented. He gathered
into himself and uttered all these activities and
grandeurs. The utterance was worthy of the fact
and the occasion. The voice was responded to in
a thrill that ran through every breast

At the session of 1849 he was elected on the
reserve list to the General Conference. A vacancy
occurring among the regular delegates, he took
his seat as a member of the General Conference
at the session of 1850, in St. Louis. At every
subsequent election, while he lived, he was chosen
by a heavy vote, and was in the General Conference in the sessions of 1854 and 1858, at Columbus,
Ga., and Nashville, Tenn. He took no very prominent part in the discussions nor in the business,
feeling himself to be one of the younger men of
that great representative assemblage of the Church.
He was growing into this body, however, as he had
grown into the business of his own Conference.

He never thrust himself into affairs. By another session he would have been active and prominent, for there was the power in him. He would not have done this by any effort. It would have come to pass in the most natural way

At Columbus he preached one or two sermons in a small church with good liberty. I have mentioned in another chapter his sermon at the McKendree Church at Nashville. From some untoward causes he was not at all himself on that occasion. He failed to become known, as he was, to the Church at large.

I was twice with him in the Bishop's Council when he represented the Weston District. He was full of his work. The burden of Northwest Missouri was on him. It was to be the most populous and powerful region within the limits of the Conference. The foundations must be broadly and strongly laid there. I never felt the force of his will so fully any where else. In prosecuting his views with respect to this region he was stubborn. He would never yield a point. He had come up with matured plans, and they must be executed. He supported them with an array of facts and arguments, stated with so much earnestness and such deep conviction of their truth, that all opposition was brought to a pause. When the Bishop made an appointment in his District against his views he entered his protest with so much solemnity and force as to secure a reconsideration. It was no mere wilfullness, but a deep sense of duty and fidelity to the cause that actuated him. It revealed a depth of character in him I had never seen before. He was a man of immense will. He was not, however, always asserting himself. It was only when a great interest or duty called him out that the indomitable spirit appeared. His own interests might be waived, but when he stood for God and His cause I would as soon have expected him to die in his tracks as any one I ever knew.

Many of the pleasantest recollections of my life are connected with Caples at Conference. His presence constituted no mean part of the charm of those occasions. The figure of the man as he came and went on the streets, at the dinners, in the assemblies, stands out distinct and radiant in the picture gallery of memory. The flash of his eye gleams upon me to-night from the glooms of the past. The resonance of his voice lingers upon my ear now like the cadence of a great bell that has just given notice of some unusual, divine solemnity at hand. He stands before me now, in the pulpit, on the Sunday night of the session, looking down upon the vast throng crowding the whole space within the walls, his right hand extended forward, the palm downward, the fingers at a slight curve, and "the words of this life" flowing from his lips.   Sentence after sentence the thought deepens, feeling becomes more intense, tears flow, shouts ascend, and every preacher there feels that it would be an honor too great to be allowed to preach Christ on the most miserable mission in the State.

Thenceforth we will be more self-sacrificing, more constant in toil, more cheerful in suffering, more like our Master.   So felt we all under his Conference sermons.

From all I can learn his life culminated at the sessions of the Conference held at Fulton and Mexico during the war.   These sessions were held in troublous times.   The internecine struggle had raged around the preachers with concentrated fury   They had been " in perils oft."   They had been looking daily for violent deaths.   As ministers, in their pulpits and ecclesiastical conventions, they had been servants of the Lord Christ. ' As individual men most of them had been Southern sympathizers.   The very name of their Church bore, as a suffix, the word " South."   They were suspected men.   However pure their Church record might be from any political stain, even the slightest, a suspicious eye was upon all their assemblages.   No circumspection of individual demeanor could avert malignant rumor.   Private enmities and ecclesiastical jealousies were ever on their track, invoking military interference.

In these times it was a sublime courage that attempted the holding of a Conference at all. Every man who left home to attend did so under the apprehension that he might never return. They committed themselves and their families to God, at parting, "with prayers and tears" that will never be forgotten. Verily, they "sowed in tears" then. The sword was perpetually over them, held by a hand not unwilling to strike.

But they were the under shepherds of the flock of Christ. Fidelity to Him, the chief shepherd, required that they should guard the flock in these perilous times. He had given His life for the sheep, and now they must follow His footsteps, even though they led to the cross. Vital interests of His cause called them to Conference. Envious tongues would accuse them of a traitorous purpose. But they knew the integrity of their own hearts, and God knew it. To Conference they must go, though bonds, imprisonment, death, might await them.

The "diary" already quoted, for the most part very brief, is more full in its account of the Mexico Conference. I shall give the material portions of it:

"Sept. 12, 1864. Visited brother Nevil's, Hutcheson's, etc.; took Mattie and left for Conference. Stayed at Brother Monroe's.

"13. Brother Monroe, Mattie and I started at
12

7 o'clock. Mattie stopped at brother Lassiter's. Dined at brother Horner's. Brother Monroe had a chill—quite sick. Found ten or fifteen brethren on the cars. Reached Mexico in the evening and found home at sister Pilcher's, with brothers Dockery, Rush and Vincil — a pleasant home. God bless the family and the occasion.

"14. Brother Berryman preached last night. This morning Conference was to organize. The brethren, many of them, young and old, here, not counting their lives dear unto them, for none of them could leave home and come here without risking life. Some thirty-five or forty, however, met. Brother Monroe went forward to read the Scriptures, and sang the hymn commencing, 'And are we yet alive'— prayer, fervent, following."

What meaning was in that hymn then! It had been sung at the opening of the sessions from year to year, almost always, and never without much feeling. Amid the ordinary changes and uncertainties of life, after a year's separation, emotion was stirred when they all saw "each other's faces." How much more now!

"And are we yet alive?"

No wonder that the prayer which followed was "fervent." Hearts accustomed to gratitude for all the ordinary mercies of a never-failing Providence would melt now. Gratitude for life preserved filled every heart — overflowed every eye. A knowledge of present dangers brought them consciously near to God. It was for His name and cause that they were risking life and imperiling their families. How appropriate, too, that Andrew Monroe should lead their devotions. He had survived to them from the first generation of Missouri preachers. His white hair seemed silvered already by a ray reflected from the world of spirits. He stood before them a token and proof of the loving care of God. That "fervent," effectual prayer of a righteous man availed much! They "were heard in that they feared." Elijah's God was at hand. The fellowship of prayer had, probably, never been more fully realized. These hearts, in the furnace, were fused, and flowed together. They were melted into one. All these forty men "agreed on earth as touching the one thing" they asked for. It was done for them. Some of them, perhaps all, are aglow with the fire of that morning's baptism still. Their enemies were, unwittingly, furnishing them the conditions of a spiritual growth, soon to appear in light and beauty, under happier auspices and brighter skies. Surely it was compensation for many sorrows to participate in that song and prayer and blessing.

This auspicious beginning of the session was followed by military interference. The diary, under date of the 14th, continues:

"The Provost-Marshal came forward and informed the brethren that they must take an oath, as prescribed in special order No. 61, Provost-Marshal General's office, 1864. The officer appeared not to know of a modification of this order, and commanded the brethren not to organize until they had taken the oath. A dispatch was sent to the Head Qu. Prov. Gen. office. Answer indefinite. So brother Savage went forward to St. Louis, and we improved the day in preaching and prayer. Brother Austin preached at 3 P. M. and H. H. Hedgepeth at night.

"15. Prayer-meeting at 9 A. M. A good time, melting into love. A holy unction rested on the brethren. All appeared blessed. . At 3 P. M. brother Jo. Pritchett—on the teachings of grace—a strong, turgid presentation of truth and duty. I tried at night to offer a few thoughts on 'The servant is not above his Master,' and pressed upon a large audience the acceptance of an undivided Christ."

The wonderful power of this sermon became known to me last year in Oregon. At Corvallis I found brother A Cauthorn and his family. They never tire of talking about this Conference, and about this sermon especially. Truly as they had served God from their youth, Christ became *more* to brother and sister Cauthorn from that transcendent sermon. The gospel became greater and more glorious. The very light of heaven seemed to have baptized the place. All that is loveliest and most exalting in spiritual beauty and immortal hope came within the sphere of vision. It was no mere passionate raving—it was a grand progress of thought from exordium to peroration—not *mere* thoughts, though, cold and luminous, but a lava-flood, bursting up from unknown, unfathomable, mysterious fire-depths.

The preaching of this occasion had a twofold advantage. The preachers, purified by fire, preached better than they had ever done, and the people, purified also by fire, heard better than they had ever done. There was a deeper sympathy between the preachers and the people. They had read about persecution in the fabulous old times. Now they themselves felt it. Thanks to the Provost-Marshal! he had deepened the sensibilities of the hour, and God restrained him from doing more. The word of God meant more to these bruised hearts than it does to the proud and prosperous. Sorrow drooping upon the breast of Jesus feels the throbbing of the Infinite Heart. Tears clarify vision.

Garrulous gray hairs, seventy years hence, will charm the ear of childhood with the story of the wondrous preaching at the Mexico Conference in 1864—preaching the like of which has never been since and probably never will be—preaching by rare men whom God had greatened in the furnace, and by Caples, the greatest of them all. The children will gape and wonder if the Lord will ever send such men into the world again.

Instead of taking the oath which the Provost-Marshal required of them the brethren sent a trusted messenger to headquarters. By the next morning this messenger, Rev. F A. Savage, had returned with an order permitting the Conference to organize. The preachers of Missouri set themselves resolutely against any interference of the civil or military authorities with their work. They would take no oath, as preachers. Whatever they might do as individual men, or in their character as citizens, they would submit to no such terms as a condition on which they should be allowed to transact the business of the Church. Most or all of them, I presume, had taken some form of oath to the Government since the beginning of the war, as other citizens had done When it was imposed as a condition of holding the Conference they declined. They owed it to posterity to take this stand in favor of the independence of the Church and in favor of religious liberty. Through years of persistent persecution they stood firm. Their attitude was sublime, their courage equal to the crisis, and in the end they triumphed.

The Provost-Marshal General had the good

sense not to require the oath in this instance. I return to the diary:

"16. Conference organized. Brother Monroe elected President and Brother Vincil Secretary Forty members present. Brother Shackelford preached at 3 P. M. and James Penn at night, strong, effective discourses A fine state of religious feeling in the Conference and congregation.

"17. Examination of Elders took up most of the time. Monroe sick. Berryman in the chair. Brother Wm. Penn preached at night, Jordan at 3 P. M. Quite a storm of wind and a little rain, leaving the air cool."

The entry for Sunday, the 18th, mentions the different places of preaching. The following brethren occupied various pulpits: Caples, Bird, Spencer, Pinckard, Savage, Newland and Vincil. He adds, "A day of good, we trust, to the large congregations." All the churches, it seems, were opened to them, and the people thronged the houses.

"19. Business of Conference proceeds smoothly Downing preached at 11 o'clock, Jordan at 3 and myself at night, on 'Felix trembled and said,' etc.

"20. Conference completed its business, and brother Monroe, in great feebleness, read the appointments for the coming year. Brother Vincil preached at night. A very pleasant Conference session. The preaching was more spiritual and

of a higher order than I ever heard before at a
Conference. The people were deeply interested.
May rich blessings follow these labors."

I rejoice, as all his friends will do, to find so
much from his own hand in reference to the last
Conference he ever attended. In a few weeks he
was dead. His voice was never heard by the
assembled brethren again. They had grasped
his hand for the last time on the earthly shore.
When they next met in Conference he was with
"the general assembly and Church of the First-
born."

How apparent will his love and his deep interest
in the preachers be to those who knew him, from
these casual pencilings in his diary A stranger
will not see it so clearly, but his old friends will.
What a vacancy there was when the brethren
assembled in their next session!

But the echo of his sermons was in their ears,
and the mention of his name melted all hearts.

Since preparing this chapter I have received
the following account of Mr. Caples' presidency
over the session of 1861, at Glasgow, from Rev. J.
D. Vincil. It was prepared at my request, and
will conclude the chapter appropriately:

"The eighteenth session of the Missouri Annual
Conference, M. E. Church, South, convened in
the city of Glasgow on the 11th day of September,
1861.

"By vote of the preceding session, Hannibal had been chosen as the seat of the Conference for 1861. But, owing to local causes and influences, it was deemed best to move the Conference. The question of change was agitated early in the season. Many thought Glasgow the most desirable point in our jurisdiction at which to quietly assemble. The writer was in charge of Glasgow Station at that time. Being written to respecting the matter, he submitted it to the Quarterly Conference on the 6th of July, 1861, Brother Caples presiding. A resolution was unanimously adopted tendering to the Annual Conference an invitation to meet in Glasgow, if found necessary to change. With the invitation was a tender of the *hospitalities* of the Church and assurances of a warm welcome. The preachers knew what was *meant* by such offers, having enjoyed the generous kindnesses of that people four years previously.

"Their invitation was subsequently accepted and arrangements made to receive and entertain the brethren. Accordingly the Conference assembled as above stated, it being the time set by Bishop Pierce who was appointed to visit and preside at that session. In consequence of the dark war-cloud, so ominous, hanging over the land, our beloved Bishop did not reach Missouri, and we were without a superintendent. The Conference met in the City Hall and was called to order by Rev. Andrew Monroe, who conducted the religious devotions of the morning. The election of a presiding officer, in accordance with the law of the Church, was first in order. A ballot was taken and resulted in the election of Wm. G. Caples as President of the Conference. He took the chair with great dignity, and expressed, with unaffected simplicity, his sense of the responsibilities imposed by the confidence of his too partial brethren.

"Business was entered upon and dispatched with an ease and facility which clearly evidenced that the brethren *knew* their man in placing him in the chair. In truth it seemed so natural to him to act in the capacity of a presiding officer that we felt less than otherwise the absence of the Bishop we all delight to honor. The writer has somewhat closely studied 'the make up' of presiding officers in various deliberative bodies of the day and of the country With no pretentiousness he ventures the opinion, from close observation, that but comparatively few men combine all the necessary qualifications to fill the station of presiding officer. The thought has been frequently presented that our Church has displayed remarkable discretion and judgment in the elevation of men to the Episcopal bench of rare administrative abilities. Endowed with a deep knowledge of the legislative, judicial and executive departments of Church government, and possessing the experience of years, our Episcopal Fathers are, with fewest exceptions, very superior presiding officers. Of some of them it may be safely affirmed they have no superiors in any sphere of life. To say all these things of Caples would be injudicious. But it is the firm conviction of the writer that he possessed a combination of qualifications fitting him for the Episcopal chair that no occupant of it could ever depreciate or be ashamed of. These qualities he displayed in his presidency over the Conference in Glasgow and proved himself every inch a Bishop except in *official* title. Amid the most trying surroundings and delicate labors the business of Conference, both in session and in the cabinet, was conducted in a highly satisfactory manner.

"During the session delegates to the General Conference were selected for the quadrennial meeting of 1862. On the first ballot Caples was chosen at the head of the list. Brothers Monroe, Vandeventer, (Dr.) Anderson, Dines and Spencer were his co-delegates. E. K. Miller, P M. Pinckard and Jesse Bird were chosen alternates.

"Brother Caples was re-appointed Presiding Elder of the Brunswick District for the following Conference year, and remained in charge till Oct., 1863, when he was stationed in Glasgow, as stated elsewhere.

" Aside from the many warm personal expressions of high appreciation of Caples as President of Conference, the following, adopted by a rising vote, is a matter of record:

"'*Resolved*, That in the spirit and fraternal manner of conducting the business of our annual session, our superintendent, Wm. G. Caples, has more than ever endeared himself to the members of this Conference.   S. W. Cope,

E. K. Miller.'

"The closing address of brother Caples to his brethren was characteristic. As viewed and remembered through the crowding events of following years, the writer cherishes that address as one of the richest treasures of life. To reproduce it here might be gratifying to many, but expediency forbids."

CHAPTER X.

PECULIAR VIEWS.

I have said elsewhere that Mr. Caples' views were strictly Wesleyan. In regard to Church polity he was a conservative, yet not of the most rigid class. What is essential to the itinerant system he would not have touched. He was jealous of any changes that might check the force of its administration. He would preserve it intact as it came from the fathers. He could see no remodeling of it, no readjustment of its parts that would not probably create friction. All friction involves a waste of power. The structure as it is is homogeneous. When changes begin to be made no doubt some elements will creep in that are not in harmony with the whole system. The system itself is a distribution and direction of Christian agencies in the way of organized activity of the most efficient character. Mr. Wesley he thought the most consummate legislator of modern times, and that the Episcopal Methodism of

America realized the Wesleyan idea most completely.

Yet he believed that some such addition might be made as he himself attempted in the District meetings—not as a change of the structure, but to supplement it, with a view to greater activity in the established agencies of the Church. To augment the power of agencies already at work was desirable. There is often a tendency to dullness or apathy in individuals. To collect them together once a year in each district so that the vigor of the best workers might excite the more sluggish to enthusiasm, and that all might provoke each other to love and good works, was not to change or mend, but only to bring into greater activity the agencies already provided. He was in favor of anything that would secure more *work*. Work was what the Church needed. We had the best distribution of work; the thing needed was only to animate the workmen.

Such is about the substance of views I once heard him put forth in a private discussion of the subject. I mention this only to show that in Church government he was a pronounced Methodist.

In doctrine he was no less pronounced. In another place I have said that he was strictly an evangelical Arminian. Yet he did not just accept what came from others. He had his own views. But his mind was so broad and comprehensive that he was not in peril of heresy at every step in his speculations. He did speculate boldly, but at the same time he comprehended the scope of evangelical doctrine and saw the everlasting foundations on which it rests too clearly to allow any mere speculation to come into collision with it.

That he did think independently and with great force and truth will appear from the following statement of Rev. William Holmes. I make the quotation from a communication sent me by Brother Holmes, and as the matter I refer to stands in immediate connection with other statements confirmatory of what I have said in a former chapter, I will give more than that which bears immediately on this point:

"Brother Caples' education, like my own, was very limited. But he had supplied the deficiency as best he could by levying contributions from every source of knowledge within his range, and few men have such a peculiar mind for arranging and classifying what they learn for future use. He possessed an extremely fruitful mind in expanding ideas, and extending the application of the same idea to every relation of life. He devoted the entire powers of his mind in one direction, and that was to present the gospel in the most forcible and clear manner. He had wonderful powers of mind, but they were peculiar. All his ideas he took second-hand from living minds or books, but the arrangement, illustration and imagery were his own. Watson's Institutes and Sermons and the Bible were almost solely his text-books. He scarcely read any work except those named, and if he consulted other books it was only to gather the author's plan and leading ideas. A usual method was to read a portion of the opening chapter, or just so much as revealed the author's plan and the leading idea or ideas of the work, and he then had no further use for it. I recollect getting hold of a new work I had read with great profit and pleasure and went to his house with it. He took it, read the plan of the work, read parts of two chapters, and with all my persuasion I could not get him to read it through or take any further interest in it. He said to me: 'No, I don't want to read it; I am afraid. I've got his plan; I like it; I want to arrange the details myself.' I was astonished in hearing him preach often during the following year to find that he had mastered all the author's ideas, and had extended the application of them with more force, as I thought, than my favorite author. Yet I know he had only read as I have stated."

I concur fully with Brother Holmes, except that I think he took hints from nature as well as from men and books. I think it is also true that he became a greater reader after the period of Brother

Holmes' association with him. He procured, in later years, every important publication coming from the press in the line of theology. He was among the first to get and devour Bledsoe's Theodicy and Young's God and Evil, and The Christ of History, by the same author. And while there was to the last much reading in the manner indicated in the statement given above, yet books of a high order of thought were often studied by him with care.

Of Bledsoe and Young he was a great admirer. He luxuriated in their writings. But from what I know of his mental habitudes, if he had lived to see "The Life and Light of Men," by the latter of these men, he would have repudiated as essentially heretical his views of the Atonement. The fact of *guilt* as an essential incident of sin, the correlative fact of the condemnation of the sinner under a Divine judicial administration, his well-poised understanding could never have been beguiled to relinquish by any, the most specious sophistry. The correlative of guilt and condemnation again is penalty, and all these involve the great fact of *justice*—administrative justice. Sin is not just merely an abnormal condition of the soul, a fatal reality in personal consciousness. It is not just subjective, a dreadful incident of which is spiritual death. Beside and beyond all this, it is active and has an objective bearing. It is a

13

violation of law.   It is an obtrusion of malignant forces upon the universal order which God has established in the spiritual sphere.   It does not terminate upon the sinner himself, but is a breach of the peace of the universe.   God, in his character of Infinite Justice, the conservator of universal order, must hold the violator of his law guilty.   There must be an arrest of the offender. There must be an executive and penal administration.   These propositions are all grounded in reason.   No less are they distinct affirmations of Scripture.   "The wrath of God is revealed from heaven against all unrighteousness and ungodliness of men."   "The Lord shall be revealed from heaven in flaming fire, taking vengeance on them that know not God and obey not the gospel of the Lord Jesus Christ."

The incarnation and sufferings of Christ are not simply an expression of the Divine love to win the sinner to God, but also a vicarious sacrifice for his sin.   Great numbers of passages declare this, and the most ingenious and sophistical explication is ever more resorted to by those who deny it.   "He bore our sins in His own body on the cross."   "The Lord hath laid on Him the iniquity of us all."   No man ever felt this more deeply than Caples, or gave a more distinct or fuller utterance to it than he in his public teachings. He saw in these great facts the very foundation of the Christian structure. They constitute the everlasting truth as it appears in the plan of salvation. He had mastered and repudiated most of the sophistries which assail this doctrine.

But he was no slave of other men's thoughts. There were some things in the old books (for, as I have elsewhere said, in his latter years he read many of the best old English authors) which have become incorporated with the popular theology that he controverted. Some views universally accepted as belonging to the evangelical doctrine he considered mere fungous attachments. These he did not hesitate to attack. One or two instances I will mention as indicating his independence as a thinker. Whether he was right or wrong the reader will, of course, decide for himself.

He gave me at one time, with great interest, an account of a sermon he had preached not long before, in which he controverted the prevalent idea that God had created man for His own glory. More precisely, his hypothesis was, that to glorify Himself was not *the motive* of the Maker in creating intelligent beings. He had been led to this view by the repugnance he felt to certain phrases in the Westminster Confession. That God had foreordained some men to eternal life *for the praise of His glorious grace,* and others to eternal damnation *for the praise of His glorious justice* was a statement that he could not bear. Yet if you

concede the postulate, that His own glory is the
actuating motive of the Creator in His work, the
extreme Calvinistic conclusion must be accepted.
If the glory of God is the final object, it matters
little what becomes of man, whose destinies
are neither here nor there, in the light of this
theory, except as they may enhance the glory of
God.

This he met by denying the postulate. Man
was *not* created for the Divine glory—at least this
was not the motive of the Creator, not the end
proposed by Him. This motive would disparage
the Almighty It represented Him as a selfish
Being, looking to selfish ends, whereas the great
fact of His nature was love. His motives are
benevolent, not selfish. His glory, in fact, consists
in this. To assign a selfish end to His work is to
destroy His glory. If He should create for His
own glory His glory would be lost in that very
fact, for His true glory is found in the beneficence
of His nature. We must believe, then, that He
created man that He might bestow good. The
purpose of creation was a beneficent one, therefore a purpose that looked *out* of himself, and not
in upon himself.

He illustrated thus : A man sees his neighbor's
child exposed to instant death. At imminent
hazard of his own life he saves the child. He
never pauses to examine his own motive, but

obeys an impulse—a generous impulse. It never occurs to him that this act will be greatly to his credit, and that he will lay the parents under obligation. He just has a right impulse and acts upon it instantly. He desires *to save the child*, and acts accordingly The motive is one that looks *without* and not *within*.

Now, this is a *good deed*. It is of the *highest class* of good deeds. His praise is in the mouth of every one.

But let it come to be understood that he deliberately proposed it to himself as a motive of the act *that he would be glorified* in the community—that he cared nothing for the child, but desired to become a hero with his acquaintances—and every praiseworthy feature of the act is lost. The glory of the act was in the fact that it was an expression of generous alarm for the child. Assign a selfish motive and your admiration of the deed is gone. *The glory of a deed is in the unselfishness of it.* The man who toils and encounters danger *to do good* is a hero : the man who toils and encounters danger *to make a hero of himself* is none. He is just a common, selfish-man. A man is glorified in doing a glorious work so long as he does not propose his own glorification as the end.

So, he maintained, God *is* glorified in His work, but He is so because His purpose is beneficent and does not spring from a motive terminating in

Himself. To work for glory, as a motive, would be to destroy His own glory and to forfeit the praise of His creatures. No man, therefore, was foreordained and created with a mere deliberate design of the Creator to give Him eternal life for the praise of His glorious grace. Much less is the other one of the Westminster propositions true.

I asked him what he would do with those Scriptures which declare that all things are and were created for the glory of God. He did not hesitate for a reply Every thing connected with the matter had passed through the alembic of his mind. His answer was that all things *do* glorify God, and this as a result, of course, He foresaw. He is omniscient These passages state a fact. The fact is that all of His works glorify Him, and it is right for us to see them as for his glory But the actuating source of His work is given in another statement—"God is love." I have given the substance of his statement without any attempt to recall the exact language. But I am very certain that as to the substance my statement is accurate.

He did not accept the common theory as to the origin and design of *natural death*. He maintained that physical death was not the penalty, nor any part of the penalty, of the first transgression. "In the day that thou eatest thereof thou shalt surely die," he affirmed, did not contemplate this species of death at all. On the contrary, natural death was not denounced against man until *after both the fall and the promise of redemption.* "Dust thou art and unto dust shalt thou return," comes historically *after* the seed of the woman had been provided. The penalty, "thou shalt surely die," gives just what will befall the impenitent in their final estate. Soul and body in hell will realize its import. The phenomenon which we call physical death—the separation of soul and body—belongs to another administration altogether. The arrest of judgment in the case of the first offenders, by the intervention of redeeming mercies, made place for a new state of things. Natural death is a part of that modified condition which supervened upon the introduction of the reign of grace. It is just the disposition that is made of a man between the moment when his probation ceases and the day of judgment. *It is not the penalty of the law.* To the incorrigible and finally impenitent it may have some penal significance, as all they suffer has, but this was not the design.

It is, in fact, rather a part of the remedial system. A result of sin it certainly is; but an *indirect*, not a *direct* result. The necessity for any remedy comes of the fact of disease. Evil, in this world, is in a form subdued to the purposes of redemption—that is, natural evil. All suffering, under the reign of grace, is corrective, not penal. Natural death has its place in this system of disciplinary agencies. It is called by the apostle an enemy indeed, and in one sense it is so. The surgeon's knife has never a friendly aspect to the patient, however beneficent the result of its use. "Now no chastening for the present seemeth to be joyous, but grievous; nevertheless, afterward it yieldeth the peaceable fruit of righteousness to them that are exercised thereby" "All things are yours," even "death."

Upon my giving the substance of this view in the St. Louis *Advocate*, some years ago, Caples accused me, in a good natured way, of having gotten it from him, referring me to a conversation we had on the subject when we were both very young men. The conversation I remembered, but I remembered also another thing, which was that I already held this opinion at that time. Our views in the matter were coincident. But he never would give it up. I was his "disciple" in this doctrine. He would hear to nothing else, and I never took the trouble to dispute the point further, but told him he should be my Rabbi. The results of my more mature reflection upon the subject I will not take the space to give here.

Among other things that he found in old authors, which he affected so much in the latter

years, was a theory of the Tithe, which he adopted
and advocated with great enthusiasm. When
Rev. T. M Finney was agent of the Book Depository, before the war, he instituted a course of
lectures under the auspices of the Young Men's
Methodist Union, of St. Louis. The object was
to give life and interest to the Union, to do good
by the lectures, to make something for the Depository, if possible, by the fees, and to publish the
lectures in a book, which should at once be a
valuable contribution to religious literature in the
West and a source of revenue to the Depository.
Caples was engaged for two lectures in the course.
He responded readily, chiefly for the reason that
it would afford him an admirable opportunity to
get his doctrine of the Tithe before the people.
Both of his lectures, if my memory is not at fault,
were on this subject. I had hoped to secure a
copy of them, that I might give the most important
portions of them here. But the book was never
published, and I have not been able to get a copy
of them. Nor can I recall the elaboration of the
theme adequately The clew he had gotten hold
of in some book, but he threaded the labyrinth
for himself. The substance of the theory, as I
remember it, was about this:

The Tithe is the *tenth part*. The law of the
Tithe prescribed that one-tenth part of the "increase"—that is, of a man's income, should be

devoted to God. The law of the Sabbath required one-seventh part of a man's time for the exclusive service of God. The object was to impress the claims of the Creator on man. Our time is all His, and while by His ordination a large part of it must be used in the necessary affairs of this life—and while thus used, if the right disposition be maintained, He is glorified—one part of it is reserved to His especial service, lest in our worldly avocations we should become engrossed and forget God. He thus recalls us, perpetually, at short intervals, to Himself. He reminds us that our time is all his, and that all appropriation of it, even to secular affairs, must contemplate Him. It is the assertion of the supremacy of God. He makes use of the relation we bear to time as an occasion of asserting Himself in our thought and arousing us to an habitual worshipful regard of Himself.

The law of the Tithe makes the same use of our relation to property. However legitimate and necessary to civilization the acquisition and individual appropriation of property may be, in our depraved condition it proves a snare to many It becomes the supreme object of pursuit. God is put aside by it. The true spiritual ends of existence are forgotten. Men live in the flesh and for the flesh That which is really accidental in our conditions takes ascendant position in thought and pursuit. The man delivers the whole force of his faculties upon this end. Life loses all meaning except that which is expressed in percentages. The spiritual nature is ignored. Eternity goes into an eclipse behind the dollar.

There is that in our fallen condition which responds most strongly and acutely to the charm of wealth. The ear is ever keenly set to receive the clink of silver. There is no music the melody of which commands such universal and clamorous applause. Men will dance to its notes who can be moved by nothing else. Even sincere Christians often find this propensity the chief hindrance of religious growth. The love of money not unfrequently keeps them in a gross, carnal state, when, to all appearances, they would otherwise come into the full liberty of the Gospel.

Those who *have* riches are by no means the only class who are in danger from this cause. Very often the greatest love of money is seen in those who have but very little. Not only those who *are* rich, but " they that *will be* rich, fall into temptation and a snare, and into many foolish and hurtful lusts which drown men in ungodliness and perdition." Nor is it only that form of the love of money that looks to *hoarding*, but that other form of it which looks to spending for the gratification of our lusts and pleasures, that is sinful and debasing. In all money-making, money-hoarding and money-spending there is occasion of temptation.

To counter-work this fatal tendency to grossness and carnality of life arising out of our relation to property, God asserts Himself directly in this relation. While He graciously gives us, for food, and raiment, and education, and all the exigencies of a civilized, cultivated condition, the greater part of the fruits of our industry and enterprise, He demands an appreciable portion for Himself. The results of our labor must not all be turned upon *self.* We must "honor God with our substance." He demands recognition here. He will not consent that we should make a god of the world. He asserts Himself against the dominion of Mammon in the law of the Tithe. All time and money are His But he allows us the greater part of both our time and property for the exigencies of our present condition, being glorified thus indirectly by a wise use of them for ends that have been ordained by Himself. Yet one-seventh of time and one-tenth of property He takes *directly* to Himself, lest otherwise His right in these matters should be forgotten or denied.

There is a deep feeling in men that they have a *right* to the fruits of their labor, and perhaps the divine authority is never more fully established over a man than when he has freely conceded this right. When a man of about average instincts

with regard to property has surrendered his possessions to God, and is fully ready to acquiesce
in any, the largest, demands of the Creator upon
his property, it is high proof of perfect fealty.
Hence the Tithe. It was a pronounced, perpetual
demand of God directly upon property. It was an
assertion of divine claims in a particular that
would test the depth and truth of the response.

There is a popular belief that the law of the
Tithe was part of the Mosaic Institute, and, therefore, passed away with the coming of Christ.
This he maintained was an error. This law was
not peculiar to the Mosaic dispensation. The
reason of the law is too deep for this. It was no
expedient to meet a temporary condition. It is
founded in essential, permanent states of the soul
and of society. It is called for not only by the
facts already stated, but also by another no less
important. The spiritual life must express itself
in organic forms. There must be a Church, with
ministers of the sanctuary A due proportion of
the property of men must be put to this use. It
must provide an organized utterance — a local
habitation and ·a name — for religion. Religion
can not make way in the world otherwise. It can
have no footing in a world where all life is in
organic forms except it also be embodied. To
this end there must be property in the immediate
service of God. To secure a desirable result, this

appropriation of property to religious uses must be under the operation of a *law*. Otherwise every thing will be at haphazard and the world will realize but little of religion in any form of property.

He affirmed that we have ample illustration of this. Men had come to believe that the law of the Tithe was done away with, and that they were at liberty to give much or little, or nothing, at their option or convenience. Hence no adequate proportion of the property of the world, or even of the Church, in our country, was consecrated to God. In most places there is a want of adequate provision for the worship of God and for Christian education. Ordinary Church expenses drag. Even the wealthy city churches are often in a stew to bring up arrearages. The stewards are in painful consultation every now and then over an empty treasury, with an unpaid preacher anxiously asking how he is to get a barrel of flour. Not unfrequently the most questionable expedients are resorted to in order to supply deficiencies. The vanities of this life are appealed to for relief. Fairs, charades, tableaux, with their concomitants, are put into requisition to supplement the charities of the Church. The conscience of the people of God, under a well-understood law of divine authority, would secure a revenue at once regular and ample. All expenses would be adjusted to

resources which would meet every reasonable demand. The law of the Tithe would solve all the
knotty financial problems which have vexed the
stewards of the Church from immemorial times.

As to the *fact* of this law being only a part of
the Jewish ritual — a fact which he denied — he
affirmed that it had been incorporated, as the
Sabbath had been, into that ritual, but that, like
the Sabbath, it is to be traced to a higher origin.
Many things found in Moses' law are of permanent
obligation. It was not all mere ritual. It embraced
the moral as well as the ceremonial code. It also
embraced principles fundamental in ecclesiastical
legislation. It incorporated into itself customs
divinely ordained among the Patriarchs. Amongst
these are the Sabbath and the Tithe. The consecration of the *tenth* to religion dates back at least
to Abraham, for that greatest of the Patriarchs,
the father of the faithful, gave the the tenth of
all the spoils of the campaign against the kings
to Melchisedeck, the priest of the Most High God.
The incident is mentioned in the narrative in a
matter-of-course way, not as an extraordinary case,
but as if it were a customary thing. No doubt
Melchisedeck was in the habit of receiving such
recognition of his official character. God was
thus habitually acknowledged by men appropri-
ating to His priest one-tenth part of their goods.
St. Paul, in mentioning this incident, seems to

understand that the only extraordinary thing about the case was that Abraham, the friend of God, should have found a priest having precedence of him—one so great that even *he* paid the Tithe.

From this case, and perhaps other hints in the Scriptures, he maintained that this law antedates the Mosaic economy, and rests on no ground of obligation that the Christian era has not as well as the Jewish. Like the Sabbath, it rests on a firmer ground. It is no less necessary now than in the time of Moses or of Melchisedeck. Everywhere recognized and acted on in the Church, it would heal the infirmity of ecclesiastical finances and put a new face on Christian enterprise.

But there was another proposition which he announced on this subject with great emphasis. It was this:

The Tithe does not give the full measure of Christian obligation in the use of money for religious purposes.

On the contrary, it was imposed and intended only to *provide for the worship of God where it was collected.* It was given to the priest to defray the expenses of the sanctuary   Nothing beyond the *expenses of local worship* is to be provided for in this way   This, he maintained, the whole history of the law would show. Every man *owes* God the tenth part of his income to meet the expenses of the Church where he worships—to support the pastor and provide for the decent, appropriate worship of God in the public congregation. From the poorest to the richest, the law was in force over all. If any man received ten dollars and no more, one of them belonged to God for this purpose. If he received ten thousand, the *law* demanded the *tithe* of it for the honor of God in the maintenance of worship for his own family and his neighbors.

All claims of charity and Christian enterprise in the form of Missionary labors, church extension, aiding the poor and providing for the orphan, are over and above the Tithe—quite in another category of virtues. Christian charity, where there is wealth, can by no means satisfy itself with the one-tenth which God has levied upon to keep the most essential forms of religion alive in the world. The man who receives but a small salary, with a family to support and children to educate, after meeting this divine assessment, may feel that for charities beyond this he can spare but little. But where a bountiful Providence has blessed a man's enterprises until ten thousand dollars a year, more or less, flows into his hands, will an enlightened conscience and a soul made perfect in love allow the remaining nine thousand to go to the uses of avarice or vanity? The suggestion is preposterous! Above this regular revenue for the maintenance of religion at home God has given no specific
14

legislation, but only the great law of love—"Thou shalt love thy neighbor as thyself."

The fact is (I have heard him use very nearly this language), the Church does not *begin* to realize her obligation in this matter. Even among professed Christians the devil gets the use of ten dollars where God does not get one. The *Church* actually pays, ten times over, more to support avarice, vanity and family pride than to advance the kingdom of the Prince of Life. Those who make the loudest profession will pay a hundred dollars to gratify the vanity of one child, and growl half a day if they have to pay *ten* in the course of the year to support the Gospel. If ever you see a man shouting at a camp-meeting and you wish to test the quality of the shout, just take up a Missionary collection. Ten chances to one he would turn sulky, and with an ungracious air drop in a battered dime, or else be singing so devoutly, with his eyes shut while the plate passed, that he would not see it. You might know that that shout came from no very deep place in the soul. Every effort to get anything up from the money-depths fails. His religious character does not go down there. It is shallow—all on the surface. It is a religion of the sentiments, not of the affections. These cling to earthly things. True religion subdues the whole man to God. The affections of the soul that take hold of property are not exempt from the gracious, transforming power. They, with the whole nature, become sanctified, and property is held for God. When He calls for any part of it for His immediate use, it is surrendered freely, joyfully. The fact is, when a man comes to comprehend his duty and privilege in this respect, there is no part of the Christian life that he will enjoy more than this glorifying of God with his substance.

He would, on occasion, deliver a heavy rebuke upon men who were getting rich and all the while keeping themselves in debt by fresh investments, so having a perpetual excuse, when divine claims were made upon them, that they had no money. They must pay their just debts. Honesty first and generosity afterward. All the while they take care to keep in debt. They make money by going in debt. They are all the time "making provision for the flesh." Thus they manage to get rich and defraud their Creator of His just claims. They will not be held guiltless in the day of eternity It is the bounden duty of every man to make thoughtful provision beforehand to have money for Christian purposes. He has no right to keep himself so cramped, while his resources are so abundant, as never to be able to make a full return from his means to the Great Giver of all things. If it is right to go in debt in order to make money, it is right to go in debt to do good.   This latter is by far the more important investment.   It will go on yielding its per cent. in eternity   Let a man know that while he keeps his capital fully absorbed in speculations looking solely to the increase of it, he is to suffer heavy loss in the " true riches."

I have, in fact, known no man whose ideas of duty with respect to the use of riches were so positive, or who delivered himself on this subject with so much emphasis.   He saw, with that distinct vision of spiritual truth which so eminently characterized him, that the covetousness of the Church "clogs the wheels of Zion."   The movements of the Church are hampered.   There are no adequate means of enlargement and enterprise.   Prophetic inspiration anticipated the honoring of the Son of God by "gifts."   The silver and gold were to be His, furnishing large revenues to be administered for the increase of His kingdom.   His treasury was to overflow from the offerings of a joyful multitude.   The wise men brought their tribute— gold and frankincense and myrrh.   But, alas! a mercenary Church to-day reduces the administration of the Son of God to the utmost straits and furnishes no adequate resources for conquest. While Heathenism and Mohammedism and Romanism dominate the world with their imperious and corrupting superstitions, and array the agencies of wealth against the work of Christ, His people, who really command to a great extent the commerce of the world, refuse the supplies necessary to any aggression on a grand scale upon the territories of darkness. The Kingdom of Christ in this world can succeed, and does succeed, only so far as the active agencies of the world are touched and sanctified by it. It is triumphant among men only when domestic life, social life, political life and business life are sanctified by it, and when all the forces of society contribute to its development. One of the most potent of these is money. There is no agency of evil that has wrought more moral ruin than money But money is not inherently evil. It is evil only as it is made to serve the ends of avarice and pride and lust. It may be turned to most beneficent uses and made active as an agent of redeeming mercies amongst men. Even the mammon of unrighteousness is to be subjugated to Christ and put to service in the sublime movements set on foot by Him for the salvation of lost men. "The world," in the Christian meaning of that word, is, perhaps, concentrated in money, and expressed by it more fully than in any other one thing. The measure of the Redeemer's conquest of the world, then, will appear in the extent to which the wealth of the world is brought into Christian conditions. The meager revenues of the Church are in proof of a most imperfect spiritual life even amongst

His professed followers.   When once He gains a requisite ascendency over the hearts and resources of His own people, then even worldly means, transformed into evangelizing forces, shall hasten the dawn of the millennium.

There is no adequate consecration that does not take money along with it.   So long as this is held back from God our offering amounts to very little indeed.   It is mere hypocrisy to talk of giving up soul and body to God while we withhold our property   Soul, body, property, family, *every thing* must be felt to be at the disposal of the Creator.   Nothing must be common or unclean. The touch of grace must be on every dollar— every dime.   The commonest outlay even for food and clothing must have His glory in view, and large, painstaking arrangements must be made to carry on His work.   A sanctified spirit will dress plainer and set down to a more frugal table in order to swell the tide of Missionary agencies and increase the energy of the Church.   To take possession of new conquests in China or Madagascar for Christ, or to contribute in the smallest measure to such a victory, will give a true Christian heart infinitely greater satisfaction than costly entertainment.

But with the great majority the Savior and His work are put off with the odds and ends –the leavings — after the thirst of avarice and the clamor of appetite have been satisfied.

All these things he delivered with a clearness and force of statement, and an opulence of illustration and imagery, that this narrative will utterly fail to realize. Many of his sermons and addresses on these topics were unique and striking in the highest degree. They were never tame. He spoke with authority as one who consciously represented the Great King. There was nothing apologetic in tone or manner. He had no apology to make for urging the claims of God. To make duty clear and bring the conscience up to an enlightened standard was the aim. What I am writing is but a feeble echo of his grand utterances on this important subject. He is with God now, and I trust that his word, so imperfectly repeated, will convey a deeper meaning from that fact. Being dead he still speaks to us in Missouri. He warns us against the dominion of a mercenary spirit. He commands us not to rob God.

Of the Missionary cause he was a most earnest advocate. His charity was as large as the world, his views co-extensive with the boundaries of the Redeemer's kingdom. He felt that the Church which failed to bring out its resources for the conversion of the world must incur the displeasure of the Lord. Apathy in this cause was sin. Not to be in sympathy with the purpose of Christ was

to be dead to all that is divine. He who came to
redeem the world requires all His people to join
Him in love and sacrifice for the great result. We
are to be workers together with Him. In this He
has conferred high honor upon mortals, and the
soul is dead that does not thrill under the high
impulse of this divine partnership of labor and
of glory

He was keenly alive to the delinquency of Missouri Methodism in Missionary labors. The
country was new, indeed. The Church had a
great work to do at home. Everywhere churches
were to be built. Schools were to be provided.
New ground was to be occupied. There had not
been time for the accumulation of capital as in
older countries. For all this allowance was to be
made. Yet after the largest allowance the Church
was undeniably culpable. Much more might have
been done. There was often money for every
luxury, money for pleasure, money to be wasted,
even by members of the Church. The money
given to send the Gospel to the heathen, in the
meantime, amounted to nothing. Less than nothing, in fact, for during his lifetime the Missouri
and St. Louis Conferences consumed more Missionary money than they raised. With forty
thousand members, or thereabout, we were a tax
on the general treasury We ought to have

supplied every home demand and sent some thousands abroad.

The reproach is not removed from us to-day. It is the sin and shame of our Church in Missouri that scarcely any of our members feel an enlightened sense of duty in this matter. Every man in the Church ought to lay aside, as he may be able, a sum each year for Foreign Missions. If he is poor let it be ever so little, but let *something* be consecrated to this holy object. If he is rich, let it be in proportion to his wealth. We are positively narrow. We have kept our sickly charities concentrated upon home objects until we are shriveled. While a New Orleans Sunday School, under the impoverishment of the war, has sent contributions once and again to China, and come into rich, world-wide sympathies, we have been drying up under the assumed inability to do more than attend to our own wants.

It is high time for Missouri to come up to a nobler elevation and get an outlook upon a dying world. We want a broader spirit. The words of the great commission have never taken effect upon us: "Go ye out into all the world and preach the Gospel to every creature."

I am a Missourian by birth, and in my spiritual life the offspring of Missouri Methodism, and therefore speak plainly. For the shortcomings of the Church I am, perhaps, as much at fault as any other man. While this book which I have undertaken the labor of writing may be a monument to the memory of Caples, I propose to the whole Church to join me in erecting a better and worthier one. Let us inaugurate an era of Missionary zeal. Let every man, woman and child in the Church in Missouri from this day make a contribution every year to *Foreign Missions.* With the poorest, if it be but the two mites which make a farthing, still let it be cast into the treasury with prayer. God will receive in it the odor of an acceptable sacrifice, a sweet-smelling savor, well pleasing to Him.

Mr. Caples laid no burdens on other men's shoulders that he was not himself willing to bear. He was a princely giver according to his means. Indeed, many of his friends thought him too generous. But he did it in faith. In the eternal world it will be seen that he acted from a high motive—that he acted also wisely and well for himself and for his children. Well he knew that money hoarded for children is often a curse and not a blessing. The name and memory of a noble father are a better inheritance for children than money, inspiring in them a high purpose and an honorable sentiment which lead to the achievement of better fortunes than wealth can secure.

I have wandered. Yet not far, for in his views of the use of money for the glory of God Brother

Caples went a length that justifies their classification as *peculiar*. What I have said comes fairly under the caption of this chapter.

But just in so far as they were peculiar they approached nearer to the measure of the truth as it is in Jesus. May the mantle of this Elijah fall on many surviving prophets!

CHAPTER XI.

———

DENOMINATIONAL EDUCATION.

I have already given Mr. Caples' views of the education required for the ministry While he strongly opposed making a classical course a condition of reception into the traveling connection, and was averse to theological schools, he did not undervalue educational opportunities for the young. In the entry in his diary on his last birth-day, given elsewhere, he laments with evident feeling his own limited attainments. He felt that, in many situations, he could have accomplished more with the advantages of a thorough education. As he advanced in years and in knowledge he felt this more and more keenly.

He did not, however, imagine that the sum of all excellencies is to be found in the mere acquisition of knowledge. With " all knowledge " there might be the absence of every virtue. "Knowledge is Power," but it may be power for evil as well as for good. In the hands of the

Jesuit it will extend the domain of superstition and misbelief. In the infidel it will be the source of unbounded mischief. In the service of corrupt passions it will spread the malaria of vice and licentiousness far and wide, and invest the grossest indulgences with an air of respectability. It will give plausibility to the narrowest fanaticism and an air of dignity to the meanest and most mischievous enterprises.

It is of the utmost consequence, then, that the education of our youth should be in the right hands. The best possible conditions must be brought into concurrence in the formation of character.

One fact is apparent in all ages, and yet men seem not to have been duly impressed with it up to this hour—that is, that no amount of mental training or culture can guard a man against error. The most gifted and highly educated are just as liable to embrace erroneous creeds in religion and ethics as the most ignorant. The falsest and most disorganizing and debasing doctrines have never wanted for accomplished advocates. The pride of opinion which so often accompanies learning is a state of mind most unfriendly to the reception of truth. A boy is very likely to embrace the opinions of his instructor, and when once he comes to consider himself "educated" he feels his character for learning at stake in his creed. He fortifies himself in it, and always has his lance leveled for any antagonist. He is never reluctant to prove his skill in dialectics, and the more adroit he proves himself in sophistry the more he will cherish the falsehood in defense of which he has made himself illustrious. His learning makes him an ingenious sophist, but confers no power of infallible discrimination between truth and falsehood.

But where mental culture may be brought to the support of truth immense advantage is secured. There will be at once acuteness and force in the advocacy. Truth, unfortunately, is not so popular amongst men that it may wantonly adventure into the arena without sword or helmet. It requires to be full-panoplied in the conflict. Every possible advantage must be secured, every possible alliance effected. In the natural sciences and mathematics men seem to take to the truth readily enough. But even in these, the moment you ascend into the more abstruse and complex regions, investigation becomes difficult and error abounds. Much more in the sphere of philosophy and religion. Except in the most obvious matters there seems to be an affinity rather for error than truth. Only he who holds firmly by the Word of God is safe from fatal blunders.

It is not enough, then, to educate the intellect alone. The moral and religious side of our nature must be looked after. The mind must be taken possession of for God at the earliest possible moment, and through the whole period in which fundamental beliefs are commonly formed it must be guarded against both unbelief and misbelief. A high moral tone must be secured and a sensitive conscience toward God. Religion must be dominant. As the intellectual force is augmented it must be turned into a direction that will promote the harmonies instead of aggravating the discords of life. Otherwise this augmentation of force acquired by mental development and discipline will contribute to extend the domain of evil, while it intensifies and greatens the ruin into which the man himself will plunge.

The youth of the country will be educated by somebody. Every man that is able to do it will give his sons and daughters a liberal education. He will not stop to ask about the consequences, moral and religious, that are to follow He will send his children to *college*, no matter how pestilential the spiritual atmosphere of the place. They may be manipulated into Romanism or Infidelity, but *to school they must go*. Parental partiality will take it for granted that they will escape contamination.

Nor is the general estimate of the value of education exaggerated except in the particular I have named. It enlarges the area of consciousness, quickens the faculties, and evolves power. It makes a man neither a saint nor a sinner, but it enables him to become either the one or the other on a large scale. He is more *in* himself and *to* himself than he could otherwise be, and delivers himself upon society and events with much greater force and effect. He can do more good—he can do more harm. The youth ought to be educated—*must be*—WILL BE.

Who shall do it? The Romanist? The Infidel? Both will do it so far as they can, especially the former. They are striving to the utmost of their power and their vast resources to get possession of the young mind of the country. And parents—thoughtless Protestant parents—are constantly sending their sons, and especially their daughters, into the midst of this religious infection—this spiritual small-pox—stupidly hoping that they will escape the plague. Just at the most impressible period of life, when opinions are almost wholly the offspring of the sentiments and the imagination, the incipient woman is placed under the exclusive control of those who will take possession of her through her affections, and in constant contact with a ritual contrived by the sagacity and experience of ages to impress the imagination. If she is not led by her affections and imagination to embrace this stupendous distortion of the Christian faith it will be a miracle.

But the children ought to be educated, and must; and somebody will do it. No one saw more clearly than Caples these two facts: first, that a solemn obligation rests on the Church to supply a Christian education to her own children, and as many others as possible; and secondly, that the Church that does most in this field of enterprise and opportunity will reap the richest harvest. *The Church* must educate the young. The rising generation must be taught religion and science at the same time. This is not a contest with the devil over the *body* of Moses (and even an archangel thought a human body too sacred to be relinquished to the wicked one) but over *immortal souls.*

Methodists he held to be under peculiar obligations in this regard. Methodism was born in a college. Mr. Wesley would have been but poorly qualified to do the great work to which God had called him had he been a man of limited attainments. As it was he had achieved incalculable results in several fields. The *intellectual* was almost equal to the *spiritual* quickening that attended his labors. The rage for learning became epidemic among his followers. From the college he brought an influence to bear that made many a man a scholar who scarcely ever saw the inside of a college building. Mr. Wesley's preachers,

15

however crude at first, almost all became in some substantial measure educated men, many of them highly accomplished. Clarke and Drew and Olivers, and a great multitude, became erudite under influences coming from the Wesleys. The movement had extended to this country. The Methodist impulse had raised thousands of young men from the ranks of poverty to cultivation and eminence.

The Methodists, as a people, both in England and America, had done much in the field of education proper. Mr. Wesley early founded a school. In this country, even in the days of Coke and Asbury, a college was founded, and since that time Methodist colleges and high schools had sprung up everywhere. Herculean labors and immense sums of money had been devoted by them to this object.

There had been much abortive effort, indeed. But this, even, must be said to their honor; for these failures had occurred in instances where their zeal had anticipated the resources of the country. But already many institutions founded by them were established on a permanent basis and doing a great work.

Views such as these he often gave in public addresses on the subject of education, elaborating them with great clearness and urging them upon the conscience of the Church with great force.

If the labors of men devoted to the profession of teaching and the protracted service of Rev. P. M. Pinckard as agent of Central College be excepted, no man amongst us in his day did so much for the cause of education as Mr. Caples. Indeed, in the history of Missouri Methodism he still holds this pre-eminence.

His arduous devotion to this cause commenced while he was the Presiding Elder of Weston District. I have already spoken of his having inaugurated the District Conference. I have just learned from Rev. M. R. Jones that in addition to the preachers, traveling and local, he invited all official members, especially exhorters and stewards, to participate in the business of these meetings. From the same source I learn that he intended to give practical value to these occasions beyond what I have indicated in a former chapter. In one of them he originated the movement which resulted in the establishment of both the Weston and Plattsburg High Schools. Various localities were invited to compete for the location of a school of high grade. The community making the largest subscription was to be honored with the school. Caples, then living at Weston, took charge of the subscription for that place, and Jones, being in charge of the Plattsburg Circuit, raised one there. These two points were far in advance of all others, and Weston ahead of Plattsburg, but only by a very small amount. It was finally determined that each of these places should have a school.

Of the school at Weston he was a trustee, and to a very large extent the responsibility of the business rested on him. In addition to the labors of the district, which he never neglected, there was the letting of the contract for this building, a large brick edifice; collecting subscriptions, some of which gave him great trouble; meeting financial obligations, and doing all other things incident to so large an enterprise. The house finished at last, through much toil and the wear of a thousand anxieties, suitable teachers must be employed and the school put upon a good footing. Then a debt, in spite of all his efforts, rested upon the house; and house, school, debt and all rested upon his heart.

His affection for the Weston High School was like that of a father. It was, indeed, his offspring. He had given it existence. The pride he felt in it was natural and inevitable. And he did take pride in it. It was one of those agencies by which he hoped to keep the Church abreast of the wonderful progress of the remarkable country in which it was located. Much of the best and freshest part of his life had gone into it. He expected it to be an evangelizing power in the country after he should be dead. It was to preach for him long after his tongue should be silent.

At the expiration of his term on the district he was for one year stationed at Weston, and at the same time acted as superintendent of the school. In this relation to the institution he was not expected to teach any of the classes. His mental habitudes and studies had not prepared him for this. But a general control was vested in him, and he was looked to for the moral discipline and government of the pupils. He often gave them a short lecture with great effect. The young people regarded him with filial respect. They loved him. His words went down into their hearts. Many things he said they will never forget.

There were two men associated with him in this school whom he loved and admired greatly—Rev. L. M. Lewis and Prof. A. C. Redman, eldest son of W W Redman, so long a leading man in the Missouri Conference. They both had the mental and social endowments that attracted Caples. They were intellectual, vivacious, candid, outspoken, generous. Men of that sort he loved with a luxury of feeling known only to big, mellow natures like his.

The latter of these gentlemen went to an early grave. "Coke Redman." Many an eye will moisten upon meeting this name here It is but right that some memorial of him should appear in this memoir of his friend Caples. He was a man of fine presence, born a gentleman, with intellectual powers of a high order, unbounded courage, and as generous a heart as ever throbbed against human ribs. I first saw him when he was a mere youth, and "took to him" at once. He and Caples were always enthusiastic admirers of each other. His untimely death must remain among the unsolved problems of Providence.

But for the war both of these schools would, no doubt, ere this have been out of debt, and had a history of prosperity and usefulness to justify the hopes of the man who projected them.

Caples' plans were never merely local. They were always comprehensive. His eye swept the whole field of his Conference. He contemplated and urged an educational system that should be co-extensive with the State. It was, in brief, just this: That there should be one College, to become in the course of time, as the resources of the country and the Church might be developed, a University, and only one, to be patronized by both the Missouri and St. Louis Conferences. Then in each Presiding Elder's district he proposed a high school, an institution to meet local wants and at the same time be a feeder to the great Central College These more local schools should be required, so far as their curriculum extended, to conform to that of the College, and to use the same text books, so that students might take their place at any time in the latter without embarrassment.

When the system should be perfected and the local schools become prosperous, they might advance many of their pupils, who would be too poor to bear the expense of a long course at College, to the junior year, so that many a one unable otherwise to attain the end might graduate. These schools would turn attention everywhere to the College, and greatly increase its patronage, while they would afford a substantial education to thousands who would never be able to go beyond them to the College.

The committee on education in the Missouri Conference of 1867 reported the same plan substantially, with the additional recommendation that the District High Schools should be directly under the patronage of the District Conferences instead of the Annual Conference. This I consider an excellent plan, for several reasons. It will relieve the Annual Conferences of a large amount of business that may be better done elsewhere. This relief is not unimportant, for there is a constant tendency to accumulate business in those bodies until, in many cases, it becomes burdensome. Beside, it will place the patronage of these schools in form where it is in fact, and concentrate attention on them in the region upon which they must depend for support.

When a convention of preachers and laymen was called, by the joint action of the St. Louis and Missouri Conferences, to consider the question of establishing an institution of learning of the highest grade, under the united patronage of the two Conferences, he saw in it the dawn of a day he had longed for. He entered into the project with enthusiasm. It served as the nucleus of his system, and I think suggested it to him. Some were apprehensive that the country was too new and the resources of the Church not yet such as to justify an undertaking so heavy as this. He thought otherwise. He knew there was sufficient wealth in the Church to build and endow a "first class College," and believed that an enterprise so grand would wake the intelligent men of the Church and of the country, so as to command the means. On the question as to whether the work should be undertaken, he voted aye. For us in Missouri it was at the time a big undertaking. For that very reason Caples advocated it. As long as we attempted little things only we would do less, and that in a languid way He would never fall behind the general advance of the country in Church enterprises. We doomed ourselves to littleness by such inanition. Our true policy was to lead the times, and not be dragged along in the rear. We must not only be up with the times, but ahead of them. All progress is in activity. If we get to the front we must push ourselves there. If we wait till the enterprise **is** *easy* we will find ourselves perishing from sheer inactivity. The resources of the country will flow into other channels.

The Convention, by a large majority, resolved to establish a first-class college, with the proviso that it should not be organized until there should be a cash endowment of at least fifty thousand dollars.

Only two points competed for the location of the college—Fayette and St. Charles. Caples' vote was cast in favor of Fayette. The majority was with him—a large majority. This was the origin of Central College. Brother Pinckard informs me that Brother Caples would probably have been appointed at the first the agent of the College but for his involvement in school enterprises up the country The enterprise was committed to the agency of Rev. P M. Pinckard. Howard county was first called upon to contribute an amount sufficient to provide a suitable edifice, and responded with great generosity The present building was soon erected. The whole territory of the two Conferences was to be canvassed for subscriptions to the endowment fund. To accomplish this the St. Louis Conference gave to the agency at different times Revs. W M. Prottsman, W M. Wharton and J. F Truslow. In the Missouri Conference Brother Pinckard was assisted for two years by Mr. Caples. His agency commenced in the fall of 1856 and closed in the fall of 1858.

Upon receiving this appointment he promptly removed his family to the town of Fayette, the seat of the College, and entered upon the duties of the agency without delay His heart was in it. He traveled extensively and delivered many sermons and public addresses. To this public advocacy of the claims and demands of the College he was better adapted than any other man we had. In private efforts with individuals he had less tact, perhaps, than some other men. But with an audience such as his reputation would command almost anywhere he was at home. If he had raised no money he would still have done a great work in arousing the Church upon this subject. In the financial result his hopes were not met, yet he accomplished much. I have no means of knowing how much money he raised in the course of the two years, but the amount was considerable. A great task lay upon the agents. The public mind had to be educated on the subject of Colleges. Men could not see why there must be a large endowment. They thought tuition fees ought to pay all expenses. Private classical schools paid their own way and prospered. Why must the expenses of a College be so great? Many, again, could not see why the Church should have a great College. Liberal ideas had to be introduced, a large-minded public opinion to be created. Immense brain power was requisite to accomplish this. Immense brain power was brought to bear. But it was hard work, and progress was not rapid.

The College and its agents labored under many embarrassments. The fifty thousand dollars was not realized as early as was expected. The scholarship system had been adopted by the Board of Curators, and many subscriptions had been made by men who desired to educate their sons there, and who understood that they were paying tuition in advance. They expected the College to be organized in a short time. But year after year they suffered disappointment. Many of them became clamorous. Yet the endowment fund had not reached the minimum, and the organization could not be effected.

The Curators feared the consequences of delay. Men who had taken scholarships were becoming disaffected. The public was becoming restless. It seemed that the enterprise was about to become demoralized. A High School was already opened in the building. Rather the old High School that had been maintained at Fayette for many years by the Church was continued and removed into the new edifice. But this was not what the public had bargained for. It was to be a College—a College of the highest grade. Fear was entertained by those immediately charged with the responsibility of managing affairs that delay, which had already bred discontent and discouragement, would end in distrust and apathy, which would defeat the hopes of the Church. But yet they could not organize the College proper until the full amount of fifty thousand dollars should be in hand as an endowment fund. The very terms of their charter forbade it.

In their anxiety to meet all emergencies they fell upon the expedient of a *provisional organization*. But, unfortunately, this measure excited strong, not to say violent, opposition. It was asserted that the Curators had at once violated their charter, or at least the published terms, acting in bad faith with contributors, whose liberality was based on the high character of the proposed institution, and degraded the College by organizing it on the basis of an inadequate endowment. This feeling was participated in honestly and deeply by several of the best men in the bounds of the St. Louis Conference. Widespread disaffection was the result. The subscription for the endowment was greatly embarrassed. The enterprise dragged heavily. It almost seemed that all the toil and liberality already concentrated in it would go for nothing. Yet its friends hoped on, labored on, and the goal, though distant apparently, was coming in sight. Rev. W H. Ander-

, n, M D., was President of the College, and Rev.
U. W Pritchett, A. M., in charge of the Mathe-
matical department. They had established a high
reputation already as teachers, and the patronage
they commanded was large. The situation was
hopeful, upon the whole, though the complications
were serious and the burden heavy. Current expenses were not met, salaries fell into arrear, and
meetings of the Board of Curators were full of
perplexity and anxiety There are many living
who have a lively recollection of those meetings,
and these recollections are softened and saddened
by the thought of some who are gone—men whose
names are the heritage of Missouri Methodism.
Among them Captain W D. Swinney was a
leading spirit. He had been a generous supporter
of our schools in Fayette from the first. In the
destiny of this College he felt the liveliest interest
and hope, but was disappointed and grieved that
the endowment lingered as it did. He had given
much money to meet expenses as they accrued,
and was ever ready to meet responsibilities, of
which he took a large and Christian view. He
felt that not only the honor of the Church was
involved (and to that he was ever sensitive), but
that there was here an agency for good, commanding and far-reaching, for the present and for coming ages, and to falter in the work would be a
dereliction nothing short of criminal. He was a

man who not only gave money to the cause of God, but also thought for it and laid plans for it with painstaking solicitude He was with this Board of Curators in its darkest days and most anxious meetings. Though he died, like Moses, before the promised land was reached in this great undertaking, I doubt not that his influence will reappear in the consummation, and that his work will reach places and ages in which his name will be unknown.

Thus things wore on until the war came. The disorders of the times reached every thing. Bro. Pritchett persevered in maintaining the school as long as possible. But even his earnest devotion to the cause could not carry it forward through the violent and lawless times upon which it had fallen. During the last years of the war the College doors were closed.

As soon as practicable, after the war closed, Rev. H. A. Bourland re-opened the school. This experiment was successful beyond the most sanguine hopes of its friends. The two Conferences, in the autumn of 1867, took the history and claims of this institution into earnest consideration. The Lay Delegates contributed, by the earnest deliberation with which they approached this vital question, to the happy issue at last reached. The reports of the committees on education in both the Conferences were admirable documents, and belong to the history of the Church.

A joint committee of the Conferences met in St. Louis soon after the adjournment of the St. Louis Conference and called a convention, to meet in the town of Fayette in June of 1868. The whole matter was canvassed with a serious and prayerful sense of its importance. The Convention was addressed in the most impressive manner by Dr. W A. Smith. Hon. Trusten Polk also delivered an address, impromptu, which contributed much to the deep sense of the importance of the hour. It was felt by all to be a crisis in the history of Central College, and, as such, also in the history of the Church in Missouri. The voice of the Methodist public was unanimous as to the magnitude of the interest. The doubt was not as to the *end* to be pursued, but as to the *means*.

The desideratum was a *man* to take charge of the fortunes of the College, whose name would give confidence and be at once the pledge and augury of success. There was a man present, a member of the Convention, whose power to accomplish the object no one doubted, and yet of whom no one seemed to think in connection with it. He was not thought of, for the sole reason that no one supposed he would undertake the task. Twenty of the best years of his life had been devoted to the building up of one College. The war had disorganized and scattered the fruits of all this labor. He had looked around him hopelessly upon the wreck, and feeling that he was too old to begin the work anew, he yielded to a call for aid in the pastoral work in the West. Leaving twenty years of himself in the wreck of Randolph-Macon College, he came to St. Louis and was appointed pastor of Centenary church. His reasons for leaving Randolph-Macon were known in Missouri.

But in the crisis at Fayette, as if by a sort of inspiration, he was thought of. Two of his friends, after full consultation with each other, called on him and proposed to him to take the Presidency of Central College, with the understanding that his first work would be to raise an endowment of one hundred thousand dollars, the Conferences having already agreed upon this as the minimum of endowment upon which the College should be organized.

He was taken wholly by surprise. His view of the labor involved was clear. He grasped the conditions of the undertaking fully The magnitude and the difficulty of the undertaking were fully present to his mind. He thought of his own advanced age. He thought, also, of the grandeur of the result, if it could only be achieved. After a pause so solemn that it was *felt*, he said, in substance, to the two friends who had made the proposal, "You know Missouri; I do not. You know the extent of my influence in Missouri; I do not. You are *my friends*. You will not trifle with me. I am too old to be wasting time. If I can accomplish this object it will be the *greatest thing I can do*. It will be the crowning work of my life. But I can not afford to devote my last years to a work that must fail. If you, my personal friends, knowing Missouri as you do, and knowing me, believe I can raise this endowment in ten years, I will undertake it. I am lame. I am getting old; traveling is a great labor to me. But if you think I can do this work in ten years I will undertake it." They told him that it was their conviction that he would accomplish the whole work in *two years*. After further most earnest conversation, he gave his consent for them to offer his name to the Convention.

The Convention was just then assembling for its last session. All was doubt and anxiety in most minds. There had been much talking, much thinking, much prayer.

At an appropriate moment in the session the name of Dr. W A. Smith was offered to the Convention for the Presidency of the College, with the statement that he had already consented to serve if elected.

I will not undertake to describe the scene that followed. Of course he was elected as if by acclamation.

16

I shall never forget that hour. The subdued tone and well chosen words in which Dr. Smith acknowledged the honor and accepted the labor conferred and imposed are still fresh in many minds. The congratulations which a hundred men looked and spoke and felt, the deep sense of relief, the new-born sense of confidence, the flush of a great hope, constituted one of those occasions that lift life out of its commonplaceness—an occasion to be held in memory forever after.

What followed is too recent to require detailed statement here. The extraordinary labor of that great man, and the result, must be held as an epoch in the history of the Church. Let us hope that the activities of the Church will take higher tone, and her plans and methods be projected and carried forward upon a broader and more adequate conception of Christian obligation from this time forward. Who can doubt that God raised up the man and in His providence brought him to the work just at the juncture when success or failure hinged upon the action of an hour?

But, alas! the aged man did two or three years' work in one, and the overtaxed nervous system broke down. He is dead, and the cause of Christian education in Missouri bears the consecration of his *last labor*. That great life culminates in Central College! Its last work and last prayers were for this chief of Missouri educational institutions in the Methodist Church. Though he carried it so near to completion, and accomplished so much beyond our hope, in a few months, yet, like Captain Swinney, he, too, died before the promised land was reached. But he stood on the mountain and *saw it*

In this agency Brother Bourland contributed in no small measure to the result, and now Brother Rush is before the public to finish the work that the Doctor dropped from his dying hand. Let us not forget that it has to be finished this year, or all that has been done will be lost. All the subscriptions are made upon the condition that the endowment shall reach the amount of one hundred thousand dollars by the first of January, 1871. But surely the few thousands remaining to complete the sum will be forthcoming The Church will not allow so much to go for nothing.

Is there not some man who will contribute twenty-five thousand dollars to endow a professorship which shall bear the name and be a monument of the labors of the martyr to Methodist education in this College?

For the great success of the labors of Dr. Smith there had been not a little preparation in the years and labors that had gone before. No doubt the personal influence and public addresses of Brother Caples had produced an effect that was still felt. It required all the great powers of Dr. Smith to

bring the influence into fruition, but such an influence there was. The very fact that Caples was
dead revived the memory and gave emphasis to
the tone of his labors in the interest of denominational schools, and especially of this College.
In all justice he must be held as one of those
men without whose devotion this institution could
never have attained to power and permanency.
His name belongs to its history in no obscure way.
His public discourses in its behalf combined a
philosophic breadth with a popular manner that
was peculiar to him. He grasped the whole idea
of popular education and brought it out in a way
that impressed men of good sense most profoundly   Views presented in the beginning of
this chapter, and many others, he enforced with
irresistible spirit. Upon the more sober truth,
there was in his discourses the flash of genius that
set it in a clear light before all. Then came in
the play of a happy conceit or the touching pathos
that swept all before it.

The following, from Rev. Wesley G. Miller, will
illustrate this, and give some idea of the ingenious adaptation of his appeals in behalf of the
College to the time and circumstances. He felt
perfectly at home before this audience. The people of this part of the country knew him and
admired and trusted him in the highest degree.
He was perfectly free among them, and knew that

they would be prepared to receive the form of attack upon meanness and stinginess which is given at the close. Brother Miller says:

"I remember, among many, one very remarkable discourse, which, under the circumstances, produced a wonderful effect. It was delivered in the fall of 1857, at a camp-meeting in Daviess county, while he was on a tour collecting money for Central College, as its agent, and it was in advocacy of the claims of that institution. He was dwelling on the subject of the reflex and personal benefit of benevolence, and the gratification the remembrance of our charities would give us. In the course of his remarks he drew a most vivid picture of our Lord's entrance into Jerusalem riding on the colt, beginning with the man's permission given to the disciples to lead his colt away for the 'Master.' He was so surprised by the request that, half stupefied, he gave his permission without consideration, but after they were gone with the colt he began to soliloquize thus: 'Why, I was very foolish to let them take my colt off so. It is true I love Jesus, and it was very good in Him to open the eyes of our neighbor's son; and then I like so much to hear Him talk. But there is no other man in all the village that would have given Him such a fine colt as that of mine was, and now I am afraid I will never see it again. I really wish I had thought a little before I let them have him.' Just here he begins to hear the general, confused shout: 'Hosanna to the Son of David: blessed is he that cometh in the name of the Lord! Hosanna in the highest!' The man looks out, and the vast multitude are coming right up by his little shop, and the shout goes up louder still, 'Hosanna to the Son of David!' 'Why, what can all this be about?' He runs out. The vast crowd moves up upon him. He sees Jesus on the colt. He runs out into the crowd and breaks into a stentorian shout: 'Hosanna! Blessed is he that cometh in the name of the Lord!' and turning, slaps his neighbor on the shoulder and exclaims: 'That's my colt he is on!' And now, louder than ever, he shouts: 'Hosanna to the Son of David!'

"This is the merest outline of what he gave, filled up with such inimitable wit, such naturalness, and occasionally such a tender pathos, that the crowd in one moment would be convulsed with laughter and on the point of a general outburst, then they would weep like children. I saw the rough old backwoods farmers stand — for the crowd was too large to find seats — with a broad grin on their faces just then, and now with their faces convulsed and the big tears chasing each other down their bronzed cheeks Many broke down and wept like children. And the wonder was from the fact that all this was produced by a discourse about money, one of the hardest subjects to reach the feelings with in the world.

"He then drew the counterpart of the picture—a poor, little, stingy soul, having saved a large fortune by his parsimoniousness, yet never satisfied; but with all his lands, his herds and flocks and money around him, he still bawls out '*More! more!*' He said if we approached such a man with the claims of suffering humanity, at once he began to feel a twitching of the nerve of the pocket and took the *puckers* instanter. His nose would become sharp, his mouth pinched, his face wrinkled, and his soul would collapse within him and become transformed into an old puckered purse, into which he would seem to creep and try to pull the world in after him. If such a being could get into heaven he would stand for a thousand years and gaze at the golden streets. And thus, with such keen sarcasm and satire, such bitter invective, such burning scorn, did he treat those characters, that it would have been impossible not to have felt an unutterable scorn and contempt for them. Many men who had seldom given for any purpose, that day found themselves the subjects of deeds of most marvelous benevolence. They gave, and seemed to enjoy it wondrously

"To this day the address is remembered and talked of in that country, and when men solicit a

contribution they will say, 'Come, now, you will
be glad to see the Lord on your colt after a while,'
or, 'Don't take the puckers now.' "

He was heard with equal interest by all classes.
The man of education and high culture was no
less impressed than the "rough backwoodsman"
referred to by Brother Miller. . Even when in the
abandon of his happiest moods he used terms
that are commonly ostracized from elegant speech,
as in the case given above, the most refined for-
gave the approach to coarseness for the sake of
the point and power with which they came.
Indeed, there was a charm in the whole spirit of
it that redeemed a low word, and he was one of
the rare men who could use such terms without
offense.

He and Pinckard once visited St. Louis and
remained several days with a view of arousing
the Methodist public of the city upon the subject
of the College. The plan was to get a large public meeting on some night in the week, that
Caples might deliver a public address that should
bring the enterprise home, and cause the magnitude and importance of it to be truly appreciated.
But it is next to impossible to rally the people of
that community in that way There never was
anything like an adequate audience secured for
him, and the address he made to the people of St.
Louis, though full of broad views and important

suggestions, wanted enthusiasm. He felt that the occasion was flat. The audience was small and everything seemed to move heavily. His friends and the friends of the College were profoundly mortified that they could not get a good hearing for him—not on his account, but on account of the cause he represented. If he could have delivered himself at that time upon St. Louis with the full power that was in him the endowment fund would have been set forward at once to a point that would have brought the final result within easy reach. As it was, the agents went away discouraged and with a heavy task on hand. But the great Methodist College was talked of a good deal in Methodist circles, as a result of the effort, and possibly a train of agencies was started that has had more or less effect. I feel very sure that the knowledge of Caples' zeal for its success has at this day, in the bounds of the Missouri Conference, the effect of producing a deeper interest and a larger liberality. It would not surprise me if some one of his old friends, in making a large contribution to the endowment, should erect a monument to him that would be as lasting as the College.

One fact has come to my knowledge since I have been engaged upon this biography, of which I had not been aware before. Toward the latter part of Mr. Caples' life he was much concerned upon the subject of a provision for indigent orphans. The feeling amounted to anxiety The Church, he believed, had this resting upon her as an imperative obligation. Here was a very large class of the young, exposed to any fate that might befall amid the corruptions of the world, ready to be gathered into the fold of Christ by a little care and charity. Thousands of lambs abroad in all weather call piteously upon the Church for shelter and care that will prepare them for the joys of the world to come. Left to themselves they will scarcely escape the jaws of the wolf, or a more lingering and pitiful death in the storm.

It was in his mind to agitate this enterprise so soon as the immediate crisis of Central College should be passed. With some trusted friends he communicated freely on this matter. He could not rest in view of the apathy of the Church with respect to such charities. Where a field so wide and inviting lay in sight he could not comprehend the indifference of those who professed to love God. Children were special objects of the Savior's love, and surely His people would look tenderly upon such as were fatherless in the world. Even in the ruder period of the Old Testament times God proclaimed himself a Father of the fatherless and the Judge of the widow. The sorrows of bereavement have ever been held to have a peculiar claim upon sympathy; how much more so when the lost friend was also the natural protector and provider.

What his plans were, or whether he had any that were at all mature, I do not know. He never mentioned this matter to me, and as his purposes did not ripen into public effort at all I have nothing in detail. A personal friend, to whom he did speak of it with great interest, has given me what I have written, but knows nothing more than the general fact that he felt much, and upon the earliest opportunity intended to move with vigor.

I can well believe it. It was like him. Sagacious and generous, from motives both of duty and impulse, he was just the man to originate such a movement in the Church. He would have done it for the sake of the Church and for the sake of the children. The Church he knew would grow by its own activity, and many of the children would be saved. Work done for God never loses its reward, if it be done with a pure motive and in faith. Surely work done for the comfort of the fatherless poor and for their salvation is peculiarly done for God.

Our Church in St. Louis has at last entered upon this field of Christian labor. Many are doing nobly. Christian women, whose names are in the Book of Life, are devoting time and thought and labor. The service done by them in support of the "Home" is arduous, and sometimes even humiliating. But they do it "for His name's sake." These poor children will "rise up in the last day and call them blessed."

Shall we not now very soon see a house owned by this Home, in a pleasant situation and of ample capacity for all wants? God and the Church would be alike honored by it.

CHAPTER XII.

THE WAR

It would have been impossible for such a man as Mr. Caples to pass through a period so stirring as that of our great civil war clear of all involvement. Alive as he was to all great human movements, he could not possibly hold himself indifferent to one which touched every true man to the quick. Only the callous or the supremely selfish could stand coolly balancing questions of safety and interest. Vital questions of *right* were involved. With his *sense of justice*, which was inwrought into every fibre of his moral nature, he could be no silent spectator. Although his conception of the Christian ministry was too correct to allow the prostitution of the holy office to political ends, yet privately and in his character of *citizen* he did not hesitate to commit himself. In this, as in every thing else, he was outspoken—perfectly so—and delivered himself with an emphasis which the character of the events would evoke from such a soul.

So far as the subject of slavery was involved in the contest he was well prepared to decide the question for himself. In his Church relations he had been forced to investigate that matter. He had done so thoroughly. He had read every thing in our current literature on the subject, and brought to bear the poweis of analysis for which he was so remarkable. As a question involving conscience he had answered it long before. I had ample opportunity to know his mind from long conversations on several occasions within the few years preceding the war. There were two points on which he delivered himself with great emphasis.

The first was that the Bible did not condemn slavery, but clearly in the Old Testament authorized it and in the New allowed it. It was established by statute in the civil code of Moses. It was recognized, and the duties it involved defined and enjoined, by the Apostle Paul. It is, therefore, not a question overlooked by the sacred writers, but distinctly under their cognizance and treated of by them. Clearly, if the ownership of slaves were sin, they had occasion to pronounce upon it. The Holy Spirit, speaking by them on this very topic, deals with the relation of master and slave, but never once condemns it. What, then, must be the audacity of the man who professes to accept the Bible as the *word of God*, the divine and ultimate standard of morals, and impeaches the Holy Ghost in His teaching on this subject.

He saw that the writers of the New Testament Revelation left this relation to be determined by the civil law. They recognized it as within the domain of the civil magistrate. Slaveholding was not, like stealing or adultery, wicked even if tolerated by civil statute. It was a relation, on the contrary, not lying at the foundation of essential morals, and which might be established by the law of the land, and in that case is beyond animadversion from the teacher of religion. This was, in substance and very briefly, his view on this point.

The second was, that Abolitionism was the deadliest sin of modern society. Its direct tendency was to subvert the Christian faith. That done, the only divine safeguard of virtue perishes. He heard the insane cry for "an anti-slavery God and an anti-slavery Bible" with the most profound alarm. He had even heard members of so-called Christian Churches say, "If you should convince me that the Bible justifies slavery, I would throw it away and trample it under my feet." Nor was this a mad outburst of one or two fanatical spirits, but a wide-spread sentiment of Abolitionism, in and out of the Church. This "higher law," the law of reason, or humanity, or whatever else, that might set itself above Holy

Scripture, he saw to be a deadly infection of society, under which all simple faith in the Word of God must perish. That done, man falls back into the utter darkness and chaos of unchecked, erratic thought, and having no divine centre to hold him in the orbit of truth, each individual must become a law to himself, and society be ultimately disorganized. Worse yet, religion dis credited in her supreme law, the Bible, the gloom of the everlasting darkness sets in upon the human soul.

That faith rests upon a poor foundation which is shaken by humanitarian sentimentalities. With Caples the authority of *the Book* was sufficient. No *theory* of abstract right was to be taken as against it. Its statements were all *true*, its laws all *right*, its teachings all *divine*. When you have heard its voice the last word has been spoken. Eliphaz the Temanite, and all the rest of them, to the generous and intellectual Elihu, may contend and dogmatize, and Job may answer and assever- ate, till *God* speaks. Silence and submission must follow His voice. The philosophy that finds fault with *His* word is blasphemy. That word is articulate in the Bible to-day, and the philan- thropy that sets itself up to be purer than the teachings of an apostle of Christ is of the wicked one. The clamor for an "anti-slavery God" is infidel in the last degree. Faith bows before the

Bible, worships God and exclaims, " Speak, Lord,
for thy servant heareth." To the soul that realizes
its true relation to God he may say *anything*.
Even Isaac will be sacrificed. But the Abolitionist will not sacrifice *his ideas* to the God of the
Bible. Of course, he is an infidel.

Just so the socialist *has ideas*. He sees intolerable hardships and evils in the institution of
marriage. Many hard cases occur. Many a
Socrates finds that his spouse is another Xan-
tippe. Men and their wives become distasteful to
each other sometimes. It is dreadful to bind them
together till death. So says the oracle of free
love. But the institution of marriage is recognized by the Bible. " Then away with the Bible."
And Free-loveism rests on the very same foundation as Abolitionism. Both assail the Bible from
the same ground of attack. With both it is dis-
credited as recognizing an institution incompatible
with *their ideas of right*. They are alike systems
of infidelity.

To Mr. Caples the Bible was the depository of
everything that is good. The conditions of society
given under its sanctions, though the evils of a
depraved humanity may evermore appear in them,
were the best possible in the present state. An
"incompatible" man and woman might feel it to
be intolerable to continue through life in the
sacred relation of man and wife, but an infinitely

17

worse thing would be the destruction of the family, the very corner stone of civilization and virtue. The father of a family may be a monster, and his administration of home affairs may be most disastrous to domestic peace, but the children that are in the world are in infinitely better case than could be possible in the absence of the paternal relation. He who would cure the evils of society by abolishing the institutions of the Bible but throws himself from the reeling ship, which will yet survive the tempest, into the devouring waves of the sea.

Mr. Caples did not deny that there was evil connected with the relation of master and slave. There is evil in all the forms in which the relation between capital and labor appears. Capital, and especially in overcrowded populations, has immense advantage of labor. The evil is everywhere. But it is the evil that is inherent in the depravities of a fallen world.

Aside from all reasoning on the subject, the fact that Abolitionism bred disrespect for the Bible was to him cause of anxiety   In this Book we have the will of God. Our hope of heaven is in it. All that is worth having in time or eternity is there. As a question involving religion, then, he opposed the Abolitionist theory with all his power, and felt that Churches infested with it were in league with the infidel. This was the more alarming to him when those Churches began to take action in their ecclesiastical assemblies on political subjects. He saw that it was the entering wedge of ruinous tendencies. When the Conferences of the Northern Church began to appoint committees on the state of the country and adopt resolutions bearing on the political issues before the people, he thought that the American mind would spurn them as encroaching on the vital traditions against ecclesiastical interference in civil affairs which he believed to be sacred in the eyes of the people. But as this and political preaching began to become a recognized fact, and the anti-slavery fanaticism clapped its hands, he learned that nothing was sacred to *it* but its own success. The Constitution of the United States, an instrument as sacred with him as anything not emanating directly from the Bible could be, they denounced as "a league with hell." For it they seemed to have lost all respect. At length a President of the United States was elected with the celebrated declaration before the people that "the Union could not continue to exist part slave and part free." He was the candidate of a *section* in avowed hostility against an institution of the other section, which was guaranteed by constitutional compact. He was, in fact, elected by the Abolitionist vote.

Mr. Caples participated fully in the alarm felt

throughout the South. A party which was purely
sectional, in which many of the most influential
men were avowedly hostile to the Constitution,
and all of them determined to defeat the Constitution in its protection of Southern institutions,
though they proposed to do it under "constitutional forms," had attained supreme power in the
Government. He felt that the Southern States
were justified in resorting to the extreme measure
of secession. They had graver grievances, to use
his own language, "than the thirteen Colonies
had when they resisted the encroachments of the
British Government upon their chartered rights."
He was a States-Rights Democrat, and believed in
the right of secession. Even if that doctrine were
not correct, he believed "the occasion justified
revolution."

No justice can be done him with respect to this
period of his life without referring to these matters. Officially, he kept to his work as a
preacher of the Gospel; privately, he declared
himself on the questions involved in the war.
This was inevitable. Being such a man as he
was, he felt as only great souls can the greatness
of the wrong (as he saw it) done to the Southern
people by the party in power. He saw that the
Administration was ready to destroy the Constitution. The South was in the minority. Consti-
tutions are made for minorities. Majorities do

not need them. The Constitution was the pan-
oply of the South. Stripped of this, she was
ruined. A sectional mob would do whatever its
interest or its hatred might dictate. From the
first he was fully committed on the side which, as
he supposed, afforded the world its only hope of
"constitutional freedom ;" and as for mob freedom,
that was worse than any despotism. It was itself
a despotism—the despotism of the majority ; and
in this case the more intolerable as it was
charged with all the passions and interests of
a section, which it was ready to assert without
remorse. It is all well for the majority to rule so
long as all essential rights and interests of the
minority are guarded by constitutional provisions. But with that protection gone, the majority
is the most fearful of all despots.

He had studied politics more closely than I
had, and I confess that I listened to him on these
topics with the most intense interest. Events
already transpiring had aroused an interest I
never before felt. It had always seemed to me a
matter of course that things would go on right in
"the Government." What he said was a sort of
revelation to me. Hence it was engraven on my
mind, so that I could not forget it if I would.
With such views, and his strong sense of justice
and right, he could not but be a pronounced
advocate of the Southern cause.

Yet was he just and generous toward those who differed with him. If he was sometimes harsh in denunciation (and he was) it was against *acts* that he witnessed, and not against opinions. He honored men who identified themselves with the Administration when they pursued a just course of conduct. This I know. That he condemned any vicious and cruel acts committed by men of his own party I can not doubt.

The beginning of the war found him on the Brunswick District as Presiding Elder. During the first months of the war he attended faithfully to his work. That he talked about the war more than he ought I do not doubt. But let him that is without sin cast the first stone. That he was more vehement and demonstrative than his relation to the work of Christ would justify I shall not deny But, as I have already said, his nature, so decided, so ardent, rendered this almost inevitable. I can not doubt that it would have been better if he had never named politics, even in private. But a man could scarcely talk at all at that time if he did not talk politics. People talked about little else. All were excited. The feeling was intense, and if a man had any heart he would feel the glow of the warmth that was on all sides of him. But the minister who denied himself for Christ's sake at that time, and kept his mind and tongue employed about the gospel, and that alone, was surely in the path of duty

He continued on this district, faithfully discharging the duties of his office, until in the fall when the Conference met at Glasgow. There was no Bishop in attendance. The war had fully set in. The Bishops were cut off from us in Missouri by hostile armies. Several battles had been fought. Americans were cutting each others' throats. Peace had spread her white wings and sought another home. The vulture gorged herself with human flesh from the Potomac to the Western plains.

But amid the tumult the Missouri preachers assembled in their annual convocation to do the Master's work. They were in the midst of great alarms. During the session Gen. Martin E. Green entered the town and made his famous crossing of the Missouri river. When his command was reported as approaching the preachers, many of them, were excited, not knowing who they were nor what might happen. The presence of the troops, however, did not interrupt the business of the Conference.

In the absence of the Bishop Mr. Caples was elected President of the Conference. This, I believe, was the first and only time he ever presided over the Conference. As will be seen elsewhere, his presidency gave great satisfaction, both in the general conduct of the business and in the stationing of the preachers.

Being already on the Brunswick District he returned to that field from this Conference. This work, as I have good evidence, he took in perfect good faith, intending to fill it the year through. He returned home from Conference with this purpose and, I think, actually entered upon the labors of the year. But the war furore increased. The battle of Wilson's Creek had been fought and won by the Confederates. Price was moving upon Lexington. The Southern people were exultant. Central Missouri rushed to his camp with great enthusiasm. The country within Caples' district sent immense numbers to join him. Gen. Price lived in that region, and his great popularity and recent successes, followed up by this bold move upon Lexington, turned all the young men wild. The people expected him to cross into North Missouri, and, keeping pace in the West with victories to be gained in the East, to bring the war to an end in a very short period. There was no ear for the gospel. The public mind was pre-occupied. The young men were all going to Price. It was a disgrace not to go. In that region there were no Union men, or at least very few

In this state of affairs Mr. Caples felt that he could do more good in camps than on his district. He ever asserted that his object in going was to preach. He could preach 'to many more in the army than he could at home. The young men there, multitudes of whom knew and loved him, would need the gospel. To counteract, so far as might be, the demoralizing influences of camp life, he would go and be with them. He believed he could do them good. Nor was he wholly disappointed. Eager thousands crowded to his sermons, and to this day they do not tire of talking about the wonderful preaching of Caples when he was with them in the field.

He reached the army while it was at Lexington, after the place was captured. I am indebted to Capt. Harry W Pflager for the following account of his connection with the army during the short time he remained with it. Though he saw but little of him, yet, being at the same time connected with Price's command in the commissary department, he knew the most important facts, and has kindly furnished them to me. He had known him intimately, loved him deeply, and felt a lively interest in his movements.

The Captain deplores the paucity of materials in his possession, but his account is the fullest I have, and is as follows:

"A few days after the surrender of Lexington, Missouri, while we were encamped around the city enjoying the fruits of our victory, a number of our friends from Brunswick came up to see us, some with the intention to join the army and some only to visit their friends. We had now been out some three or four months, and were glad to see our friends and have an opportunity once more to hear direct from home. The Rev W G. Caples was among the number who came to join us, and there was none whom we were more pleased to see. He had many warm friends in the army, and he was warmly received by his friends, and also by Gen. Price, especially when it became known that he had come with the intention to join us. In a few days Gen. Price received information that there was a large force of Federals coming up the river from St. Louis, and other forces concentrating from other points, and while he had men enough he had comparatively few arms and less ammunition for them, and was consequently not in a condition to meet a large force, well armed and supplied with ammunition, and a day or two after we received orders to be in readiness to march, which we did the next day. There were many sad hearts and disappointed hopes when the line of our march was taken up southward. Many who had come with the intention to join us remembered suddenly that they had business at home which they could not possibly leave, and they would have to return home. Alas! such was the case with too many, and the main cause of our final expulsion from the State. They were willing to remain with the army while it remained near their homes, but they were not willing to leave home to share its fortunes and fate. Mr. Caples, however, was not one of those. He remained with us on our march south, and although he had no regular appointment as chaplain (as far as I can remember) he preached among the different commands as often as he had opportunity, doing much good, not only by his preaching, but also by his example. He was ever lively and cheerful, and had a kind word to say to every one. After the day's march was over there would generally a crowd of friends gather around him to hear him discuss the incidents of the day, and to hear him relate anecdotes, of which he had a rich store. On the march he was always ready to lend a helping hand where there was a bridge to build across a small stream or a wagon to lift out of a mud hole, thereby encouraging others.

" Gen. Price seemed to regard him very highly, not only as a personal friend, but being a man of quick perception and good judgment, he would frequently converse with him about the condition of affairs and surrounding circumstances. While in camp at Jack river (I think) some of the regiments were re-organizing and he was strongly solicited by some of his friends to run for Colonel of one of the regiments, and I have no doubt would have been elected, but he declined—not that he was afraid to fill that position, but he believed that his duty called him in another sphere, where he could accomplish more real good. Somewhere about the last of November, 1861, Mr. Caples, under instructions from General Price, returned to Chariton county to assist in raising and bringing out some recruits. Captain Barr, from Brunswick, was then organizing a company, and about the 18th of December they were ready to start for the army, and crossed the river with the intention of joining some recruits then rendezvousing in Saline county, under the command of a Colonel Robinson. They joined Colonel Robinson's command the next day, and he being the senior officer took command of all the recruits. They then took up their line of march south to join the army, and proceeded as far as Blackwater, where they arrived in the morning, after having marched all night.

"Colonel Robinson gave orders to remain in camp all day, intending to march again at night. I afterward learned that Mr. Caples was opposed to remaining in camp all day, as they were encamped in a place from which there would be no way of escape (as was afterward proven) in case of an attack. The Federals had learned of the camp in Saline county and were keeping a sharp lookout for them, and were concentrating their forces at Warrensburg and several other points, and they were not long in receiving intelligence of the camp at Blackwater Bridge. Colonel R. felt so secure in his hidden retreat that he even failed to send out pickets any considerable distance, consequently the enemy came down upon them like a thunder-clap, without any warning, and but very few were able to make their escape. Our friend, Mr. Caples, was among the unfortunate who fell into the hands of the enemy, and was sent to St. Louis. (I regret that I am not able to give a better description or a more accurate and detailed account of the capture of Blackwater; but not being present I, of course, know only what I afterward learned from some of those who made their escape, and most of what I then learned in regard to it I have forgotten.) The next I saw of Mr. Caples was at Glasgow, after he had received that fatal wound. I went with the party who went to capture the town. Soon after we entered the town I learned of his misfortune and went to see him. I shall never forget my feelings when I saw him. I had seen many a one wounded before, but never was I so much shocked as when I saw him. He seemed glad to see me, received me with a smile, and although he was much exhausted and very weak from loss of blood, he conversed quite freely, told me how he had been persecuted and his life threatened, how hard it seemed that just as deliverance was at hand he had to be stricken down, and that, too, by friends. But his Christian fortitude and resignation did not forsake him in this trying hour. He said it was the Master's will, and he was ready to obey the call. I called again later in the evening, but he was asleep, and I did not see him. I left town that evening and did not get to see him again."

There is one fact not mentioned in this narrative. During the time he was out he made a tour in Northen Arkansas, with Judge Atchison, delivering public addresses, with a view of inducing the men of that State to volunteer and assist Gen. Price to prevent the advance of the enemy into their territory

Though he had gone with the express purpose of *preaching*, and this alone, he was led into this direct participation in the contest. There was no man at hand who could make popular speeches with such effect as he. His services were deemed essential. He yielded to importunity and undertook to "stump" some counties in Arkansas. I regret that he did so. Yet with the pressure that was upon him it would have been next to impossible for him to refuse. His great personal popularity led the General to engage him in the recruiting expedition in which he was captured. He desired to see his family and arrange, as well as might be, for their well-being in his absence.

The army was in great need of supplies at the same time, especially of winter clothing. His own necessities in this particular were pressing. All these motives led to his visit to Chariton. While there he did what he could to collect supplies and enlist volunteers. The disastrous end of the effort is given in Capt. Pflager's narrative.

Mr. Caples told me he could, for himself, have escaped capture. His friends strongly advised him to do so. Being well mounted he could have retreated under cover of a skirt of woods with the utmost ease. But many of the young men who must inevitably fall into the hands of the enemy had been by their parents committed especially to his care and oversight. They had been given up to the service for the reason, in part, that they would be, in a measure, under his guardianship. And now that the evil day had come he could not think of abandoning them. At whatever cost he would share their fate with them.

That fate was hard enough. They were all marched off to the railroad for shipment to St. Louis. In vain did he plead for the use of his own horse. In vain did his friends urge his inability to make the march on foot. There was little mercy in those days. In the weary march he felt that he would fall to the earth. I heard him say that just when he was ready to drop young Watts came up, generous as he was robust, and said: "Here, Brother Caples, take my arm." How gratefully he spoke of this! With this aid he dragged along and reached, at last, the end of the road.

They were all crowded into box cars on the rail-road, and slowly trundled off to the city. Not the slightest regard was had for their comfort. They were pressed into these close cars until they were so packed that all were compelled to stand upon their feet. There was no room to sit. There was almost no ventilation. Though the weather was bitter cold they became moist with perspiration. There was a sense of suffocation. He was happy who could place his nose at a little opening. The air became noxious. Accumulating excrement added to the misery. Slowly the train moved on, making frequent and long stops for wood and water and other trains. No pains were taken to relieve their distress. Hours grew into days. There they stood on their feet, weary, suffocated, and no hand opened a door to let in the fresh air. Nothing, absolutely nothing, was done looking to any mitigation of the horrors of their situation. Cattle brought to market would have been treated with more humanity.

At last they are in the city. Now relief will come. Now they will get air! An hour passes. Another. Hour after hour there they stand after the cars arrive. I can communicate no such impression of the horror of the situation in writing as he did to me in a detailed narrative of it.

At last out of the pent air, moist with perspiration—out of the steaming boxes in which they had been so long confined—they were turned into a bitter winter wind from the northwest. Instantly they were chilled through and through. In a few minutes their teeth chattered. The revulsion was fearful.

From the cars they were marched off to Gratiot street prison, which had been prepared with great economy of space and means. They were already chilled in their moist clothing, and with the nervous system relaxed from the impure atmosphere and warmth of the crowded cars. Their present quarters were inadequately heated. The floors soon became damp. In a day or two pneumonia appeared. Great numbers were soon prostrated. No medical attendance was provided for several days. There were several physicians among the prisoners. They asked for medicines but got none. The patients began to die. Their own medicine chest, captured with them, lay in sight from their windows. They implored the privilege of a supply from its contents. No attention was paid to their prayer. The sickness increased. The mortality became frightful. *In three weeks they were more than decimated.* If the treatment of the

18

prisoners had had this end in view it could not have been more sagaciously ordered.

In a week or two Mr. Caples addressed a note to two of his friends in the city, informing them that the food he received was loathsome to his palate and rebelled against by his stomach. He begged them to send him fruit and pickles. They took a jar of pickles to the headquarters of the regiment which was guarding the prison. The officer in command hesitated, deferred the matter, and after two days let them know that the pickles could not be sent in. The contemplated barrel of apples was, therefore, never sent.

His incarceration lasted, I think, not more than five or six weeks. In this time he preached whenever circumstances would allow. It was about the first of February, I believe, that the prisoners captured on Blackwater were transferred to the Alton Penitentiary. Mr. Caples was made an exception, in view, no doubt, of his high character as a clergyman. He was released on parole.

Suddenly, unannounced, he appeared on the corner of Pine and Fifth streets. A number of the members of the Church were in attendance upon the afternoon meeting. He was well known to them. I was then the pastor of the Centenary Church. The joy we all felt was like that of the Disciples when Peter stood at the gate, and they all " believed not for joy and wondered." At night he was at Church and concluded the service, which fact was duly criticised by the newspapers. He spent the night with me at Brother Ricords' Our hearts were full. We had many things to talk of, and were little disposed to sleep. The clock struck one, two, three, and we had not yet thought of repose. I never saw him in a better mood. You would not have believed that he could have any occasion of anxiety. Yet he expected soon to be exchanged and go South, leaving his family. I never saw such power to cast off trouble in any other man. Even while in prison he never fell into a gloomy state of feeling.

The camp, the prison, even the hospital and the battle-field will furnish, now and then, its joke. While in the Gratiot street prison one of the officers, whose negro servant had been captured with him, came to Caples with a very serious expression and told him that Tom was in great distress, and that as he was a minister he would be glad for him to talk with the boy. They accordingly went to the officer's apartment and there stood Tom, with his back to the fire, a coal black young negro, six feet high, raw-boned, cadaverous, and the very picture of grief. "Mr. Caples," said the gentleman, "Tom was to have been married up in Saline county, Christmas eve; that's to-morrow, and here he is. If he were released even now it would be impossible for him to meet his engagement His trouble is almost killing him, and I thought as you were a preacher you might offer him some consolation." "Never mind, Tom," said C., "this won't last always. You'll get home some day, and if it should be forty years you will find her the same loving girl she is now." At the mention of *forty years* Tom broke completely down and blubbered out: "I never *can* stand it!" Poor boy, whether he ever saw his wedding day or not I do not know. The last I ever heard of him he was standing there before the fire, sobbing. Most likely he is dead now.

That night—the first after his release from prison—was the last we ever spent together. Much of the matter of this chapter must be credited to the conversations of that interview Though he was cheerful, yet much of the conversation was profoundly serious. He felt! His first sanguine hopes as to the duration of the war had been dispelled. He then foresaw years of distress and bloodshed. Like so many other religious men of the time, however, he looked confidently to a happy issue. The cause, they said, was just, and God would see to it that the just cause should triumph! As if every just cause had triumphed in this fallen world! Before this can be, the depraved conditions in which society moves along its course must be removed, or at least greatly mitigated from any state of things realized in the past. It must be in another world that justice and truth shall be crowned. He will yet witness his long-delayed hope, not in the low conditions of an earthly triumph, which must yet in its best estate contain much evil, but in the ultimate elimination of all the evil that is in even the best human movements, and the final coronation of Truth and Love. Had his cause succeeded he would have found unexpected evils appearing in the very hour of victory Before he died he had learned to wait, with a purified trust, God's own good time for all consummations, and to accept God's own methods with a deeper sense of the unapproachable wisdom of His ways.

The next morning we walked together down Olive street to Sixth and parted. I never saw him again. Our hearts had been fused and flowed together yet more perfectly than before in that last meeting. From that day we went our several ways. They diverged and we met no more. I scarcely ever think of him but that I recall that last walk and the parting on the corner of the street. Through infinite saving mercy I hope to walk with him again along the streets of another city.

From that time, so far as this world is concerned, Mr. Caples' life was under a shadow. He was never exchanged, as he expected to be. Soon after reaching home in Brunswick the ill health of his eldest daughter, Charlotte, assumed a character which indicated clearly her approaching death. Every consideration of parental love and duty forbade his leaving her. The circumstances of his family were such that he could not be spared. By taking an oath prescribed by the authorities he might remain. The oath was most distasteful to him. To take it was humiliating. But to leave his family in the circumstances would be to violate the highest considerations of parental duty and domestic obligation. Duty to a man's own family is paramount. Their claims stand first Failure here is worse than infidelity. When a man like him is under the leverage both of conscience and affection there can be no question as to the result, no matter how strong the motive may be to take another course.

He took the oath, and his conscience was bound by it. He took no sophistical sedatives with it. He did not admit to himself that he might innocently trifle with the name of God to which he had appealed. He was not *forced* to swear. He did it freely as the alternative to be chosen in preference to something worse. The necessity was an incident of the war. He submitted to it and all it involved. He took the oath, and, to the best of my knowledge and belief, kept it inviolate.

Another motive for taking the oath was, that by doing so he would obtain liberty to preach.

He might, perhaps, have remained at home on his parole an indefinite length of time. But the privilege of preaching was denied him.

The following facts have been supplied, for the most part, by Rev James O. Swinney, relating to the time that elapsed between his release from imprisonment and the close of his life.

The conditions of his release were that he should give his parole not to bear arms nor recruit for the Southern army, and that he should not leave the State of Missouri. Soon after he was forbidden to preach under pain of imprisonment. Hard as was the condition he yielded to it, believing that it would not be long required of him and because of his anxiety to be with his family, and for the further reason that privately and by correspondence he could still work for the Church and exert some influence for good in various ways, which would be utterly impossible if he were confined in prison.

How irksome such restraint was to a man of his spirit and habits can well be imagined. To see the dangers of the Church, the rapid decline of piety around him and the alarming increase of vice of every-description, and not be allowed to raise his voice in such time of need was more than he could bear. He applied to the nearest officer for a release. After considerable delay and correspondence with the Provost-Marshal General, in St. Louis, he was told that his request would be granted providing he would take the oath of allegiance to the United States Government. This was the crisis with him the grand point of his trial. A States-Rights Democrat, fully committed and ardently espousing the Southern view of the questions then at issue—believing implicitly that the South would be eventually successful—he hesitated long to accept a condition which would sever him from the people he loved and impliedly make him their enemy For months he prayed and reasoned, wept and sought for the line of duty Banishment or self-exile seemed preferable. But the pressing demands of the Church in Missouri, the interests of his family and the warning voice, "Wo is me if I preach not the gospel," so terrible to him at times, all combined at last to bring him to the determination to take the prescribed oath and stay at home and *preach*. There was no "*mental reservation*" in this oath-taking with him, as others by wicked sophistry have asserted might be done with impunity Had there been he could not have hesitated so long.

He preached irregularly until the Conference at Fulton, which met in October, 1863, from which he was appointed to Glasgow station. Here he had many vexations. Ingenious efforts were made to entangle him, publicly and even in the pulpit, in political issues. With great forbearance and good sense he avoided it, preaching only the clear doctrines of the Word of God. His enemies were baffled, and his friends felt that he had met the emergency in the true spirit of the Christian ministry. During the whole term of his pastorate he was assiduous in the discharge of its duties, visiting much, especially the poor and sick, holding prayer-meetings, leading the classes, attending the Sunday-school and doing with his might what his hand found to do for the salvation of the souls committed to his charge. There was, within this time, a revival of considerable interest in the Church and quite a number professed conversion, in spite of the uproar of war in the country.

The charges and censures of enemies he met mildly and kindly. However unreasonable or aggravating the accusations brought against him, he retained a constant equanimity of temper, which placed him above criticism. All military orders, though made expressly to annoy him, he obeyed promptly and cheerfully.

His friends, knowing the animosity of certain parties against him and fearing for his safety, advised him to leave the State. He refused to do so, declaring that he would rather die at his post than desert the Church at such a time.

From the Mexico Conference, Oct., 1864, he was re-appointed to Glasgow. He was still unremitting in his visiting and praying with the people. But the sky darkened above him. There was much sickness in his family He was full of anxiety on their account. Much of his time was taken up in nursing. In the midst of it all his house was almost turned into soldiers' quarters. It was with difficulty he could get enough to feed them and his family He always received them cheerfully and fed them with the best he could procure. Yet these very men, while consuming his substance, openly threatened his life. His enemies were becoming more and more malignant. All felt, and he knew, that his life was in constant peril In spite of the perfect propriety and the unimpeachable integrity of his course, in spite of the conscientious observance of his oath, there were men whose malignity could be satisfied with nothing short of his death. Of this he was not ignorant. Yet never for a moment did he lose either his courage or his cheerfulness. Even when partisan fury was so insane and the reign of terror so complete that his friends did not dare to defend him against the unjust and unfounded suspicions of his enemies, the self-possessed dignity of his bearing was the wonder of all. You could not have imagined that the thought of danger was in his mind. Perhaps the real greatness of the man was never so fully seen as in the sustained courage with which he bore himself amid the terrors of that most unhappy time. He rested with perfect tranquillity in the consciousness of his own integrity and in the assured mercies of his God.

True to his oath but steadfast to his principles, while he was neither spy nor informer, he was just as far from being a truckler to the petty despotism of the hour. He never lowered his head in unworthy supplications for mercy from the men who had no just ground of accusation against him. He did his duty, gave no cause of offense, and awaited the issue without trepidation. In the presence of those who had his life in their power, and at the same time were not indisposed to take it, he never cringed nor gave the slightest token of unworthy fear. He gave them the respect due to their position, but nothing more. His deportment was self-respecting, and in the trying and delicate situation he was in, every way becoming. So strikingly true was this that his friends were greatly impressed by it and speak of it with gratulation to this day

"A merciful Providence," says one of them, "directed the shell that removed him before the increasing malice of cruel men had ventured to murder him. Had he lived until after Shelby's men left Glasgow, I doubt not his had been a worse fate than Robberson's."

All this while God was finishing his work in the man. The Divine Artificer was giving the last strokes, bringing his soul into forms of grace and beauty for a place in the house not made with hands. The work was almost done. These were the final humiliations which were the prelude of the glory just at hand. From the insults of men he was about to be taken into the society of angels. He had come, consciously, very near to God in faith. He was now just ready to see Him face to face. The shadows were heavy, but the dawn had already touched the East. The gates of glory were in sight. Pulses of heavenly music fell upon his ear. He was upon the threshold of immortality

CHAPTER XIII.

THE MAN, CAPLES.

I should judge that Mr. Caples was about five feet nine or ten inches in hight, and weighed a hundred and forty-five or fifty pounds. His shoulders drooped forward considerably The head was rather thin through the temples, but from the front backward it was very deep, giving ample brain-room. His hair was black, rather thin, and, although never worn long enough to indicate affectation, was never trimmed close. The general impression was that his eyes were black, but a very intimate friend, who was with him much and who loved him deeply, agrees with me that they were a very dark brown—not quite black. The under jaw was heavy, with an angular curve which gave a decided expression—an expression of quiet strength. The nose was not Roman, nor yet was it of the opposite type. It was rather broad, and at the lower extremity heavy. The forehead was high, the complexion sallow. When in repose he would be considered homely, though the forehead and eye were always imposing. When animated in the pulpit he was remarkably fine looking. At such times his presence was commanding in a very high degree, and was in keeping with the wonderful sermons he preached.

He was, in the fullest meaning of that word, *an honest man*. If there was no other proof of it, the fact given elsewhere that he paid a debt contracted in the first two years of his ministry by chopping cord wood would be sufficient. Some men see dishonor in hard work, and imagine themselves to be gentlemen while their creditors go unpaid. By him the dishonor was seen on the other side. There could be no honor where there was not honesty, and honesty required payment of debts, at whatever cost of labor.

His "diary" contains abundant evidence of thoughtfulness in expenditures. A man on a limited salary may be dishonest just through carelessness. There must be prudent forethought. He well understood this and was careful not to allow expenses to outrun receipts. Every thing was carefully noted and paid for when purchased.

His generosity to the poor has been mentioned in another place. His gratitude for kindnesses shown to himself was not less marked. In that last sad year of his life through which his diary runs, mention is made, with simple hearted ten-

derness, of several instances of thoughtful attention shown him by various friends. I can not
forbear citing one or two instances, there is so
much heart in them. I quote from the diary:

"1863, Nov. 9 Set up housekeeping. Sister
Swinney shows her kindness by sending" house-
hold supplies," the various items all mentioned.
He then adds: "Heaven bless her."

"1864, April 4. Bro. D. White brought me a
very large load of wood. God bless him, for he
would take nothing from me."

No truer hearted friend ever lived than he.
Some are more demonstrative, more given to pro-
testations, but none could be relied on more fully
in the day of trial. The warmth of his nature
led him to form many warm friendships, both
among the preachers and private members of the
Church. He never seemed to say to himself, and
certainly never to them, that there was special
partiality Yet it was very apparent to all that
there were some whom he loved with uncommon
tenderness. I could name several, but it is not
necessary. His heart, indeed, was warm toward
all in whom he reposed confidence. But even the
Perfect Man, the Son of Man, indulged certain
special endearments. John was the "disciple
whom Jesus loved." In the lovely family of Beth-
any he found congenial spirits to whose home
he repaired in the evenings and under whose

roof he found shelter at night when on his visits at Jerusalem. "Jesus loved Martha and her sister, and Lazarus." A man may "love his neighbor as himself" and yet recognize personal affinities as the basis of a peculiar intimacy

The generous spirit of the man and the fidelity of the friend are equally illustrated in a case to which Bro. Vincil refers in his narrative. There is one fact connected with the case which probably never came to Brother Vincil's ears, and is, I suppose, known to but few to this day. The case is mentioned in the diary, but the fact to which I refer, so honorable to himself, he does not notice. The statement in the diary is as follows:

"1864, Sept. 28. I am put in possession of an order making me responsible for the telegraph from this place to Boonsboro by Gen. C. B. Fisk."

Thus calmly he states the fact. He makes no comment upon the malignant despotism of the order, nor any reference to the great personal hazard to which he might be exposed in executing it.

But the fact to which I refer is this: It was the purpose of the authorities to designate to the charge of the telegraph line Rev A. Monroe, a man seventy years old, and at the time prostrate from long and severe illness. Caples, hearing of this purpose, went to intercede for his aged friend. He plead his age and honorable character in vain.

He urged his sickness to no purpose. "I would not be surprised," said he, "if he should be in heaven before your order reaches him." At last he said: "If nothing will do but you must have a Southern Methodist preacher for this service, I pray you *take me* and let that aged and sick man be excused." The General took him at his word. When did Caples ever fail a friend in the hour of danger or of need? This fact was communicated to me by Brother Monroe himself.

This was near the close of his life. Within the next month he went to heaven. His friends will find sad pleasure in reading the few references he made in his diary to the new responsibilities imposed upon him by the military authorities. I find the following:

"Oct. 3. Telegraph all right on my line."

This was at the time of the last Confederate invasion of Missouri under Gen Price. His troops were then making their way along up the Missouri river. The excitement was intense. His duties on the line of telegraph must have occasioned great solicitude on the part of his friends and himself. But his entries betray no weakness. He never lost his poise. All the testimony I get is to the effect that through the whole he bore himself with a dignity and self-command well befitting his character. The juncture gives great meaning to these extracts:

19

"Oct. 5. Excitement and my orders to attend to the telegraph absorb all my attention.

"8. Called out on the line of telegraph and spent most of the day busied about such matters. No stirring news. Made some preparation for the pulpit."

Six days later he made his last entry, and soon after was released from all military orders by the "Captain of our salvation," who was Himself "made perfect through suffering."

This act of friendship toward the "patriarch of Missouri Methodism" well became the last days of a generous son in the Gospel. To the very last and in times of greatest peril, which brought into play the latent selfishness of so many men, Caples showed himself the *faithful and unselfish friend.* For this one deed, if there was no other reason for it, his name would be a word of honor in Missouri.

No account of the man would be at all complete that did not recall him as a companion. Already, however, I have said enough on this subject. His wit delighted young and old, and in sober moods he instructed and entertained his friends at once. There was at the same time a thorough good sense and adaptability which at once established him on a good footing wherever he went. On the occasion of his first visit to the town of Mexico he, with several other preachers, stopped at the house of Brother A. Cauthorn, which was a great *preachers' home.* To Brother B. R. Cauthorn, then a boy, and now residing at Mexico, I am indebted for the incident. The preachers' horses were taken to the stable by the boys. Very soon Caples appeared in the stable, laid aside his coat and went to work on his horse with the curry-comb in good earnest, entering at the same time into a pleasant chat with the boys. They voted him, on the spot, the best man amongst the preachers, and he never lost his hold upon their affections. Thus did the genial spirit of the man assert itself in all circles and circumstances, and over the hearts of all classes. No man had better self-command. Rev. W Holmes writes me that when he was stationed at Weston he witnessed in him an instance of meekness and forbearance which, in view of the native independence of his character, was quite remarkable. Caples was Presiding Elder and lived in Weston. There had been a case of administration to which he stood in a delicate personal relation, and in which, in spite of the greatest caution, both he and Bro. Holmes had incurred the displeasure of a large and influential class of the members of the Church. They were so bitter that they would pass the preachers without speaking, but Brother Caples never failed to speak to them politely and kindly

He never lost his balance under the most trying provocation.

I remember an incident connected with the same affair, which Caples himself told to me not long after it happened, and which Rev. B. H. Spencer has reminded me of. He and Holmes were walking along the street together, and meeting some of the disaffected party he greeted them in an unconstrained manner, one after another as he met them, in every case getting either no response or a very gruff one. At last Brother Holmes expostulated with him, saying it did no good to speak to them in the temper they were in, and only gave occasion to indignities toward himself. He replied: "It will never do to let this devil that is in them get dumb, for 'this kind (that is dumb devils) can come forth by nothing but by prayer and *fasting*' (Mark ix. 17–29), and I have no time to fast." He was at the time in charge of a large district, which was of itself sufficient labor for one man, and beside this was involved in heavy responsibilities with the High Schools. This explains the remark above.

This self-command, this holding himself free from passion, gave him great influence and ascendancy over other men.

A marked trait of his character was *buoyancy of spirit*. He never sank down even under the greatest burdens of responsibility or grief. This was not for want of sensibility. He *felt* more than most men. But there was the spring in him that would rise under any load. In the hands of his enemies, in a loathsome prison, where his companions in misfortune were dying every day, he was cheerful. The night after his release he spent with me. I never knew him more genial. In the last year of his life, while the clouds were thickening around him, while enemies were laying snares in his path, and he knew it, though there was now and then a touch of sadness upon him, he still cheered his friends by the light of his hopeful, happy spirit. Even the flash and corruscation of his wit still played among the shadows, but especially a deepened sympathy, made radiant by a faith that triumphed more and more as the darkness deepened, poured sunshine on all around him. Himself consciously treading on the edge of death, he yet brought cheer and consolation to many hearts. The joy of faith, added to his native joyousness, held him erect to the very last.

Added to all this there was an openness, a candor that made him a most decided man You were never in doubt as to his sentiments or opinions. It would have been impossible for him to play a part. He could be no schemer. What he was he was. He affected no unreal friendship. He never played fast and loose. He took his attitude toward men and measures promptly, boldly. There was not the slightest trace of the *fox* in him. If he laid his hand on your shoulder and said, "old fellow," you might rest. He was your friend.

He was an earnest man. The great purpose of his life was pursued with sustained energy through all temptations and discouragements.

He was an industrious man. Living in Weston several years, he had, chiefly by the labor of his own hands, made a most delightful home, with ornamented grounds, and this amid district and educational labors that would have fully engrossed an ordinary man. He cultivated a large garden, and was rarely idle for a moment.

In that sad "last year," having removed from his home near Brunswick to Glasgow, his diary shows the same industry. The ice-house is repaired one day and filled the next. There are several trips to the farm near Brunswick, and days spent in necessary labors—stripping tobacco, repairing fences, and so on. In the spring there is the inevitable gardening. The diary shows him at work.

I have lingered over this diary for hours. To me there is a charm in it that is almost a fascination. There was evidently no thought of its ever seeing the light when it was written. But his old friends at least will thank me for extracts at this period. His wife was very ill, and these unpremeditated entries from day to day show him as he was—at the bedside of his wife, in pastoral labors and in the garden. The scene is hallowed. The domestic affections are deep, tender and pure. This trait appears through his whole life

"1864, March 29. The ground covered with snow. Still stormy and cold. Wife but little better. Attended Bible class.

"30. Did little but wait on Mrs. C. and entertain company. Wife better.

"31. Did but little except nurse. Wife keeps much the same. Did not attend class at night.

"April 1. Made garden, planted beets, parsnips, onions, etc. Mrs. C. still in bed, but a little better. At prayer-meeting; but few there.

"2. Visited Sister Marr. Went with Brother Pitts to the country for butter, etc.

"3. Attended S. S. Met the Bible class. Preached on John x. 11: Christ the good Shepherd. Rained; no further service. Mrs. C. better, but still in bed.

"5. Worked some in the garden. Entertained Brother Swinney. Spent some time with Dr. and Dick Vaughn. Met Bible class at night.

"6. Visited Sister Thompson, Bro. Errickson, Sister Cason, Bro. Perry Errickson, Bro. Shackelford, Mother Errickson, etc.

"12. Made garden. Mrs. C. much worse.

"14. Made asparagus bed.

"15. Spaded in the garden."

I suppose the diary contains the names of all the members of the charge and speaks of visits paid them.

From all I gather I think his Christian life was deepened during the war. The troubles of that unhappy time had a hallowing effect. Rev. C. Babcock writes me that being with him at one time during the last year of his life, for several days, he heard him speak freely of his experience. He said that sometimes he could scarcely refrain from shouting aloud the praises of God.

With regard to his general character his tried friend, Amos Rees, Esq., of Leavenworth City, writes: "I can say, from an acquaintance of twenty years, part of the time very intimate, that he was one of the most useful men I have ever known. He was a man of many, indeed constant, labors and much prayer. His great object in life always seemed to me to be to do good. He was a pleasant companion, a good preacher and a warm and unfailing friend."

Rev. B. H. Spencer writes: "He was my Presiding Elder two years, and I never had one that pleased me better. In *social life* he was exceedingly agreeable and entertaining. In *Conference* he was a great favorite and a leading man. In the pulpit he was peculiar. He never, I believe, announced his plan except as he proceeded in his discourse, and after hearing him in his happiest efforts I have never been able to recall his plan, because the brilliancy of his style and the soul of his eloquence had rendered me oblivious to everything else. Though I heard him a great many times, yet I am unable to recall the skeleton of a single sermon that I ever heard him preach."

Mr. J. B. Dameron, of Moberly, says: "When Bro. Caples was on Huntsville circuit he was well received and dearly loved by the Church, and admired by all. He commanded large congregations, was listened to with unusual interest by those who seldom attended the house of worship, and is still spoken of as one of the leading spirits of our Church. No one lays aught against Bro. Caples. His untimely death cast a shade over all who knew him. Bro. Caples was much at my house, was a Bible student, and instructive in the family circle. The children all loved him, and even the servants were glad to see him, for he always had a kind word for them."

In this connection, as indicating the personal character of Bro. Caples and confirming some things already written, I give another extract of a communication from Bro. Holmes, who was with Caples as Jonathan with David:

"My first acquaintance with Bro. Caples was in the fall of 1841. We met at Hannibal, on our way to Conference at St. Louis, where we were detained two days waiting for a down boat. We spent those days together pleasantly, and he formed for me, as I for him, a love and attachment that strengthened and grew in all the after years of our acquaintance. Our contrast of qualities seemed to rivet us more closely—he full of humor, I grave and sedate. We were in the same class, and were ordained deacons and elders together.

"I remember, in strolling over the hills of Hannibal during the days mentioned, of his relating his struggles to repress the strong conviction of his duty to preach, and how, at the end of his second year on trial, he declined attending Conference, wrote to the Bishop of his intention to locate, of chopping cord wood, and his contention with poverty, and, as he then thought, adverse providence; of his struggles with his convictions that he was out of the line of duty, and his final determination, with an increasing family and the certain prospect of a meager support on any circuit to which he might be assigned, to re-enter the itinerant ranks for life."

I give two more extracts from the diary. Having been written on important occasions near the close of his life, they will be of special interest to his old friends:

"1864, July 4. This day twenty-six years ago I married. Time in passing has carried many loved ones away, I trust to the better home above, and I, too, am hastening away. Lord help me so to live that I, at last, may die in peace and join the good above!"

Hastening away! He was living daily under the wing of death—was consciously in the valley of the shadow. The times were evil, and he knew that evil eyes were upon him.

The following was written on his last birth-day. I have lingered over it with tears:

"April 23. As this is my forty-fifth birth-day I have been reading Southey on Henry Kirk White, who died at twenty-one years of age. O! my Father in heaven, is it so that I have been forty-five years on earth? I used to write to my mother on my birth-days, but years have passed since. Oh! what years have mine been—a conflict sometimes with poverty bordering on want, with domestic cares and afflictions burdening and almost heart-breaking—always with a sense of ignorance and want of qualification for any great enterprise, and yet a longing desire to be useful, if not great. My father died when I needed him most, when I was not yet sixteen. My mother left earth to join him in heaven near a dozen years since, and I, a parent, about whose heart hang ineffaceable images, not only of parents gone from earth, but dear, dear children, too. And is it true that I have reached the summit of my strength, and must my

steps hence grow feeble, and with so little done? 1
sigh for the rest of the grave, with no other claim
upon the Church or the world than the exercise of
charity in forgetting my follies and neglects.

"God hath not dealt with me but in mercy, and
only in that mercy, through the Crucified, do I
hope for the future. O! my gracious God, be
compassionate to my weakness, and let not my
family nor thine suffer for my ignorance or neglects. O! my Savior, wash me from all impurity,
and permit me to join my loved ones in heaven,
and bring, oh! bring, at last, those I love on earth
to that blessed home. Thine be the praise.
Amen."

What humility is here! We thought he had
accomplished much; to him it seemed as nothing.
How touching this sense of his own want of early
opportunities. He felt himself to be "ignorant"
to the very last, though in matters pertaining to
religion he had been recognized on all sides for
many years as a master. Indeed, he had acquired
a vast amount of general knowledge, and, on occasion, knew how to use it. Yet to himself he
seemed ignorant.

At life's summit he contemplated the descent
with sensibility. He was a man of fine muscular
power, and dreaded the "feeble steps" of old
age. God decreed that he should be spared
this humiliation. While yet at the summit, in

the fulness of his strength, he was taken to the "loved ones" he longed so much to see. May all those for whom he prayed on his last birth-day, when their time shall come, be ready to join him also in the skies!

As a fitting conclusion of this chapter, I give a few communications which have been kindly sent me by men who knew Bro Caples long and loved him much. The first is from Rev. B. R. Baxter, formerly of the Missouri, now of the Columbia Conference:

"DEAR BISHOP: I sit down to write you my recollections of our mutual friend and fellow-laborer in the vineyard of our Master, Rev. Wm. Goff Caples. If what I write shall not be of any service to *you*, it will serve to revive in my own *mind* and *heart* the memory of him whom I *esteemed* and *loved* more than any other man I ever knew, my own father excepted. I first saw Brother Caples in the month of August, 1839, at a quarterly meeting held in a grove near my father's house, in Clay county, Mo. (The same place on which he lived when *you* traveled Liberty Circuit, 1844.) By reference to the minutes of the Missouri Conference, in Dr. M'Anally's Life of Rev. W Patton, you will find we were embraced in Lexington District, Jesse Green, P E., Richmond Circuit, D. T. Sherman, circuit preacher. On Saturday he presented Bro. Green his certificate of membership and license as an Exhorter, and on the afternoon of that day he delivered his *first* exhortation. Two things impressed me under that exhortation that marked the man in all his after life and labors—*simplicity* and *earnestness*. The exhortation made a favorable impression upon the congregation, especially upon the members of the Church. During the summer of 1840, while he was in charge of Plattsburg Circuit, his appointment for a two-days' meeting in the town of Plattsburg came in collision with the appointment of Duke Young, at that time one of the great lights of Campbellism in Northwest Missouri. On Saturday Young proposed to preach first, to which Bro. Caples assented. Young occupied something over *two hours*, wearying the congregation and virtually depriving Caples of preaching at all. He then proposed that as Caples was a young man, and would not want to occupy much time, that *he* should preach *first* on Sunday and Young would follow To this arrangement, of course, Caples consented. He began services at 11 o'clock and held the congregation till *half-past one*, making retaliation, in that case, a *complete success*.

"In September, 1840, he attended the first camp-meeting ever held at Pleasant Grove camp ground, Clay county, Richmond District, Rev. W W Redman, P E., Conley Smith, preacher in charge. Bro. Smith was sick, and Bros. Redman and Caples did most of the preaching. Caples preached with great acceptability The result of the meeting was between forty and fifty conversions and additions to the Church. On Monday night he preached from Rev. ii. 7, 'Him that overcometh will I give to eat of the tree of life which is in the midst of the paradise of God,' and closed with an earnest appeal to sinners to begin the Christian warfare *then.* The altar was crowded with penitents, and the writer well remembers kneeling at the seat *outside* the altar to ask the prayers of the Church. My mother and Bro. Caples came and knelt beside me and prayed for and instructed me in the way of life. While Bro. C. was pointing me to the 'Lamb of God that taketh away the sin of the world,' I was enabled to trust in Him and feel *my* sins forgiven. In that hallowed hour was laid the foundation of that friendship which was never interrupted to the close of his life, and which I hope to renew beneath 'the tree of life in the midst of the paradise of God.'

"During the summer of 1841, when he was traveling Platte Circuit, his appointment on Saturday, on one occasion, came in conflict with the appointment of Rev Mr. Kline, of the Baptist Church. Mr. Kline preached first, setting forth pretty clearly the final perseverance of the saints. Mr. C. followed, taking for his text Heb. xi. 14, 15 and 16, and while describing the heavenly country a Baptist lady got happy and shouted. The congregation was dismissed, the Baptist Church meeting organized and the good sister arraigned for trial for shouting under the preaching of a Methodist preacher. She left the house and went out into the yard where Bro. C. still was and said: ' Brother, they have arraigned me for trial for shouting under your sermon, and I want to join the Methodist Church.' 'Very well, sister, I will receive you,' and he commenced singing, 'Am I a soldier of the cross,' and that lady and one other from the Baptist Church, and two others who had not been Church members, gave him their names, and the Baptists proceeded to expel the two ex-members for violation of Church discipline. These two circumstances Brother Caples related to me frequently

"My next association with Bro. Caples was at Platte City, in the fall of 1848. Our house of worship was completed just before the session of the Missouri Conference at Weston, and I got Bro. C. to spend a week with us on his way to Conference and dedicate the church. His text for the dedication service was II Chronicles, 6th chapter, 40–41 verses. It was a sermon full of power and unction, setting forth the presence of the Lord in the Church for the safety and comfort of his people. At night he preached from the 110th Psalm. It was one of the happiest efforts

I ever heard him make. The priesthood and dominion of Christ. On Monday he preached from John, 14th chapter 1st verse: 'Ye believe in God, believe also in me.' I remember one point in the sermon: A man might be a *believer* in the existence, wisdom, power and providence of *God*, and an *infidel* in reference to his Son, our Lord Jesus Christ. That any system of faith that did not embrace Christ in his divine character and mediatorial office, and salvation through Him as the *only* and *all-sufficient* sacrifice for sin, was essentially defective and could not secure the salvation of those who embraced it. At the Weston Conference, 1848, I was transferred to the Indian Mission Conference, and did not meet Bro. Caples again until in the summer of 1852, when I found him P E. on Weston District. I attended his quarterly meetings in St. Joseph Station and on Savannah Circuit. It was at the camp-meeting on Savannah Circuit that I first heard him preach a missionary sermon. His text was Isaiah, 2d chapter, 2d, 3d and 4th verses. It was one of his finest efforts, produced a deep impression on the large congregation, and was followed by a handsome collection for missionary purposes. This was at 11 o'clock on Monday In the afternoon we went in company to Savannah, some 13 miles, and at night he preached a very effective sermon, in the N. S. Presbyterian Church, from Heb. xii.

20

18–24. During the summer of 1853 I lived in Hainsville, Clinton county. Caples was P E. on Weston District. I attended several quarterly and two camp-meetings with him. One of his chief excellencies as P. E. was his uniform courtesy toward, and appreciation of, his brethren in the ministry, both traveling and local. He would invite all to preach, however limited their ability in the pulpit. He was, as you know, the devoted friend of missions and the unflinching advocate of the support of the gospel ministry. I have often heard him argue the point, that any man who attended regularly upon the gospel ministry and did not contribute to its support was 'a *pauper on the preacher.*'

" In the summer of 1856, while he was stationed in Weston, he visited me in Savannah and preached with great power and and acceptability. That was his last visit that far up the country The last time I saw him was in Glasgow, in January, 1863, after he had been released from prison in St. Louis and *permitted* to resume preaching. We spent some two weeks together in a gracious revival of religion in Glasgow, Rev. J. D. Vincil pastor. He preached with liberty and power, as many will remember. He preached a very impressive sermon on the Judgment. On the second Sabbath of the meeting, while assisting in administering the Lord's Supper, he became very happy and requested Bro. Vincil and the writer to sing, 'I would not live alway,' during which he shouted the praise of God. When we were alone he often referred to his past life as a man and a minister; spoke of his trials and triumphs in the past and his hopes in the future; conversed freely in reference to his connection with the Southern army; said the motive that governed him in so doing was to preach Christ crucified to the thousands of Missourians' sons who were going to the field of conflict and to the bed of death. I shall never forget the manner in which he spoke of his treatment and that of his fellow prisoners from the time of their capture until they reached McDowell College, St. Louis. Propriety forbids its insertion in his life. In the last conversation we ever had, at Brother Thompson's, in Glasgow, he referred to his lifelong disposition to cheerfulness. Said he: 'I *believe* I have lived to convince even Bro. —— that a man can be as cheerful as I am and yet be a Christian.' And added, with emphasis, 'I pray my Heavenly Father that I may not live to be a captious, querulous old man.' Next day we bade each other adieu, little thinking it was to be our last meeting on earth.

"He was a favorite with myself and wife, dedicated four of our children to God in baptism, and often tarried with us in his journeyings in his

Master's work. We cherish his memory with strong affection, and hope to join him in that

> "Glorious land where no bright dream is broken,
> No flower shall fade in beauty's hand,
> And no farewell be spoken."

The following is from Rev. W A. Mayhew:

"My acquaintance with Rev. W G. Caples commenced at the Conference held in Glasgow, Mo., in the fall of 184/ That was the first Conference I ever attended. Bro. Caples was the pastor of the church, and upon him devolved the duty of providing homes for the preachers during the session of the Conference. When introduced to him by Rev. B. R. Baxter he met me kindly, and pleasantly remarked that he failed to get my name, but would provide me a good home, and immediately sent me to Bro. Dunnica's, at whose house, in company with some half dozen of the members of the Conference, I found a very pleasant home, indeed. During the session of the Conference I was much pleased with his attention and affability to the preachers and his exhortations in the public services had in the church. The more intimately I became acquainted and associated with him the more I learned to value him as a man of noble, generous impulses and a Christian of warm, gushing sympathies. Bro. Caples was a man of large benevolence. His hand was ever ready to help the needy and destitute about him. Many have been made glad by the timely assistance, in various ways, which his thoughtful and ready benevolence afforded. Numerous instances might be mentioned. It was no unusual thing for him to send from his little place near Brunswick, Mo., wood and other articles of necessity to those who were in need. At his home he was courteous and hospitable, and always glad to have his friends and acquaintances with him. He was a man of high social qualities, communicative, entertaining and quite instructive, which occasioned his presence in the social circle to be hailed with delight wherever he went. He possessed a fund of rich incident and anecdote, collected during the years and from the extended field of his ministerial labor, which he related with so much facility and effect that they charmed and instructed all who listened to them. He never seemed more at home than when surrounded by his brethren in the ministry, and no one enjoyed the society of his co-laborers in the ministry more than he did.

"On the Conference floor and in the deliberations of the body he was a leading spirit, always deeply interested in whatever tended to the advancement of the Church and the glory of the Lord throughout the length and breadth of our Zion. In the deliberations of the Conference his influence was felt as much, if not more, than any one in the body. His views on all questions which demanded the attention of the Conference were almost always correct. He entertained grand ideas of the work of the Church and took enlarged views of the plans and means of her success. These he advocated with strength and clearness. He was always listened to by the preachers with respect and interest, and the effect of his appeals and arguments could usually be seen in the action of the Conference on whatever question was before the body To all the great interests of the Church he was fully alive. To some of them he was quite in advance of his time. He was deeply interested in behalf of the widows and orphans of the ministry who died in the regular work of the Church, and labored to devise plans and provide means to meet the necessary wants of those who, by death, were left widowed and fatherless among us. I have heard him say that a great burden would be removed from his mind were some plan devised by which ample provision for the support of the widows and orphans of our deceased and constantly dying preachers would be secured. In the cause of missions, foreign and domestic, he was ever greatly interested, and he was one of our finest and strongest advocates for the destitute portions of our work, and for the millions who were held, by false systems, spell bound in Pagan idolatry and kept in ignorance of the Savior who redeemed them. On the subject of education among us he was one of our ablest advocates. In behalf of this cause he labored extensively and was liberal almost to a fault, as his efforts for building a Weston High School and one in Plattsburg will abundantly testify. .At the Conference of 1861, there being no one of our Bishops present, Bro. Caples was elected to preside over the deliberations of the body. He was thus placed in a situation which he had never occupied before, and called upon to discharge the delicate and responsible duty of making, with the assistance of the Presiding Elders, the appointments for the year. The result proved him to be fully competent for the position to which his brethren, by their votes, had called him. He presided over the deliberations of the Conference with kindness and dignity, and to the entire satisfaction of the preachers. His charge to the Deacons elect, delivered before the Conference, was very impressive, and it was remarked by several that they had scarce ever heard a more appropriate one. He occupied the highest positions in the gift of the Conference, filling her best stations and districts, and representing his brethren in the General Councils of the Church.

"In the pulpit he scarcely had an equal, and certainly no superior, among us. As a preacher he was earnest, his doctrine sound, his illustrations striking, and his arguments strong and forcible. On the platform and in the pulpit he seemed ever ready, and it was there his powers of intellect were more fully called forth and appeared to greatest advantage. In the delivery of his sermons he used no manuscript and but seldom a brief note.

"He has, I believe, left but little written account of his travels and labors. The absence of such manuscript papers is a felt difficulty in writing the life of one who filled so large a place among us, and who was for so long a time identified with the development and movements of Methodism in Northern Missouri. While his discourses were almost always able, there were times when he seemed to rise entirely above himself and all cramping circumstances, and then his pulpit efforts assumed a majesty and his eloquence and pathos became overpowering. He drew crowds wherever he went, and many flocked to hear him who were not in the habit of attending the house and worship of God. It was thought by many that he preached with greater power and effect at his quarterly meetings in the country than he did in the large towns. At one of his quarterly meetings in the country several brethren from an adjacent Station heard him deliver a powerful discourse, and ventured to ask him why he did not favor them with such sermons in their town. With a pleasant smile and a mischievous twinkle of the eye, he simply replied: 'Ah! you town people have been fed so long on nubbins that you would not know what to do with a full ear.'

"As a Presiding Elder he was diligent in the management and work of his District. Under his labors the Church was edified and prospered. Especially was this the case in the Weston District, which he traveled for four years. His intercourse with the preachers in his District was always kind and pleasant, which made his quarterly visits to their charges be looked forward to with a great deal of interest, anticipating as they did a rich feast of Gospel instruction, social intercourse and friendship. While he was not regarded a painstaking pastor, still he did not altogether neglect this field of ministerial labor and usefulness. As a pastor he was kind and sympathetic, and always had a word of counsel for the erring, of sympathy for the distressed, of hope for the desponding, and of consolation for the afflicted and bereaved. His numerous friends who knew him best, and knew the value of his counsels and sympathies, regretted that his domestic duties and ministerial labors prevented him from being with them more frequently, both pastorally and socially He had a large and growing family which demanded his attention, and for whose support he had to labor no little on his small place. This, of course, operated to hinder him in his pastoral work. The people loved him and were anxious to have him much with them at their homes. The name of Caples through the Platte and Grand river country, and from the Mississippi to the Missouri, almost throughout the length and breadth of North Missouri, has become a household word, and the influence of his character and ministerial labors is still felt, and will be for long years to come. I think I may say, without disparagement to others, that Rev. W. G. Caples possessed more influence and was more popular with preachers and people than any one among us. It is no unusual thing to hear, throughout the Fayette District, his labors referred to with emotions of pleasure and interest. His presence among us was always a pleasure, and his absence is greatly missed. His remains lie buried in the cemetery in Brunswick, Mo. It was my sad duty, in company with Revs. A. Monroe and J. D. Vincil, to assist in performing the last sad rites at his burial."

From the Rev. C. I. Vandeventer I have received the following:

"Rev. William G. Caples was a comparatively young but growing and honored member of the Misssouri Conference at the time of my admission into the same on trial in the fall of 1844. At about this time our acquaintance commenced, but our spheres of operation being necessarily different and our fields of labor not contiguous, this did not amount to much more than a *Conference* acquaintance, until, in Sept., 1852, I was appointed to the St. Joseph Station, with Bro. Caples for my Presiding Elder, which relation he sustained to me the three following years. During this period, and up to the time of his lamented death, an intimate, ardent and Christian friendship was mutually cherished and cultivated by us—a friendship unbroken and unimpaired by the lapse of time—which still lives, and which, I trust, will be strengthened and matured in the home of the Redeemed. I announce but the verdict of the masses in this Platte country and of the sections of the State generally which shared in his ministerial labors, of the people in the Church and out of the Church, of friends and enemies (if he had any) that William G. Caples was, in the true import of the word, *a great man*, a man of vast mental capacity, and, what is an immeasurably more valuable record of him, that he was the very impersonation of magnanimity and Christian benevolence. He was a charming *preacher*, who would not only interest and please with his peculiarly attractive *manner*, but often under his ministration of the Word the fountain of the heart would be opened, the tempted child of God would be comforted and edified and the careless sinner awakened and converted.

"Brother Caples was a model Presiding Elder. There were no complaints about *that office* when he filled it. If there were any I do not remember having heard of them. The quarterly meetings were occasions of general interest and of much profit. His profound and touching proclamations of Gospel truth held the listening multitudes at times almost spell-bound, especially, as thousands will remember, when, in his happiest moods, he discoursed upon the ultimate triumph of the Redeemer's kingdom, of the Resurrection of the Dead, of the General Judgment, and of kindred themes.

"He was emphatically a *Methodist* preacher. Of *original* thought and *speculative* turn of mind, he was sound to the core in the doctrine and essential polity of the Church as received from our fathers. Yet so broad was his Christian charity, so free was his spirit from bigotry and offensive sectarianism that he was a favorite of all denominations, and was spoken of with kindness and respect by those with whom it became, as he thought, necessary to '*contend* earnestly for the *faith*.' During the period referred to Bro. Caples manifested a zeal worthy of the faithful minister of Christ, and a degree of enterprise in behalf of the interests of education and religion which was in advance of the times. He had inaugurated the District Conference and held two Annual District camp-meetings, one of which, at least, was a time of great spiritual power. A considerable number of churches was erected within the bounds of his District and several High Schools established through his agency. The last year that he was on the District I was stationed in Weston, where he also resided. Here, in connection with Rev. Robert G. Loving, then in charge of the Weston High School, it was my privilege more frequently to meet Bro. Caples, and often at his own house. Here we and our families, amid uncommon trials, took sweet counsel together and walked unto the house of God in company In the summer of this year I was extremely ill, and was favored not only with the visits and prayerful sympathy of my dear brother, but believe that, during the unavoidable absence of my physician, his knowledge of my condition and prompt and appropriate suggestions were, with the blessing of Providence, instrumental in my recovery

"Bro. Caples was truly, in the various departments of life—domestic, social and religious—a loving and lovely man and useful minister—'a bright and shining light' While constitutionally cheerful, and sometimes manifesting almost an excess of vivacity, you had but to know him well to be convinced that this was but the *outgushing* of an innocent and happy heart, and of one that would, if possible, even under the most gloomy surroundings, render all about him happy. The whole tenor of his life made this impression upon my mind (without claiming that for him to which none are entitled—entire exemption from error in judgment or in practice), that, in his relations to God and to his brethren, it was his invariable aim to *do right*.

"He was pre-eminently a *laborer* in his Master's vineyard, a workman that needed not to be ashamed, rightly dividing the word of truth. If such language will not be misconstrued, I would say he possessed a proper denominational ambition; he desired that the Church of his love and of his choice, which he regarded as but the exponent of 'Christianity in earnest,' should be in the front of the great battle with the powers of darkness and first in every good work, and it was his chief delight to *lead* the Lord's militant hosts in this holy warfare. He told me, on one occasion, that he dreaded more than anything else the prospect of becoming old and superannuated, of living to be in the way and of no benefit to mankind, and that it had been a frequent prayer with him that before that time should come the good Lord might take him out of the world. O, may we meet him in heaven."

The last communication which I will give in this connection is from Rev. J. C. Parks:

"I first became acquainted with Brother Caples in the fall of 1859. He was then stationed at Brunswick, on the Missouri river, and there, for the first time, I heard him preach; there, for one year, I listened with much interest to his efforts as a Gospel minister.

"I was a stranger at that time among the people to whom he ministered, and shall ever feel grateful for the interest he manifested for my welfare and success. While he was preaching to that people I was trying to educate their children, and it is but just to attribute to him much of the influence that gave me success.

"Bro. Caples was a man easy of approach, and could make a stranger feel familiar with him at once. If ever I knew a man who conscientiously regarded the rights of others, he was that man. I had frequent opportunity of testing that quality of his heart. He was a true friend, a faithful, thoughtful, judicious adviser. Knowing the difficulties that surrounded me in managing the educational interests of that people, he was my refuge and defense, and by the position assumed with his own children while attending school, exerted an influence over the whole community which made the government of the school-room comparatively an easy task.

"With children Brother Caples was never very familiar, yet I never saw him in any family circle where the children did not seem to be interested by his anecdotes and listen attentively to all he had to say, and somehow or other advice from Brother Caples was always regarded by them as sacred.

"It was my privilege often to visit him at his own house, and there, if anywhere, he might be regarded as a teaze (I don't like the word). The remarks he frequently made would, if made by many a parent, have encouraged a spirit of resentment and disobedience; but in his family while his words would seem to plague, they would at the same time amuse. His children always seemed to venerate the opinion of their father, and always spoke of him with the greatest confidence and regard.

"During the year he was stationed at Brunswick I attended two protracted meetings held by him, at one of which three of his family were converted and joined the Church. Two of that family— his son William, and Alonzo Bailey, his wife's son—are now ministers of Christ, each holding an itinerant relation in the Missouri Conference. During the presence of his children at the altar of prayer his mind seemed much agitated, and upon the conversion of his son William so deeply was his mind impressed with the thought that William would be called of God to preach that he mentioned the fact to me while standing in the altar and frequently afterward. One would suppose that a man of so much ease in approaching others upon the subject of religion could easily approach his own children, but it was not so. He was timid in saying anything upon the subject. He remarked to me that, for some cause unknown to himself, it was the hardest cross he had to take up.

"Nearly two years ago I met his son William at the Gallatin District Conference and learned from him that his father had tried to ascertain from him if he did not feel it his duty to preach. If I remember rightly his son never gave him any positive assurance of his intention to do so, and, for aught I know, he died without knowing the impressions of William's heart in reference to his call to the ministry

"As a minister Bro. Caples was expository and argumentative rather than topical in his method of presenting truth. His style was earnest, and sometimes truly eloquent. He aimed, and succeeded, too, in convincing the judgment as well as assailing the heart. Self-possessed, he seldom failed to place his audience at ease and in the best condition to listen to the truths he uttered, and win at once their admiration and confidence.

"It so happened that in all the efforts I ever heard him make he never made what is called a

21

failure. His talents seemed to be of a commanding order every where, with all classes. A student
he was, but not of books. Plodding after the
thoughts of other men he regarded as the veriest
drudgery He seldom, if ever, read an author
through with close attention. He aimed to get
their positions, and then, rather than confine himself to the drudgery of reading and studying
their style and mode of reasoning, chose to do the
thinking himself and form the argument after his
own style.

"If there is anything to be regretted, it is that
he did not avail himself of the helps at hand furnished by others. He studied nature, men and
principles, in all of which he would have become
more proficient and would have saved much time
by using the material furnished to his hand by
others, especially upon scientific subjects.

"I once inquired of him what he thought of
the probability of any one giving us a true interpretation of the prophecies. He replied that
God's government of the material world and His
providential dealings with nations and men were
Jehovah's commentary upon the prophesies, and
until the commentary was written we should not
be able to prophesy correctly

"I presume you have his views upon the subject
of the tithes, as he once prepared and pronounced
a lecture upon that subject in St. Louis. The

lecture did not do him justice upon that subject, and the reason is to be attributed to the fact that he seldom wrote anything in the form of a lecture or a sermon. He gave that subject a great deal of attention. His conversations upon it were of the most interesting character, and the inferences he drew from the facts collected upon the subject were such as to produce the finest moral effects upon the efficiency of the Church in the evangelization of the world, could the system be again restored to the Church. I hope we may have his views in his forthcoming life.

"In 1861, upon the breaking out of the war, Brother Caples became a partisan to that ever-memorable conflict—not willingly, as he said, but of necessity I shall never forget the night we sat upon a log, in the suburbs of Brunswick, until after one o'clock, talking of the then-commenced conflict, consulting as to what we ought to do. He seemed to survey the whole struggle, and looked upon the then existing Government as at an end. He believed the States ought to separate, as constitutional liberty would only be preserved by the Southern States organized into a confederacy. With this conviction fully fixed in his mind he felt it his duty to identify himself with the Southern cause, be his personal fate what it might. No one was more attached to the spirit of the Constitution than was he. He was among the few that then seemed to h.ive a clear and just view of the rights of the States (or States-Rights doctrine). He advocated them earnestly, and fully believed in the ability of the Southern States to effect their secession and maintain their independence. All his hopes for a truly republican form of government rested right there, and for that purpose he was willing, if need be, to sacrifice his life. I called his attention that night to the unequal conflict, provided the North were united. He replied (in substance), a bad cause left men without courage, and that the North would not stand before the determined bravery of the Southern soldiers. On this point, perhaps, few men with the same amount of intellect were more mistaken. For a long time he believed in the final triumph of the South, and in fact, so far as I know, he was possessed of that feeling until he fell a victim to the destroying element of war, at the city of Glasgow, where the saddest hour of his history meets us.

"He became identified with the army at the battle of Lexington, and on the first Sabbath after the surrender of that place, in Col. Price's regiment, he preached his first sermon. He addressed the soldiers earnestly upon the necessity of immediate and constant preparation for death. He found it difficult for awhile to adjust himself to his new position, as army life was in strange contrast with the sumptuous boards at which he was accustomed to feast as the Church's favorite minister; but he soon became accustomed to all the inconveniences of army life, and his jovial disposition soon made him a favorite with the soldiers.

"Upon Gen. Price's retreat from Lexington he was made chaplain at headquarters, after which I saw him only occasionally. He was commissioned by Gen. Price as a recruiting officer and returned home. After raising a regiment, in connection with others, he again started to the army and was captured at Blackwater and sent to Gratiot street prison.

"Prison life was intolerable to Bro. Caples, and he made every honorable effort to be paroled, but the authorities regarded him as a man of too much influence to grant him his request. Accustomed as he had always been to the largest liberty, confinement in a prison was anything but pleasant. He obtained permission to preach to the soldiers, which seemed to be the only green spot in his prison life.

"At the time the Blackwater prisoners were sent to Alton, through a friend he obtained a parole to return to his family, after which he gave himself to his former work, preaching Christ to the people, and returned no more to the army

"I may say of Bro. Caples that, fair reasoner

as he was, his arguments were never a parallel to his perceptions of truth. No man that it was ever my good fortune to associate with possessed greater ability to perceive the force of truth than did he, and but few men could urge the consequences of erroneous views with greater strength. Had he studied authors and formulas of argument more he would have made one of the most convincing reasoners in the Church. He surely possessed the native genius and talent to do so."

The sum of the matter is, that *William Goff Caples* was a man of rare force of character, intellectual power and purity of heart; that he was supreme in the pulpit of Missouri, enjoying immense personal popularity and wielding his great influence in favor of God and the Church. He had as few faults as most men, and they were such as " leaned to virtue's side."

He was my friend. I record it with gratitude. The writing of his life is a labor of love. His name ought to survive the present generation of Methodists in Missouri. I desire to be his voice, now that he is dead, in order that he may " still speak." The utterance is inadequate, but it is given in prayer. May the Spirit of God, through this memoir, edify the Church and bring sinners to repentance.

Since this chapter was prepared I have received the following from Bro. Baxter. It will be read by those who believe in a prayer-hearing God with much interest:

"INDEPENDENCE, POLK CO., OREGON.,}
"*January 13, 1870.* }

"DEAR BISHOP: I fear you will think me intrusive, but the associations of to-day called up an 'incident' in the life of Caples that I had forgotten, but while attending the funeral service of Col. Ford, of Dixie, to-day, it came fresh to my memory. It is illustrative of his faith in God and his belief in *direct* answer to prayer.

"You are, doubtless, aware that while stationed at Brunswick (I do not remember which year) he was given up to die of cholera. He often told me that his consciousness never forsook him, and that he never thought he would die at that time. He said he did not attribute his recovery on that occasion so much to the remedies used by his physicians as to the prayers offered in his behalf. He said he believed the Lord raised him up from the very gates of death in direct answer to the prayers of Rev. R. G Loving, who wrestled all night in prayer in his behalf. I have never known a man who had a more unwavering faith in the providence of God over those who put their trust in Him."

CHAPTER XIV.

FACE TO FACE WITH DEATH.

Mere courage in the presence of death is not a test of moral or religious character. The worst men sometimes meet their fate bravely. Abandoned and unrepentant criminals have been known to go to the gallows cheerfully. Such instances are, no doubt, cases of mere bravado. Others are the result of stolid insensibility. Some men maintain their poise by force of will. Death is sometimes met with resignation, probably, from inexpressible weariness of life. The unhappy spirit, beat about by waves and currents until the failing hand lets go the helm, drifts with desperate calmness in the dark, ready to cast anchor in any harbor or drive upon any reef, as chance may shape the event. To it any future is welcome as a refuge from the insufferable past and present.

Every healthy mind, however, looks upon death with a feeling of solemnity; and when the assured hopes of religion are absent this solemnity, when death is imminent, is, in men of strong will, an oppressive dread. In weak men it grows into terror. If a man is not desperate, nor under the curse of insensibility, nor sustained by a proud effort of will, he will tremble in the presence of the "last enemy," unless there is a deep-felt assurance of pardon and preparation to meet God.

It seems to be an ambition in some men to die *in character.* They have been playing a part in life; they must sustain it in death. There has been going the rounds of the papers an extract from Curtis' "Life of Daniel Webster," giving his "last words on religion." There are many well considered and noble utterances in it. There is a candid admission of the fear of death. "No man, who is not a brute, can say that he is not afraid of death." He turned, also, in his helpless fear, and looked upon Christ. But, plainly, there was no joyful trust. The cross was heavily shadowed, yet he felt that it was the only ground of hope. Perhaps we may say he rather *saw* than *felt it.* He *saw it.* He confessed it in solemn and fitting words.

But suddenly he expressed the apprehension that some unworthy weakness had been betrayed in what he had said. Face to face with death as he was, still he must maintain his dignity He must die great. He must act in keeping—not with his character as a sinner before God, but with his distinguished reputation as a man. The following is the extract:

"'My general wish on earth has been to do my Maker's will. I thank Him now for all the mercies that surround me. I thank Him for the means he has given me of doing some little good; for my children — those beloved objects — for my nature and associations. I thank Him that I am to die, if I am, under so many circumstances of love and affection. I thank Him for all His cares. No man who is not a brute can say that he is not afraid of death. No man can come back from *that* bourne; no man can comprehend the will or the works of God. That there *is* a God, all must acknowledge. I see Him in all these wondrous works; Himself how wondrous! The great mystery is Jesus Christ — the Gospel. What would be the condition of any of us if we had not the hope of immortality? What ground is there to rest upon but the Gospel? There were *hopes* of the immortality of the soul running down, especially among the Jews. The Jews believed in a spiritual origin of creation. The Romans never reached it; the Greeks never reached it. It is a tradition if that communication was made to the Jews, by God Himself, through Moses and the fathers. But there is, even to the Jews, no direct assurance of immortality in heaven. There is now and then a scattered intimation, as in Job,

"I know that my Redeemer liveth;" but a proper consideration of *that* does not refer it to Jesus Christ at all. But there *were* intimations — crespuscular—twilight. But, but, but, thank God, the Gospel of Jesus Christ has brought life and immortality to *light—rescued* it—brought it to *light.* There is an admirable discourse on that subject by Dr. Barrow, preacher to the Inner Temple. I think it is his sixth sermon. Well, I don't feel as if I am to fall off. I may '

"He paused a short time; a drowsiness appeared to come over him, and his eyes were closed. In a moment or two he opened them, and, looking eagerly around, he asked: 'Have I—wife, son, doctor, friends, are you all here?—have I on this occasion said anything unworthy of Daniel Webster?' 'No, no, dear sir!' was the response from all. He then began the words of the Lord's Prayer; but after the first sentence, feeling faint, he cried out earnestly, 'hold me up; I do not wish to pray with a fainting voice.' He was instantly raised a little by a movement of the pillows, and then repeated the whole of the prayer in clear and distinct tones, ending his devotions with these words:

"'And now unto God the Father, Son and Holy Ghost be praise forever and forever! Peace on earth and good will to *men—that* is the happiness, the essence—*good will toward men.*'"

"Unworthy of Daniel Webster!" Attitudinizing before the world in the very act of going to the bar of God! "How can ye believe which receive honor one from another, and seek not that honor that cometh from God only?"

"Except ye become as little children ye shall in no case enter into the kingdom of heaven." This consciousness of observation, and the affectations that come of it, are fatal to faith and piety. The man is adjusting himself to the world, to its criticisms, to its standard, and not to God. The eye is not single. The motive is not pure. There is not perfect candor with God.

Is it not a melancholy spectacle—this great spirit, occupied with its relations to God, occupied with the name of Christ, suddenly becoming startled with the apprehension that he had said something that might be open to criticism! As if it were anything to *him* what should be said of his dying words. As if the *only* thing worthy of the human soul were not found in God.

No wonder that the shadow was never lifted. His intellect turned to Christ, but his heart clung to the world. He must play out this last hour in the puppet-show of life becomingly. Cæsar must gather his robes about him and fall with dignity. Even the thought of God, and sin, and Christ, in his mind could not attract attention from that.

Any just idea of dignity and greatness, the

greatness of the soul, would have induced, at such an hour, the utmost indifference to the attitude in which he might appear before men. To an eye that could see, God would have filled the whole field of vision. The only thing that is becoming is to act in keeping with the high nature of man as he is related to the government of God. This statement has augmented meaning in the dying hour. The pride of the statesman, betrayed at such an hour, turns the last act of the drama into a mere farce, which can not be redeemed by a few stately commonplaces of religion. Even religion is taken as an incident of the play, to be rendered in a way that shall not be "unworthy" of the distinguished actor.

No doubt the stupor into which he had fallen will account in part for this last utterance. After his mind had been fully turned to the great theme of religion, a momentary unconsciousness broke the train of thought, and at once the old worldly habit and desire of fame asserted themselves, and the debility of disease accounts, in part, for the effect.

Such is man, in his best estate, without a simple-hearted trust in our Savior.

How that *trust* lifts a man out of the human littlenesses that so degrade us in time! Consciousness and capacity are enlarged by direct communion with the Infinite Being. Just relations are assumed toward God on the one hand, and the world on the other. What value there is in the world is taken from its relation to God. The man triumphs over the world as he comes near to God. "This is the victory that overcometh the world, even our faith."

What a contrast with the last hours of the worldly man, the great statesman and orator, does the death of Whitfield present. A divine radiance is upon the spirit of the man. He has lived not for this world, but for that which is to come. He has not sought the praise of men, but of God. He has been *doing a work*, not acting in a drama. Having done his work he was going to give an account of his labor and receive the reward of it. His attitude before others in this supreme hour was matter of no moment. God was "all and in all." Man was nothing to Whitfield, only as he stood related to God.

Here was a man as far from being "a brute" as Mr. Webster, yet he was "not afraid of death." He had been, but he was not now *Something had taken away that fear*. What was it? It was Christ! This man had seen Christ, not in a philosophical sort of way, as bringing something higher than heathenism, more perfect than Judaism, but in the personal vision of faith. In this vision of faith Christ had become the one great fact of life In Him was salvation. In Him was man reconciled to God. In Him was Life. He was the destroyer of the works of the devil. And believing on Him with the heart unto righteousness men came into fellowship with Him. They received His Spirit. They were *born again*—became children of God by faith in Him. Then they were one with Him as He with the Father, and where He was they should be also. These are no Websterian platitudes about Christ and Moses—they are very pulsations of the heart of Christ. Whitfield did not speculate about Christ; he believed in Him.

Jesus of Nazareth, the Son of God, was his Savior He had given Him unfaltering *trust* and undivided fealty. He had not asked any questions as to what might be "unworthy of Whitfield," but desired only to know what was the will of God. And now he realized a glorious truth of revelation: "The sting of death is sin and the strength of sin is the law, but thanks be to God who giveth us the victory through Jesus Christ our Lord." His was the faith that overcame death, and cast out the fear of it. Read the following simple account of his last hours:

"The time came for Whitfield to die. The man had been immortal till his work was done. His path had been bright, and it grew brighter to the end, like that of the just.

"'You had better be in bed, Mr. Whitfield,' said his host, the day he preached his last sermon.

"'True,' said the dying evangelist, and clasping his hands, cried: 'I am weary *in*, not *of*, thy work, Lord Jesus.'

"He preached his last sermon at Newburyport. Pale and dying, he uttered therein one of the most pathetic sentences which ever came to his lips:

"'I go to my everlasting rest. My sun has risen, shone, and is setting—nay, it is about to rise and shine forever. I have not lived in vain. And though I could live to preach Christ a thousand years, I die to be with him—which is far better.'

"The shaft was leveled. That day he said: 'I am dying!' He ran to the window; lavender drops were offered; but all help was vain; his work was done. The doctor said: 'He is a dead man.' And so he was; and died in silence. Christ required no dying testimony from one whose life had been a constant testimony

"Thus passed away, on September 30th, 1770, one of the greatest spirits that ever inhabited a human tabernacle. The world has ever been an immeasurable gainer by his life. He had preached *eighty thousand sermons*, and they had but two key-notes: 1. Man is guilty; he must be pardoned. 2. Man is immortal; he must be happy or wretched forever."

Thus ascended a human soul aglow with the light of God. No earth-spot was to be seen upon it. So fully does Jesus save where he is wholly trusted. So does the Sun of Righteousness dissipate the darkness of death when His beams are not shut out by human pride. "I go to my everlasting rest. My sun has risen, shone, and is setting—nay, it is about to rise and shine forever."

No, a man need not sink into the insensibility of the brute to overcome the fear of death. He may rise to the higher sensibilities of faith and of divine love, in which case not only is fear overcome, but "death is swallowed up in victory" "O! death, where is thy sting? O! grave, where is thy victory?"

> "Death is the gate to endless joy;
> Why should we dread to enter there?"

But the life of the proud, the sensual, the vain, the flippant man never kindles into this blaze of light as it passes out of sight. Only those who have been dead with Christ in the world live with Him in death. It is the Christ-like spirit that passes into life instead of death. It is the path of the *just* that is as the light that shineth more and more unto the perfect day. Life, realizing itself in fame, or wealth, or pleasures of this life, when it goes into death passes out of the sphere of all these sources of its illumination. It goes into darkness—into the blackness of darkness forever. Only the life that realizes itself in God comes into that light which shines every where

22

and evermore. Death has no caverns which it does not penetrate. He who lives in Christ is dead to the world while he lives, and lives to God still when he dies. "Ye are dead, and your life is hid with Christ in God. When Christ, who is your life, shall appear, then shall ye also appear with Him in glory"

Such an instance of victory over death in a man of the highest sensibility has been furnished recently from our own ranks. Rev. W A. Smith, in the last hours, declared that he could compare his feelings to nothing but "a quiet lake, in a deep forest, under a clear sky." What an image of peace—of the absence of fear! "Thou wilt keep him in PERFECT PEACE whose *mind is stayed on Thee*, because he TRUSTETH IN THEE." I love to contemplate this great soul in absolute repose upon God. The following account of his death is from a brief sketch furnished by Rev. J. C. Granberry to the Richmond *Christian Advocate:*

"With sad hearts we looked on the ghastly face of our venerable father and friend; unchanged in mind and heart, in body he was the wreck of his former self. The last two months of his life he was confined to his room, and for the most part to his bed. He did not suffer much physical pain, but his nervous system was shattered, and his restlessness and depression on this account was often extreme. He received the greatest attention from numerous friends, both of his own Church and of the general community, and they spared no pains to make him as comfortable as possible. He delighted in society, and would seem himself again, the noble Christian sage and leader, as with kindling eye and voice that had not wholly lost its old tone of authority, he discussed at length the sublime truths of the Gospel and the interests of our Church. With special unction and power did he dwell on the declaration of John, 'God is love.' His friends saw that he steadily grew worse, but this fact he did not understand. He felt that there was life in him yet, and he hoped soon to return West and complete the enterprise on which his heart was set—the building up of the great Missouri College. He had a hard fight with death, and if strength of will could have availed in the struggle, he would not have been conquered. He believed that his work was not yet finished, and therefore he was loth to die. But this desire to live did not conflict with entire resignation to the will of God and an assured hope of eternal life. He expressed himself fully on this subject. In his youth he had given his heart to Christ, and though he had often erred, he had never recalled that act of self-surrender, nor did his trust in his Savior waver. His mind was full of peace in the prospect of the eternal hereafter. It was a lake embosomed in a deep forest; the rough winds could not find it, but there it lay with an unruffled surface. This is the beautiful figure by which he described the state of his mind. He was fond of hearing the sweet songs of Zion, and they wafted him to the pearly gates of the New Jerusalem. The last few days he was so feeble, and a bronchial cough so constantly harassed him, that he could say little. 'I have so much to say to you,' he whispered in my ear, 'but I can't say it now.' He retained the clearness of his faculties until a few hours before his death; almost without a struggle he fell asleep in Jesus."

It is often the case that Christ becomes more and more to a man as he nears death. Indeed, I think this is the common experience of His people. Rev. George W Bewley, of the Missouri Conference, died in the autumn of 1846. He was a leading man amongst us in his day Endowed with an incisive intellect, acute, brilliant, full of resources, intrepid and intense, he was much given to controversial preaching. In all questions at issue between our Church and others he was adept. We had at the time few men of equal cultivation. On the mode of baptism, infant baptism, justification by faith, the Divinity of Christ, the universality of the atonement and the free agency of man in receiving Christ, he was a master. He wielded his blade with a dextrous hand when any comer made battle on these issues. In

fact he relished the fray   His religious beliefs
were very deep, his convictions strong.   The *truth*,
as Christ and the Apostles taught it, was a thing
most holy.   The faith once delivered to the saints
was to be contended for.

He did a great work.   In many communities in
Missouri he laid the doctrinal foundations broad
and firm.   This is a service done by the fathers
which we do not always rate at its true value.
Bewley was a man of feeble health, laboring under
pulmonary disease for years.   He was once preaching in the court-house at Richmond on the
Divinity of Christ, which great fact was habitually
assailed in that region.   A small blood-vessel was
ruptured.   The blood came into his mouth and
was wiped off with a white handkerchief   The
bloody white handkerchief spoke volumes to the
hearts of the hearers.   It gave emphasis to the
fervent words of the preacher.   Tears flowed
from unaccustomed eyes.   There was sobbing all
through the house.   Redman, sitting behind him,
sprang to his feet, seized his arm and begged him
to desist, for he preached on as if nothing had
happened.   Rousing his slight frame with the
strength of a lion, Bewley pushed his friend
aside, exclaiming, "Let me alone; I would rather
die defending my Lord and Master from these
aspersions than in any other way"   Years afterward I was told that the Divinity of Christ had

never been publicly questioned in that community since that day.

When he was near his end, in Hannibal, his friend, Rev. J. Lanius, then Presiding Elder of the Hannibal District, asked him if he would change his course in any material respect were it granted him to live his life over again. After a pause of some minutes he replied in effect: "There is only one particular in which I could wish to amend my ministry I have preached the true doctrine. I have defended it earnestly. I would change nothing. *But I would preach Christ more.*" Thus, at the gateway of eternity, did this earnest man see in a new light that to preach Christ is the one great business of the ministry At that moment he would, if possible, have put all of *self* out of every sermon he had preached and filled the place with Christ.

His friend Lanius, also, gave a dying word to the Church in Missouri, especially to the preachers, that ought never to pass out of mind. He died at Fayette soon after the adjournment of the Conference which met there in 1851, when Bewley had been with God five years. Bro. Lanius had often said he *feared death.* I have several times heard him make the statement in love feasts. He affirmed distinctly that he did not—he felt he did not—fear to go into the presence of God. He felt that his peace was made. He trusted the Son of God without any misgiving on that point. What he dreaded was "the *death struggle*—the pain, the agony, *in articulo mortis.*" These were his very words. Many now living will remember them.

His last illness *was* painful in the extreme. But the *last hours* were not. His body was at ease, his mind in peace. He knew that he was dying. His own conviction was confirmed by friends and by his physician. When the last doubt on the point was removed, and he knew that he was then actually dying, he called on a brother present to bear a message from him to the preachers of his Conference. "The preachers," he said, "have all heard me say that I feared death. I want you to tell them all for me, now that I know the fact, that it is *nothing for a Christian to die.*" He suffered no bodily pain, and his heart was full of that peace which the Savior gave to His disciples when He breathed on them and said, "Peace be unto you."

In point of fact, as attested by the history of Christian experience from the first, the disciples of Jesus do confront death without fear. That is, I mean, His true followers—those who have been born again and come to know in their own lives the "power of his resurrection."

Not unfrequently, while yet in the flush of health, they look forward to the hour of death with dread. I have known many who did so.

Death is a fact against nature. A natural repugnance to it is common with men. All feel it. Very earnest Christians often feel it. It is the voice of our nature that cries out against death—not our *sinful* nature, but our essential nature. That a mind in healthy tone, while yet life is flush, and all its relations happy and its endearments unembittered, should welcome death, is due to that God who caused the light to shine out of darkness, and who now, by the Spirit, shineth in our hearts, giving the light of the knowledge of the glory of God in the face of Jesus Christ. It is an astounding fact that evil in some of its deadliest forms has the power to crush out the love of life, so that the victim of it accepts death, in spite of the deep repugnance of nature to it, as a deliverer from something more dreadful than itself. So faith in Christ secures the manifestation of God in such a degree as to master the dread of death, deep-rooted as it is in the very essence of the soul. In this instance it is not one evil sought as a refuge from another felt to be greater. It is death consciously overcome by a higher life. The life of faith is realized to be so full in God that death is seen as a mere incident in the course of its progress and development, which operates, in fact, no check upon it. In the hand of the Prince of Life it has, indeed, been reduced to a place among the very agencies that perfect the man in the vital attributes that constitute him an heir of celestial destinies. Death is overcome.

Yet the full vision of truth which gives victory is not always realized in the midst of life and health. Many excellent persons are troubled with the fear of death, and troubled about themselves because they are not fully delivered from this fear. They infer a want of preparation for death from this fact. "If I were really a child of God, surely I should have no fear of death." I have known many very earnest Christians to be troubled and perplexed at this point.

A common answer, and the true one, is, that in full health we do not need dying grace. God gives the grace that is needed. What we have to do now is to *live*, not to die. For duties, trials, temptations, we need grace now. If we live right we will have it. When the hour comes, the faithful servant of God will have grace to die.

As a matter of fact and observation I have never known it to fail. Several notable instances have come under my own observation. Nervous women, who have held their own Christian character in doubt because they could never get the better of their fears, I have seen sweetly welcome the messenger when he came at last. *I have never known a consistent life to end in gloom.* Temptation sometimes prevails to a late hour, but the light springs up in the darkness before the spirit takes its flight. "Though I walk through the valley of the shadow of death I will fear no evil, for thou art with me; thy rod and thy staff they comfort me."

Surely a "cloud of witnesses" assures us of final triumph if we are faithful.

Mr. Caples' theory of death has been given in a former chapter. He held natural death to be a part of that condition into which the world was brought by the intervention of Christ after man fell, every element of which is made an agency of grace through Him. Suffering in this world is not punitive, but corrective. Physical death he saw to be a part of that discipline through which a faithful Creator is preparing His creatures for high ends. These views gave character to the sentiments he realized in contemplating the grave. Though an enemy, death was conquered and in chains—a slave, doing service that none else could do.

Yet "no chastening for the present seemeth to be joyous, but grievous." He did not trifle about death. It is a solemn necessity, welcome only in view of its relation to the Christian faith. But in this relation it is welcome—most welcome—as all pain is. It is welcome because it is a part of that "furnace-heat" which softens our hearts for the chisel of the Divine Artificer.

Pain's furnace heat within me quivers,
  God's breath upon the flame doth blow,
And all my heart in anguish shivers,
  And trembles at the fiery glow;
And yet I whisper, "as God will!"
And in the hottest fire hold still.

He comes and lays my heart, all heated,
  On the hard anvil, minded so
Into his own fair shape to beat it
  With his great hammer, blow on blow;
And yet I whisper, "as God will!"
And at the heaviest blows hold still.

He takes my softened heart and beats it—
  The sparks fly off at every blow;
He turns it o'er and o'er, and heats it,
  And lets it cool, and makes it glow;
And yet I whisper, "as God will!"
And in his mighty hand hold still.

Why should I murmur? for the sorrow
  Thus only longer lived would be;
Its end may come, and will to-morrow,
  When God has done his work in me.
So I say, trusting, "as God will!"
And trusting to the end, hold still.

He kindles, for my profit purely,
  Affliction's glowing fiery brand,
And all his heaviest blows are surely
  Inflicted by a Master hand.
So I say, praying, "as God will!"
And hope in Him, and suffer still.

The pain is fearful, but with the eye of faith upon the great end there is a sustaining power realized which makes it possible to say,

"Labor is rest, and pain is sweet,
  If Thou, my God, art here."

By the alchemy of faith every basest thing is transmuted. "Your sorrow shall be turned into joy." The sorrow does not give place to a joy which comes from another source, but is itself "*turned into joy.*" Even death becomes the condition of a higher, divine life. "Except a corn of wheat fall into ground and die, it abideth alone, but if it die it bringeth forth much fruit." Though this passage does not in its connection, as it stands in the sacred text, bear upon the question of natural death, yet it postulates a truth that covers the whole ground. Life is conditioned upon death. Caples saw all this, felt it, preached it. It affected his heart. It nerved him for the coming of the final hour. Not with the affected indifference of a stoic, not with the reckless despair of a desperate man, nor yet with the sullen acquiescence of a helpless victim, did he meet death, but with the cheerful courage of a Christian.

He had been in close quarters with the monster many times. He had often been under the same roof. His father died when he was a boy. Later his mother had fallen. He had grappled with the enemy still closer. His first wife had been taken into the captivity of the grave. The children of his body had gone into the dust. So many contests had he had with death, so many defeats had he suffered; yet ever with the consciousness of victory, for to him the defeat was partial, momentary, and to add to the trophies of the final triumph. He had even in his own person wrestled with death when all his friends were in despair. But he had been raised up.

In all these instances the sustaining faith of the Gospel had saved him from both terror and despair. More, it had given him a cheerful and self-possessed courage that diffused itself through the domestic circle and enheartened all who were around him His spirit diffused itself.

Toward the close of the war he felt himself at all times to be face to face with death. How he deported himself has been seen in a former chapter, and will be in the following.

From all I can learn he never flinched. He responded to the scowl of the enemy with a quiet, level eye.

Hope brightened in the shadows. What moment death should strike heaven would open. He was nearing home, and longings after immortality became more ardent. He would see the risen Lord. He would see father, mother, children, wife. He would see the Patriarchs, Prophets and Kings of the primeval Church. He would see the holy angels. He would be received into the holiest place. He would go in and out like one at home in the Palace of God.

Death threatened, but it only brought him near to the world where there will be *no more death.* The most fatal blow that he could strike would most effectually defeat himself.

Yet there *was* a reason for dreading death. He must leave a wife and little children, helpless and without resources, in the dreadful war times. How should they battle with the raging elements? Here was a test of faith, severer than his personal exposure. To be able to commit a tender wife and helpless children to God at such a time seems to me to be the very highest expression of inspired trust. But why not? Is any thing too sacred to be given up to God? And there are special promises to justify our fullest confidence.

There is an emphasis in the promises made to widowhood and orphanage scarcely to be found in any other. "A Father of the fatherless and a Judge of the widow is God in His holy habitation." Well may we commit our "fatherless children to Him."

We often note how unexpectedly well widowed mothers manage and secure their households against want. When human resources all seem wanting, every day, somehow, there is bread; she herself can scarce tell how. God *does* fulfill His promises.

So, even in this most dreadful aspect of his coming, Mr. Caples met death with composure and trust. He would not dishonor God by questioning even His care over an orphaned and widowed household, cast adrift on the tempestuous ocean of civil war.

At length the fatal blow descended. There was

no way of escape. The bony hand was on his very heart. He must die.

After long expectancy the fatal event came at a moment when it was not anticipated. It came in unexpected circumstances, and from an unlooked for source. So that much as he had been kept, by apparent dangers, on the watch, he was destined in the end to realize the truth of the Scripture, "At such an hour as ye think not, the Son of Man cometh." He had just then, when the fatal stroke came, a feeling of security that he had not known for months. The dread Reaper, who had been swinging his scythe in sight so long, had just now gone out of view. Before he knew it the bolt had fallen and he lay quivering under the foot of the destroyer. But he was ready. "He fell, but felt no fear." Wife, children, friends—all save himself— were in consternation. He lay at the gateway of eternity, calm, peaceful, happy He rested in God. "Though He slay me, yet will I trust Him." The shadow of the Almighty was over him, and the very darkness was a beneficent presence. It is ineffable, this·child-spirit, this feeling of the Father's arms around us in the dark, this resting in Almighty Love at midnight. Life culminates in such an hour. Where there is such faith, dying is *not dying*, but only falling asleep—falling asleep in the Father's arms. Our brother, helpless on the bed of death, knew how blessed it is just to sink into God—

> "To *feel*, although no tongue can prove,
> That every cloud which spreads above,
> And veileth love, *itself is love*."

Rev. J. D. Vincil, who was with Mr. Caples at the time of his death, and well informed with regard to the closing events of his life, has, at my request, prepared the following chapter.

CHAPTER XV.

LAST DAYS.

It will be remembered that Bro. Caples was appointed Presiding Elder of Brunswick District at the Conference session held in St. Charles, September, 1860. He was re-appointed to the same field at the Conference which met in Glasgow, September, 1861. Owing to the disturbed condition of the country the Conference did not assemble in 1862.

In the autumn of 1863 Bishop Kavanaugh made an appointment to hold a session of the Missouri Conference, but subsequently revoked it, for causes unknown to the writer. It was then generally supposed that there would be no meeting of Conference, as was the case the previous year. About that time Bros. Savage and Vandeventer addressed Bishop Kavanaugh, earnestly requesting him to make another appointment for the Conference to convene. The Bishop readily consented, and directed the brethren to assemble on

23

the 14th day of October, in Conference capacity, at the place chosen at their last meeting.

According to the authority and order of the Bishop, Conference assembled in Fulton, October 14, 1863. The fatal illness of Bishop Kavanaugh's wife prevented his attendance. Brother Monroe, being elected President, presided over the Conference deliberations quite satisfactorily. But it will derogate nothing from Bro. Monroe's character as a presiding officer in the Conference room and in the Cabinet to say that the ripe judgment, rare ability and varied experience of Wm. G. Caples contributed largely to facilitate business and appointments. It is due to truth and to his memory to say that he was *felt* more than any man in that Conference assemblage. He participated in the business and labors of the session much more actively than was his wont. He seemed to feel the necessity for a *leading* spirit in the body, and most worthily did he meet the wants of the hour And it will be regarded by those present at that session as no disparagement to other ministers to say that he did THE preaching of the occasion. Two sermons will long live in the memory of those who heard him.

The Synod of the Old School Presbyterian Church was in session in Fulton at the time of our Conference. Rev. Dr. Farris, of that Church, present editor of the *Old School Presbyterian*, was attending the Synod. On Sabbath morning he attended service at the Methodist Church to hear his cherished friend and brother, Caples. The sermon was on the text, "What think ye of Christ?" Dr. Farris, seated in the pulpit with the preacher, was a delighted and deeply interested listener. On no former occasion was Brother Caples more fully master of the subject. The sermon was characteristic. An analysis or outline is not admissible here. But it was a grand vindication of the Divinity of "Jesus, the Christ."

On Monday afternoon of the session, "according to the dying request of Bro. Robt. C. Hatton, late a member of our Conference, his funeral was preached by his friend, Rev. William G. Caples. The occasion will never be forgotten by those who were privileged to hear the discourse." So said the committee in their memoir of Rev. R. C. Hatton. Surely the *sermon* "will never be forgotten" by many who heard it. And the glory that was revealed will never fade from the minds of those who realized the power of the Highest on that ever-memorable evening. In his peroration the mightiest powers of Caples' great soul were unchained, when he rose, in grandest moods, far above anything remembered in the most glowing efforts of his life. The contrast drawn between Hatton as seen when taken from a Federal prison to die, and as seen amid the glories of the upper sanctuary, was singularly grand and powerful.

Said he: "Could the sainted soul of Hatton, all dripping with glory, walk into this sanctuary to-day and speak to the Conference he loved so well from the blissful *experience* of heaven, he would say, your 'light afflictions, which are but for a moment, shall work for you a far more exceeding and eternal weight of glory.'" The manner and matter of his peroration produced an effect rarely ever witnessed in these days. To describe accurately the scenes of that evening is simply impossible. It was *heaven* realized in mighty power on earth. Little thought those present then that in one year Caples and Hatton would be together, sharing that "eternal weight of glory," an earnest of which was then enjoyed by so many brethren beloved.

On the 20th of October Conference closed its labors, when Bro. Caples was appointed to Glasgow Station. He moved there from his farm, near Brunswick, in November, and took charge of the Church. That he was, as ever before, a most acceptable preacher to the great majority of the people in that community is a truth too well known to admit of doubt or require proof. And yet, in some respects, that was not the most pleasant year of his life. A few persons in the Church, being controlled by strong political feeling more than by that charity which "thinketh no evil," in connection with the military authorities, caused him no little trouble and annoyance. It was a year of trial to his lofty spirit. Aside from the deep and prolonged affliction of his wife, which produced constant anxiety and apprehension in his mind, there were many other external surroundings of a character calculated to render his condition most unpleasant. A spirit of fierce opposition, of deep dislike, and of petty persecution, existed among his enemies. He had the manliness to *think* for himself, independent of the dictates of partisan behests. That was a crime then with the ruling power not to be tolerated. The feeling of hate shown in acts of the most infamous kind against such a man typed the bitterness of the times and the ascendency of passion. The various methods employed to annoy him need not be mentioned here. Let such things and their authors be forgotten rather than honored with the perpetuity of history. Having passed through that eventful and trying year in Glasgow, he closed his labors and repaired to Conference, which convened in Mexico, September 14, 1864, the last he ever attended. The brethren assembled in Mexico, and on the morning of the 14th September gathered at the church to begin their Conference labors. The business of the session was peremptorily forbidden, as well as any organization, un-

less the members would severally take and sub-
scribe an oath of loyalty as a condition precedent.
The demand was made by the Provost-Marshal
of the Military Sub-District.   When his military
highness, Corporal Gannet, Provost-Marshal afore-
said, made his demand in person, the brethren
quietly dispersed.   They resolved not to conform
to *any* requirement of a political or military character as a qualification to sit in a court of Christ.
Bro. Caples was looked to for advice in the matter.
His counsel was wise and prudent.   He suggested
that an organization of the Conference for business should be deferred until a " greater than "
Gannet would interfere, and that in the meantime
the brethren give themselves to prayer.   The
Provost-Marshal General of Missouri, being informed of the pert doings of his subordinate,
issued an order to Corporal Gannet directing him
to present no such test, but " allow the Confer
ence to organize and proceed with business.'
Mr. Gannet and our enemies, whom he was serv·
ing, having been defeated in their bad designs to
prevent our session being held, we joyfully assem
bled on Friday morning, the 16th, when Brother
Caples opened the *nineteenth* session of the Missouri Annual Conference with the customary religious services.   In the absence of Bishop Kavanaugh, the Conference elected Andrew Monroe
President   Brother Caples was appointed on two

most important committees at this session. He was chairman of the committees on Education and on Books and Periodicals. The report on Educacation rendered by him was of a high order, and well deserves to be preserved by the Conference as the last document ever produced by the strong mind of Caples. Its introduction here, however, is not deemed advisable, as it would swell this chapter to undue proportions.

During this session the preaching of Caples was very superior. On Sabbath morning he filled the Presbyterian pulpit, and discoursed to a vast audience from the words of Christ uttered in presence of Pilate: "My kingdom is not of this world." The sermon was strong, original and powerful, and withal most remarkably *appropriate* to the times and circumstances in which we were placed.

A few years since a living writer and preacher treated the Church and the world to a *lecture* on the above mentioned text. It was regarded by those who heard its delivery as a finished and masterly production. Its publication was earnestly called for, and it appeared in print. While reading it the writer did not wonder at the impression produced on the congregation by the lecture, because it was the sermon of Bishop D. S. Doggett, found in the Southern Methodist pulpit, preached by that scholarly divine on the text:

"My kingdom is not of this world." With Dr. Doggett the sermon, "Christ and Pilate," was *original*. With the lecturer, the production was *plagiarized*.

When Caples preached on the text, "My kingdom is not of this world," the sermon was peculiarly his own, and original. An outline of the sermon was sketched at the time of its delivery and is now in possession of the writer.

"The chief points distinguishing the kingdom of Jesus Christ are: 1. SPIRITUALITY. 2. UNIVERSALITY. 3. UNITY."

The kingdom of Christ is *Spiritual*, "not of this world." *Universal*, open to *all* mankind as its subjects. Its *unity*, or *oneness*, is seen in that it admits *all* to its *privileges*, and to EQUAL privileges, *all* being the *children* of GOD by faith in Jesus Christ.

The sermon was delivered "in demonstration of the spirit and of power." The effect was deep, and doubtless lasting. It will be remembered by some who heard it as the last they ever listened to from the beloved Caples.

He preached one other discourse during the sitting of Conference. On Monday the committee superintending public worship, through their chairman, the lamented Edwin Robinson, made the following announcement: "Preaching to-night by Bro. Caples, at the request of the *outsiders*." To the "outsiders" he did preach. And such a sermon! Who has forgotten the mighty appeals of that solemn hour? May the seed sown that evening yield an hundredfold.

The Conference adjourned on Tuesday P. M., but many of the preachers could not leave until the morrow, for want of a train west. At night a sermon was preached by one of the brethren on the Priesthood and Mediation of Christ, and followed by an exhortation from Caples. The theme was Caples' glory and delight. How glowing the faith and enraptured the soul of the speaker while following our "Great High Priest" as he "passed into the heavens." 'Twas then he uttered those sublime words: "Take away my life and in a few moments I will raise a shout on the other shore that will astonish the angels." The closing prayer offered by him that evening will be treasured as a precious memento by many who heard his voice for the last time on earth. He bore to the Divine Throne his brethren beloved of the Conference, " whose faces we may see no more in the flesh." How sadly prophetic those words! Ere another gathering of the Conference three of those present that night had "passed into the heavens" and met on "the other shore," to raise "a shout" unheard among "the angels" before. A Caples, a Robinson, and a Young were called hence to be with Christ.

Brother Caples was re-appointed to Glasgow Station, and returned to his work at once, reaching home on Thursday, the 22d day of September.

The following Sabbath his pulpit was occupied, morning and evening, by the writer, so that he did not preach. The succeeding Sabbath, the same visiting brother being in town, found Bro. Caples quite indisposed, but did not occupy his pulpit, having promised to preach for the Presbyterian congregation. Bro. Caples preached his last sermon that morning. His indisposition increased so as to prevent the occupancy of the pulpit at night, which was filled by his friend and brother, who was still on a visit there. This was the 2d day of October. This brother minister visiting Glasgow was with him from the assembling of Conference at Mexico until he passed away During this last week of his life they were together every day. Many cherished interviews are remembered, and will be ever. We were in the midst of perilous times. Military despotism reigned supreme. Southern men, or men suspected of Southern sympathies, were marked and evil was determined on concerning them The more prominent the man, the greater the injury sought to be done him. Hence, Caples was a conspicuous target for malevolence to shoot at. While he was a man of undissembled Southern feelings, yet no more quiet and law-abiding citizen lived in the

land. But this was not sufficient. He must yield
convictions of right and give up principles or
suffer. The former Caples never did. The latter
he was prepared to do. At that time lawless
bands—marauders or bushwhackers, as they were
styled—were roaming through the country, perpe-
trating many outrages upon peaceable citizens.
As to the soldiery of the land, they and the bushwhackers were not on terms sufficiently good to
come in sight of each other when it could be easily
avoided. An intimate acquaintance or personal
interview was not desirable. Hence, when the
bushwhackers would make a raid on the telegraph lines and cut the wires, citizens instead of
soldiers were detailed to repair the damages.
The danger attending the performance of such
work was evidently very great, as those engaged
were liable to be attacked and shot down at any
time by the bushwhackers. Brother Caples was
sent on such duty by military authority, at the
instance of *citizens* of Glasgow, who had formerly
professed great friendship and admiration for him.
There is not an existing doubt but those who
offered him such indignities expected and desired
that Caples would fall by the hands of those who
were raiding through the country, preying alike
upon Union and Southern people. The joy of
such, had he met the fate they hoped for, would
have been akin to that secret satisfaction felt by

them when he fell by a stray shot from Confederate cannon.

On Saturday morning, October 8, 1864, at early dawn, the thunder of artillery broke in startling peals upon the ears of the citizens and soldiery of Glasgow. Many were awakened from their morning slumbers by the roar of cannon which opened fire on the town from the opposite side of the river, manned by "Shelby's" command. Some awoke that morning from their last sleep, until the grave became their bed. Some were aroused from peaceful slumbers to fall suddenly by the hand of war to rise no more, others to fall wounded, to linger amid sufferings, and to die by degrees. Amongst the latter was our own beloved Caples. When the Confederates began their cannonade many of the people of Glasgow fled the town. Perhaps all left who could do so with any safety, and those who did leave were certainly very much exposed. Shells came screaming and screeching across the river, falling here and there, endangering the lives of non-combatants more than those at whom the fire was supposed to be directed. At times shot as well as shell fell in unwelcome proximity to men, women and children, who,

"Hurrying to and fro in hot haste,"

sought to find asylum from the frightful storm of death-dealing missiles which hurtled over the devoted town. Scarcely had the flying fugitives reached the suburbs of the town and gotten out of danger from the fire on the opposite side of the river, until they were surrounded by Clark's Division of cavalry that swept around from another point. This command had crossed the river below Glasgow some miles and marched up on the same side of the town. When at a proper distance Clark's artillery opened fire upon the Federal camp, which was stationed near the outskirts of the town. The Federal soldiers hurriedly left camp and retreated to their intrenchments on an eminence near the center of Glasgow. The Confederate forces moved forward to an advanced position, and, with artillery and small arms, opened a heavy fire. Thus Glasgow was between *two* fires, Shelby's command thundering from the West side (*across* the river), and Clark's Division completely belting the place on the town side with a cordon of men. The artillery from both commands played upon the place in merciless fury. Shot and shell went crashing through the town with ill-directed aim, striking houses and tearing up the private residences of citizens. What they were firing *for*, or *at*, in many instances, is a question more easily asked than answered.

What were the conflicting and painful emotions of the people of Glasgow during those terrible hours may be imagined faintly, but described never. To fly was next to impossible. To remain was attended with imminent peril. Thus forced to stay amid such scenes as unwilling spectators of a fearful drama was a trial none will ever forget or desire to endure again. Added to the surging storm of battle raging in their midst was another appalling calamity. The fire·demon was turned loose by order of a miscreant who, reckless of consequences, applied the torch to the City Hall. Soon the flames communicated to other buildings and the surges of destruction rolled on, carrying away the homes and fortunes of many. Family residences, churches, public buildings and business houses alike melted before the fiery destroyer as he stormed over the fairest and best portion of the city The scenes and events of that terrible day linger with fearful distinctness in the memory of those who were so unhappily situated. Sad and gloomy were the hours as deep uncertainty hung over the fates of loved friends who were prisoned within the war-desolated city To those who fled when the first alarm was given the anxious inquiry occurred time and again through the day, "Who has fallen?" While waiting to hear from town, as we lingered in the vicinity, fearful was the suspense respecting many exposed to the perils of the battle. At last intelligence came of the surrender, and with it the most sorrowful tidings to be met with in a lifetime: "Bro.

Caples is mortally wounded." Hurrying to town
we found that the news was fearfully true. He
was shockingly injured, and was suffering unutterable agony It was during the early part of
the day that this most sad calamity took place. It
occurred in this wise: When the cannonade from
the west side of the river began — by Shelby's
command—Bro. Caples and family descended to
the *basement* of the parsonage for safety They
were joined by a near neighbor, Dr. Cropp and
family, and all together found a safe refuge in the
dining-room. The basement wall was stone, and
served as a protection against war missiles. The
west end of the basement wall was protected by
a heavy embankment, where the cellar had been
dug, so that in that part of their retreat there was
complete immunity from danger. Had Brother
Caples remained within doors the misfortune here
recorded had not befallen him. At what precise
hour of the morning this fatal disaster occurred
is not now remembered. But while the parties
named were occupying the dining-room in the
basement, Bro. Caples ventured out of their retreat
on to the pavement fronting the parsonage basement. From the pavement a stairway ascends
to the porch and to the rooms above. When he
stepped out of the basement room to the pavement, the stairway was between him and the
river. He evidently advanced so far on the pave-

ment as to be able to look around the stairway in the direction of the rebel battery. This was shown by the range of the shot which felled him. Fatal look! While standing thus a cannon from the opposite side of the river was fired, it is supposed, at the Federals in the City Hall. The gunner carelessly or awkwardly aimed his gun, and the shell missed the hall. Passing on northeast it took the parsonage in its range and went crashing through the stairway behind which Bro. Caples was standing. From the manner in which the ball struck him he must have been leaning forward, the weight of the body thrown upon the left leg, which was in advance of the other, the head inclined to the right, looking around the stairway toward the artillery. In that attitude he was stricken by a shell of probably twelve pounds. The ball, on passing through the stairway, struck the studding and carried off a heavy sliver or splinter of several inches in length. This was driven with fearful force against the side of his leg above the knee, making an ugly wound, laying bare the flesh to the bone. At the same instant the shell struck the thigh, at the most fleshy part, a few inches above the other wound. While the flesh was fearfully torn, yet the bone was not broken. The wound was of the most ghastly kind, and the shock to the nervous system was terrible, from which it never recovered. The

physicians said reaction never fully returned.
Thus in a moment was stricken down the great
and noble Caples, to rise no more. Amid sufferings unutterable he was finally—so soon as help
could be procured—borne up to his room. As
soon as dangers permitted several physicians were
called, and all was done that human power could
do to alleviate the deep agony that was riving that
once powerful frame. From Saturday morning
till Tuesday night there was seen in his case the
mightiness of suffering. But it was all *physical.*
When not under the influence of powerful opiates
his mind was not only clear, but calm and in sweet
repose. At no time did the writer hear him utter
a murmur. Scarcely an exclamation of pain
escaped his lips. There was a quiet *grandeur*
and almost massive self-possession in his bearing
throughout, softened by a gentleness and sweet-
ness of spirit that told the greatness of his soul
and the triumph of faith. Being with him from
Saturday to the closing scene, the writer knows
whereof he affirms. The faith of years and the
principles of a grand ministry shone out in hallowed beauty as he neared the shadowy vale.
To the closing of that grand life attention is now
invited. It is needless to say that "hope, which
comes to all," cheered our tortured hearts, even
while we greatly feared and apprehended the
worst But on Tuesday, the 11th of October, hope

24

died out of our hearts, and we felt that his end was close at hand. Loving and deeply devoted friends were around him. At times during the afternoon drowsiness overcame him, and it was with an effort that he could converse. Singing was proposed, when a few faltering voices joined in singing:

"On Jordan's stormy banks I stand."

We felt ourselves singing for *him* a final song, who had often sung for us, and cheered the Israel of God in the weary journey he was now completing. We sang amid tears. When the song was commenced he roused himself from the gathering stupor, and with beaming face smiled his pleasure and joy The writer then approached him and said: "Bro. Caples, shall we pray?" "Yes, pray, Bro. Vincil," was his calm response. We all, in deep solemnity, knelt around his bed to weep and pray with him, whose prayers had so often blessed and gladdened our hearts. The plea of the "sisters" of Lazarus was urged with sinking hearts: "Lord, behold, he whom thou lovest is sick." Oh! *could* the friend of those loving sisters have consistently interposed in behalf of *our* dying Caples, surely the prayers of that evening, with the "cries and tears" of the grief-crushed wife and children, would have brought him nigh— "our *brother* had not died."

Bro. Caples engaged earnestly in the devotions, and responded audibly and frequently during prayer. When we arose his face bore that calm, sweet and happy expression which told of the deep peace and holy serenity dwelling within. Knowing his fondness for a certain hymn, the writer sang it for him to a tune which he always enjoyed. Eighteen months before, while he and the writer were laboring together in Glasgow Station, we sang the same song for him to the tune of "Summer," which was then new He became exceedingly happy, and rejoiced with demonstrations rather uncommon for him—going through the congregation shouting the praises of God. Ever after he was delighted with the song:

> "I would not live alway, I ask not to stay,
> When storm after storm rises dark o'er the way."

When we had concluded the prayer, wishing to cheer his last hours with the inspirations of sacred song, we all united in singing the last strains he ever heard till the music of the heavenly songsters broke upon his ear. While we sang his face brightened into a glowing radiance, reminding us of the countenance of Stephen in the council when he preached his last sermon. Bro. Caples attempted to join in the melody that was bearing his soul up to the place "where the saints of all ages in harmony meet." He was too weak, however, to sing, but *repeated* the *words* with deep feeling. When the song was ended the following conversation passed between him and the writer:

"Bro. Caples, we fear we are soon to lose you. Much as we love you we feel that we must give you up. Tell us how stands the case with you now, in view of your approaching end?" With the most settled composure and sweet serenity he replied: "My brother, my race is about run— suddenly cut short. I have unexpectedly reached the end. *'I shall soon be on the other shore.'*" These words occurred in that sublime sentence uttered by him at Conference in Mexico, *three* weeks before that very evening: "Take away my life and I will raise a shout on the other shore that will astonish the angels." How near we all felt he was to "the other shore" in this last conversation! Realizing that a few more pulsings of that noble heart would land him among the angels, we desired his final expressions to cherish as sweet mementos in the future.

"Bro. Caples, when we meet again at Conference you will not be with us. We will miss you. What message have you to send to your brethren?" Rallying his sinking energies he replied with much feeling: "Tell my brethren, from me, to cleave unto their work." Oh! the depth of meaning that was in those words, as we listened to them coming from lips soon to close forever. So earnestly, calmly and deliberately uttered, as a last admonition to the brethren he loved. Would that they sounded ever in our ears.

Seeing that he was much exhausted from the protracted interview, we inquired: "Bro. Caples, can you still say that 'all is well?'" "Ah! yes," said he, "all *is* well, and has been for many years. Long ago this matter was settled. I have lived for this. Though suddenly grown weary in the journey, I will soon be at rest."

With this our conversation ceased, and he soon relapsed into a quiet slumber, in which he continued until after nightfall. Between seven and eight o'clock he roused up and spoke quite audibly He said: "I have been sleeping." "Yes, you have been resting quietly for some time. How do you feel now, Bro. C.?" "Easy, but weary," said he. "Give me some water." It was given him, and he drank a little, remarking, "I swallow badly." It was with difficulty that he drank the water. After a few moments he remarked to the writer: "Brother Vincil, I am weary lying in one position so long; please turn me a little on my left side." He had lain on his back from the first. We tenderly moved him as desired. In that position he remained but a minute. His breathing became labored upon his left side, and we assisted him to turn upon his back again. Then it was we saw the *last* struggle commence, so soon to terminate. Then it was his great, lustrous eyes shone, as thousands had seen them shine, with the fires immortal that burned within his soul when swayed by the mighty truths to which he gave utterance. Then it was that his always expressive, speaking countenance beamed with glory, kindled intelligence and expression unwitnessed before. Then, with eyes upturned and filled with light unearthly, he raised his hands and waved them gently; looking and pointing upward, he exclaimed in full, rich tones: "I feel that I am going, going." It was painfully evident that he *was* "going" fast, and no power here could detain him. Oh! the sad scenes of that death chamber! There stood the agonized and deeply loved wife of his heart plunged in sorrow unsyllabled. There were the children of his love, weeping—some at the great and gathering gloom overshadowing their young lives, some unable to comprehend or know their loss. There were friends, tried and true, sorrowing most of all that we should see his face no more. Oh! cruel death! what hast thou not done? From all these dear ones he was going. Realizing that to live was Christ, to *die* was *gain*, he fixed his eyes upon the "eternal weight of glory" in view Oh! who can paint the scenes that passed before his mind then! For the moment he lost sight of wife, and children, and loved friends, in the enrapturing glories of the breaking future. Standing there, on the outer limits of mortality, he gazed with brightening vision upon the scenes of beauty which swelled across the fields of view like a sea of golden glory,

> " Where the rivers of pleasure flow o'er the bright plains,
> And the noontide of glory eternally reigns."

He must have caught a glimpse of the heavenly rest and heard entrancing melody from "the other shore, for while he swept his eye around and upward he uttered his final words of victory on earth: "Oh! what I am gaining, gaining, gaining." With the last note of triumph, feebly yet distinctly spoken, his hands fell powerless, his eyes closed, a convulsive shudder shook his frame, and in a *very* short time the great soul of Caples was gone, doubtless, to "the other shore." Our loss—how keenly felt—was his *gain*. In the loneliness of "that stilly night" the writer sat and gazed up among the stars, thinking of the *path*—swept by angels' wings—our dear Caples, on spirit pinion, had traveled to "the other shore." There, amid silence so deep that it was painful, with upturned ear, I listened to hear the song and shout of Caples among the angels. What I *heard* not I imagined, as "the newly arrived" took high rank among the intelligences of the heavenly company and gave a deeper swell to the anthems of the redeemed. Farewell, dear Bro. Caples! Earth has been sad and lone since thy departure. But oft in dreams thou art with me still.   Farewell, loved friend, thou art gone,

> But my heart is turning ever
>   Where thou dost happy dwell;
> And in thy blissful home we'll never,
>   Never again say farewell.

On the day following his decease (the 12th) we carried his remains to Brunswick.   On Thursday, the 13th day of October, A. D. 1864, all that was mortal of Wm. G. Caples was laid away to sleep beside his loved daughter, "Lottie," and his former wife.

CHAPTER XVI.

___

"THY DEAD MEN SHALL LIVE."

The doctrine of the immortality of the soul was among men in the earliest ages. It was not set in that clear light in which it stands in the Christian Scriptures, but the most ancient mythology as well as the oldest and crudest philosophy contained it. In all ages men have believed that they would survive death. The rudest savage casts his eye forward to a mysterious life to be enjoyed beyond the grave.

But with the ambitious Greek and Roman immortality was often looked for in fame. To make a name that should not perish out of the records of men, to play a part in human affairs that should be historic, seems sometimes to have appeared more real to them than any actual life of the soul in the world to come. Hope looked forward to that rather than this. Their perception of spiritual truth was dim. A name still living among men upon the earth was a fact fully in their vision. The soul living among the immortals in an invisible world seemed shadowy and unreal. It was not sufficiently within the range of vision to be an actuating fact—to be the source of motives or give color to expectation. Yet the instinct of immortality was strong, and looked to the airy shadow of an imperishable name. It *must* look to something, and to the depraved imagination of an ambitious heathen, fame was a fact more evident than any spiritual essence to rise out of the ruins of death and live forever.

How grand is the Christian conception in contrast with this! To us the living soul is everything, a living name nothing. To live with God and in the company of holy angels is a fact, to live in fame is the most miserable fiction. Life and immortality have been brought into the light—into clear disclosure—by our Lord Jesus Christ. We stand upon the boundary of a world more real than this. Death but introduces us into life.

"The life everlasting" was no remote, unreal thing to him whose name is commemorated in these pages. Little thought he of any posthumous reputation. This book, "The Life of Caples," however humble in pretension, was never thought of by him. If it had been it would have offered a miserable substitute for the immortality on which his eye was fixed. He knew that he would enter upon a course of celestial activity and achievement and realize life in a fullness of conscious power and pleasure beyond the highest possibilities of earthly imagination. Any laudation of him by us dwellers in the dust, if he had anticipated it, would have seemed most trivial.

The love of applause, indeed, is innate in us, and Mr. Caples shared it with all other men. But he rated it at its true price. It would have been impossible, with his clear vision of eternity and of God, to see in it an object of high import or a substitute of personal, actual immortality

But there is a fact within the vision of faith that was wholly unknown to the ancients. The fact of the *resurrection of the dead* is found in the Christian revelation alone. Of it the heathen. knew nothing. It is hinted, and little more than hinted, in the Jewish Scriptures, and that in later periods of prophetic inspiration. To this last statement one passage in the Book of Job forms the solitary exception. "In my flesh shall I see God," and this after worms should have destroyed his body No affirmation could be more definite or unequivocal. But it is by no means a prominent feature of the Old Testament writings. The New Testament is full of it. It appears both in the Gospels and in the Epistles. The Son of God proclaimed Himself "the Resurrection and the Life." Coming up Himself out of the grave, He became "the first fruits of them that slept." His

resurrection is the prophesy and promise of ours
He will bring "His people with Him."

The fact of the resurrection is brought more
distinctly to our thought and faith by the resurrection of the Lord than it could have been in any
other way It is represented to us by a great
event of history. This one instance of it stands
in the past. Not in any mythical past, but in a
period and amid events distinctly, eminently his-
torical. It is actually under observation. Nothing could be more imposing, more impressive.
"The third day He rose again." So all the dead
shall rise.

There is an astounding tendency to perverse
thinking on the subject of religion. One form in
which this tendency discovers itself is, a disposition to subject the Holy Scriptures to a sophistical
species of interpretation, and thus get rid of their
plainest declarations. This is done by men who
profess to accept the Bible as the authoritative
disclosure of Divine truth. There is a strong disposition in man to make his own mental predilec-
tions the standard of truth. Even when he formally
admits the incapacity of his own mind to reach
the truths of religion by its own intuitions, or by
any process of rational induction, and professes to
make the Word of God the standard, he will destroy all reliance on that Word and virtually set
aside its authority by the most perverse interpre-

tations in cases where his preconceptions are contradicted by it. If he take it into his head that there ought to be no hell he will stickle at no absurd exegesis to put it out of the sacred text. So if he gets the notion that a final Judgment Day is not the best arrangement, or that slaveholding must be wicked, he will make any havoc of language in order to force Scripture to say what he thinks it ought to say

Nothing could be more clearly put in human language than the doctrine of the resurrection of the body is in the Bible. Any species of interpretation that will get rid of it will unsettle the meaning of language and leave us uncertain of anything that may come to us through this medium. If this fact is not in the Scriptures, then all speech is deceptive and the attempt to put facts into any form of words is mere folly and child's play. Yet you will find men who take the Bible as containing the matter of their religious beliefs flatly denying the fact of the resurrection of the body. They will contend that nothing more is taught in Scripture than the immortality of the soul; that the resurrection is predicated of the soul and not of the body, and this in the face of St. Paul's affirmation of the body: "It is sown in corruption, it is raised in incorruption;" and of the formal declaration that our "vile bodies shall be raised and fashioned like unto Christ's glorious body."

The resurrection of Christ, which pledges and types the resurrection of men, was a resurrection of the body. Indeed, to predicate this great fact of the soul is an absurdity of language, for the soul does not die: it just lives on when the body dies. But the very word *resurrection* means *living again.* The *dead* are *raised up.*

To all doubts and perplexities as to the possibility of the fact, the triumphant interrogatory affirmation of the apostle is a final and sufficient answer: "*Why should it be thought a thing incredible with you that* God should raise the dead?" If some metaphysical·wiseacre could have been in existence before any world was made the fact of creation would have seemed impossible to him. But since the power and wisdom of God have appeared in this first stupendous miracle, it is absurd to question the possibility of any work He has promised to perform. The only question is as to whether He has promised to raise the dead. Indeed, this is not a question, for if language means anything, if speech was not invented to deceive, we have the pledge of our Creator that our bodies shall be brought forth in the last day immortal. "For the trumpet shall sound and the dead shall be raised, incorruptible."

"But some man will say, how are the dead raised up, and with what body do they come? Thou fool, that which thou sowest is not quickened except it die; and that which thou sowest, thou sowest not that body that shall be, but bare grain; it may chance of wheat, or of some other grain; but God giveth it a body as it hath pleased Him, and to every seed his own body " " It is sown a natural body, it is raised a spiritual body. There is a natural body, and there is a spiritual body "

I have met with men who affected an elevation from which they looked down with contempt on all material things. Their hope contemplated a pure spiritual existence in eternity They had no affection for their bodies, no desire to recover them out of the domain of the destroyer. The grossness of matter was odious to them. It was too heavy, too clumsy, a mere embarrassment of spiritual activities. It was the occasion, if not the very source, of all corruptions. The resurrection of the body was not a thing to be desired.

Alas! for poor human reason, how it will rattle away when it gets fairly a-going with some proud, foolish conceit, as if it knew everything, and as if God could not choose our conditions for us with infinitely more wisdom than we can for ourselves. No doubt the ideal man is given in the duplex nature with which he was created. The spiritual essence finds its appropriate vehicle and expression in physical organs. Nor is matter necessarily so very gross and clumsy. It often exists in highly sublimated forms. Take the electric fluid as an example. May not some such sublimated form of matter compose the substance of the resurrection-body? May it not have been this which the apostle referred to in that statement: "There is a natural body and there is a spiritual body;" a body so refined as to be in some close affinity with spiritual substances.

We may very well believe that a body thus constituted would be a fit habitation of the immortal soul, for several reasons:

First, we may well believe it to be so subtle and vital as to be independent of accidents, and to have power of self-preservation against all violence. We may well believe that such a substance, vitalized by a spiritual occupant, will have a power of rejuvenescence which will insure immortality

Secondly, we know that matter in highly sublimated conditions is capable of an activity and force unknown in grosser forms. This is seen, for instance, in electrical phenomena. What a vehicle of spiritual activities would a body formed of some such substance be? Only think of it! What work might not be accomplished by some potent spirit in such a body?

Thirdly, it is altogether rational to suppose that matter in such forms, vitalized, would be sensitive and responsive to spiritual touches in the highest degree. What movements might not be anticipated from the power of volition delivered upon such a body? The momentum of a simple wish might transport it from one world to another in a moment of time. What explorations of space will be practicable then!

Fourthly, how *vital* a body thus constituted must be when brought into identity with a soul! Even our gross bodies now are full of life. There is power in the soul to quicken them consciously in every part, to every extremity But one constituted as we have supposed, so susceptible of spiritual touches, so receptive of spiritual communication, must be inexpressibly vital. There can be no languor, no stupor, no stupidity Activity will bring no fatigue. Sensation, secured against abnormal conditions, will suffuse each member and muscle with pleasurable consciousness. From bone to epidermis, every organ and every membrane will be replete with the joy of life.

Fifthly, such a body must be a transparent medium of spiritual expression Even the coarse stuff of which we are now made is capable of miracles of expression. The soul sometimes floods the face with its own light. The eye gives most subtle and varied reflection of thought and sentiment and passion. From the gentlest ripple of reverie to the grandest swell of thought, from the quiet sense of complacency to the fervor of

25

unbounded love, from the shadow of a half-felt repugnance to the fury of unbridled revenge, what myriad complexities and shades of the inner life come into the light of revealment in this organ. Even the attitudes of the body, the step, the placement of a limb, the set of the head, may indicate the state of the mind or character of the man. How much more when in the resurrection the material structure shall be so nearly assimilated to spirit! How transparent to spirit-light it may be!

The body of the Lord when he was incarnate was formed as ours are now. But in the transfiguration his countenance became as the sun, and so did the inner effulgence shine through all the flesh that his very garment became "exceedingly white, so as no fuller could whiten it." It was radiantly white—"white as snow," as the new-fallen virgin snow glowing under the glare of the sun. After His resurrection, inspired speech labored in vain to intimate the glories of His person in the first chapter of the Apocalypse. "Like unto His glorious body" shall ours be fashioned,

> "And every shape and every face
> Be heavenly and divine."

We shall be thus greatly changed in the resurrection. Yet shall each one be himself, and form and feature and expression, though raised to heavenly beauty, will be the same essentially as now. Even in this life we have witnessed something of the same. How different a face in repose, and the same in the rapture of some moment of supreme joy! Yet it is the very same face. Identification is easy I have seen some men almost transfigured in the pulpit. I have seen Caples so. He was the *very* same, yet how changed! Even in the Transfiguration the disciples knew the Lord. They did not for a moment confound Him with Moses or Elias

I have a theory that every human form and face are cast upon some type of beauty. Even the adjustment and set of the features in each case are upon a perfect model. In many instances the ideal is far from being realized. Perhaps it is fully realized in none. The depravities of our present state have made sad work with many forms and faces. But we are "waiting for the redemption of the body " When that shall come each one shall reach the exact ideal of the Creator. The change will not be radical. We will be surprised to find what slight variation of the lines of the face will bring the ugliest into perfect beauty— realizing the ideal of its type.

Beauty is more in expression than in feature. An exalted soul coming into expression in the plainest face redeems it. I have often seen this. Some notable instances are in my mind as I write. They are hints to me. They intimate the miracles of beauty that will be realized in the bodies of the saints after they are rescued from all the consequences of sin, made "spiritual bodies," and modeled upon the glorious form of our risen Lord.

Mr. Caples lived in the hope of the resurrection of the dead. When his father died, and his mother, he expected to see those venerated faces again. When he surrendered a wife, and the very children of his body, to the dishonors of death, it was with the assurance that they would be triumphantly brought forth again at last by the Captain of our Salvation. In those dreadful days when his own mangled body was sinking down into death the same hope cheered and consoled him. And now, a disembodied spirit in the highest glory that a disembodied spirit is capable of, he

> "Longs perfection to inherit,
> And to triumph in the flesh."

He watches "the sleeping embers" until they "shall rise and live anew" For certainly the consummation of the work of Christ is not reached short of the resurrection. The dead in Christ are happy now. They go to Him at once. Exactly what their state is we can not know. How the faculties may find exercise in the absence of the physical organs created to be their instruments, we can learn only by our own experience after death. But that it is an imperfect state, though a happy one, seems certain. The faculties are not in full power and play Perhaps the blessedness enjoyed before the resurrection is found largely in *repose.* "They *rest* from their labors." The state of the righteous dead, before the resurrection, is called *sleep.* "They that sleep in Jesus shall God bring with Him" in the last day. There is sufficient intimation of the fact that they are not wholly unconscious. They live. They are in ineffable peace. But it seems probable, at least, if not certain, that the great pursuits of eternity will not be fairly entered upon until after the resurrection and the Judgment Day. Then the spirit, restored to the conditions for which it was created, furnished again with proper organs of communication and action, in a body perfected by divine skill and power, will realize the sublime ideal of the Creator and start forth to achieve and enjoy what God intended.

What part such a man as Caples may then perform, what fruition of former labor done in time he may then enjoy, we will see if we are faithful. With what power he may deliver himself upon the forces of that high condition, how far he may give shape and type to the celestial phenomena surrounding him, we must wait to know. I make no doubt that I shall see him moving forward upon a magnificent course of destiny, pursuing plans and working upon methods that will require eternity for their consummation, and be great among the grandeurs of the City of God.

My conceptions of the heavenly state have been greatly modified since I commenced the Christian course. Then the poetic descriptions of the Apocalypse constituted the medium through which I viewed it. The physical features of heaven predominated. The walls, great and high; the Throne; the sea of glass; the streets, paved with gold; the river of life, flowing through groves of the tree of life; the music, like the sound of many waters; the heavenly inhabitants, clothed in fine linen, clean and white—these constituted at that time the staple of thought in contemplating the future home of the people of God. And the thought of them is no less enchanting now. The outward beauty of heaven will be the source of untold delight. The place has been prepared. Creative wisdom appears there in its highest expression. Think of the magnificence of the city in which the very foundations of its walls—the meanest stones—are emerald, jacinth and topaz

But glorious as heaven is, viewed in its external splendors, this is the lowest conception of it. The true glory of it is found in the *nature* we shall inherit and in our near access to God. The great thing is not *where* we shall be, but *what* we shall be. Washed in the blood of the Lamb, we shall appear before the presence of God's glory *faultless*, without spot, or blemish, or any such thing. Heaven is chiefly subjective.

"Beloved, it doth not yet appear *what we shall be*, but we know that when He shall appear WE SHALL BE LIKE HIM, for we shall see Him as He is." This likeness to Christ will be physical, intellectual and spiritual. If we are indeed consecrated to God, we are even now being transformed into the very image of the divine humanity—into the image of Christ. "*It doth not yet appear what we shall be.*" Our most adventurous imagining comes far short of it. Such passages as this give me my highest hopes of the eternal state now. I linger not so much upon the enchanting visions of external glory. It is not so much a glorious state as *glorified being* that attracts me.

"Now we see through a glass darkly, then we shall see face to face; now I know in part, then shall I know even as also I am known." What a high subjective condition is here intimated! A man face to face with God, unrebuked, unfearing. To know as we are known, even as God knows us! Perhaps a pure spirit realizes the imperfections of time no more oppressively now than in the fact of ignorance. We know so little. There is so much lying at our very feet touching upon our own being and destiny, involving the Divine administration—so much that is vital to us—that we can not know. There is, indeed, a deep-felt blessedness in *trusting* and walking by faith. But it will be a joy to *know* when the key of knowledge is at last put into our hands. Then we shall see all the ways of God in the light of His own wisdom and love.

Not only the government of God and the mysteries of life will be laid bare to us, but the physical universe in all its laws and forces will be comprehended and express to us the very nature of the Creator. With such bodies as we shall then have the tour of the universe will be no task The exploration of a world will be the recreative occupation of an hour. The most complex relations and subtlest movements will be understood at once, and the sweep of worlds and the history of ages grasped without an effort.

Holiness is the supreme fact of the heavenly state. Second to it is knowledge. The incident of both is happiness.

All men desire to reach heaven at last, but most of them, I fear, under a mistake as to the thing of which they think. To them heaven and happiness mean the same thing. Of the essential fact in the heavenly life they never think. Let it never be forgotten that that fact is holiness. " *Without holiness no man shall see the Lord.*" "Except a man be born again he can not enter into the kingdom of God." " What are these that are arrayed in white robes, and whence came they? These are they who came out of great tribulation and have washed their robes and made them white in the blood of the Lamb." Let no man in an unregenerate state, living in sin, indulging his pride and lust and passion; no mercenary man; no lover of pleasures more than God; no man who lives to the flesh and not to God, dream of heaven at last. From such a dream he must wake up in torment. Heaven is found in a holy nature. Holiness is of the essence of heaven, and happiness an essential incident of holiness.

But the creature, even when holy, is not self-sufficing. The blessedness of the state of such is not in the mere fact of holiness, but in the relation into which this brings them toward God; in the communion with Him which it secures. He alone is sufficing to the soul. He is all in all. There could be no heaven without His presence; with it heaven is complete.

"The smile of the Lord is the feast of the soul." To the Christian God is everything. His approbation is life, His frown is death. To know Him, to feel the baptism of His presence, to receive, consciously, His love, is to realize the end of being.

But in His love we love also His followers. Fellowship of saints is a source of pure and exalted happiness. The hope of meeting the loved dead is a worthy and holy sentiment. To be sure, the relations of time will not subsist in the world to come. There "they neither marry nor are given in marriage." There are no blood ties there. The affinities of that life are purely spiritual. Yet I can not question that friendships begun in Christ on earth will ripen under His smile in heaven. The husband and wife who were related to each other by faith here, in a common spiritual life, will, not from natural, but from divine affections, be especially dear to each other in heaven. They passed through the Christian warfare together and their souls are knit in Christ. These soul affinities will survive and be deepened when all the loves that sprang from a carnal source alone shall perish. Thus many a friendship, incipient here, will be perpetuated amid the high associations of eternity Who can doubt that heaven will be hightened by this fact.

At least it seems nearer to us now that Caples has gone up. It seems brighter, too. His presence is another attraction, even of that holy place. He is our brother still. We bore the cross together. He remembers us with a deeper love.

Will he not meet us at the bank, on the other side, when we cross the river? Will he not lead us through the gates into the city? Will he not guide us in the unknown pathways? Will he not conduct us into the presence-chamber of the King?

We shall hear his voice again, deeper, richer, fuller than it was on earth. It was already practiced in the strains of worship when he ascended. What a vehicle of praise it was even here! There it will melt into the melodies of the new song so richly that an angel might pause to hear it.

We shall see his face. It will be radiant with the light of the soul. We shall know him. Recognition will be instant and perfect. That face! O! it will be joy to see it again, and to see it there; to see it in perfected beauty

The voice and face will be restored to us by the resurrection. Not until that morning will the fullness be realized. We shall meet him when we cross the river. But we must all await perfection until the redemption of the body shall complete the work of Christ, and His people together shall be gathered in. Then shall the heavenly Bridegroom take home His bride, and at the marriage supper we shall see the face and hear the voice of our departed brother.

A noble company will be there from the old Missouri Conference. May we all follow them as they followed Christ! May we join them in that day when the "Lord Himself shall descend from heaven with a shout, with the voice of the archangel and the trump of God."

"Lo! it comes, that day of wonder;
   Louder chorals shake the skies:
Hades' gates are burst asunder;
   See! the new-clothed myriads rise.
Thought, repress thy weak endeavor,
   Here must reason prostrate fall;
O, the ineffable *forever*,
   And the eternal ALL IN ALL!"

CHAPTER XVII.

After the greater part of this book was written Rev. W P Caples found, unexpectedly, and forwarded to me, the manuscript of his father's two lectures on The Law of the Tithe. Not only will his old friends be gratified by their publication, but I trust also that great good may be done thereby.

I find that my memory was at fault in one particular with regard to his views on this subject. My impression was that he taught that the tenth in each Church was to be paid for the support of its own pastor. I remembered distinctly that he excluded the support of the poor and all general charities from a claim upon the tithe, and it was in my mind that missions were also put into the list of charities to depend on voluntary contribution. But I see that, according to his view, all that preach the Gospel are to live by the Tithe.

The theory is this: The tenth of property, as

the seventh of time, is the *Lord's*. This tenth part of property, or of income more properly, which God demands as His own, to remind us of His absolute proprietorship of us and ours, He has appropriated to the support of that class of men whom He calls away from secular pursuits to serve Him in the ministry The law, faithfully observed by all, rich and poor, would be ample for the support of the home ministry and to carry on a grand system of evangelizing agencies abroad. The tenth is the Lord's, and those whose time He demands exclusively in spiritual labor are to be fed out of this fund.

There has been a suggestion made to me that the publication of these Lectures would not do justice to Mr. Caples—that they are not a fair representation of the man. One brother thought they had better not be published; another suggested that I should rewrite them and *edit* them freely. But I have determined to publish them, and that as he wrote them, with only such corrections of orthography and punctuation as were necessary. A few other corrections have been made (very few), such as I am sure would have been made by himself if he had carefully revised the manuscript.

But in publishing these Lectures it is only right to say that Mr. Caples was no writer. He had never practiced writing. He never wrote sermons.

I have no doubt that these compositions are the longest he ever wrote. Every one who has any experience knows how essential practice is to success in writing. Let it be understood, then, that these Lectures are mere apprentice work, and are not at all on paper what they were as he delivered them from the pulpit. They contain but the material out of which the sermons were made. For, although these are in the form of lectures, he often preached on the subject with great effect.

While these productions give no adequate idea of the power of their author, they do equal injustice to his style. Unaccustomed to the pen, he could not, it seems, attain to that elevation which he maintained in the pulpit His sentences here are rather heavy and clumsy. I have heretofore noticed the fact that in his heavier moods in the pulpit his style betrayed the want of early cultivation. But when he was well sprung his sentences were grand, and not wanting in elegance. The following specimen of his writing reminds me of him when his mind was *dull* in the pulpit.

Yet the Lectures show a great mind. There is much solid thought in them, and I am by no means ashamed to give them to the public. They are upon an important theme, and I will venture to say that any man would find it a difficult task to answer his arguments. It seems clear to me that the Law of the Tithe does not belong to the

Levitical code, any more than that of the Sabbath. It has its root in essential, divine claims.

I trust the publication of Mr. Caples' views at this time will wake up inquiry, and that the Church at large may come to feel this law to be binding on conscience now as it was in the Old Testament times. I can not doubt that great grace would be on all in that event. Even worldly affairs would be lifted out of their insignificance, and labor would learn to connect itself with the saving import of the Cross.

A poor man works hard, gets poor wages and has his family to support. He feels that there is nothing left for God. The merchant gets a share of it, and the shoemaker, and the butcher, and the teacher, and the doctor, but God never gets His share. He never sues for His part, which, by a law always in force, is the tenth. The man will die greatly in debt to his Maker. And while he lives his life is devoted to unblest labor. The Law of the Tithe may seem hard to him, but in fact he would find that God has ordered all things graciously, as well as wisely, if he would only conform to His law. Many a baffled life in this world would have been blest if the Creator's right over our property had been conscientiously and systematically recognized.

I commend these Lectures to the prayerful consideration and good sense of the Church.

LECTURE I

The fact of the existence of God is the great fact, the first in grandeur and importance; and all correct thought of Him is exalting. In all true science He is the great first cause and universal ruler. In all true religion "He filleth all in all." To deny Him in His relations to us is to avow our depravity; to forget Him in anything is to evidence the weakness of our piety Both in science and in religion He is the absolute and universal Sovereign. With this recognition of God it is not only wise in the sense of policy or prudence, but our bounden duty in all things to obey Him; and true obedience recognizes His absolute proprietorship in all things. There is no just recognition of the Sabbath except upon the ground that all time is His, and by us possessed as his bounty, and that, consequently, it is His right to say how we shall employ it; and that He does require us to keep one-seventh of it holy Any appropriation of property to His glory presupposes His ownership of all, and a declaration of His will as to the use to be made of it; otherwise there is no piety in the act. It will be sufficient to say to all Christians that the God of the Bible claims absolute proprietorship in all property "All the earth is mine." "The earth is the Lord's and the fullness thereof." "Sanctify unto me all the first born, both of man and beast—*it is mine*." And of the land of covenant—the land to be reached by toilsome travel and possessed by hard-fought battles—"the land shall not be sold forever, for the land is mine." "Every beast of the forest is mine, and the cattle upon a thousand hills." "The silver is mine, and the gold is mine," saith the Lord of hosts; "all souls are mine." Who will dare contest, in whole or in part, this claim with his Maker? The Almighty not only asserts this claim theoretically, but practically Does He require men for His ministry? His demands are: "Leave all and follow me," and His claim is honored when nets, and boats, or office, houses or lands are forsaken. Again he asserts this right when he says to the young man, "Go, sell what thou hast and give to the poor." And His claim is practically dishonored when the young man goes away sorrowful. Would you know the extent to which this claim of God is held? Read and study with care the Parable of the Talents recorded in the 25th chapter of the Gospel by St. Matthew. Observe, the servants and the goods both belong to Him ; and although he bestows upon the servants the goods, and the use or abuse of them is for the time left to their agency, yet the right is in Him. He gives direction as to their use and improvement, and holds each to an account accordingly From all these and many more passages in the holy Scriptures we conclude that although man has right of property toward his fellow man, he has and can have none toward his Maker. All we can claim is, that we are the Lord's stewards. We can not be more in relation to property, and soon, very soon, He will say to each of us, give an account of thy stewardship.

Without any further examination of this subject we might very reasonably premise that God requires of us some practical acknowledgement of Himself as the rightful owner of our property, especially in view of our proneness to claim independence in its possession and control, and the sordid selfishness engendered by such assumed independence, together with an intense love of riches for their own sake, which dries up every refreshing fountain of benevolence, casts gloomy shadows over every endearment of social life, and withers all that is lovely in the soul of him that indulges it, as well as the happiness of those in any way dependent upon him. But when we find a law given to man, *as man*, to remind him that God is the author of time, and that to him it is a gift, and that in its enjoyment he is dependent—the law of the Sabbath demanding at his hand a practical acknowledgement of his obligation to God in this regard—it would appear strange indeed if God had given us no law in obedience to which we might acknowledge his right in our property and secure to ourselves the constant recognition of our stewardship. So strong is this presumption and so explicit are the Scriptures of the Testaments of God in regard to it, that all Christians recognize, in some form or other, to some extent at least, the right of God in their property. Nor will it be contended that the command of God, as given in Prov. iii. 9, "Honor the Lord with thy substance and the first fruits of all thine increase," has become obsolete. Yet, perhaps, the majority of Christians will contend that the Almighty Giver has left the amount to be given, as well as the objects for which it is to be given, to be determined by each man's sense of propriety and the dictates of his own conscience. I will leave it to the observation of my auditors to say whether multitudes acting on this supposition are not making to the Church and the world humiliating concessions on the obtuseness of their sense of propriety and the imbecility of the dictates of their consciences. I grant there are many objects of benevolence brought to view in the Scriptures wherein God leaves us to determine what amount we will give, and in all such cases he brings forward the most powerful motives to battle with our cupidity. Take the following as examples: "He that giveth to the poor lendeth to the Lord and He will repay him again." "Blessed is he that considereth the poor; the Lord will deliver him in time of trouble"

"Inasmuch as ye have done it unto one of these my servants ye have done it unto me." More than one hundred and fifty times in the blessed Bible does God warn his stewards not to oppress but to remember the poor—to use the substance he has given us to relieve their distresses. The measure of our contributions must be determined by the necessities of the case and our ability to help in view of the incentives set before us. Again, when Moses was about to build the tabernacle—a work of piety, for which God gave command—it was in this wise (Ex. xxv. 2): "Speak unto the children of Israel that they bring me an offering. Of every man that giveth it willingly with his heart ye shall take my offering." The extent of the offering and its acceptability, in this instance, is determined by the willingness, the hearty willingness, of the offerer, for Moses must not accept it for the Lord unless it be given with the heart. And again, when David would prepare material for building the temple (see I Chron. 29th chapter): "And who then is *willing* to consecrate his service this day unto the Lord? Then they offered willingly The people rejoiced for that they offered willingly, because with a perfect heart they offered willingly unto the Lord; and David, the king, also rejoiced with great joy; and in this joy he blessed the Lord, saying, Thine, O Lord, is the greatness, and the power, and the glory, and the victory, and the majesty, for *all that is in the heaven and in the earth is Thine;* Thine is the kingdom, O Lord, and Thou art exalted as head above all. Both riches and honor come of Thee. But who am I, and what is my people, that we should be able to offer so willingly after this sort? for all things come of Thee, and of Thine own have we given Thee." Here we find every principle stated above entering into—yes, constituting—the piety of these offerings. For the poor, for the erection of places of worship and public instruction, in all the benevolence which God enjoins that has direct respect to our fellow man, we are left to determine the amount, and the act is acceptable to God in proportion as it regards His revealed will as the supreme law and our willing hearts enter into it. "If there be first a willing mind, it is accepted according to that a man hath." This use of the property God has given us is a test of our gratitude to Him as the giver, and His beneficence to us is made the model after which we should pattern. "Be ye therefore merciful as your father also is merciful;" and the ability which He has given us, as well as the necessities of the case, will guide us in the measure of our responsibility. If "freely ye have received, freely give." "Let every one of you lay by him in store on the first day of the week as the Lord hath prospered him." "Every man according as he purposeth in his

heart, so let him give, not grudgingly or of neces
sity, for God loveth a cheerful giver." It is thus,
in part at least, that we are to "honor God with
our substance." We merely suggest whether there
are not thousands who make contributions and
call it honoring God with their substance on a
scale that would be an insult to a common pauper.
And will not God be avenged for these things?
Yea, verily, for He has characterized it as robbery—the basest of robbery—a robbery of God—
and charged the guilt of it upon ancient Israel.
"Ye have robbed me of offerings." This entire
class of Christian charities is called offerings;
and because the per cent. or proportion of the
property possessed that is to be thus appropriated
is not definitely fixed by law, they are sometimes
called free will offerings, votive offerings, gifts,
alms, etc. We are not to conclude, however, that
because God has left us a margin in these duties
for the exercise of our free will, and the expression
of gratitude toward Him, and our sympathy for
our fellows, that He made no definite law to direct
us in regard to the use of any part of our property
He who has said so definitely, "Remember the
Sabbath day to keep it holy; six days shalt thou
labor and do all thy work, but the seventh is the
Sabbath of the Lord thy God, in it thou shalt do
no work," would not likely bestow his goods upon
his servants without some positive law to remind

them that He is the proprietor of them. The necessities of the governed require a positive and definite law at this point, and just such a law we find recorded in Lev. xxvii. 30: "All the tithe of the land, whether of the seed of the land or of the fruit of the tree, *is* the Lord's; *it is* holy unto the Lord." And we remark of the law of the tenth, thus explicitly stated, that it is not an ordinance to meet the peculiar wants of the times nor the special circumstances of the people to whom it was thus published. Indeed, it is but the announcement of a previously existing law—a law, as we are called upon to show, made *for man as he is man*, not as he is a Patriarch, or Jew, or Christian, to the exclusion of others, *but as he is man*, just as Christ says of the Sabbath, "The Sabbath was made for man, and not man for the Sabbath." It is worthy of special notice that the positive law of God claiming a *tenth* of property as his own is introduced by Moses into the written law precisely in the same form in which he introduces the law of the Sabbath: "The tithe is the Lord's." "To-morrow is the Sabbath of the Lord." In both instances it is the recognition of a law already in force, and not the enactment of a new statute. But it may be more satisfactory, however, to trace the history of this law a little further back, for if we can be assured that it was a law in force anterior to the giving of the law by Moses, recognized and observed by the Patriarchs, then it will follow that it is not merely a part of the ceremonial law, and does not, consequently, with it, vanish away. Nor are we to conclude that, unless we find some earlier record than the one above cited, it did not previously exist as a divine requirement. We might ask, where is the earliest recorded command for animal sacrifice? It may justly be answered, that God's acceptance of Abel's offering is proof sufficient that he required this at his hand. The reasoning of Archbishop Magee, in his work on "The Atonement," in support of the divine origin of sacrifices, it will be found, holds equally good on the subject before us. Hence we quote them:

"That the institution was of divine ordinance may, in the first instance, be reasonably inferred from the strong and sensible attestation of the divine acceptance in the case of Abel, again in that of Noah, afterward withal of Abraham, and also by the systematic establishment of them by the same divine authority in the dispensation of Moses."

Let us examine for a moment this case of Abel's offering, and Cain's, too, if you please. "Cain brought of the fruit of the ground an offering." If we may trust the criticism of Dr. Adam Clarke, the Hebrew word used means, as explained in Lev. ii. 1, etc., an offering of fine flour with oil and frankincense. "It was merely," says the same author, "an eucharistic, or gratitude offering, and is simply what is implied in the fruits of the ground, brought by Cain to the Lord, by which he testified his belief in Him as the Lord of the universe and the dispenser of secular blessings." "Abel *also* brought of the firstlings of his flock." Hear Dr. Clarke again. He says: "Dr. Kennicott contènds, and I am of the same opinion, that the words he *also brought* should be translated Abel brought *it* also—i. e., *a gratitude offering*, and beside this, etc.; and St. Paul supports this view when he says God testifying with his gifts, which certainly shows that he brought more than one." Now, if God's acceptance of his sin offering is sufficient to prove a law requiring it, why, we urge, does not the acceptance of his thank (or tithe) offering show a law requiring this also? And if any should inquire, why, then, was not Cain's accepted, seeing he respected the law? we might retort, if there were no law why did he offer at all? The reason of his rejection is very apparent. While he did well in acknowledging the right of God in his property he ignored the fact of his sinfulness in the sight of God, and, consequently, all faith in the promise of a Redeemer. "If thou doest well," or, as rendered by another, if thou art righteous, this thy offering is acceptable; but if not, this offering does not look for forgiveness, makes no confession of sin, and, consequently, can not be acceptable. Your sin still lieth at the door. Or if thou wilt do well in order to acceptance, meeting my requirements of you as a sinner (it is within your power to do so) (according to Dr. Clarke), a sin offering lieth at the door (of your fold) or is at hand. From these cases of acceptance and rejection, with the reason given by God himself for the rejection of the one and the acceptance of the other, it is quite as apparent that God required an acknowledgement of His sovereignty over the property he gave man as that he is the author of animal sacrifice; and if any of my hearers doubt the pertinency of this case because the tenth is not stated to be the amount required, I answer, neither may we infer from it that it was not; but we hope to show from other parts of the history of this law that a tenth was required and offered with acceptance before the days of Moses; and for this purpose I will now introduce a case—a very noted case—of the recognition of the law, afterward recorded by Moses. The case we refer to is stated briefly, but with great precision, in the 11th chapter of Genesis. The points to which special attention is desired may be stated thus: Chedorlaomer and his confederate kings make war on the King of Sodom and his associates and prevail in battle. The victors seize upon the persons and goods of the vanquished and start with them to their country., Abram, hearing of the capture of his nephew, arms his trained servants, in number three hundred and eighteen, and pursues them unto Dan, smote them, and recovered all the goods and the captives. Here let it be noted that all these goods were legally Abram's property. The King of Sodom met him on his return, in the valley of Shaveh, and Melchizedek, King of Salem, brought forth bread and wine. Note with what emphasis it is stated: " And he was *the priest of the most high God*, and he blessed him and said, Blessed be Abram of the most high God, *possessor* of *heaven* and *earth*, etc., and he (Abram) gave him *tithes of all*. And the King of Sodom said unto Abram, give me the persons and take the goods to thyself. And Abram said to the King of Sodom, I have lifted up my hand unto the Lord, the most high God, the *possessor of heaven and earth*, that I will not take from a thread even to a shoe-latchet." And why? "Lest thou shouldst say I have made Abram rich." Might not the King of Sodom ask, why, then, did you give a tenth of all to the King of Salem? Will Abram *make a present* to a king with this oath upon him? Alms it could not have been. But he asks no such question. He knew well there was a divine law which the piety of Abram would prompt him to keep, and had he not heard the great truth upon which that law was founded and the remembrance of which it was intended to perpetuate, stated both by the priest of God in his blessing and Abram in his oath, that the most high God was *possessor of heaven and earth.* Yes, idolater as he was, he knew full well that a tenth of every bestowment of Providence was to be consecrated to the powers that gave it. And both Melchizedek and Abram acknowledged this victory and these spoils to be of His providence, who was the possessor of heaven and earth, and Abram dare not withhold the tenth from Him and be guiltless. But now that it is tithed, Abram may use his pleasure as to its return or use; but until this is done Abram can not exercise any discretion in the premises, for "*the tenth is the Lord's*"

Although these cases might sufficiently demonstrate the pre-existence of the law recorded by Moses, yet I wish to state and briefly examine another case, one in itself full of thrilling interest. It is recorded in the 28th chapter of the Book of Genesis. Jacob, the son of Isaac and Rebekah, is restless by reason of his fear of Esau, his brother, who conceives himself wronged by Jacob in the matter of the birthright. His mother shares those fears with him, and with her advice and his father's blessing he takes leave of the home of his childhood and youth, at Beer-sheba, and goes toward Haran. As the day was closing, the sun having set, he selected a place to rest, and taking some stones for a pillow he lay down to sleep. How changed the circumstances of the young man in one short day! His last waking thoughts may have been of Rebekah's cheerful tent, now left behind, perhaps forever, of wearisome travel yet before him until it should bear him far away among strangers, with no other companion but "this staff." But God seized on this propitious time to instruct and encourage him, and in the dreams of that eventful night showed him a ladder reaching from earth to heaven, and passing angels thronged the way, and above it stood the Lord, who said, "I am the God of Abraham, thy father, and of Isaac," and made him large promises of family and possessions, and repreached to him the Gospel as he had preached it to Abraham. And Jacob awaked out of his sleep and said, Surely the Lord is in this place, and in his fear he said, 'tis dreadful! it is the house of God and the gate of heaven. He rose early and set up the stones on which his head had laid, and pouring oil upon them called the place Beth-el. And Jacob vowed a vow, saying, "If the Lord will be with me and will keep me in this way that I go, and will give me bread to eat and raiment to put on, of all that Thou shalt give me I will surely give a tenth to Thee."

You will perceive in this case, again, the recognition of the great principle upon which the law of the tithe is founded, to-wit: That all the property we possess is His bounty, and He is acknowledged to be its proprietor in the observance of this law. There is in this case one peculiarity to which I call your attention. Abram gave the tithes, at least in one case, to the priest of the most high God, and under the Mosaic economy God gave the tithes to the sons of Levi. But in this case they are not given to any priest, and we are taught by it that the law requiring the tenth to be devoted to God is entirely independent of the direction it may please God to give it. The use to be made of the tithes must be matter of revelation. Jacob deferred for a long time the fulfilment of his vow, but at length he repents, and, being himself a priest, he offers them upon the altar.

We will claim your attention to but one more branch of evidence in support of the Divine institution of tithes anterior to Moses, and to this but briefly, which is the almost universal belief that one-tenth of all income belongs to the gods. "The custom of giving or paying tithe is very ancient."—*Chambers.*

Xenophon, in the Fifth Book of the Expedition of Cyrus, gives us an inscription upon a column near the Temple of Diana, whereby the people were warned to offer the tenth part of their revenues every year to that goddess. The Romans offered a tenth of all they took from their enemies to the gods. The Gauls gave a tenth to their god Mars, as we learn from the commentaries of Cæsar. And Festus assures us that the ancients gave a *tithe* of every thing to their gods.

We make these quotations from Chambers' great dictionary, and we might multiply them if necessary, but these are sufficient. Authors have been strangely perplexed to find the original of a custom established among so many people of different manners and religions—to give a tenth to their kings, their gods, or their ministers of religion. Says the above quoted author: "Grotius takes it to arise hence, that the number ten is the most known and the most common among all nations, by reason of the number of fingers, which is ten." On this account he thinks it is that the commands of God were reduced to ten for the people to retain them with greater ease, that the philosophers established ten categories, etc.

This attempt at answering the inquiry we think labored, and withal very far from being satisfactory Why not assume that the number two was the best known, by reason of the fact that men walk on two feet and have two hands; or four, because so large a proportion of animals have four legs; or five, because of the five senses. How much more rational to accept the reasoning which so well satisfies the Christian world in regard to the origin of animal sacrifice, that it was revealed by God himself to our first progenitors, and thus spread among the families which became nations, and although corrupted, long retained some of its original features. But originate as it may, *God, as we have seen, enjoined it* as a *law upon Israel.* Now, we ask, did God borrow his law from the vagaries of men, or did men receive this idea from the revelations of God? The answer can not, with any sane mind, be dubious.

We conclude this lecture with this remark, that unless we have entirely mistaken the subject before us, or the nature of evidence, or the mental calibre of our patient audience, the minds of all are satisfied that the law of the tithe was given by the Almighty to the early Patriarchs as involving a great moral principle, and that in giving this law He acted "not as the God of the Jew only." And the establishment of this fact puts it beyond cavil that, unless He has repealed the law, it *is, in its original purity, to all intents and purposes, in full force* And if you will honor us with another hearing we will answer some objections to its perpetuity, examine it in the light of the New Testament, and show its bearing upon the future of the Church and the destiny of the world.

LECTURE II

An objection has been urged to our view of the great moral principles involved in the law of the tithe and the consequent perpetuity of the obligation to observe it, on the assumed ground that it is not found in the ten commandments, or moral law. To give any force to this objection it must be assumed that the entire moral law is expressed in the ten words or commands, but this assumption is in *fact false.* It is true that the ten commandments written upon the tables of stone are an epitome of the entire moral law and contain its great principles, which are as changeless as the Eternal Law-giver. Indeed, upon the principles of the two first hang the entire law and the prophets. And is not this statute of the tithe covered fully by the first article of this great moral constitution: "*I am the Lord thy God.*" "*Thou shalt have none other gods before me.*" "Thou shalt not make thee any graven image, or any likeness of any thing that is in heaven above, or that is in the earth beneath, or that is in waters beneath earth. Thou shalt not *bow down thyself unto them, nor serve them,* for I, the Lord thy God, am a jealous God, showing mercy unto thousands of them that love me and keep my commandments."

Sin is well defined to be "a want of conformity

27

to, or a violation of, law." Did not the Ephesians violate this command when they gave the tithe to Diana, the Romans when they gave it to their gods, the Gauls when they bestowed it upon Mars, and all the ancients (if Festus be credited) when they gave it to their gods, and the tribes of Jacob when they consumed it upon their lusts? For although they regarded not an idol, yet they "robbed God in withholding the tithe." And why? Because "the tithe is the Lord's, *the possessor of heaven and earth.*" Look at the universal custom of the heathen world, especially of old, and read the command again: "I am the Lord thy God. Thou shalt have no other gods before (or beside) me." And in fear of that God, who is the possessor of heaven and earth, who hath fed you all your lifelong, and claims to be your God, and to whom you are glad to say, My Lord, and my God, tell me whether the devotees of the mythological daughter of Jupiter, and Latona, and the sister of Apollo, the Gauls, in their devotion to the son of Juno, the ancient Chaldean offering his tithe to the heavenly luminaries, the Epicurean denying allegiance to all else, hiding it in the treasury-house of his appetites, the Jew, who robs God, and the professed Christian who, turning from the law of the tithe, cries, My property is my own, and it is lawful for me to do with it as *I will*—are not all guilty of a positive violation of the first great command of the ten?

Another objection which we notice is, that the tithes of the children of Israel were offered as sacrifices and were to be eaten in Jerusalem, etc., and that being thus ceremonial they can not be perpetual. This objection is certainly more specious than formidable, and grows out of the supposition, doubtless, that there was but one tithe enjoined upon the tribes. But beside the tithe which is the Lord's there was a second tithe, which was, says Chambers, a tenth part of the nine remaining after payment of the first tithe. This tithe was set apart in each family, and the master of the family was obliged to carry it to Jerusalem and use it there; or, in case he could not, he was to redeem it or convert it into money, in which case he was to add a fifth part to it and carry it to Jerusalem. A third tithe was a tithe of the first, to be given by the Levites to the priests of the house of Aaron. The fourth was the tithe of the third year; not much different from the second tithe, except that it was less troublesome, because they did not carry it to Jerusalem, either in kind or in money, but kept it by them for the Levite, the strangers, the fatherless and the widows of the place (Deut. xiv. 28, 29). This was also called the tithe of the poor, and the third tithe and these third years when it was paid were called the tithe

years.   Several learned Jews and Christians, however, conceived that this was not a distinct tithe,
but the same as the second, so that, as Mr. Mede
apprehends, what was meant in other years to
be spent in feasting was every third year spent
upon the poor.

Dr. Clarke thinks the reason why God required
this last named tithe to be eaten at Jerusalem
was to establish uniformity of worship, which,
says he, was very important in those idolatrous
times; and his comment exactly corresponds with
the opinions I have gathered from Chambers.
(See C. Com. on Deut. xiv. 28, 29.)

The bare statement of the facts as above explodes the objection.   Yes, it does more, for it
again shows the tithe of all, *which is the Lord's,*
standing out in bold relief, independently of all
that is merely ceremonial.

The next argument we present will be on the following proposition, namely : That the Jews, as people, converted to Christ, their Savior, will, according to their own prophesy literally observe the law
of the tithe.   And we would not have you forget
that the tithe is not a type of anything whatever,
but an acknowledgement of the sovereignty of
God and the recognition of present existing relation to His providence and bounty; and as this
relation is absolute between the Creator and the
creature, so no covenant God has ever made with

man ignores this law. But, on the other hand, the great truths upon which this law is based, and of which it is the exponent, underly every covenant God has been pleased to enter into with man. In view of these facts, and a Jew's familiarity with the law in its relation to them, let us consider a Jew as converted to the true Messiahship of Christ, and under the light of the truth received in this conversion, reading the 20th chapter of Ezekiel's prophesy, in which he traces the dealing of the God of Abraham with his fathers; how He showed them wonders in Egypt and mercies in the wilderness, and how they rebelled against Him and provoked Him to anger; how He scattered them among their enemies, and at their repentant cry He brought them out of their troubles; but again and again they rebel, until He gives them up to their delusions and refuses to accept their offering or acknowledge their sacrifices, and they vainly say we will be like the nations around us. But God preserves them distinct among the nations until the nations among whom they sojourn acknowledge His hand upon them—until He pleads with them as he plead with their fathers. "And I will cause you to pass under the *rod*, and I will bring you into the *bond* of the *covenant*. And I will purge out from among you the rebels, and them that transgress against me; there will I accept them and there will I require your offerings and the first fruits of your oblations, with all your holy things." He understands very well that passing *under the rod* they acknowledge that they and theirs belong to God, and thus God brings them *into the covenant*, and then accepts, yea, requires, their offering, their first fruits, with all their holy things. He reads, again, Jeremiah, 33d chapter. How the word of the Lord comes to his imprisoned prophet, filled with encouragement to the scattered tribes to hope in the covenant of God made with Abraham their father and David their king, declaring that so long as the covenant with Noah shall stand so long should this remain; that Jerusalem, so long desolate and sad, should again rejoice for the return of her children, and the voice of the shepherd should once more make glad the desolate land and the numerous flocks take rest within its vales. And in the time of this restoration the Lord is to be acknowledged in the universal observance of the law of the tithe. "In the cities of the mountains, in the cities of the vale, and in the cities of the south, and in the land of Benjamin, and in the places about Jerusalem, and in the cities of Judah, shall the flocks pass again under the hands of him that telleth them, saith the Lord." "Behold the days come, saith the Lord, that I will perform that good thing which I have promised unto the house of Israel and to the house of Judah." But when, O, when shall it be?

"*In the days of the righteous branch* that I will cause to grow up unto David. He shall execute judgment and righteousness in the land. In those days shall Judah be saved and Jerusalem shall dwell safely, and this is the name wherewith she shall be called *the Lord our righteousness.*" A Jew would not (much less a Christian) deny that this prophesy refers to the glorious days of the last time or times of *Messiah.* And although, as Mr. W.atson says, the predictions may have a permanent fulfilment in the return from Babylon, its ultimate and glorious accomplishment must be referred to the times of the Messiah. This granted, we have but to inquire, what shall take place in these times? The answer is given in the 13th verse. In the cities of the mountains, of the vales, of the south, in the land of Benjamin, about Jerusalem, and the cities of Judah, shall the flocks pass under the hands of him that telleth them. It is not necessary that we determine whether Jerusalem is here used literally or for the Church of God, of which it was the type—the argument is the same. W.e only have to inquire what is meant by passing *under the rod,* or the *hands of him that telleth them.* We find this same form of words in Lev. xxvii. 32: "And concerning the tithe of the herd, or of the flock, even whatsoever passeth under the rod, the tenth shall be holy unto the Lord."

Dr. A. Clarke says the signification of this verse is well given by the Rabbis. When a man was to give the tithe of his sheep or calves to God, he was to shut up the whole flock in one fold, in which there was one narrow door capable of letting out one at a time. The owner about to give a tenth to the Lord stood by the door with a rod in his hand, the end of which was dipped in vermilion or red ochre. The mothers of those lambs or calves stood without; the door being opened, the young ones ran out to join themselves to their dams, and as they passed out the owner stood with his rod over them and counted one, two, three, four, five, &c., and when the tenth came he touched it with the colored rod, by which it was distingushed to be the tithe sheep, calf, &c. We gather first from these and other prophesies of similar character that they will be accomplished in the times of Messiah; and secondly, that in their fulfilment the law of the tithe will be observed. We now merely ask, will the Jews converted to Christ form a part of the Christian Church under the New Testament dispensation? or will there still be one law for Christian Jew and another for Gentile converts? No, verily; "there shall be one fold and one shepherd." For there is neither Jew nor Greek, there is neither circumcision nor uncircumcision, but ye are all one in Christ Jesus. Will any one undertake to show why it is that a descendant of Abra-

ham after the flesh, made heir of the promise by
faith, is required to honor God with the tenth of
all his revenue, and the spiritual seed, made heir
of the same promise by the belief of the Gospel,
is left to use his own will as the standard to determine what he gives, or whether he will give at
all or not. In the absence of a positive revelation
from God to this effect such a supposition is *mon-
strous presumption*, and without an explicit repeal
of the law in the New Testament we can not avoid
its obligation. To the New Testament, then, for
a few moments at least, let us turn and see if there
be any repeal. But first let us ask, can there in
the nature of things be a repeal of this law unless
there be first a change of the relation upon which
it is founded? The only mention Christ makes
of tithe is a recognition of the law and a com-
mendation of obedience to it, even in the smallest
matters (Luke xi. 42): "Ye tithe mint, and rue,
and all manner of herbs and pass over judgment
and the love of God: these ought ye to have done,
and *not to leave the other undone.*" Christ here
says that the tithing of mint and rue and all manner of herbs ought not to be left undone. Is this
repeal? (See, also, Matthew xxiii. 23.) If so, it is
couched in strange language.

The Pharisee made a boast in his prayer: "I
give tithes of all that I possess." Let it be observed that it is not the payment of tithes that is

held up by the Savior as improper, no more than is fasting, or freedom from extortion, or adultery, but in his making a boast before God instead of feeling and confessing as did David : "That *of thine own have we rendered thee, for all came of thee.*" This rebuke of self-exaltation is the farthest removed from a repeal of the obligation or denial of the God asserted fact—"*the tithe* is *the Lord's.*"

It will hardly be pretended that the obligation to give tithes under the priesthood of Christ is annulled by St. Paul in his powerful argument on the superiority of his priesthood over that of Levi by reference to his great type in the person of the King of Salem. The sacred history but three times opens the veil and gives us glimpses of this mysterious character, but in these it gives the most certain information. First, he is shown to us blessing the patriarch Abraham, and receiving at his hand the tithe ; secondly, David tells us that the priesthood of his Lord (our Jesus) was by the oath of God forever after the order of Melchizedek. Upon these facts St. Paul builds his argument. The priesthood of Christ being by the oath of God after the order of Melchizedek and not after the order of Aaron, consider the greatness of this man (the type) to whom even the patriarch Abraham gave the tenth ; and verily they that are of the sons of Levi, who receive the office of the priesthood, *have a commandment* to take tithes of the people according to the law, that is of their brethren, though they be the children of Abraham. But he whose descent is not counted from them received tithes of Abraham and blessed him that had the promises. And without all contradiction the less is blessed of the better. And here were men that did receive tithes, but then he receiveth them of whom it is witnessed that he liveth. And, as I may so say, Levi, also, who receiveth the tithes (having had a *command* to do so) paid tithes in Abraham. If, therefore, this priesthood given to Levi was perfect, what need of another after the order of Melchizedek? But this change of the priesthood from the imperfect one given to Aaron to that which abideth forever, the first being annulled, there is a disannulling of the commandment also. So that the sons of Levi, by reason of their call to minister at the altar, which now ceases, have no longer a commandment to receive tithes, for as their priesthood is changed so there must be a change also of the law or commandment. But the law of the tithe is not thereby disannulled. Indeed, we gather from St. Paul's reasoning that it is entirely independent, not only in its origin, but also in its obligation, of the Levitical or Aaronic priesthood. And now that the priesthood of Aaron has merged into the perfect and perpetual priesthood of Christ, and as tithes were required under the dispensation of the Gospel in the days of the Patriarchs, and as they were received by that illustrious type of Christ, Melchizedek, even from him to whom God preached the Gospel and to whom he gave the promises, how is it that we have come to conceive that they are no longer required of us, who draw nigh to God through this perfect and ever abiding priesthood, our highest claim being that we are Abraham's spiritual seed and blessed with him that was faithful, in that we are partakers of the promises? Once more we beg leave to remind our audience that God's claim on our property of. a tenth stands (as we have already shown in several instances) entirely independent of every inquiry as to what God may be pleased to do with it, and the direction to be given to it must be matter of revelation. This fact kept before us, of itself explodes the idea entertained by some that the tribe of Levi, by God's command, cut off in a large degree from the possession of the lands among their brethren and from secular pursuits; that the law was a necessary provision for their maintenance, but that this necessity passed away with the priesthood of Aaron, and that hence the obligation to observe the law has expired. In this objection or statement there is a great deal of plausibility, especially to those who have thought but little upon the subject; but to the close thinker it will be sufficiently apparent that there is not one particle of truth in it. First, it wholly ignores the fact of the pre-existence of the obligation; and, secondly, the great principle upon which it rests. Its fallacy will be further apparent as we proceed. Let us hear once more the voice of the Lord on this subject: "And all the tithe of land, whether of seed of the land or of the fruit of the tree, is the Lord's." "And concerning the tithe of the herd or of the flock, even of whatsoever passeth under the rod, the tenth shall be holy unto the Lord." Lev xxvii. 30–32. "And the Lord spake unto Aaron, Thou shalt have no inheritance, neither shalt thou have any part among them; I am thy part and thy inheritance among the children of Israel. And, behold, I have given the children of Levi all the tenth in Israel for an inheritance for their service which they served, even the service of the tabernacle of the congregation." You can not fail to observe how perfectly distinct God's *claim* is from the *appropriation* which He here makes of it. He unquestionably calls Levi's family away from land and secular employments. This is His right, for all are His; but He as unquestionably gives them His tenth as the chief item for their support; and mark, He says it is for their service which they serve. But in view of the last stated objection I wish to inquire, Has the antitype of Melchizedek no ministers? Did he

not as emphatically call men to minister for him
as God called Aaron? And does not Paul say no
man taketh this honor to himself but he that is
called of God, as was Aaron? Is not the call
equally imperative, "*Follow me?*" Does it not
as positively separate from secular employments?
"Let the dead bury their dead." "Go, sell all
that thou hast and give to the poor and come follow me." "Lo, we have left all." "No man that
warreth entangleth himself with the affairs of this
life." Is not the labor as onerous and the field as
large and the charge to duty as stern? "Go ye
into all the world and preach the Gospel to every
creature." Does he leave them to look after their
own support? "Who goeth a warfare at any
time at his own charges?" Does He feed and
clothe them by miracles from heaven? "Take
neither purse nor scrip for your journey—neither
two coats." "The workman is worthy of his meat
and *the laborer of his hire.*" Read I Cor. ix. 13:
"Do ye not know that they which minister about
holy things live of the things of the temple, and
they that wait at the altar are partakers with the
altar? *Even so hath the Lord ordained that they
which preach the Gospel shall live of the Gospel.*"
Verse 8: "Say I these things as a man, or saith
not the *law* the same also?" "If we have sown
unto you spiritual things, is it a great thing if we
shall reap your carnal things?" Will any one

undertake to show me the law in the New Testament that the apostle refers to? No, the apostle looks right to the provisions that by command Levi received while he ministered for God, and with the abolishing of this ministry the embassadors of Christ became the ministers of God, and Jesus tells them the workman is worthy of *his meat* and the *laborer of his hire*, and the commandment or law on this subject, as we have seen in our examination of Paul's argument on the priesthood of Aaron and Christ, is changed of necessity with the priesthood. God gave them His *tithe for their service which they served*, and does not Christ teach His disciples to look directly to God for their support, having thus ordained that they that preach the Gospel *shall* live of the Gospel? Let me inquire what you would think of a government that would make, by just and positive revenue laws for a term of years, ample provision for the support of its soldiery while it was acting on the defensive; but when the plan of the campaign required that the army should take a more active position should issue its imperative orders to enter the enemy's country, and then pass a law or ordinance that the army should still live out of the treasury, but at the same time abolish the revenue laws and leave it discretionary with the subjects of the government how much—*if anything*—they would give to meet its expenses? Our own General Government menaced the country some years ago with something like this, when in party strife they refused for a time to pass the army appropriation bill. We with united voice would condemn it as most cruel, oppressive and silly But have we not, in setting up our own wills as the standard by which we will be governed in our contributions to the Lord's treasury and ignored the obligation to give the tenth to the Lord, charged Him, practically at least, with this species of legislation? If, indeed, we have thus charged God foolishly, may we not say, "I wot, brethren, that ye did it ignorantly, as did also your rulers." But say you the law of the tithe must, to a great extent, remain a dead letter unless you wed Church and State and enforce its claims by the arm of civil law? I answer, there would be just as much propriety in invoking the civil power to make men pray, go to church, or perform any other act of obedience to God's re quirements, and just as much scriptural authority for it, too. Herein is the manifest folly of all the tithings and systems of tithing known at the present day in all Christian countries where they are thus enforced; and being thus enforced and otherwise abused the grounds of obligation to it are obscured and the moral results are entirely destroyed And hence many good men have cried out against them as evil. The history of the legislation of Christian nations on this subject would form an interesting theme for a lecture, and might be profitable in showing therein the cause of the evils now existing in the Church, in various respects, throughout the Christian world; and although it does not enter into the design of this lecture to review such legislation, our position being that all civil intermeddling with it is unscriptural, subversive and consequently ruinous, yet we may suggest a point or two that may lead to further inquiry Modern authors are much divided in opinion as to the time of their first being observed in the Christian Church, and no one has ever been able to show their first introduction. Some good men, impressed with the evils already noticed, are fond to believe that they were comparatively of modern origin and a departure from the apostolic constitution; but the belief that the obligation continues under the Gospel, is of great antiquity, can not be denied. Chambers says: Origen, Hom. 11th on Numbers, thinks that the law of Moses touching the first fruits and tithes, both of cattle and the fruits of the earth, are not abrogated by the Gospel, but ought to be observed on their ancient footing. In the second Council of Matiscona, held in 585, it is said expressly that the Christians had a long time *kept inviolate* that law of God whereby tithe of all their fruits was enjoined, etc.—*Ibid.* The fifth canon

28

orders tithes to be paid to the ministers of the Church according to the *law of God and the immemorial customs of the Christians*, etc. At a provincial synod at Cullen, in 356, tithes are voted to be God's rent. Judge Blackstone says that possibly tithes in this country (England) were contemporary with the planting of Christianity among the Saxons, by Augustin, the monk, about the end of the sixth century; but the first mention of them that he has met with in any written English law is in a constitutional decree made in a synod held A. D. 786, wherein the payment of tithes in general is strongly enjoined.

With these authorities before us, it devolves upon those denying the continuance of the obligation to show that their observance is an innovation in the Christian Church; but if this can not be done, then it follows that the Church (as asserted by the Council of Matiscona) has always acknowledged it, and that its neglect is a departure from the practice of the primitive Christians. This same course of argumentation is considered incontrovertible in regard to other practices (to instance the baptism of infants); why not equally so here? Unless the premises are successfully attacked the apostolicity of the practice is fairly presumed. That there is some obscurity about its practice in the primitive Church is not strange. In this it is only like every other practice of the

times. We know but little of the history of the
Church, comparatively, until she, to a greater or
less extent, becomes entangled in civil alliances.
The Gospel gained its first victories mainly among
the poor, and these were made to pass for ages,
with but little rest, through confiscation and
bloody persecutions, so that it is not strange that
but little of her detailed history has come down
to us. The alliance of the Church with the civil
powers of the earth was, doubtless, the fruitful
source of her rapid corruption. Not only is the
collecting of tithes by the civil power contrary to
the Scripture, but the claiming of the tithes of any
given district or parish, by the ministers that may
minister to the people of the same district, is altogether wanting in scriptural authority and, more-
over, repulsive to its teachings.

It may not be amiss just here to show that those
Churches or bodies of Christians called Protestant,
and, still more specific, called dissenting by those
who still cleave to their carnal alliance with civil
powers, have not only thrown off the unjust exercise of civil law in the collection of tithes, and,
consequently, of the unrighteous monopoly of the
tithes of a given district by the minister of that
district, but they have sufficiently tested the in-
efficiency of having no definite rule on this subject, and have found, I am sure, trouble enough
and sorrow enough to lead them to inquire, can-

didly and earnestly, for the mind of the Lord in regard to it. A brief glance at those troubles may not be amiss just here. And, first, it is complained that in a very large number of instances, amounting perhaps to nine out of ten, the increase of riches, with individual Christians and with congregations, is attended with decline in vital piety and the sweet simplicity of Christian character, and the few that escape these dreadful results do so by a degree of liberality that to others is truly astonishing. Extravagance in dress and personal ornaments, in furniture, equipage and style of living is growing to an extent that alarms both the divine and civilian; and what is it all but a practical declaration of independence in the possession and use of property. And who is clear in this matter? *I*, says the preacher, and *I*, exclaims the editor. Aye, we have preached, and written, and published, against all this with marked ability and wondrous strength. But let me ask, of all you have preached or published, what definite idea have you given your people on this subject? And if, perchance, you have half startled some soul with the inquiry, "Will a man rob God?" and they have inquired wherein, you have perhaps told them of prayer, and Church, and sacrament neglected, and that they ought to give *something to the poor*, and have left them with only vague conceptions instead of the defi-

niteness of God's truth—"*The tenth is the Lord's.*"
"*Ye have robbed God in tithes*" How generally
do we hear this complaint from the most ex-
emplary members of the Church: Our congregation is abundantly able to support our minister
without any one being at all oppressed, but so
few of our members help that the few upon which
the burden falls feel it very sensibly. Now, why
is it that so many in the Church are content to
let others bear this burden for them? Well, in
the first place, what they hear on the subject is
usually a misapplication of the Scriptures. The
duty is generally presented as one we owe to the
preacher, hence the partiality we have for the man
has much to do with our liberality in his support.
If the Bible be called up to support the appeal,
ten to one if some text in reference to alms-giving
or free-will offerings is not quoted and the law of
the Lord is not invoked to give light to the mind
and authority to the appeal. These people have
a Christian conscience on other subjects, such as
prayer, attention to the means of grace and the
observance of the Sabbath; but "where there is no
law there is no transgression," and they have not
been taught the law on this subject and they have
no conscience toward God in this whole matter.
Once more, it is complained of as a humiliating
fact that there is no just proportion between the
effort made to collect funds for the support of

missions and the results realized. We have but
to glance at the subject to feel this. The theme
of the solicitor of funds for a Gospel mission sur-
passes every other that has ever stirred an audience from a platform. The most exalted subject
ever discussed in the Roman forum in comparison
with this was the merest trifle. The finest class
of talents God has ever given to the Church have
tested their utmost power here, and the eloquence
of the missionary platform for the last twenty-five
years beggars the brightest displays of ancient or
modern senates. And with what results? We
would be the last to despise the day of small
things, but when we look at the results we are
almost ready to inquire, was Christ in earnest
when He said, "Go ye into all the world and
preach the Gospel to every creature." Yes, verily,
in earnest; for this He groaned in earnest in the
garden, for this He founded the command upon
the fact, "All power is given unto me in heaven
and earth, go ye, therefore." Yes, verily, for this
His providence has worked in earnest, opening in
the wake of His Gospel chariot the channels of
commerce and trade, pouring His treasure of
wealth and power into the laps of those that embrace Him, and ever beckoning them to the fields
beyond them; and this, too, by the measure of a
definite will—a will the power of which we have
broken, and in vain do we attempt to compass the

field by another of our own make. We have en-
snared ourselves in perverting the blessing of God.
Wealth to us is unsanctified—it has not passed
under the hand of Him that telleth it. We worship the creature more than the Creator. We
have robbed God, and our wealth is unclean. As
well might we expect joy and peace on the earn-
ing of the Sabbath as on our untithed substance.
Let the Church arise and cause to pass under the
rod all their possessions and God will bring them
into the bonds of the covenant. Then shall be
written on the bells of the horses and every pot
in Jerusalem and Judea, *Holiness unto the Lord.*
But says one, the treasury of the Lord would overflow, and there would not be preachers enough.
Ah! if this were so, one prayer to the Lord of the
harvest for more laborers would bring them into
the field as they never came before. With what
propriety can a Church that has robbed God until
the treasury is empty pray Him to send more laborers into the field? I have actually known in
our own beloved Church resolutions passed calling upon the whole Church to fast, and pray the
Lord of the harvest to send more laborers into the
harvest, and this was timely, for, perhaps, the
ranks of the ministry was that day thinned by
the retirement of six of the best laborers, compelled to this by long fasting. And yet how slow
to see our folly. But says another, what would

become of other parts of the Church's labor? We answer, when this law is observed they will be sustained. A people that will not keep the first commandment will not be likely to keep the second. But cries a third, such a policy would beggar the Church. Let Him respond who is the possessor of heaven and earth. *"Bring all the tithes into the storehouse, that there may be meat in my house, and prove me now herewith, saith the Lord of hosts, if I will not open the windows of heaven and pour you out a blessing that there shall not be room enough to receive it. And I will rebuke the devourer for your sakes, and he shall not destroy the fruits of your ground, neither shall your vine cast her fruit before the time in the field, saith the Lord of hosts. And all nations shall call you blessed, for ye shall be a delightsome land, saith the Lord of hosts.* Mal. iii. 10, 11, 12.

THE END.